THE

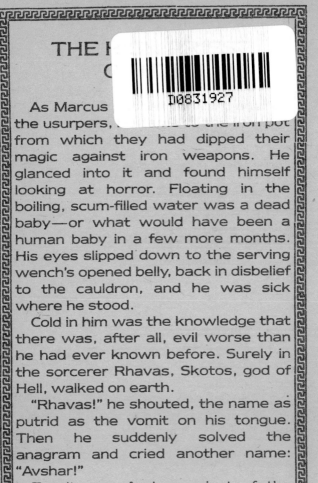

As Marcus [...] the usurpers, [...] to the iron pot from which they had dipped their magic against iron weapons. He glanced into it and found himself looking at horror. Floating in the boiling, scum-filled water was a dead baby—or what would have been a human baby in a few more months. His eyes slipped down to the serving wench's opened belly, back in disbelief to the cauldron, and he was sick where he stood.

Cold in him was the knowledge that there was, after all, evil worse than he had ever known before. Surely in the sorcerer Rhavas, Skotos, god of Hell, walked on earth.

"Rhavas!" he shouted, the name as putrid as the vomit on his tongue. Then he suddenly solved the anagram and cried another name: "Avshar!"

For it was Avshar, priest of the god of Hell and Videssos' greatest foe—and it was to him that the Pretender had turned as chief upholder of his rule!

By Harry Turtledove
Published by Ballantine Books:

The Videssos Cycle:

THE MISPLACED LEGION

AN EMPEROR FOR THE LEGION

THE LEGION OF VIDESSOS

SWORDS OF THE LEGION

NONINTERFERENCE

Book Two of *The Videssos Cycle*

An **Emperor** for the **Legion**

Harry Turtledove

A Del Rey Book

BALLANTINE BOOKS • NEW YORK

To Judy-Lynn del Rey, for calling
to let me know they sold.

WHAT HAS GONE BEFORE:

A scouting column of three cohorts of Roman legionaries, led by military tribune Marcus Aemilius Scaurus and senior centurion Gaius Philippus, was returning to Julius Caesar's main army when they were ambushed by Gauls. To prevent mass slaughter, the Gallic commander Viridovix offered single combat, and Marcus accepted. Both men bore druids' swords, that of Marcus being battle spoil. When the blades crossed, a dome of light sprang up around them. Suddenly the Romans and Viridovix were in an unfamiliar world with strange stars.

They soon discovered they were in the war-torn Empire of Videssos, a land where priests of the god Phos could work real magic. They were hired as a mercenary unit by the Empire and spent the winter in the provincial town of Imbros, learning the language and customs.

When spring came, they marched to Videssos the city, capital of the Empire. There Marcus met the soldier-Emperor Mavrikios Gavras, his brother Thorisin, and the prime minister, Vardanes Sphrantzes, a bureaucrat whose enmity Marcus incurred. At a banquet in the Romans' honor, Marcus met Mavrikios' daughter Alypia and accidentally spilled wine on the wizard Avshar, envoy of Yezd, Videssos' western enemy. Avshar demanded a duel. When the wizard tried to cheat with sorcery, Marcus' druid sword neutralized the spell, and Marcus won.

Avshar tried for revenge with an enchanted dagger in the hands of a nomad under his spell. The Videssian priest Nepos was horrified at the use of evil magic. Avshar forfeited the protection granted envoys.

Marcus was sent to arrest Avshar, accompanied by Hemond and a squad of Namdaleni, mercenaries from the island nation of Namdalen. But Avshar had fled, leaving a sorcerous trap that killed Hemond. Marcus was given Hemond's sword to take to his widow, Helvis.

Avshar's offenses served as justification for Videssos to declare war on Yezd, which had been raiding deep into the western part of the Empire. Troops—native and mercenary—flooded into the capital as Videssos prepared for war. Tension rose between Videssians and the growing number of Namdaleni because of differences in their worship of Phos. To the religiously liberal Romans, the differences were minor, but each side considered the other heretics. The Videssian patriarch Balsamon preached a sermon of toleration, which eased the tension for the moment.

But fanatic Videssian monks stirred up trouble again. Rioting broke out, and Marcus was sent with a force of Romans to help quell it. Going into a dark courtyard to break up a rape, he discovered that the intended victim was Helvis. Caught up in the moment, they made love. And after the riots subsided, she and her son joined him in the Romans' barracks. Other Romans had already found partners.

At last the unwieldy army moved west against Yezd, accompanied by women and dependents. Marcus was pleased to learn Helvis was pregnant, but shocked to discover Ortaias Sphrantzes commanded the army's left wing; he was only slightly mollified on finding the young man was a figurehead, hostage for Vardanes Sphrantzes' good behavior.

More troops joined the army in the westlands, including those of Baanes Onomagoulos and Gagik Bagratouni, a noble driven from his home in mountainous Vaspurakan by Yezda. Two other Vaspurakaners, Senpat Sviodo and his wife Nevrat, were acting as guides for the Romans. All Vaspurakaners were hated as heretics by a local priest, Zemarkhos. Zemarkhos cursed Bagratouni, who threw him and his dog into a sack, then beat the sack. Fearing a pogrom, Marcus interceded for him.

The Yezda began hit-and-run raids against the imperial army as it moved closer to Yezd. Then an advance force of Onomagoulos' troops was pinned down near the town of Maragha. Leaving the army's dependents behind at Khliat, the Emperor moved forward to rescue them.

In a great battle, Avshar commanded the Yezda. By sorcery, he slew the officer who truly commanded the imperial army's left wing. Ortaias Sphrantzes, suddenly thrust into real command, panicked and fled.

The whole wing collapsed. The battle, till then nearly a

draw, turned to disaster. Mavrikios fell fighting, and Thorisin's desperate counterattack from the right failed, though he did manage to escape with a fair part of the army.

Roman discipline let the legionaries hold their ranks. They withdrew in good order and encamped for the night. Toward midnight, Avshar taunted them by throwing Mavrikios' head into their camp. As Gaius Philippus commented, the wizard should have pursued the forces of Thorisin instead.

The game was not over yet.

I

THE ROMANS' TREK EAST FROM THE DISASTROUS BATTLE-field where the Emperor of Videssos lost his life was a journey full of torment. The season was late summer, the land through which they marched sere and burning hot. Mirages shimmered ahead, treacherously promising lakes where a mud puddle would have been a prodigy. Bands of Yezda invaders dogged the fugitives' tracks, skirmishing occasionally and always alert to pick off stragglers.

Scaurus still carried Mavrikios Gavras' severed head, the only sure proof the Emperor was dead. Foreseeing chaos in Videssos after Mavrikios' fall, he thought it wise to forestall pretenders who might claim the imperial name to aid their climbs to power. It would not be the first time Videssos had known such things.

"Sorry I am I wasna there when that black spalpeen Avshar flung you himself's noddle," Viridovix said to the tribune, his Latin musically flavored by his native Celtic speech. "I had a fine Yezda one to throw back at him." True to the fierce custom of his folk, the Gaul had taken a slain enemy's head for a trophy.

At any other time Marcus would have found that revolting. In defeat's bitter aftermath, he nodded and said, "I wish you'd been there, too."

"Aye, it would have given the whoreson something to think on," Gaius Philippus chimed in. The senior centurion usually enjoyed quarreling with Viridovix, but their hatred for the wizard-prince of Yezd brought them together now.

Marcus rubbed his chin, felt rough whiskers scratch under

1

his fingers. Like most of the Romans, he had stayed clean-faced in a bearded land, but lately there had been little time for shaving. He plucked a whisker; it shone golden in the sunlight. Coming as he did from Mediolanum in northern Italy, he had a large proportion of northern blood in his veins. In Caesar's army in Gaul, he had been teased about looking like a Celt himself. The Videssians often took him for a Haloga; many of those warriors forsook their chilly home for mercenary service in the Empire.

Gorgidas worked ceaselessly with the wounded, changing dressings, splinting broken bones, and dispensing the few ointments and medicines left in his depleted store. Although hurt himself, the slim, dark Greek doctor disregarded his pain to bring others relief.

Covered by a screening force of light cavalry from Videssos' eastern neighbor Khatrish, the legionaries tramped east toward the town of Khliat as fast as their many injuries would allow. Had he led a force in the lands Rome ruled, Scaurus would have moved northwest instead, to join Thorisin Gavras and the right wing of the shattered imperial army. Hard military sense lay there, for the Emperor's brother—no, the Emperor now, Marcus supposed—had brought his troops away in good order. The fight against the Yezda would center on him.

But here Marcus was not simply a legionary officer, with a legionary officer's worries. He was also a mercenary captain. He had to deal with the fact that the legionaries' women, the families they had made or joined since coming to Videssos, were left behind in the Vaspurakaner city that had been the base for Mavrikios' ill-fated campaign. The Romans would disobey any order to turn away from Khliat. So, even more, would the hundreds of stragglers who had attached themselves to his troop like drowning men clinging to a spar.

For that matter, he never thought of giving such an order. His own partner Helvis, carrying his child, had stayed in Khliat, along with her young son from an earlier attachment.

That was to say, he hoped she had stayed in Khliat. Uncertainty tormented the legionaries as badly as the Yezda did. For all Scaurus knew, the invaders might have stormed Khliat and slain or carried into slavery everyone there. Even if they had not, fugitives would already be arriving with word of the catastrophe that had overtaken the Videssian army.

In the wake of such news, noncombatants might be fleeing eastward now. That was more dangerous than staying behind Khliat's walls. Marcus ran through the gloomy possibilities time after time: Helvis dead, Helvis captured by the Yezda, Helvis struggling east with a three-year-old through hostile country . . . and she was pregnant, too.

At last, with a distinct effort of will, he banished the qualms to the back of his mind. Not for the first time, he was grateful for his training in the Stoic school, which taught him to cast aside useless imaginings. He would know soon enough, and that would be the time to act.

About a day and a half out of Khliat, a scout came riding back to the Roman tribune. "A horseman coming out of the east, sir," he reported. His staccato Khatrisher accent made him hard for Scaurus to understand—the tribune's own Videssian was far from perfect.

Interest flared in him when he realized what the scout was saying. "From the east? A lone rider?"

The Khatrisher spread his hands. "As far as we could tell. He was nervous and took cover as soon as he spotted us. From what little we saw, he had the seeming of a Vaspurakaner."

"No wonder he was leery of you, then. You look too much like Yezda." The invading nomads had ravaged Vaspurakan over the course of years, until the natives hated the sight of them. The Khatrishers were descended from nomads as well and, despite taking many Videssian ways, still had the look of the plains about them.

"Bring him in, and unhurt," Marcus decided. "Anyone fool enough to travel west in the face of everything rolling the other way must have a strong reason. Maybe he bears word from Khliat," the tribune added, suddenly hopeful in spite of himself.

The scout gave a cheery wave—the Khatrishers were most of them free spirits—and kicked his pony into motion. Scaurus did not expect him back for some time; for someone in the furs and leather of a plainsman, convincing a Vaspurakaner of his harmlessness would not be easy. The tribune was surprised when the Khatrisher quickly reappeared, along with another rider plainly not of his people.

The scout's companion looked familiar, even at a distance. Before the tribune was able to say more than that, Senpat

Sviodo cried out in joy and spurred his horse forward to meet the newcomer. "Nevrat!" the Vaspurakaner yelled. "Are you out of your mind, to journey alone through this wolves' land?"

His wife parted company from her escort to embrace him. The Khatrisher stared, slack-jawed. In her loose traveling clothes, her curly black hair bound up under a three-peaked Vaspurakaner hat of leather, and with the grime of travel on her, only her beardless cheeks hinted at her sex. She was surely armed like a man. A horseman's saber hung at her belt, and she carried a bow with an arrow nocked and ready.

She and Senpat were chattering in their throaty native tongue as they slowly rode back to the marching legionaries. The Khatrisher followed, still shaking his head.

"Your outrider has a head on his shoulders," she said, switching to Videssian as she neared Scaurus. "I took him and his comrades for Yezda, for all their shouts of 'Friends! Countrymen!' But when he said, 'Romans!' I knew he was no western jackal."

"I'm glad you chose to trust him," Marcus answered. He was fond of the intense, swarthy girl. So were many other Romans; scattered cheers rang out as the men realized who she was. She smiled her pleasure, teeth flashing white. Senpat Sviodo, proud of her exploit and glad beyond measure she had joined him safely, was grinning, too.

The question Senpat had shouted moments before was still burning in the tribune's mind. "In the name of your god Phos, Nevrat, why did you leave Khliat?" A horrid thought forced its way forward. "Has it fallen?"

"It still stood yesterday morning, when I set out," she answered. The Romans close enough to hear her cheered again, this time with the same relief Scaurus felt. She tempered their delight by continuing, "There's worse madness inside those walls, though, than any I've seen out here."

Gaius Philippus nodded, as if hearing what he expected. "They panicked, did they, when news came we'd been beaten?" The veteran sounded resigned; he had seen enough victories and defeats that the aftermaths of both were second nature to him.

The Romans crowded round Nevrat, calling out the names of their women and asking if they were all right. She told them, "As I said, I left early yesterday. When last I saw them, they were well. Most of you have sensible girls, too; I think they'll have wit enough to keep from joining the flight."

"There's flight, then?" Scaurus asked with a sinking feeling.

Nevrat understood his fears and was quick to lay them to rest. "Helvis knows war, Marcus. She told me to tell you she'd stay in Khliat till the first Yezda came over the wall." The tribune nodded his thanks, not trusting himself to speak. He felt suddenly taller, as if a burden had been lifted from his shoulders. Helvis, he knew, had no such reassurance that he lived.

There were messages from Khliat for some of the other Romans as well. "Is Quintus Glabrio here?" The junior centurion was almost at Nevrat's side, but as usual quiet nearly to the point of invisibility. He took a step forward; Nevrat laughed in surprise. "I'm sorry. Your lady Damaris also told me she would wait for you in the city."

"And much else besides, I'm sure," he said with a smile. The Romans who knew Damaris laughed at that; the hot-tempered Videssian girl was able to talk for herself and Glabrio both.

"Minucius," Nevrat continued in her businesslike way, "Erene says you should know she's stopped throwing up. She's beginning to bulge a bit, too."

"Ah, that's fine to hear," the burly legionary replied. After less than a week without a razor, his beard was coming in thick and black.

Nevrat turned back to Marcus for a moment, amusement in her brown eyes. "Helvis has no such message for you, my friend. I'm afraid she's green as a leek much of the time."

"Is she well?" he asked anxiously.

"Yes, she's fine. There's nothing at all to worry about. You men are such babies about these things."

She was so full of comforting, reassuring words from Khliat that someone finally called out, "If all's so well back there, why are they fleeing the city?"

"All's *not* well," she said flatly. "Remember, the messages I bring are from the folk with the wit to stay and the heart to think I'd find you and they'd see you again. All too many are of the other sort—they've been scurrying like rabbits ever since Ortaias Sphrantzes came galloping into the city with word all was lost."

Curses and angry shouts greeted the young noble's name. Command of the Videssian army's left wing had been his, and his terror-striken flight turned an orderly retreat into rout. Nevrat nodded at the Romans' outburst. She might not have seen Ortaias flee the battlefield, but she had been in Khliat.

She said contemptuously, "He stayed just long enough to change horses—the one he'd ridden died next day of misuse, poor thing—and then he was flying east again. Good riddance, if anyone cares what I think."

"And right you are, lass," Gaius Philippus nodded. A professional soldier to the roots of his iron-gray hair, he asked, "On your way hither, what did you see of the Yezda—aye, and of our fellows, in the bargain?"

"Too many Yezda. They're thicker further east, but there's no order to them at all—they're like frogs after flies, striking at anything that moves. The only thing that brought them together was the imperial army. Now they've crushed it and they're breaking up again, looking for new land to push into . . . and all Videssos this side of the Cattle-Crossing lies open to them."

Marcus thought of Videssos' western lands laid waste by the nomads, the rich, peaceful fields put to the torch, cities so long at peace they had no walls now the playthings of invading barbarians, smoking altars heaped high with butchered victims for Yezd's dark god Skotos. Searching for any straw to contradict that horrid picture, he repeated the second half of Gaius Philippus' question: "What of the Empire's troops?"

"Most are as badly beaten as Ortaias. I watched three Yezda chasing a whole squad of horsemen, laughing themselves sick as they rode. One broke off to follow me, but I lost him in rocky ground." Nevrat dismissed two hours of terror in a sentence.

She went on, "I did see what's left of the Namdalener regiment still in good order, most of a day's ride ahead of you. The nomads were giving them a wide berth."

"That would be the way of it," Viridovix agreed. "Tough as nails, they are." The Romans concurred in that judgment. The warriors from the island Duchy of Namdalen were heretics in Videssos' eyes and as ambitious for themselves as any other mercenary soldiers, but they fought so well the Empire was glad to hire them.

"Did you see anything of Thorisin Gavras?" Scaurus asked. Again he thought of linking with Thorisin's forces.

"The Sevastokrator? No, nor heard anything, either. Is it true the Emperor's dead? Ortaias claimed he was."

"It's true." Marcus did not elaborate and did not mention his grisly proof of Mavrikios' passing.

Gorgidas caught something the tribune missed. The physician said, "How could Sphrantzes know? He was long fled when the Emperor fell." The Romans growled as they took in the implications of that.

"Perhaps he wished it true so badly, he never thought to doubt it," Quintus Glabrio suggested. "Men often believe what they most want."

It was like Glabrio to put as charitable a light as possible on the young noble's action. Marcus, who had been active in politics in his native Mediolanum, found another, more ominous interpretation. Ortaias Sphrantzes was of a house which had held the imperium itself; his uncle, the Sevastos—or prime minister—Vardanes Sphrantzes, was Mavrikios' chief rival.

Gaius Philippus broke into Scaurus' chain of thought. He demanded, "Have we chattered long enough? The sooner we're to Khliat, the sooner we can do something more than beating our gums over all this."

"Give a body a bit of a blow, will you now?" Viridovix said, wiping his sweaty, sunburned forehead with the back of his hand. "You're after forgetting not everyone's like that sleepless bronze giant I once heard a Greek tell of . . ."

He looked questioningly at Gorgidas, who gave him the name: "Talos."

"That's it," the Celt agreed happily. He was excitable, energetic, in short bursts of strength well-nigh unmatchable, but the senior centurion—indeed, many Romans—surpassed him in endurance.

Despite Viridovix' groans, Marcus decided Gaius Philippus was right. Progress was too slow to suit him anyway; there were many walking wounded, and others who had to be carried in litters. If Khliat still stood, the Romans had to get there as fast as they could, before the Yezda mounted an assault to overwhelm its feeble and no doubt demoralized garrison.

That thought led to another. "One last question before we

march," he said to Nevrat: "Is there any word of Avshar?" For
he was sure the wizard-prince was trying to organize the unruly nomads he led to deliver just that attack.

But she shook her head. "None at all, no more than of
Thorisin. Curious, is it not?" She herself had seen war and
skirmished against the Yezda when they first conquered Vaspurakan; she had no trouble following the tribune's logic.

By nightfall the Romans and their various comrades were
less than a day from Khliat. Granted a respite by the Yezda,
the legionaries erected their usual fortified camp. The protection had served them well more times than Marcus could recall. Men bustled about the campsite, intent on creating ditch,
breastwork, and palisade. Eight-man leather tents went up in
neat rows inside.

The Romans showed the Videssians and others who had
joined them what needed to be done and stood over them to
make sure they did it. At Gaius Philippus' profane urging,
order was beginning to emerge again in the legionary ranks.
Now the newcomers, instead of marching where they would,
filled the holes fallen Romans had left in the maniples.

Scaurus approved. "The first step in making legionaries of
them."

"Just what I thought," Gaius Philippus nodded. "Some will
run away, but give us time to work on the rest, and they'll
amount to something. Being with good troops rubs off."

Senpat Sviodo came up to Marcus, an ironic glint in his
eye. "I trust you will not object if my wife spends the evening
inside our works." He bowed low, as if in supplication.

Scaurus flushed. When the Videssian army was intact, he
had followed Roman practice in excluding women from his
soldiers' quarters. As a result, Senpat and Nevrat, preferring
each other's company to legionary discipline, always pitched
their tent just outside the Roman camp. Now, though— "Of
course," the tribune said. "After we reach Khliat, she'll have
plenty of company." He refused to say, or even to think, If we
reach Khliat. . . .

"Good," Senpat said. He studied the tribune. "You can
loosen up a bit after all, then? I'd wondered."

"I suppose I can," Marcus sighed, and the regret in his
voice was so plain he and Sviodo both had to laugh. So it's to
be our women with us wherever we go, is it? the tribune
thought. One more step along the way from legionary officer

to head of a mercenary company. He laughed at himself again, this time silently. In the Empire of Videssos, captain of mercenaries was all he'd ever be, and high time he got used to the notion.

The Yezda were thick as fleas round Khliat; the last day's march to the city was a running fight. But Khliat itself, to Scaurus' surprise, was not under siege, nor was any real effort made to keep the Romans from entering it. As Nevrat had remarked, in victory the nomads forgot the leaders who had won it for them.

That was fortunate, for Khliat could not have repelled a serious attack. Marcus had expected its walls to be bristling with spears, but only a handful of men were on them. To his shock, the gates were open. "Why not?" Gaius Philippus said scornfully. "There's so many running, the Yezda would be trampled if they tried to get in." A gray-brown dust cloud lay over everything eastward, the telltale banner of an army of fugitives.

Inside, panic still boiled. Plump sutlers, calculating men who could smell a copper through a wall of dung, threw their goods at anyone who would take them, so they could flee unencumbered. Singly and in small groups, soldiers wandered through the city's twisting streets and alleyways, calling the names of friends and lovers and hoping against hope they would be answered.

More pitiful yet were the women who crowded close by Khliat's western gate. Some kept a vigil doomed to heartbreak, awaiting warriors who would come to them no more. Others had already despaired of that and stood, bejeweled and gowned, offering themselves to any man who might get them safely away.

The Khatrishers were first into Khliat. Most of them were without women here, as they had taken service with Videssos for the one campaign alone and thus left wives and sweethearts behind in their forested homeland.

The tribune passed through the squat gray arch of stone and under the iron-spiked portcullis which warded the city's western gate. He looked up through the murder-holes and shook his head. Where were the archers to spit death at any invader who tried to force an entrance, where the tubs of bubbling oil and molten lead to warm the foe's reception? Likely, he

thought bitterly, the officer in charge of such things fled, and
no one has thought of them since.

Then any concern over matters military was swept from
him, for Helvis was holding him tightly, heedless of the pinch
of his armor, laughing and crying at the same time. "Marcus!
Oh, Marcus!" she said, covering his bristly face with kisses.
For her, too, the agony of suspense was over.

Other women were crying out with joy and rushing forward
to embrace their men. Three, comely lasses all, made for Viridovix, then halted in dismay and dawning hostility as they
realized their common goal.

"I'd sooner face the Yezda than a mess like that," Gaius
Philippus declared, but Viridovix met the challenge without
flinching. With fine impartiality, the big Gaul had kisses,
hugs, and fair words for all; the blithe charm that had won
each girl separately now rewon them all together.

"It's bloody uncanny," the senior centurion muttered en-
viously. His own luck with women was poor, for the most part
because he took no interest in them beyond serving his lusts.

"The Romans! The Romans!" Starting at the western gate,
the cry spread through Khliat almost before the last legionary
was in the city. Their dependents flocked to them, and many
were the joyful meetings. But many, too, were the women
who learned, some gently from comrades, others by the simple brutal fact of a loved one's absence, that for them there
would be no reunions. There were Romans as well, who
looked in vain for loved faces in the excited crowd and hung
their heads, sorrow sharpened by their companions' delight.

"Where's Malric?" Marcus asked Helvis. He had to shout
to make himself understood.

"With Erene. I watched her two girls yesterday while she
kept vigil here at the gates. I should go to her, to let her know
you've come."

He would not let her out of their embrace. "The whole city
must know that by now," he said. "Bide a moment with me."
He was startled to realize how much for granted he had come
to take her beauty in the short time they had been together.
Seeing her afresh after separation and danger was almost like
looking at her for the first time.

Hers were not the sculptured, aquiline good looks to which
Videssian women aspired. Helvis was a daughter of Namdalen, snub-nosed and rather wide-featured. But her eyes were

deepest blue, her smiling mouth ample and generous, her figure a shout of gladness. It was too soon for pregnancy to mark her body, but the promise of new life glowed from her face.

The tribune kissed her slowly and thoroughly. Then he turned to Gaius Philippus with orders: "Keep the single men here while those of us with partners find them—the gods willing—and bring them back. Give us, hmm—" He gauged the westering sun. "—two hours, then tell off a hundred or so good, reliable men and rout out anyone fool enough to think he'd sooner go it alone."

"Aye, sir." The grim promise on the centurion's face was enough to make any would-be deserter think twice. Gaius Philippus suggested, "We could do worse than using some Khatrishers in our patrols, too."

"There's a thought," Marcus nodded. "Pakhymer!" he called, and the commander of the horsemen from Khatrish guided his small, shaggy horse into earshot. Scaurus explained with he wanted. He phrased it as request; the Khatrishers were equals, voluntary companions in misfortune, not troops formally subject to his will.

Laon Pakhymer absently scratched his cheek as he considered. Like all his countrymen, he was bearded; he wore his own whiskers full and bushy, the better to cover pockmarks. At last he said, "I'll do it, if all patrols are joint ones. If one of your troopers gets rowdy and we have to crack him over the head, I want some of your men around to see it was needful. It's easier never to have a feud than to stop one once started."

Not for the first time, Scaurus admired Pakhymer's cool good sense. In shabby leather trousers and sweat-stained foxskin cap, he looked the simple nomad, a role many Khatrishers affected. But the folk of that land had learned considerable subtlety since their Khamorth ancestors swept down off the plains of Pardraya to wrest the province from Videssos eight hundred years ago. They were like fine wine in cheap jugs, with quality easy to overlook at a hasty drinking.

The tribune ordered the buccinators to trumpet "Attention!" The legionaries stiffened into immobility. Marcus gave them his commands, adding at the end, "Some of you may think you can steal away and never be caught. Well, belike you're right. But remember what's outside and reckon up how long you're likely to enjoy your escape."

A thoughtful silence ensued. Gaius Philippus broke it with

a bellowed, "Dis-*missed!*" Partnered men scattered through the city; their bachelor comrades stood at ease to await their return. Some moved toward the women clustered at the gates, intent on changing their status, permanently or for a little while. Gaius Philippus cocked an interrogative eyebrow at Scaurus. The tribune shrugged. Let his troops find what solace they could.

"Minucius," he said, "come on with Helvis and me? Erene is looking after Malric, it seems."

The legionary grinned. "I'll do that, sir. With three little ones running around, I'm sure of my welcome—seeing me's bound to be a relief."

Marcus chuckled, then translated for Helvis. Among themselves, he and his men mostly spoke Latin, and she had only a few words of it. She rolled her eyes. "You don't know how right you are," she said to Minucius.

"Oh, but I do, my lady," he answered, switching to Videssian for her. "The little farm I grew up on, I was the oldest of eight, not counting two who died young, and I still don't know when my mother slept."

Even in the most troubled times, some things in Khliat did not change. As Helvis, Marcus, and Minucius walked through the town's marketplace, they had to kick their way through the pigeons, blackbirds, and sparrows that congregated in cheeping, chirping hordes round the grain merchants' stalls. The birds were confident of their handouts and just as sure no one meant them any harm.

"They'll learn soon enough," Minucius said, sidestepping to avoid a pigeon which refused to make way for him. "Come a siege, there'll be a lot of bird pies the first day or two. After that they'll know their welcome's gone, and you won't get within fifty feet of one on the ground."

Beggars still lined the edge of the market place, though it seemed most of the able-bodied vagabonds had vanished for safer climes. In an expansive mood, Minucius dug into his pouch for some money to toss to a thin, white-bearded old man with only one leg who lounged in front of an open tavern door.

"You'd give him gold?" Marcus asked in surprise, seeing the trooper produce a small coin instead of one of the broad bronze pieces Videssos minted.

"That's what they'd like you to think, anyway. It's that

pen-pusher Strobilos' money, and it's not worth a bloody thing." Ortaias Sphrantzes' great-uncle Strobilos had been Avtokrator until Mavrikios Gavras ousted him four years before. His coinage was cheapened even beyond the lows set by previous bureaucratic Emperors; the "goldpiece" on which his pudgy features were stamped was more than half copper.

Minucius flipped the coin to the beggar, who plucked it out of the air. Debased or no, it was a finer gift than he usually got; he dipped his head and thanked the Roman in halting, Vaspurakaner-flavored Videssian. That completed, he popped the coin into his mouth and dragged himself into the grog-shop.

"I hope the old boy has himself one fine spree," Minucius said. "He doesn't look like there's many left in him."

Scaurus gave the legionary an odd look. Minucius had always struck him as sharing Gaius Philippus' single-minded devotion to the army, without the senior centurion's years of experience to give a sense of proportion. Such a thoughtful remark was not like him.

"If you're as eager to see Erene as she is to see you," Helvis said to Minucius with a smile, "it will be a happy meeting indeed. She hardly talks about anything but you."

Minucius' thick-bearded Italian peasant's face lit up in a grin that lightened his hard features. "Really?" he said, sounding shy and amazed as a fifteen-year-old. "These past few months I've thought myself the luckiest man alive. . . ." And he was off, praising Erene the rest of the way to the small house she and Helvis shared.

Listening to him as they walked along, Marcus had no trouble deciding where his unexpected streak of compassion came from. Here was a man unabashedly in love. In a way, the tribune was a trifle jealous. Helvis was a splendid bedmate, a fine companion, and no one's fool, but he could not find the flood of emotion in him that Minucius was releasing. He was happy, aye, but not heart-full.

Well, he told himself, you'll never see thirty again, and it's not likely Minucius has twenty-two winters in him. But am I older, he asked himself, or merely colder? He was honest enough to admit he did not know.

Helvis wore the key to her lodging on a string round her neck. She drew it up from between her breasts, inserted it into its socket, and drew out the bolt-pin. The door opened inward;

Malric shot out, crying, "Mama! Mama!" and reaching up to seize his mother round the waist. "Hello, Papa!" he added as she lifted him and tossed him up in the air.

"Hello, lad," Marcus said, taking him from Helvis.

"Did you bring me a Yezda's head, papa?" Malric said, remembering what he'd asked of Scaurus before the imperial army left Khliat.

"You'll have to ask Viridovix about that," the tribune told him.

Minucius barked laughter. "There's a warrior in the making," he said.

His voice brought a delighted cry of recognition from inside the house. Erene, a stocky little Videssian girl who barely reached his shoulder, came running through the door and almost bowled him over with her welcoming embrace.

"Easy, darling, easy!" he said, holding her out at arm's length. "If I squeeze you as tight as I want, I'd pop the baby out right now." He stroked her cheek with a sword-callused hand.

"Are you all right?" Erene asked anxiously. "You weren't hurt?"

"No, hardly even a scratch. You see, what happened was—"

Marcus gave a dry cough. "I'm afraid all this will have to wait. Erene, round up your girls and pack whatever you can carry without being slowed. I want to be out of this town before sunset."

Minucius looked at him reproachfully, but was too much a soldier to argue. He expected a protest from Erene, but all she said was, "I've been ready to leave for two days. This one—" She squeezed Minucius' arm. "—knows how to travel light, and I've done my best to learn from him."

"And I," Helvis said when Scaurus turned his head toward her. "I've been with you long enough to know your craze for lugging everything around on your men's backs. What you have against supply wagons and packhorses I'll never understand." Her own folk's warriors fought mounted and were far more at home with horses than the unchivalric Romans.

"The more independent an army is of anything outside itself, the better it does. The Yezda show that only too well. Now, though, we really could use extra beasts and cars, what with all the noncombatants we'll have along. Will Khliat supply any, do you think?"

Erene shook her head. Helvis explained further: "Yesterday it would have, but last night Utprand brought his regiment through and emptied the horse-pens of what animals were left. He headed south at dawn this morning."

Likely, Marcus thought, the Namdalener captain was leading his troops to Phanaskert, to join his fellow easterners who were serving as a garrison in that city. From his own point of view that was a logical move: best to link all the men of the Duchy together. Utprand probably did not care—or even notice—that his march out of the path of the oncoming Yezda helped open Videssos to invasion. Mercenaries tended to think of themselves before their paymasters. As do I, the tribune realized, as do I.

His musing made him miss Helvis' next sentence. "I'm sorry?"

"I said that I suppose we'll be going in the same direction."

"What? No, of course not." The words were out of his mouth before he remembered her brother Soteric was part of the garrison at Phanaskert.

Helvis' full lips thinned; her eyes narrowed dangerously. "Why? From all I've heard, Utprand's men and yours fought the Yezda to a standstill, even after others fled." The normal contempt mercenary kin felt for the folk they were hired to defend was only made worse because Videssians and Namdaleni saw each other as heretics. Helvis went on, "Phanaskert is a stout city, stronger than Khliat. Surely behind its walls you could laugh at the scrawny nomads capering by."

The tribune swallowed a sigh of relief. He wanted no part of going to Phanaskert, and Helvis unwittingly provided him with a perfect military justification for not doing so. He also did not want to quarrel with her. She was strong-willed; her temper, once aroused, was fierce; and in any case he had no time to argue.

He said, "City walls are less protection against nomads than you think. They burn the fields outside, kill the peasants who work them, and starve the town into yielding. Think," he urged her. "You've seen it's true, in the Empire and here in Vaspurakan. May they rot for it, the Yezda are no better bargain in a siege than in the open field."

She bit her lip, wanting to disagree further but seeing

Scaurus' mind was made up. "Very well," she said at last. Her smile was wry. "I won't argue with you over soldierly matters. Whether I'm right or not, it would do me no good."

Marcus was content to let it go at that. While what he had said was true, he knew it was far from the whole truth. Great events would be brewing in Videssos in the aftermath of Mavrikios' defeat and death. He did not intend to be stranded in a provincial town on the edge of nowhere while they took place without him. In his own way, he was as ambitious as all the other mercenary captains reckoning their chances of riding chaos' wind to glory. But with only his few precious legionaries behind him, his hopes, unlike theirs, had to center on the imperial government.

None of that calculation showed on his face. He mused how much easier it would have been to remain one of Caesar's junior officers, with clearly defined duties and with someone else to do his thinking for him. He shrugged inside his mail shirt. The Stoic doctrine he'd studied in Italy taught a man to make the best of what he had and not wish for the impossible —a good creed for a quiet man.

"If you're ready," he said to Helvis and Erene, "we'd best head back."

"Sure and I'm baked to a wee black cinder," Viridovix said as he tramped along. In fact he was not black, but red as any half-cooked meat. His fair Celtic skin burned under the ferocious Vaspurakaner sun, but refused to tan. Gorgidas smeared various smelly ointments on him. They sloughed away with each new layer of peeling hide.

The Gaul swore as a drop of sweat drew a stinging track down his face. "I have a riddle for the lot of you," he called. "Why is even the silly seagull wiser than I?"

"I could think of a dozen reasons without trying," Gaius Philippus said, not about to let such an opening slip by. "Tell us yours."

Viridovix glared, but gave the answer he had prepared. "Because it has the sense never to visit Vaspurakan."

The Romans, draggled and sun-baked themselves, chuckled in agreement. Senpat Sviodo, though, took offense to hear his native land maligned. He said loftily, "I'll have you know this is the first land Phos shaped when he made the world, and the home of our ancestor Vaspur, the first man."

Some of the Videssians who had joined the Romans hooted. The Vaspurakaners might call themselves Phos' princes, but no people outside the "princes'" land took their theology seriously.

Viridovix cared nothing for theology of any sort. His objections were more immediate. Tilting his head back so he could look down his long nose at the mounted Senpat, he said, "About your being kin to the first man I'll not speak one way or t'other. Of that sort of thing I ken nought. But I do believe this land your Phos' first creation, for one look about would tell anybody the puir fool needed more practice."

The legionaries whooped to see Sviodo speechless; the imperials—and Khatrishers, too—laughed louder yet at Viridovix' delicious blasphemy. "You've only yourself to blame for the egg on your face," Gaius Philippus told the young Vaspurakaner, not unkindly. "Anyone with a tongue fast enough to keep three lovelies—and keep them all happy with him—is more than a match for a puppy like you."

"I suppose so," Senpat murmured. "But who would have thought he could talk with it, too?" Sunburned as he was, Viridovix could go no redder, but his strangled snort said the Vaspurakaner had a measure of revenge.

The Romans and their comrades pushed east from Khliat in an order reminiscent of any threatened herd. As always, the Khatrishers served as scouts and outriders, screening the main body and warning of trouble ahead or to either side. At their center marched a hollow square of legionaries, old bulls protecting the women, children, and wounded within.

The force's good order and obvious readiness to stand and fight kept it from danger. A company of about three hundred Yezda paralleled the Romans' course for more than a day, like so many wolves waiting to pick off the stragglers from a herd of wisent. At last they concluded there was no hope of catching their quarry unaware and rode away in search of easier prey.

At nightfall now, Marcus could hardly protest women inside his camp. Helvis shared his tent, and he was glad of it. Nonetheless, the principle of the thing still galled him. When Senpat Sviodo began teasing him once more, the only answer he got was a stare cold enough to end any further raillery before it could start. Acquiescent Scaurus might be, but not enthusiastic.

Late in the fourth morning out from Khliat, a Khatrisher scout came riding up from the south. Flipping Marcus the usual offhand salute, he reported, "There's something funny going on up in the hills—sounds pretty much like fighting, but not quite. I didn't take a close look. It's better country for foot than horse—the grade is steep, and there's all kinds of loose rocks."

"Show me," the tribune said. He followed the Khatrisher's pointing finger. Sure enough, he saw a small dust cloud and, below it, occasional sparks of light as the sun flashed off a blade. Even allowing that the action was a couple of miles away, it did not seem very big.

Still, if it was Videssian stragglers or Vaspurakaners meeting the vanguard of a major Yezda force, that was something the Romans had to know. Scaurus turned to Gaius Philippus. "Detail me eight men with a good, sensible underofficer to find out what the skirmish means."

"Eight men it is, sir," the centurion nodded, quickly choosing a tentful of legionaries. "And for the party's leader," he said, "I'd suggest—"

On impulse, Marcus cut him off. "Never mind. I'll take them myself."

Gaius Philippus' face froze, except for one unruly eyebrow that climbed toward his hairline in mute expression of the scandalized feelings he was too well drilled to speak out loud. But Scaurus' ears were sharper than most. As he turned to take the reconnaissance squad away, he heard the senior centurion grumbling to himself, "Fool amateurs, always think they have to lead from the front."

Leadership, as it happened, had played almost no rôle in the tribune's sudden decision. Curiosity was a much bigger part of it, a curiosity piqued by the Khatrisher's odd description of what he had heard: "Pretty much like fighting, but not quite." That deserved a closer look.

"Double march," he told his men and hurried south, his long legs chewing up the distance. Though the legionaries were shorter and stockier, they kept pace. At double march—almost a trot, really—there was scant breath for chatter. The two miles vanished in a silence broken only by hard breathing, the slap of sandals on dirt, and the occasional clank of scabbards slapping off iron-studded military kilts.

The land began sloping up from the valley floor; loose

rocks and gravel made the going hard. Marcus stumbled and had to put his hands out to save a fall. To the rear, one of his men cursed as the same thing happened to him. He realized the Khatrisher had been right in his reluctance to take his mount up the slope. Four legs might be quicker than two, but in this terrain two were far more agile.

He was close enough now to hear the noise the scout had reported, though a jumble of boulders ahead still hid its source. The Khatrisher had been right: at first it sounded like any bit of sharp fighting heard from outside, but as the Romans drew nearer they began cocking their heads and looking at one another in puzzlement. Steel on steel did not sound quite like this, nor did the shouts the combatants raised. Where was the noise of booted feet stamping and leaping, and what was the source of the high, almost inaudible keening that took its place?

Marcus drew his Gallic longsword; its weight was comforting in his palm. Behind him, he heard his men's stubby *gladii* rasp free of their brass scabbards. The Romans pushed past the last obstructions and up onto a stretch of ground flatter than that through which they had been struggling.

On the little plain, a dozen and a half Yezda, urged on by a hard-faced man in robes the color of dried blood, hewed and chopped at a double handful of Videssians clustered protectively around a plump, shave-pated fellow whose dusty garment might once have been sky blue. "Nepos!" Scaurus shouted, recognizing the rotund little priest of Phos.

Nepos' head whipped round at the cry; the struggle, going no better than most at odds of nearly two to one, promptly grew more desperate yet, the circle round the priest tighter. Neither the Videssian soldiers nor their foes appeared to notice the Romans' arrival.

"At them!" Marcus shouted. If the Yezda chose to be fools, it was none of his concern.

The red-robe who led them smiled thinly as the legionaries charged.

His men did not divert a minim of their attention from the enemy at hand, not even when the Romans were upon them. And the legionaries shouted in amazement and dread, for their swords drove through the Yezda as if through smoke, and their bodies met no resistance from the solid-seeming foe.

The Videssian soldiers, for all their bellowed war cries, for all the ringing of their blades against those of the Yezda, were as insubstantial as the wraiths they fought. Marcus' brain stopped its brief terrorized yammering—Nepos was mage as well as priest, and the tribune knew Yezda sorcerers wore red-brown by choice. His men had stumbled across a wizards' duel—and Nepos' opponent was no weakling, not if he could force the fat priest to the defensive.

Then Scaurus' sword lashed across one of the phantom Yezda warriors. The marks set into the blade flared golden as it sheared through the sorcery. Like a doused candle flame, the soldier's seeming ceased to be. Another vanished to a second stroke, then another and another. The Yezda wizard's smile disappeared with them.

As their foes blew out, Nepos' projections swung to the attack, and it was his enemy's turn to draw his powers around himself for defense. But Marcus' blade, enchanted by vanished Gaul's druids, had shown itself proof against the spells of Avshar himself; an underling's magic was no match for it. The tribune pushed forward remorselessly, striking the Yezda's wraithly warriors out of existence.

Even when the last of them was gone, the red-robe proved neither coward nor weakling. His spells were still potent enough to hold off Nepos' assault; no phantom Videssian sword reached him, though they missed now by hairbreadths. Growling an oath in his own harsh tongue, he snatched out a dagger and leaped forward to grapple with Scaurus.

That was a contest with but one possible ending, despite the Yezda's courage. The Roman turned the wizard's stab with his shield, thrust out and up with the killing stroke of the legionaries. His blade bit flesh, not the filmy figments that had so far stood against him. Blood ran from the Yezda's mouth, to drown his dying curse half-uttered.

Nepos' seemings vanished when their creator's foe fell. The little Videssian priest staggered himself, a man in the last throes of exhaustion. Sweat was pouring from his shaven crown; drops sparkled in his beard. He came up to clasp the tribune's arm. "Praise Phos, who sends the light, for sending you to me in my desperate need." The priest's voice was a ragged, croaking caricature of his usual firm tenor.

He looked down at the crumpled form of the dead Yezda wizard, murmuring, "He would have killed me, I think, had you not come when you did."

"How did you get into a sorcerers' duel?" Marcus asked.

"We were dodging each other through these rocks. I saw he had a knife and wanted to frighten him off with phantoms. But he fought back—and he was strong." Nepos shook his head. "And yet he seemed but a shaman like a thousand others, while I, I am a mage of the Videssian Academy. Can it be true, then—is his dark Skotos a mightier god than mine? Is my life's work one long futility?"

Scaurus thumped his shoulder; Nepos was normally a jolly soul, but liable to fits of gloom when things went bad. The tribune said, "Buck up. He and all his kind are riding the hem of Avshar's robe—one win and they think they bestride the world." He studied the draggled priest. "And you, my friend, are not at your best."

"That's so," Nepos admitted. He scrubbed at the sweat-streaked dirt on his face with a grimy sleeve and shook his head in dismay. It was as if he was looking at himself for the first time in days. He managed a feeble smile. "I'm not in fine fettle, am I?"

"Hardly," Marcus said. "I can't promise you any elegant accommodations with my men, but they do beat straggling home alone."

Nepos' smile grew broader. "I should certainly hope so." He sighed, then turned to the legionaries. "I suppose that means I'll have to tramp back with you long-shanked gentlemen." The Romans grinned at him; they were all taller—and leaner—than the tubby little priest.

He did his valiant best to keep pace with them, his short legs churning over the ground. "Not bad," one of the soldiers commended him as they approached the Roman column. The trooper's smile turned sly. "There's plenty of Videssians with us already. Maybe we'll find you a coat of mail and a pack and make a real legionary out of you."

"Phos forfend!" Nepos panted, rolling his eyes.

"Or we could just lay you down and roll you along," another Roman suggested. The look the priest sent Marcus was so full of indignant appeal that the tribune coughed and put an end to his troopers' fun.

Gaius Philippus had been pulling out a full maniple of soldiers to come to Scaurus' rescue. He waved when he saw the squad coming back down into the valley. As soon as they were in earshot, he bellowed, "Everything all right?"

Marcus answered with the upraised thumb of the gladiatorial arena. The senior centurion gave back the signal and returned the maniple to the ranks. Despite Gaius Philippus' mutterings over amateurs and personal leadership, Scaurus saw no signs that anyone but the centurion was going to take that maniple forward.

A spare figure in chlamys and sandals loped out from the Roman column toward the returning squad. Gorgidas ignored Marcus; as for the legionaries, they might as well not have been there. The Greek doctor's attention was solely on Nepos. "Do you know your people's healing art?" he demanded. He leaned forward, as if willing an aye out of the priest.

"Why, yes, a bit, but—"

Gorgidas allowed no protest. He and Nepos had had many soul-searching talks, but the intense Greek would not spare time for them now. He clutched the priest's shoulder and dragged him toward the litters of the seriously wounded, saying, "The gods know I've been praying for days to run across a blue-robe with his wits about him. I've had to watch men die, beyond the power of my medicine to cure. But you lads, now—" He stopped short and shook his head, a rational man compelled to acknowledge the power of forces past reason.

Curious Romans, Marcus among them, followed the oddly matched pair. He had seen a healer-priest save Sextus Minucius and another legionary just after the Romans came to Videssos. But miracles, he thought, did not go stale with repetition.

Nepos was still protesting his unworthiness as Gorgidas tugged him onward. His expostulations faded when he came face to face with the horrid facts of injury. The worst-hurt soldiers were already dead, either of their wounds or from the sketchy care and jolting they had received during the Romans' grinding retreat.

Many who still clung to life would not for long. Shock, infection, and fever, coupled with scant water and constant baking sun, made death almost an hourly visitor. The stench of septic wounds turned the stomach even through the aromatic ointments Gorgidas had applied. Men witless from fever shivered in the noonday heat or babbled anguished gibberish. Here was war's aftermath at its grimmest.

In the face of such misery, Nepos underwent a transformation nearly as great as the one Gorgidas hoped he would work on the wounded. The rotund priest's fatigue fell from him. When he drew himself upright, he seemed inches taller. "Show me the worst of them," he said to Gorgidas, and suddenly it was his voice, not the Greek doctor's, that was filled with authority.

If Gorgidas noticed the reversal, it did not faze him. He was content to play a secondary role, should that be required to save his patients. "The worst?" he said, rubbing his chin with a slim-fingered hand. "That would be Publius Flaccus, I think. Over this way, if you will."

Publius Flaccus was beyond thrashing and delirium; only the low, rapid rise and fall of his chest showed he was still alive. He lay unmoving on his litter, the coarse stubble of his beard stark and black against tight-drawn, waxen skin. A Yezda saber had laid his left thigh open from groin to knee. Somehow Gorgidas managed to stanch the flow of blood, but the wound grew inflamed almost at once, and from mere inflammation quickly passed to mortification's horror.

Greenish-yellow pus crusted the bandages wrapping the gashed limb. Drawn by the smell of corruption, flies made a darting cloud around Flaccus. They scattered, buzzing, as Nepos stooped to examine the wounded Roman.

The priest's face was grave as he said to Gorgidas, "I will do what I can. Unbandage him for me, please; there must be contact between his flesh and mine." Gorgidas knelt beside Nepos, deftly undoing the dressings he had applied the day before.

Battle-hardened soldiers gagged and drew back as the huge gash was bared. Its stench was more than most men could stand, but neither priest nor physician flinched from it.

"Now I understand the *Philoktetes*," Gorgidas said to himself. Nepos looked at him without comprehension, for the doctor had fallen back into Greek. Unaware that he had spoken at all, Gorgidas did not explain.

Marcus also realized the truth in Sophokles' play. No matter how vital a man was, with this foul a wound his presence could become intolerable enough to force his comrades to abandon him. The thought flickered and blew out, for Nepos was leaning forward to take Publius Flaccus' thigh in his hands.

The priest's eyes were closed. He gripped the mangled leg so tightly his knuckles whitened. Had Flaccus been conscious, he would have shrieked in agony. As it was, he did not stir. Fresh pus welled up over the swollen lips of the wound to foul Nepos' hands. The priest ignored it, his spirit and will focused on the injury alone.

Back at Imbros, a year before, Gorgidas had spoken of a flow of healing from priest to patient. The words were vague, but Scaurus had found none better then, nor did he now. The short hairs on the nape of his neck tried to rise, for he could feel the current passing between Nepos and Flaccus, though not with any sense he could name.

To aid his concentration, Nepos whispered an endless series of prayers. The Videssian dialect he used was so archaic Scaurus only caught a word now and again. Even the name of the priest's god shifted. The divine patron of good was Phos in the modern tongue, but sounded more like "Phaos" in Nepos' elder idiom.

At first Marcus wondered if it was his hopeful imagination, but soon he had no doubt: the evil-smelling pus was disappearing from the filthy gash, its swollen, inflamed lips visibly shrinking. "Will you look there?" a Roman muttered, awe in his voice. Other legionaries called on gods they had known longer than Phos.

Nepos paid no attention. Everything around him might have vanished in a clap of thunder, and he would have crouched, oblivious, before the still form of Publius Flaccus.

The wounded legionary moaned and stirred, his eyes fluttering open for the first time in two days. They were sunk deep in their sockets, but had reason in them. Gorgidas slipped a steadying arm behind Flaccus' shoulder and offered him a canteen. The Roman drank thirstily. "Thank you," he whispered.

When nothing else had, his words penetrated Nepos' shell of concentration. The priest relaxed his clenched grip on Flaccus' thigh; like the legionary, he, too, seemed to become aware of his surroundings once more. He reached out to take one of Flaccus' hands in his own. "Phos be praised," he said, "for allowing me to act as his instrument in saving this man."

Marcus and the rest of the Romans looked with marvel at the wonder Nepos had wrought. The rotting, stinking wound which had been about to kill Publius Flaccus was suddenly clean, free of corruption, and showing every sign of being able to heal normally. And Flaccus himself, the killing fever banished from his system, was trying to sit and trading gibes with the soldiers crowding near him. Only the fly-swarming pile of pus-soaked bandages gave any evidence of what had just happened.

His face alight, Gorgidas came around Flaccus to help Nepos up. "You must teach me your art," he said. "Anything I have is yours."

The priest was wobbly on his feet; fatigue was flooding back into him. Nonetheless he smiled wanly, saying, "Speak not of payment. I will show you if I can. If the talent lies within you, Phos' servants ask nothing but that it be wisely used."

"Thank you," Gorgidas said softly, as grateful for the boon Nepos offered as Flaccus had been for the simpler gift of water. Then the physician grew brisk once more. "But for now there is only the one of you, and many more men who need your help. Cotilius Rufus, I think, is next worst off—his litter is over here." He tugged Nepos through the crowd round Flaccus.

The priest took three or four steps before his eyes rolled up in his head and he slid gently to the ground. Gorgidas stared in consternation, then bent over his prostrate form. He peeled back an eyelid, felt for Nepos' pulse. "He's asleep," the physician said indignantly.

Marcus laid a hand on his shoulder. "We've seen that this healing of theirs takes as much from the healer as it puts into the sufferer. And Nepos had been drawing heavily on his powers before you grabbed him. Let the poor fellow rest."

"Oh, very well," Gorgidas conceded with poor grace. "He is a man, after all, not a scalpel or a stick of collyrium to grind up for eyewash. I suppose it wouldn't do to kill off my chief healing tool from overwork. But he'd better wake up soon." And the physician settled himself beside the softly snoring Nepos to wait.

Soli, when the Romans and their companions reached it a few days later, had already had a visit from the Yezda. The ruins of the wall-less new town by the bank of the Rhamnos River had been sacked yet again, probably for the dozenth time in the two-score or so years since Yezd's nomads began pushing into Videssos. Little gray eddies of smoke still spiraled into the air, though Scaurus was hard-pressed to understand what the invaders had found to burn.

On the bluff overlooking the river, the partially rebuilt Old Soli had survived behind its walls. Cries of alarm and trumpet blasts came echoing from those walls when lookouts spied the approaching force. Marcus had trouble convincing the watchmen his troops were friendly, the more so as the Yezda had driven Videssian prisoners ahead of them to masquerade as an imperial army.

When the town's stout gates swung open at last, its *hypasteos* or city governor came out through them to greet the Romans. He was a tall, thin man of about forty, with stooped shoulders and a permanently dyspeptic expression. The tribune had not seen him on the army's westward march, but remembered he was called Evghenios Kananos.

Kananos studied the newcomers with wary curiosity, as if still unsure they were not Yezda in disguise. "You're the first decent-sized bunch of our troops I've seen. Was starting to think there weren't none left," he said to Marcus. He had an up-country twang that matched his dour mien.

"Some regiments did get free," the tribune answered. "We—"

Kananos kept right on, as if Scaurus had not spoken. "Ayuh," he said, "I don't believe I've seen hardly a one, but for the miserable little band that rode in with the Emperor yesterday. On his way to Pityos, he was, and then by sea to the capital, I suppose."

Marcus stared at the *hypasteos*, his mouth falling open. Everyone close enough to hear stood similarly frozen in his tracks. "The Emperor?" It was Zeprin the Red who asked the question, elbowing his way up through the Roman ranks. The burly Haloga had been one of the commanders of Mavrikios' Imperial Guard, and his failure to save his overlord had plunged the once-ebullient northerner so deep into depression that he marched along day after day with hardly a word. Suddenly his face and voice were alive again. "The Emperor?" he repeated eagerly.

"That's what I said," Kananos agreed. He used his words sparingly; it seemed to pain him to have to go back over ground once covered.

To the point as always, Gaius Philippus demanded, "How could Thorisin Gavras have come through here without us getting word he was close? And I'd hardly call the troops he had with him a 'miserable little band'—he got clear in pretty fair order."

"Thorisin Gavras?" Evghenios Kananos stared at the centurion in surprise and a little suspicion. "Didn't say a word about Thorisin Gavras. I was talking about the Emperor—the Emperor Ortaias. Far as I know, there ain't no other."

II

"YOUR HONOR, YOU'RE A RARE STUBBORN MAN," VIRIDOVIX told Scaurus the day after Kananos' shattering news, "but you can march the legs off the lot of us, and we'll still never catch up to that omadhaun of a Sphrantzes."

Weary and frustrated, the tribune halted. His outrage over Ortaias' gall in assuming the imperial title had made him fling his small army north to drag the usurper to earth. But Viridovix was right. When looked at rationally and not through the red haze of anger, the Romans had no chance to overtake him. Sphrantzes was mounted, had no women and wounded to encumber him, and had a day's lead. Moreover, the further north Scaurus led his men, the more Yezda they met, and the more hostile the nomads were.

The legionaries clearly saw the futility of pursuit. Roman discipline kept them pushing toward Pityos, but their hearts were not in it. They were harder to get moving after every halt, and slower on the march. And only the fear that leaving would be worse kept the men they had added since Maragha with them. Everyone despised Ortaias Sphrantzes, but they all knew they could not catch him.

Laon Pakhymer sensed this stop was different from the ones before. He rode back to Marcus, asking, "Finally had enough?" His voice held sympathy—he had no more use than the Romans for Sphrantzes—but also a certain hardness, warning that he, too, was running out of patience with this useless hunt.

Marcus looked from him to the Gaul, then, as a last hope, to Gaius Philippus, whose contempt for the would-be Emperor knew no bounds. "Are you asking what I think?" the senior centurion said.

Marcus nodded.

"All right, then. There's not a prayer of catching up with the worthless son of a sow. In your heart you must know that as well as I do."

"I suppose so," the tribune sighed. "But if that's what you think, why didn't you say so when we set out?" Roman discipline or no, Scaurus rarely had doubts about Gaius Philippus' opinion.

"Simple enough—whether or not we nailed Sphrantzes, I thought Pityos a good place to head for. If Ortaias could sail back to Videssos the city, so could we, and save ourselves having to fight across the westlands. But from the look of things, there are too bloody many Yezda between us and the port to let us get there unmangled."

"I fear you're right. I wish we knew how Thorisin stands."

"So do I—or if he stands. Too many Yezda westward, though, to swing back and find out."

"I know." Marcus clenched his fist. Now more than ever, he wished for any word of the slain emperor's brother, but the choice he was forced to only made getting that word more unlikely. "We have to turn east, away from them."

They had spoken Latin; when the tribune saw Pakhymer's blank look, he quickly translated his decision into Videssian. "Sensible," the Khatrisher said. He cocked his head at the Romans in a gesture his people often used. "Do any of you know where you're headed? 'East' covers a lot of ground, and you're not from these parts, you know." In spite of his gloom, Marcus had to smile at the understatement.

Gaius Philippus said, "The Yezda can't have run everyone off the land. There's bound to be a soul or two willing to show us the way—if for no better reason than to keep us out of his own valley."

Laon Pakhymer chuckled and spread his hands in defeat. "There you have me. *I* wouldn't want this ragtag mob of ruffians camped near me any longer than I could help it."

The senior centurion grunted. He might have been pleased at gaining the Khatrisher's agreement, but hardly by his unflattering description of the legionaries.

* * *

The shrill sound of a squabble woke Marcus before dawn the next morning. He cursed wearily as he sat up in his bed-roll, still worn from the previous day's march through broken country. Beside him Helvis sighed and turned over, fighting to stay asleep. Malric, who never seemed to sleep when the tribune and Helvis wanted him to, did not stir now.

Scaurus stuck his head through his tent flap. He was just in time to see Quintus Glabrio's companion Damaris stamp from the junior centurion's tent. She was still shouting abuse as she angrily stode away: "—the most useless man I can imagine! What I saw in you I'll never know!" She disappeared out of the tribune's line of vision.

In fact, Scaurus was more inclined to wonder what had attracted the Roman to her. True, she was striking enough in the strong-featured Videssian way, with snapping brown eyes. But she was skinny as a boy and had all the temper those eyes foretold. She was, the tribune realized, as hotheaded as Thorisin's lady Komitta Rhangavve—and that was saying a great deal. Nor did Glabrio have Thorisin's quick answering contentiousness. It was a puzzler.

Glabrio, rather in the way of a man who pokes his head out the door to see if a thunderstorm is past, looked out to see which way Damaris had gone. He caught sight of Marcus, shrugged ruefully, and withdrew into his tent once more. Embarrassed at witnessing his discomfiture, the tribune did the same.

Damaris' last outburst had succeeded in rousing Helvis, though Malric slept on. Brushing sleep-snarled brown hair back from her face, she yawned, sat up, and said, "I'm glad we don't fight like that, Hemond—" She stopped in confusion.

Marcus grunted, his lip quirking in a lopsided smile. He knew he should not be bothered when Helvis absently called him by her dead husband's name, but he could not help the twinge that ran through him every time she slipped.

"You might as well wake the boy," he said. "The whole camp will be stirring now." The effort to keep annoyance from his voice took all emotion with it, leaving his words flat and hard as a marble slab.

The unsuccessful try at hiding anger was worse than none at all. Helvis did as he asked her, but her face was a mask that did as little to hide her hurt as had his coldly dispassionate tone. Looks like a fine morning already, just a fine one, the tribune thought as he laced on his armor.

He threw himself into his duties to take his mind off the almost-quarrel. His supervision of breaking camp was so minute one might have supposed his troops were doing it for the first time rather then the three-hundredth or, for some, the three-thousandth. He heard Quintus Glabrio swearing at the men in his maniple—something rare from that quiet officer—and knew he was not the only one with nerves still jangling.

The matter of guides went as Gaius Philippus had guessed. The Romans were passing through a hardscrabble country, with scores of rocky little valleys running higgledy-piggledy one into the next. The coming of any strangers into such a backwater would have produced a reaction; the coming of an army, even a small, defeated army, came close to raising panic.

Farmers and herders so isolated they rarely saw a tax collector—isolation indeed, in Videssos—wanted nothing more than to get the Romans away from their own home villages before pillage and rape broke loose. Every hamlet had a young man or two willing, nay, eager, to send them on their way . . . often, Marcus noted, toward rivals who lived one valley further east.

Sometimes the tribune's men got a friendlier reception. Bands of Yezda, with their nomadic hardiness and mobility, had penetrated even this inhospitable territory. When a timely arrival let the Romans appear as rescuers, nothing their rustic hosts owned was too fine to lavish on them.

"Now this is the life for me, and no mistake," Viridovix said after one such small victory. The Celt sprawled in front of a campfire. A mug of beer was in his right hand, a little mountain of well-gnawed pork ribs at his feet. He took a long pull at the mug, belched, and went on, "You know, we could do a sight worse than kinging it here for the rest of our days. Who'd be caring enough to say us nay?"

"I, for one," Gaius Philippus answered promptly. "This place is yokeldom's motherland. Even the whores are clumsy."

"There's more to life than your prick, you know," the Celt said. His righteous tone drew howls from everyone who heard him; Gaius Philippus mutely held out a hand with three upraised fingers. With the ruddy firelight and his permanently sunburned skin, it was impossible to tell if Viridovix blushed, but he did tug at his sweeping mustaches in chagrin.

"But still," he persisted, "doesn't all this—" He reached out a foot and toppled the pile of bones. "—make munching marching rations a thought worth puking on? Dusty porridge, stale bread, smoked meat with the taste of a herd of butchered shoes—a day of that would gag a buzzard, and we eat it week after week."

Gorgidas said, "You know, my Gallic friend, there are times you're naïve as a child. How often do you think this miserable valley can supply feasts like this?" He waved out into the dark, reminding his listeners of the poor, small, rocky fields they'd come through, fields that sometimes seemed to go straight up a mountainside.

"I grew up in country like this," the doctor went on. "The folk here will eat poorer this winter for feasting us tonight. If they did it two weeks running, some would starve before spring—and so would some of us, should we stay."

Viridovix stared at him without comprehension. He was used to the lush fertility of his northern Gallic homeland, with its cool summers, mild winters, and long, gentle rains. Cut firewood sprouted green shoots there; here in the Videssian uplands, rooted trees withered in the ground.

"There are more reasons than Gorgidas' for going on," Marcus said, disturbed that the idea Viridovix put forward half jokingly was getting serious attention. "However much we'd like to forget the world, I fear it won't forget us. Either the Yezda will flatten the Empire—which looks all too likely right now—or Videssos will somehow drive them back. Whoever wins will stretch their rule all through this land. Do you think we could stand against them?"

"They'd have to find us first." Senpat Sviodo gave Viridovix unexpected support. "To judge from the run of guides we've had, even the locals don't know the land three valleys over."

There were rumbles of agreement to that from around the campfire. Gaius Philippus muttered, "To judge from the run of guides we've had, the locals don't know enough to squat when they crap."

No one could dispute that, either. Glad to see the argument

diverted, Scaurus said, "This last one is better," and the centurion had to nod. The Romans' latest guide was a solidly built middle-aged man with a soldier's scars; his name was Lexos Blemmydes. He carried himself like a veteran, too, and his Videssian had lost some of its original hill-country accent. Marcus had a nagging feeling he'd seen Blemmydes before, but the guide's face did not seem familiar to any of his men.

The tribune wondered if Blemmydes was one of the refugees from Videssos' shattered army. The man had attached himself to the Romans a few days before, coming up to their camp one evening and asking if they needed a guide. Whoever he was, he certainly knew his way through this rocky maze. His descriptions of upcoming terrain, villages, and even village leaders ahead were unfailingly accurate.

He was, in fact, so much superior to earlier escorts that Scaurus looked from one campfire to the next until he spotted Blemmydes shooting dice with a couple of Khatrishers. "Lexos!" he called, and then repeated more loudly when the Videssian did not look up. The guide's head whipped around; Marcus waved him over.

He picked himself up from the game, though he still had his stiff gambler's face on when he came to the tribune's side. "What can I do for you, sir?" he asked. His voice had the resigned patience of any common soldier's before an officer, but the dice muttered restlessly to themselves in his closed right fist.

"Not much, really," Marcus said. "It's only that you know so much more of this country than other guides we've had, and we're wondering how you learned it so well."

Blemmydes could not have been said to change expression, but his eyes grew wary. He answered slowly, "I've made it my business to know the best ways through the land I travel. I wouldn't want to be caught napping."

Suddenly intent, Scaurus leaned forward. Almost he remembered where this frozen-faced soldier had crossed his path before. But Gaius Philippus was chuckling at Blemmydes' reply. "Your business and no one else's, hey? Well, fair enough. Go on, get back to your game." Blemmydes nodded, still unsmiling, and strode off. Marcus' half memory stayed stubbornly dark.

The senior centurion was still amused. "He's probably some sort of smuggler, or a plain horse thief. More power to him, says I; anyone with the imagination to get himself a fifteen-hundred-man armed guard to cover his tracks deserves to do well."

"I suppose so," Scaurus sighed, and shelved the matter.

That night the weather finally broke, a reminder summer would not, after all, last forever. The wind shifted; instead of the seemingly endless westerly from the baking plains of Yezd, it blew clean and cool off the Videssian Sea to the north. There was fog in the early morning, and the low gray clouds did not burn away until almost noon.

"Well, hurrah!" Viridovix exclaimed when he emerged from his tent and saw the murky daylight. "My puir roasted hide won't fry today. No more slathering myself with Gorgidas' stinking goo, either. Hurrah!" he said again.

"Aye, hurrah," Gaius Philippus echoed, with a morose look at the sky. "Another week of this and it'll start raining; and it won't let up till it snows. I don't know about you, but I'm not much for slogging my way through mud. We'll be stuck in the boondocks till spring."

Marcus heard that with disquiet, still loath to be isolated while uncertainty—and Ortaias Sphrantzes—reigned in Videssos. But Quintus Glabrio remarked, "If we can't move, odds-on no one else can either." The manifest truth there cheered the tribune, who had been thinking of his men as an entity unto themselves and forgetting that nature laid its hand on all alike—Roman, Videssian, Namdalener, or Yezda.

As requested, Lexos Blemmydes led Scaurus' band southeast toward Amorion. The tribune wanted to reach the town on the Ithome River before the fall rains made travel hopeless. Amorion controlled much of the west central plateau and would give him a base for the trouble he expected come spring—if Thorisin Gavras still lived to brew it.

Gorgidas all but held Nepos prisoner. The priest used his healing art on the legionaries and did his best to teach it to the Greek. But his efforts there were fruitless, which drove Gorgidas to distraction. "In my heart I don't believe I can do it," he moaned, "and so I can't."

Scaurus came to rely on Blemmydes more and more. The guide had an uncanny knowledge of which ways were open. Not only was he intimately familiar with the ground himself, but he also questioned everyone whose path he crossed—the few traders still abroad, village headmen, farmers, and herders. Sometimes the route he chose was roundabout, but it was always safe.

At evening a couple of days later, the Romans reached a place where what had been a single valley split into two. The rivers that carved them were dry now, but Marcus knew the fall downpour would soon make torrents of them.

Blemmydes cocked his head down each gap, as if listening. He paused a long time, longer than any similar decision had taken him before. Scaurus gave him a curious glance, waiting for his choice. "The northern one," he said at last.

Gaius Philippus also noticed the delay and looked a question at the tribune. "He's been right so far," Marcus said. The senior centurion shrugged and sent the Romans down the path Blemmydes had chosen.

Scaurus thought at first the guide had betrayed them. The valley was full of lowing cattle and their herdsmen—Yezda, or so they seemed. Dogs followed their masters' shouted commands, nipping at the cows' heels and driving them up the rocky mountainsides as the herdsmen saw the column of armed men coming toward them.

But the Romans' alarm proved unfounded. The herdsmen were Videssians who had taken Marcus' soldiers for invaders. Once they learned their mistake, they fraternized with the newcomers, though warily. Imperial armies could plunder as ruthlessly as any nomads. But when Scaurus actually paid for some of their beasts, the herders came close to geniality.

"This isn't the sort of thing you want to do too often," Senpat Sviodo remarked, watching money change hands.

"Hmm? Why not?" The tribune was puzzled. "The less we take by force, the better we should get along with the locals."

"True, but some may die from the shock of not being robbed."

Marcus laughed, but Nepos did not approve. The priest had finally managed to get away from Gorgidas for a few minutes and was wandering about watching the Romans run up their camp. He said to Senpat, "It's never good to mock a generous heart. Our outland friend shows here the same kindness he used in giving a disgraced man a chance to redeem himself."

The Vaspurakaner, not usually as cynical as his words suggested, looked contrite. But the last part of what Nepos had said made no sense to Scaurus. "What are you talking about?" he demanded of the priest.

Nepos scratched his head in confusion. He had not had any more chance than the Roman to shave, and the top of his skull was starting to get bristly. He said, "No need for modesty. Surely only a great-souled man would restore to trust and self-respect the soldier he himself ousted from the Imperial Guards."

"What in the world do you—" Marcus began, and then stopped cold, remembering the pair of guardsmen he had had cashiered for sleeping at their posts in front of Mavrikios' private chambers. Sure as sure, this was the elder of the two; Scaurus even recalled hearing his name, now that Nepos had made the association for him.

He also remembered the sullen insolence Blemmydes had shown when called to account and the way the snoozing guardsmen were ignominiously banished from the capital when their effort to shift the blame to him fell through. It was hard to imagine Blemmydes having any good will toward the Romans after that.

Which meant . . . The tribune shouted for a sentry. "Find the guide and bring him to me. He needs to answer some questions." The legionary gave the closed-fist Roman salute and hurried away.

Nepos and Senpat Sviodo were both staring at Scaurus. The priest said, "You weren't taking Lexos on faith, then?"

Pretending not to hear his disappointment, Marcus answered, "On faith? Hardly. The truth is, with everything that's happened in the months since I saw him that once, I forgot the whoreson existed. Why didn't you speak up a week ago?"

Nepos spread his hands regretfully. "I assumed you knew who he was, and thought the better of you for it."

"Splendid," muttered the tribune. He wondered if his lapse would cost the Romans, a worry that abruptly became a certainty when he saw the sentry returning alone. "Well?" he barked, unable to keep from lashing out to hold his own alarm at bay.

"I'm sorry, sir, he doesn't seem to be anywhere about," the legionary reported cautiously—unlike Gaius Philippus, the tribune usually did not take out his feelings on his men.

"That tears it," Marcus said, smacking fist into palm in disgust. "Only a great-souled idiot would take in a man like that." And if Blemmydes was gone, he must have thought he had his vengeance.

Marcus' failure to follow up on his half recognition of the guide filled him with self-contempt. He could look at others' mistakes with the easy tolerance his Stoic background gave him—they were, after all, only men, and perfection could not be expected from them. His own shortcomings, on the other hand, brought a black anger fiercer in some ways than the one he turned against battlefield foes.

With difficulty, he pulled himself free from that useless rage and began thinking what he had to do to set things right. First, plainly, he had to find out what the situation was. "Pakhymer!" he called.

The Khatrisher appeared at his elbow. "I've gotten to know that tone of voice," he said with a lopsided smile. "What's gone wrong now?"

The tribune's answering grin was equally strained. "Maybe nothing at all," he said, not believing it for a minute. "Maybe quite a lot." He quickly sketched what had happened.

Pakhymer heard him out without comment, whistling tunelessly between his teeth. "You think he's buggered us, then?" he said at last.

"I'm afraid so, anyway."

Pakhymer nodded. "Which is why you called me. I really should charge for this, you know." But there was no malice in his words, only the amused mockery with which the Khatrishers so often faced life.

He went on, "All right, I'll send some of the lads out to see what's ahead—aye, and another bunch to track down your dear friend Blemmydes, if they can." Seeing Scaurus wince, he added, "No one can think of everything, not even Phos—if he did, Skotos wouldn't be here."

That thought consoled the tribune but dismayed Nepos; the Khatrishers had a theology as free and easy as themselves. Pakhymer left before Nepos could put his protest into words. The priest was a good man, more tolerant than many of his colleagues, but there were limits his tolerance could not overstep.

Marcus wondered how Balsamon would have reacted to the Khatrisher's remark. Likely, he thought, the patriarch of Videssos would have laughed his head off.

There was nothing to do but wait for the scouts' return. The party sent out in pursuit of Blemmydes came back first, empty-handed. Marcus was not surprised. The terrain was broken enough to give the disgruntled Videssian a hundred hiding places in plain sight of the camp.

The unusual comings and goings set tongues wagging, as Scaurus had known they would. For once, rumor might be an ally: if the men suspected trouble, they would be quicker to meet it. And if what the tribune was beginning to fear came true, speed would count soon.

He saw the Khatrishers come riding back out of the east, slide off their horses, and jog over to Pakhymer with their news, whatever it was. They said not a word to the soldiers who hurled questions at them. The horsemen might not have the Romans' stiff discipline, but they were all right, the tribune decided for the hundredth time.

Their commander's scarred face had no trace of his usual mirth as he came up to the tribune. "As bad as that?" Marcus asked, reading the trouble in his eyes.

"As bad as that," Pakhymer agreed somberly. "The next valley east is crawling with Yezda; from what my boys say, they must have two or three times as many men as we do, the damned cullions."

"It figures," Scaurus nodded bitterly. "Blemmydes has his revenge, all right—he must have been looking for Yezda all along, and run off when he found a band big enough to sink us."

Pakhymer tried to keep him from falling into despair. "The count's not very fine, you understand—just a short peek over that ridge ahead to reckon up their tents and fires."

"Fires, aye," Marcus said—fires to eat the Romans up. But something else about fire teased at the back of his mind. The sensation was maddening and horribly familiar; he had felt it when he tried without success to remember where he'd seen Lexos Blemmydes. Now he stood stock-still, not forcing whatever it was, but letting it come if it would.

Pakhymer started to say something; seeing Scaurus abstracted, he was sensitive enough to keep silent a little longer.

The tribune drove his fist into his palm for the second time in less than an hour, but now in decision. "The gods be praised I learned to read Greek!" he exclaimed. It had no meaning for Laon Pakhymer, but he saw the Roman was himself again.

He started to leave, but Scaurus stopped him, saying, "I'll

need your men again, and soon. They're better herders and drovers than the legionaries ever will be."

"And if they are?" The Khatrisher was mystified.

Marcus started to explain, but Gaius Philippus strode up, demanding, "By Mars' left hairy nut, what's going on? The whole camp is seething like a boiled-over pot, but nobody knows why."

The tribune spelled it out in a few sentences; his second-in-command swore foully. "Never mind all that," Scaurus said. Now that his wits were working again, haste drove him hard. "Get a couple of maniples out there with Pakhymer's men. I want every cow in the valley down here at this end inside an hour's time."

Khatrisher and centurion stared at him, sure he'd lost his mind after all. Then Gaius Philippus doubled over with laughter. "What a wonderful scheme," he got out between wheezes. "And we won't be on the receiving end this time, either."

"You've read Polybius too?" Scaurus said, indignant and amazed at the same time; the senior centurion found written Latin slow going, and Marcus had not thought he could read Greek at all.

"Who? Oh, one of your pet historians, is he? No, not a chance." For once Gaius Philippus' smile had none of the wolf in it. "There's more ways to remember things than books, sir. Every veteran's known that trick since Hannibal used it, and known his head would answer if he fell for it."

"Will the two of you talk sense?" Pakhymer asked irritably, but the Romans, enjoying their common joke, would not enlighten him.

They did explain the scheme to Viridovix; Marcus had thought of a special role he could play, if he would. The Celt whooped when he'd heard them out. "Sure and I'd kill the man you tried to put in my place," he said.

The herdsmen who had praised Scaurus to the skies while the sun still shone cursed his name in the darkness as, without mercy or explanation, their cattle were taken away. They carried spears and knives to protect themselves against tax-collectors and other predators, but were helpless in the face of the legionaries' swords and mail shirts, and the Khatrishers' horses and bows.

Lowing resentfully at the change in their routine, the cattle shambled down the valley, prodded along by their confiscators. Some of the herd dogs, unreasoningly gallant, leaped to their defense, but reversed spearshafts drove them yelping back.

At the camp, Marcus found Gaius Philippus had been right. When he ordered the legionaries still there to chop the stakes of the palisade into arm-long lengths, they grinned knowingly and fell to like so many small boys involved in a mammoth practical joke. Their women and new non-Roman comrades watched with the same caution one gave any group of men suddenly struck mad.

The tribune did not need to give them the next set of orders. As fast as cattle arrived from the west, the Romans tied the newly made sticks to their horns.

"Marcus, if this is meddling I crave your pardon, but what on earth is going on?" Helvis asked.

"Once your brother Soteric said my men had an advantage fighting in this world because we had a bundle of tricks no one here knows," Scaurus answered elliptically. "It's time to see if he was right."

He probably would have given her the full explanation in another minute or two, but a Khatrisher scout brought him bad news: "Whatever you're playing at, it had better work soon. A couple of Yezda just stuck their heads into the valley to see what all the ruckus is about here. I took a shot at them, but in the dark I missed."

Scaurus gave his preparations a last look. Not so many cattle as he would have liked were festooned with sticks, but a good two thousand head were ready. "This is all fascinating," Pakhymer said ironically. "Do you suppose the Yezda will run from a stampeding forest?"

"I doubt it. But they just might, from a forest fire." The tribune took a burning piece of wood from a campfire's edge and walked toward the cattle.

Pakhymer's eyes got round.

"Strike them now, I say!"

"Rest easy, Vahush. They'll be there in the morning." The speaker, a stocky, middle-aged Yezda, pulled a spit from the campfire, and offered the sizzling meat on it to his nephew.

Vahush rejected it with an angry gesture. Hawk-nosed as any Videssian, he had a zealot's narrow face and moved with the barely controlled grace of a beast of prey. "When you find your foe, Prypet, smite him!" he snapped. "So says Avshar, and he speaks truly."

"And so we will," Prypet said placatingly. "It will be easy; if the scouts tell no lies, the imperials are running about like so many madmen. In any case, we outnumber them two to one at least." He waved out into the darkness, where felt tents dotted the valley like toadstools.

The flocks would grow fat in this wide new land, Prypet thought. He pulled at a wine jug, another of the spoils of war. True, he mused, Avshar had won the battle that gave the nomads room to grow, but who had seen him since? In any case, he, Prypet, led the clan, not this wizard whose face no one knew . . . and not his own wife's sister's son, either.

Still, the lad showed promise and should not be squelched. "We've had hard riding, these past weeks. We'll fight better for the night's rest. Sit yourself down and relax. Have some bread." He lifted the chewy, unleavened sheet from the light griddle that served the nomads in place of an oven.

"You listen too much to your belly, uncle," Vahush said, his confidence in his own rightness driving soft words from him—and wrecking any hope of making the older man listen.

Prypet got deliberately to his feet, the mildness gone from his face. Nephew or not, Vahush could go too far. "If you like, boy, you can find a fight closer than the next valley," he said quietly.

Vahush leaned forward. "Any time you—" He blinked. "Avshar's black bow! What's that?"

Beginning in the valley to the west, the low rumble could be felt through the soles of the feet as well as heard. Bass bellows of pain and terror accompanied it. Prypet snorted his contempt. "Get dry behind your ears, whelp. Don't you know cows when you hear them?"

Vahush flushed. "Of course. Skotos, I'm edgy tonight."

His uncle relaxed, seeing the fighting moment was past. "Don't worry about it. Farmers never could handle kine—look at them letting a batch run loose like that. It might not be a bad idea for a few men to saddle up at that, you know, and round up the stragglers as they come through."

"I'll do that," the younger man said. "It'll let me work off my nerves." He turned toward his horse, then stopped dead, horror on his face.

Prypet looked west, too, and felt ice leap up his back. The

thunder was louder now, pounding its way into the valley where the Yezda took their ease. Cattle? It was not, it could not be cattle, but the great reverberation of a rolling, chopping sea of flame washing toward them at the speed of a fast man's run. And at the edge of the wave ramped a devil, his banshee wail loud through the roar. The shifting fire struck scarlet sparks from the sword he waved above the tide.

The clan leader was a warrior seasoned in countless fights, but this was magic beyond his courage to face. "Flee for your lives!" he screamed.

Yezda tumbled from their tents, glanced west, and leaped for their mounts in panic. "Demons! Demons!" they shrieked, and set spur to their horses without another backward glance. Like an upset mug, the valley emptied of nomads. The fiery sea rolled over their tents as if they had never been.

Vahush would have fled with his uncle and his clanmates, but for long minutes his terror, far worse than Prypet's, held him motionless. You wanted to attack them, fool, his mind gibbered, when they've found a wizard who could blow Avshar out like a candle.

Nearer and nearer came the roaring ocean of flame. The young nomad stared into the shattered darkness, waiting numbly for it to sweep him away. And then at last it was close enough for him to see the grinning riders driving the cattle on, see the bare burning branches lashed hastily to horns, smell their smoke and the reek of singed hair and flesh.

Rage exploded in him, freeing spirit and body from panic's grip. He sprang onto his tethered horse. With a single slash of his saber, he cut the rope that held it. Now his spurs bit; he darted not away from the tortured herd but toward it, blade bright in his hands. "Back! Come back! You've been tricked!" he cried to his escaping comrades, but in the din and distance they did not hear.

Closer by, though, someone did. "Aren't you the noisy one, now?" an oddly accented voice said. Too late, Vahush remembered the devil-cries from the head of the stampede. There was a man on a pony in front of those frenzied cattle. A long straight blade leaped at the nomad's neck.

His last thought as he slid from his horse in death was that the imperials did not fight fair.

Had the Yezda stopped their panic-struck flight and returned to investigate, they likely would have routed the

Romans from the valley they had vacated. In the relief their deliverance brought them, Marcus' troops and Pakhymer's danced with their women in whooping circles round the campfires, clapping, stamping, snapping their fingers, and shouting with glee for all the world to hear.

Pakhymer took no part in the celebration, wandering through the camp like a man in a daze. When he found Scaurus reveling with the rest of his men, he pulled the tribune out of his circle, earning him a glare from Helvis as the dance whirled her away. The tribune was ready to be angry, too, until he saw the lost look in the Khatrisher's eyes.

"Cattle," Pakhymer said blankly. "Plainsmen who spend their lives with cattle, heathens who kill for the sport of it, running like frightened children from a harmless herd of cows." He thumped his forehead with the heel of his hand, as if trying to drive belief into it.

Marcus, who had taken on a good deal of wine, had no better answer for him than a shrug and a wide, foolish grin. But Gorgidas was close enough to hear Pakhymer's comment and sober enough to try to deal with it. He had kept the Greek habit of watering his wine and, moreover, found the pursuit of understanding a sweeter fruit than any that grew on a vine.

"We may have driven cattle against the Yezda," he said to the Khatrisher, "but do you think it was cattle the nomads saw, charging out of the night aflame? Would you, in this magic-steeped land? If you expect to find sorcery, you will—whether it's there or not."

His mouth quirked upward in something that was not a smile.

"Belief is all, you know. When I studied medicine I was trained to hate magic and everything it stood for. Now I've found a magic that truly heals, and it will not serve me."

"Perhaps you should serve it, instead," Pakhymer said slowly.

"Does everyone here talk like a priest?" Gorgidas snarled, but his eyes were thoughtful.

"Sure and they don't." Viridovix caught only what was said, not its overtones. He looked most unpriestly, with each arm encircling a girl's waist.

Marcus could not for the life of him remember which two of his three they were. For one thing, the tall Celt mostly called them "dear" or "darling," a part of his speech pattern that served him well, lessening the chance of an embarrassing slip. For another, while all three were of dainty, flowerlike beauty, none had enough character to leave much other impression on the mind.

Viridovix suddenly noticed Scaurus standing with the Greek doctor and Laon Pakhymer. He loosed his hold on the girls to fold the tribune into a bear hug; Marcus smelled the wine fumes clinging to him even through his own drunkenness.

The Gaul held him at arm's length for a moment, studying him with owlish intensity. Then he turned to Gorgidas, declaring, "Will you look at him now, standing there so quiet and all after the greatest joke any of us ever saw, the which saved all our necks besides. And here I am a hero for sitting on some smelly horse's back and scaring those poor omadhauns all to bits, and where's the glory for the fellow who thought to put me there in the first place?"

"You deserve it," Marcus protested. "What if the Yezda had decided to ride toward you instead of away? One did, you know."

"Och, that puir fool?" Viridovix gave a snort of scorn. "A week and a half it seemed he gawped at me. It's probably only when he pissed himself that he woke up. Who would have thought I'd make a horseman?"

"Cowman might be better, thinking of the herd," Laon Pakhymer said with a sidelong glance.

"Hmm. That's hardly a name for a man." But the Gaul's eyes were twinkling. "If you'd called me bullman, now, you might be closer to the truth. Isn't that right, loves?" he said, leading the girls back toward the tent they shared. Their bodies swayed toward his in mute agreement with the boast.

Pakhymer gave Viridovix' back a frankly jealous look. "What does he *do* with them all?" he wondered aloud.

"Ask him," Gorgidas suggested. "He'll tell you. Whatever else he may be, our Celtic friend is not shy."

Pakhymer watched three bodies briefly silhouetted by lanternlight as Viridovix pulled back his tent flap. "No," he sighed, "I don't suppose he is."

Next morning, Marcus thought for a bleary moment the noise of raindrops thuttering on the sides of his tent was his pulse hammering in his ears. Pain throbbed dully through his head; the taste of sewers was in his mouth. When he sat up too quickly, his stomach yelped, and his surroundings gave a queasy lurch.

His motion woke Helvis, who yawned, stretched lithely, and smiled up at him from the sleeping mat. "Good morning, love," she said, reaching out to touch his arm. "How are you?"

Even her smooth contralto grated. "Bloody awful," the tribune croaked, holding his head in his hands. "Does Nepos know how to heal a hangover, do you think?" He belched uncomfortably.

"If there were a cure for nausea, I promise you pregnant women would know it. We can be sick together," she said, mischief in her voice. But then, seeing Scaurus' real misery, she added, "I'll do my best to keep Malric quiet." The boy was stirring under his blanket.

"Thanks," Marcus said, and meant it. A rambunctious three-year-old, he decided, could be the death of him at the moment.

The downpour meant no cooking fires; the Romans breakfasted on cold porridge, cold beef, and soggy bread. The tribune ignored his soldiers' grumbles. The thought of food, any food, did not appeal.

He heard Gaius Philippus squelching his way from one group of men to the next, instructing them, "Don't forget, grease your armor, leather and metal both. Easier that than grinding out the rust and patching over the rotted hide just because you were too lazy to do what needed doing. And oil your weapons, too, though the gods help you if you need me to tell you that."

With Lexos Blemmydes vanished, there were no guides to show Scaurus' force the way to Amorion. Save for the Romans, the valley the invaders had held was empty of humanity. The angry herders whose cattle had served to rout the Yezda hid in the hills, unwilling to help the men who, from their viewpoint, first befriended and then betrayed them.

Much later than was pleasing to Marcus' senior centurion, the army finally began slogging southeast. The sky remained a sullen, leaden gray; hour after hour the rain kept falling, now in little spatters of drizzle, now in nearly opaque sheets driven by a wind with the early bite of winter in it.

There was no way to steer a steady course in those dreadful

conditions. Drenched and miserable, the legionaries and their companions struggled through a series of crisscrossing little canyons more bewildering than Minos' labyrinth. They trudged glumly on, trusting in dead reckoning.

The storm blew itself out toward evening; through tattered clouds, the sun gave an apologetic peep at the world. And when it did, some soldiers fearfully exclaimed it was setting in the east, for it shone straight into their faces.

Listening to the men, Quintus Glabrio shook his head in resignation. "Isn't that the way of the world? They'd sooner turn the heavens topsy-turvy than face up to our own blundering."

"You spend too cursed much time hanging round Gorgidas," Gaius Philippus said. "You're starting to sound like him." Scaurus had the same impression, though, thinking back on it, he did not remember seeing the junior centurion and the physician together very often.

"Worse things have happened," Glabrio chuckled. Gaius Philippus was content to let it rest. If there were things he did not understand in the younger officer, he approved of enough to tolerate the rest.

Marcus was glad the chaffing went no further than it did. His hangover was gone at last, but he had not eaten all day and felt lightheaded. A real quarrel would have been more than he was up to dealing with.

Only bits of scudding gray showed the storm's passage when dawn came again—those, and the red-brown clinging mud that tried to suck sandals from feet. It was, Marcus thought with disquiet, almost the color of Yezd's banners. He was strangely pleased to see tiny green shoots thrusting up through it, fooled into thinking it was spring.

Gaius Philippus barked harsh laughter when he said that aloud. "They'll find out soon enough how wrong they are." He sniffed at the brisk northern breeze, weather-wise from a lifetime lived in the open. "Snow's coming before long."

Quite by accident, for they were still guideless, they came upon a town early that afternoon. Aptos, it was called, and held perhaps five thousand souls. Peaceful, unwalled, unknown to the Yezda, it nearly brought tears to the tribune. To him, towns like this were Videssos' greatest achievement, places where generation on generation lived in peace, never fearing that the next day might bring invaders to rape away in hours the fruit of years of labor. Such bypassed tranquil islands were already rare in the westlands; soon, too soon, none would be left.

Monks pulling weeds from the rain-softened soil of their vegetable gardens looked up in amazement as the battered mercenary company tramped past. True to the disciplined kindness of their vocation, they hurried into the monastery storehouses, returning with fresh-baked bread and pitchers of wine. They stood by the side of the road, offering the refreshments to any who cared to stop for a moment.

Scaurus had mixed feelings about the Videssian clergy. When humane, as these monks seemed to be, they were among the best of men: he thought of Nepos and the patriarch Balsamon. But their zeal could make them frighteningly, violently xenophobic; the tribune remembered the anti-Namdalener riots in Videssos the city and the pogrom the priest Zemarkhos had wanted to incite against the Vaspurakaners of Amorion. His mouth tightened at that—Zemarkhos was still there.

The gilded sun-globes atop the monastery's spires disappeared behind the Romans. As they marched through Aptos itself, a shouting horde of small boys surrounded them, dancing with excitement and firing questions like arrows: Was it true the Yezda were nine feet tall? Were the streets in Videssos paved with pearls? Wasn't a soldier's life the most glorious one in the world?

The boy who asked that last question was a beautiful child of about twelve; flushed with the first dreams of manhood, he looked ready, nay, eager to run off with the army. "Don't you believe it for a minute, son," Gaius Philippus said, speaking with an earnestness Marcus had rarely heard him use. "Soldiering's a trade like any other, a bit dirtier than most, maybe. Go at it for the glory and you'll die too damned young."

The boy stared in disbelief, as if hearing one of the monks curse Phos. His face crumpled. Tears come hard at twelve, and scald when they fall.

"Why are you after doing that to the lad?" Viridovix demanded. "Sure and there's no harm in feeding his dreams a mite."

"Isn't there?" The centurion's voice was like a slamming door. "My younger brother thought that way. He's thirty years dead now." He looked stonily at the Celt, daring him to take it further. Viridovix reddened and kept still.

Despite the peregrinations of the day before, Scaurus learned Amorion was only about four days' march southeast. Aptos' adults pointed the way, though no one seemed eager to lead the Romans there. Still, as one plump fellow declared with the optimism of rustics everywhere, "You can't miss it."

"Maybe not, but watch us try," Gaius Philippus muttered to himself. Marcus was inclined to agree with him. All too often a landmark was a landmark because a local saw it every day of his life. To a stranger, it was just another tree or hill or barn.

Worse, the rain returned at dawn the next day, not with the vicious onslaught it had shown before, but a steady downpour riding the seawind south. The road to Amorion, in bad shape already, soon became next to impossible. Wagons and traveling cars bogged down, axle-deep in greasy mud. Straining to push forward nonetheless, two horses in quick succession snapped legbones and had to be destroyed. The soldiers worked with their beasts to move the wains on, but progress was minute. The four days' journey promised in Aptos seemed a cruel mockery.

"I feel like a drowned cat," Gorgidas complained. Dapper by choice, the Greek was sadly disheveled now. His hair, its curl killed by hours of rain, splashed down onto his forehead and kept wandering into his eyes; his soaked mantle clung to him, more like a parasite than a garment. He was spattered with muck.

In short, he looked no different from any of his companions in wretchedness. Viridovix said so, loudly and profanely, perhaps hoping to jar him out of his misery and into a good soul-stirring fight. There was more subtlety to the Gaul than met the eye; Scaurus recalled his using that ploy before and succeeding.

But today the doctor would not rise to the bait. He squelched away in glum silence, a person from a sunny land hard-pressed to deal with foul weather. Viridovix, to whom rain was an everyday likelihood, was better prepared to cope with it.

The storm closed down visibility and pattered insistently off every horizontal surface. Thus the Romans, intent on their own concerns, were not aware of the newcomers until they loomed out of the watery curtain ahead.

Marcus' sword was in his hand before he consciously wished it there. His men bristled like angry dogs, leaping back from their labors and likewise reaching for weapons. Gaius Philippus' chest swelled as he gulped the air he'd need to shout them into battle formation.

Before the centurion could give the order, Senpat Sviodo cried out in his own language and splashed forward to clasp the hand of the leading horseman ahead. "Bagratouni!" he exclaimed.

With the naming of that name, the fear fell from Scaurus' eyes, and he saw the newly come riders as they were: not a Yezda horde bursting out of the mist, but a battered squadron of Vaspurakaners, as much refugees as the Romans.

Gagik Bagratouni almost jerked his hand from Sviodo's in startlement. Like Marcus, the *nakharar* had seen what he thought he would see and was about to cry his men forward in a last doomed, desperate charge. Eyes wide, he, too, reconsidered. "It is the Romans, our friends!" he shouted to his forlorn command. Weary, beaten faces answered with uncertain smiles, as if remembering a word long unused.

As the tribune moved up to greet Bagratouni, he was shocked to see how the *nakharar* had shrunken in on himself since the battle before Maragha. His skin was looser over the strong bones of his face; dark circles puffed below his eyes. His nose seemed an old man's beak, not the symbol of strength it had been.

Worst of all, the almost tangible power and presence once his had slipped from his shoulders, leaving him more naked than a mere loss of clothes ever could have.

He dismounted stiffly; his second-in-command, Mesrop Anhoghin, was there to steady him. From the look of mute misery the lanky, thick-bearded aide wore, Scaurus grew sure his imagination was not tricking him. "Greetings," Anhoghin said—thereby, Marcus knew, exhausting most of his Vpdessian.

"Greetings," the Roman nodded. Senpat came to his side, ready to interpret for him. But Scaurus spoke directly to Gagik Bagratouni, who used the imperial tongue fluently, albeit with heavy accent. He asked, "Are the Yezda between here and Amorion too thick to stop us pushing on?"

"Amorion?" the *nakharar* repeated dully. "How do you know we to Amorion have been?"

"For one thing, by the direction you came from. For another, well—" Scaurus waved at the ragged group before him. Most of Gagik Bagratouni's men were Vaspurakaners driven from their native land by the Yezda who settled in or near Amorion with their women. They had left those women behind when they took the Emperor's service, but some were here now, looking as worn and beaten as the men they rode with.

Some were here now . . . but where was Bagratouni's wife, the fat, easygoing lady Marcus had met in the *nakharar's* fortresslike home? "Gagik," he asked, alarm leaping in him, "is Zabel—?" He stopped, not knowing how he should continue.

"Zabel?" It might have been a stranger's name, the way Bagratouni said it. "Zabel is dead," he said slowly, and then began to weep, his shoulders shaking helplessly, his tears washed away by the uncaring rain.

The sight of the stalwart noble broken and despairing was somehow more terrible than most of the concrete setbacks the Romans had encountered. "Take care of him, can't you?" Scaurus whispered to Gorgidas.

The compassion in the doctor's eyes was replaced by a spark of exasperation. "You always want me to work miracles, not medicine." But he was already moving toward Bagratouni, murmuring, "Come with me, sir. I'll give you something that will let you sleep." In Greek he told Scaurus, "I'll give him something to knock him out for two days straight. That may help a little."

The *nakharar* let himself be led away, indifferent to what fate held for him. Marcus, who could not afford indifference, began questioning the rest of the Vaspurakaners through Senpat Sviodo to learn what had happened to them to bring their leader to such a state.

The answer was the one he'd feared. He knew Bagratouni's men had got free of the fatal field before Maragha; their furious despair at Videssos' failure to free their homeland helped them beat back the Yezda time and again. The younger men and bachelors scattered to Vaspurakan's mountains to carry on the fight; the rest bypassed Khliat and marched straight for their families in Amorion.

After the rigors of the battlefield and a forced march through western Videssos' ravaged countryside, what they found there was the cruelest irony of all. Videssians had fought at their side against the nomads, but in Amorion other Videssians, using the Vaspurakaners' heterodoxy as their pretext, turned on them more viciously than ever the Yezda had.

With sickening certainty, the tribune knew what was coming next: Zemarkhos had headed the pogrom. Marcus remembered the lean cleric's burning, fanatical gaze, his automatic hatred of anyone who did not conform precisely to his conception of how his god should be revered. And he remembered how he himself had stopped Gagik Bagratouni just short of doing away with Zemarkhos when the priest taunted the Vaspurakaners by naming his dog for Vaspur, the prince they claimed as their first ancestor. And the result of his magnanimity? A cry of "Death to the heretics!" and revenge exacted from the absent warriors' defenseless kin.

The mob's fury blazed so high it even dared stand against Bagratouni's men on their return. In street fighting, ferocity carried almost as much weight as discipline, and the Vaspurakaners were already worn down to shadows of themselves. It was all they could do to rescue their surviving loved ones; for most, that rescue came far too late.

Mesrop Anhoghin, his face expressionless, gave the story out flatly, pausing every few seconds to let Senpat translate. Finally that impassivity was more than Scaurus could bear. He was drowning in shame and guilt. "How can you stand to look at me, much less speak this way?" he said, covering his face with his hands. "Were it not for me, none of this might have happened!"

His cry was in Videssian, but Anhoghin could understand the anguish in his voice without an interpreter. He stumped forward to look the tribune in the face; tall for a Vaspurakaner, his eyes were almost level with Scaurus'. "We are Phos' firstborn," he said through Senpat Sviodo. "It is only just that he test us more harshly than ordinary men."

"That is no answer!" the tribune moaned. Without strong religious beliefs of his own, he could not comprehend the strength they lent others.

Anhoghin seemed to sense that. He said, "Perhaps it is not, for you. Think of this, then: when you asked my lord to spare Zemarkhos, it was not from love, but to keep him from being a martyr and a rallying cry for zealots. You did not—you could not—force him to spare the swine. That he did himself, for reasons he found good, no matter where they came from.

And who knows? Things might have been worse the other way."

It was not forgiveness Anhoghin offered; it was better, for he said none was needed. Scaurus stood silent for a long, grateful moment, ankle-deep in doughy mud, suddenly not minding the raindrops splashing against his face. "Thank you," he whispered at last.

Fury blazed in him that the Vaspurakaners, sober, decent folk who asked no more from the world than that it leave them at peace, could find it neither in their conquered homeland nor in the refuge-place round Amorion. About the first he could do nothing; that had proved beyond all the Empire's power.

As for the other . . . The wolfish eagerness in his own voice surprised him as he asked Anhoghin, "Shall we avenge you?" The heat of the moment swept away weeks of careful calculation.

Senpat Sviodo instantly shouted, "Aye!" The headstrong young Vaspurakaner could be counted on to press for any plan that called for action.

But when he translated for Mesrop Anhoghin, Bagratouni's aide shook his head. "What purpose would it serve? Those of us who could escape have, and the dead care not for vengeance. This land has war enough without stirring up more; the Yezda would laugh to see us fight among ourselves."

Scaurus opened his mouth to protest, slowly closed it again. Were the occasion different, he might have laughed to hear arguments he had so long upheld come back at him from another. But Anhoghin, standing there in the muck with rain dripping through his matted beard and only exhaustion and defeat in his eyes, was not an object of mirth.

The tribune's shoulders slumped inside his mail shirt. "Damn you for being right," he said tiredly, and saw disappointment flower on Sviodo's mobile features. "If the way forward is closed, we'd best go back to Aptos." Turning to give the necessary orders, he felt old for the first time in his life.

III

THE HILL TOWN NORTHWEST OF AMORION WAS NOT A BAD choice for winter quarters; Scaurus soon saw the truth of that. Where the Romans would have had to storm Amorion, Aptos welcomed them. Not a Yezda had been seen in its secluded valley, but the cold wind of rumor said they were about—a friendly garrison was suddenly desirable.

More than rumor told the townsfolk of the disaster the Empire had met. The local noble, a minor magnate named Skyros Phorkos, had levied a platoon of farmers to fight the Yezda with Mavrikios. None had yet returned; only now were friends and kin beginning to realize none ever would.

Phorkos' son and heir was a boy of eleven; the noble's widow Nerse had picked up the authority he left behind. A woman of stern beauty, she viewed the world with coldly realistic eyes. When the Romans and their comrades struggled back into Aptos, she received them like a ruling princess, to the edification of the few townsmen who braved the rain to watch.

The dinner to which she invited Scaurus and his officers was equally formal. If the Romans noticed the large number of guards protecting Phorkos' estate, they made no mention of it—no more than did Nerse, at the double squad of legionaries escorting the tribune's party thither.

Perhaps as a result of those shared silences, the dinner—a roast goat cooked with onions and cloves, boiled beans and cabbage, fresh-baked bread with wild honey, and candied fruits—went smoothly enough. Wine flowed freely, though

Marcus, noticing his hostess' moderation—and recalling too well the morning after his last carouse—did not drink deep.

When her servants had taken the last scrap-laden platter from the dining hall, Nerse grew businesslike. "We are glad you are here," she said abruptly. "We will be gladder yet when we see you intend to treat us as a flock to be protected, not as victims to be despoiled."

"Keep us supplied with bread and with fodder for our beasts, and we'll pay for whatever else we take," Marcus returned. "My troops are no plunderers."

Nerse considered. "Less than I hoped for; more than I expected—fair enough. Can you live up to it?"

"What would my promises mean? The only test will be how we behave; you'll have to judge that." Marcus liked the way she put Aptos' case without pleading. He liked, too, the straightforward way she dealt with him. She did not try to use her femininity as a tool, but treated the Roman as an equal and plainly expected the same from him.

He waited for the tiny threat that was the sole pressure she could bring to bear: that Aptos' inhabitants would only cooperate with his men to the extent they were well treated. Instead, she turned the conversation to less important things. Before long she rose, nodded graciously, and escorted her guests to the door.

Gaius Philippus had been almost silent during the dinner. His presence, like that of Scaurus' other companions, was more ceremonial than it was necessary. Once outside, though, he paused only to draw his cloak round himself against the rain before declaring, "There is a woman!"

He spoke so enthusiastically Marcus raised a quizzical eyebrow. He had trouble imagining the senior centurion as anything but a misogynist.

"Cold as a netted carp she'd be between the sheets, from the look of her," Viridovix guessed, automatically ready to disagree with the veteran.

"Not if properly thawed," Laon Pakhymer demurred. As soldiers will, they argued it all the way back to the soggy Roman camp.

The tribune was inside it before he realized that Nerse's threat had in fact been made. It was merely that she had not crudely put it into words, but let him make it himself in his own mind. He wondered if she knew the Videssian board game that, unlike its Roman counterparts, depended only on a player's skill. If so, he decided, he did not want to play against her.

Wintering at Aptos, Marcus thought, was like crawling into a hole and then pulling it in after himself. He and his men had been at the center of events since spring; he had hob-nobbed with Videssos' imperial family, sparred with the chief minister of the Empire, made a personal foe of the wizard-prince who led its foes, fought in a great battle that would change Videssos' course for years to come . . . and here he was in a country town, wondering if its store of barley meal would hold out until spring. It was deflating, but gave him back a sense of proportion he had been in danger of losing.

Aptos was lonely enough at the best of times. News of the disaster before Maragha had reached it, aye; the distant king-doms of Thatagush and Agder would know of that by now. But the Romans brought word of Ortaias Sphrantzes' assump-tion of the throne, and Aptos had been equally ignorant of the persecution of the Vaspurakaners not five days' march away.

The tribune was unwilling to leave some news to chance. He talked with Laon Pakhymer outside his tent one morning not long after rain turned to snow. "I'd like to send a couple of your riders west," he said.

"West, eh?" The Katrisher raised an eyebrow. "Want to find out what's become of the younger Gavras, do you?"

"Yes. If all we have is a choice between Yezd and Ortaias, well, suddenly the life of a robber chief looks better than it had."

"I know what you mean. I'll get the lads for you." Pa-khymer clicked his tongue between his teeth. "Hate to send them out with so little hope of making it back, but what can you do?"

"Making it back from where?" Senpat Sviodo's breath puffed out in a steaming cloud as he asked the question—he was just done with practice at swords and still breathing hard.

When Marcus explained, the handsome young Vaspura-kaner threw his hands in the air. "This is foolishness! Would you throw birds in a river when you have fish handy? Who better to go to Vaspurakan than a pair of 'princes'? Nevrat and I will leave within the hour."

"The Khatrishers will be able to get in and out faster than

you could. They have the nomad way of traveling light," Marcus said. Beside him, Pakhymer nodded reluctantly.

But Senpat laughed. "They'll be able to get killed faster, you mean, likely mistaken for Yezda. Nevrat and I are of the country and will be welcome wherever our people live. We've gone in before and come back whole. We can again."

He sounded so certain that Scaurus looked a question at Pakhymer. The Khatrisher said, "Let him go, if he wants to so badly. But he should leave Nevrat behind—the woman is too well favored to waste so."

"You're right," Senpat said, which surprised the tribune until he went on, "I tell her so myself. But she will not have us separated, and who am I to complain of that?" He turned serious. "She can care for herself, you know."

After her long journey west from Khliat, Marcus could not argue that. "Go, then," he said, giving up. "Make the best time you can."

"That we will," Senpat promised. "Of course, we may do a little hunting along the way." Hunting Yezda, Marcus knew he meant. He wanted to forbid it, but knew better than to give an order he could not enforce. The Vaspurakaners owed Yezd even more than Videssos did.

The tribune had his own troubles settling into semi-permanent quarters. Campaign and crisis had let him pay Helvis and Malric only as much attention as he wanted, something suddenly no longer true.

And, under settled conditions, Helvis did not always prove easy to live with. Marcus, a lifelong bachelor before this attachment, was used to keeping his thoughts to himself until the time came to act on them. Helvis' past, on the other hand, made her expect confidences from him, and she was hurt whenever he did something that affected them both without consulting her first. He realized her complaints held justice and did his best to reform, but his habits were no easier to break than hers.

The irritations did not run in one direction alone. As her pregnancy progressed, Helvis grew even more prayerful. Every day, it seemed, a new icon of Phos or some saint appeared on the walls of the cabin she and Scaurus shared. By itself, that would have been only a minor nuisance to the tribune. Not religious himself, he was willing to tolerate—that is, to ignore as much as possible—others' practices.

In this theology-mad land, that was not enough. Like the rest of the Namdaleni, Helvis added a phrase to the creed Videssos followed; for the sake of half a dozen words, the two lands' folk reckoned each other heretics. As the lone supporter of her version of the true faith for many miles, she naturally sought Marcus' support. But to give it took more hypocrisy than was in him.

"I have no quarrel with what you believe," he said, "but I would be lying if I said I shared it. Does Phos need worshippers so badly he would not resent a false one?"

She had to answer, "No." There the matter rested. Scaurus hoped it was settled, not merely dormant.

If he and Helvis had difficulties, they managed to keep them below the level of conflagration. Others were not so lucky. One grayish-yellow morning when the fall rain had turned to sleet but not yet to snow, the tribune was rudely awakened by the crash of a pot against a wall, followed at once by a shrill volley of curses.

He pulled the thick wool blankets over his ears to muffle the fighting, but when a second pot followed the first to smithereens, he knew it was in vain. He rolled over onto one side and saw without surprise that Helvis was awake, too.

"They're at it again," he said unnecessarily, and added, "This is the first time I've ever resented having my officers' quarters close to mine."

"Shh," Helvis said. "I want to listen."

Asking him for quiet was hardly needful either; when provoked, Damaris' voice had a carry to it that any professional herald would have envied. "'Turn on your stomach'!" she was shouting. "'Turn on your stomach'! I've rolled over for the last time for you, I can tell you that! Find yourself a boy, or a cow, or whatever suits your fancy, but you'll not use me that way again!"

The door to Quintus Glabrio's cabin slammed with tooth-rattling fury. Scaurus heard Damaris splash away, still screaming imprecations. "Even when I got you to put me on my back, you were no damned good!" she cried from some distance. Then, mercifully, the wind's voice at last covered hers.

"Oh, dear," the tribune said, his ears feeling red-hot.

Unexpectedly, Helvis broke into giggles. "What's funny?"

Marcus demanded, wondering how Glabrio was going to be able to hold his head up in front of his men again.

The harshness in his voice reached her. "I'm sorry," she said. "It's just one of those silly things you think of. You don't understand women's gossip, Marcus; we've done nothing but wonder why Damaris never got pregnant. Now I guess we know."

That had never occurred to Scaurus. He felt a chuckle of his own rising unbidden, sternly suppressed it. But even as he did, he wondered again how many Romans were sniggering at the junior centurion.

At breakfast Glabrio moved in the center of a circle of silence. No one was quite able to pretend he had not heard Damaris, but no one had the nerve to mention her to him.

He drilled his maniple with grim intensity. Usually he was patient with the Videssians struggling to learn Roman ways of fighting, but not today. And he pushed himself even harder than his legionaries, not wanting to give them any opening to mock him.

But every group of men has its wit, a fellow who takes pleasure in amusing many at the expense of one. Marcus was not far away when one of Glabrio's soldiers, in response to an order the tribune did not hear, stuck out his backside with deliberate impertinence.

Already tight-lipped, the junior centurion went dead pale. Scaurus hurried forward to deal with the insolent Roman, but there was no need. Quintus Glabrio, his face empty of all expression, broke his vine-stave—a centurion's staff of office —over the soldier's head. The man dropped without a sound into the mud.

Glabrio waited until he moaned and shakily tried to sit. The young officer tossed the two pieces of his staff into the legionary's lap. "Fetch me a whole one, Lucilius," he snapped, and waited over him until he staggered to his feet and did as ordered.

Seeing Marcus approach, the junior centurion stiffened to attention. "I'm more than capable of handling these things myself, sir. No need to involve yourself."

"So I see," Scaurus nodded. He dropped his voice until Glabrio alone could hear. "It does no harm for me to remind the men you're an officer, not a figure of fun. What happened to you could as easily have befallen one of them."

"Could it? I wonder," Glabrio murmured, as much to himself as to the tribune. His manner grew brisk once more. "Well, in any case I don't think I'll have any more trouble from the ranks. Now if you'll forgive me—" He turned back to his troops. "I hope you enjoyed the rest you got, for you'll need it. And—one—!"

There was no further trouble from the maniple. Nonetheless, Scaurus was not happy. Quietly but unmistakably, Glabrio had made any further conversation unwelcome. Ah, well, the tribune thought, that one usually has more on his mind than he shows. He stood watching for another couple of minutes, but the junior centurion had everything well in hand. The tribune shrugged, shivered in the cold wind, and found something else to do.

That afternoon Gorgidas sought him out. The Greek was diffident, something so far out of character that Marcus suspected he was about to announce a major calamity. But what he had to say was simple enough: the cabin Glabrio and Damaris had been sharing was, in the junior centurion's opinion, too big for one man by himself, and he had invited Gorgidas to share it with him.

Scaurus understood the doctor's hesitation. Everyone with more sensitivity than crude Lucilius had trouble speaking straight out about Glabrio's misfortune. Still— "No reason to come at me as if you thought I was going to bite," he said. "I think that's all to the good. Better for him to have someone to talk to than sit by himself and brood. From the way you went about it, I thought you were going to tell me the plague had broken out."

"I only wanted to make sure there would be no problems."

"None I can think of. Why should there be?" The tribune decided Gorgidas' continuing failure with Nepos' healing magic was making him imagine difficulties everywhere. "It might do you both good," he said.

"I," Nepos announced, "need a stoup of wine." He and Marcus were walking down Aptos' main street. Snow crunched under their boots.

"Good idea. Hot mulled wine, by choice," the tribune said. He rubbed the tip of his nose, which was starting to freeze. Like his men, he wore Videssian-style baggy woolen trousers and was glad to have them. Winter in the westlands was not weather for the toga.

Of Aptos' half a dozen taverns, the Dancing Wolf was the best. Its proprietor, Tatikios Tornikes, enjoyed his work immensely; he was stout enough to make Nepos seem underfed beside him. "Good day to you, gentlemen," he called with a smile when priest and Roman entered.

"And to you, Tatikios," Marcus replied, wiping his feet on the rushes strewn inside the doorway. Tornikes beamed at him —the taverner was a stickler for cleanliness.

Scaurus liked the Dancing Wolf and its owner. So did most of his men. The only complaint he'd heard came from Viridovix: "May his upper lip go bald."

The Celt had reason for envy. Going against usual Videssian fashion, Tatikios shaved his chin, but his mustachios more than made up for it. Coal-black as his hair, they swept out and up; the taverner waxed them into spiked perfection every day.

The tribune and Nepos, glad of the roaring fire Tatikios had going, sat down at a table next to it. A serving girl moved out from behind the bar to ask what they cared for.

Staring into the flames, Marcus hardly noticed her come up. His head jerked around as he recognized her voice. Someone had told him Damaris was working at the Dancing Wolf, he realized, but this was the first time he'd seen her here.

He frowned a little; for his money, Quintus Glabrio was well rid of the hellcat. Today, though, he felt too good to be petty. "Mulled wine, nice and hot," he said. Nepos echoed him.

His nose twitched at the spicy scent. The handleless yellow cup stung his hands as he picked it up. The Dancing Wolf did things right. "Ahhh," he said, savoring the hot cinnamon bite on his tongue. The wine slid down his throat, smooth as honey.

"That calls for another," he said when the cup was empty, and Nepos nodded. Now that they were warmed inside and out, they could savor the second round at leisure. He waved for Damaris.

While she heated the wine, Tatikios wandered over to their table. "What's the news?" he asked. Like every taverner, he liked to be on top of things. Unlike some, he did not try to hide it.

"Precious little, and I wish I had more," the tribune answered.

Tornikes laughed. "I wish I did, too. Things get slow, once winter sets in." He went back behind the bar, ran a rag over its already gleaming surface.

"I wasn't joking, you know," Marcus said to Nepos. "I wish Senpat and Nevrat would get back with word of Thorisin Gavras, whether good or ill. Not knowing where we stand is hard to bear."

"Oh, indeed, indeed. But friend Tatikios was perhaps righter than he knew—everything moves slowly in the snow, the Vaspurakaners no less than other men."

"Less than the nomads," Scaurus retorted. He shook his head, smiled wryly. "I worry too much, I know. Likely the two of them are holed up in some distant cousin's keep, making love in front of a fire just like this one."

"A pleasant enough way to pass the time," Nepos chuckled. Like all Videssian priests, he was celibate, but he did not begrudge others the pleasures of the flesh.

"It's not what I sent them out for," Marcus said, a little stiffly.

Carrying an enameled tray in one hand, Damaris took two steaming cups from it and set them down. "Why should you fuss over a man lying with a woman?" she said to Scaurus. "You're used to worse than that."

The tribune paused with the hot cup halfway to his mouth. His right eyebrow arched toward his hairline. "What might that mean?"

"Surely you don't need me to draw you pretty pictures," she said. The undertone in her voice sent a chill through him, crackling flames and warm wine notwithstanding.

Malice leaped into her eyes as she saw his confusion. "A man who uses a woman as he would a boy would sooner have a boy...or be one." Wine slopped in Marcus' cup as he grasped her meaning. She drove the knife home: "I hear my sweet Quintus has taken no new lover these past weeks—or has he?" Her laugh was vicious.

The tribune looked Damaris in the eye. The vindictive smile froze on her face. "How long have you been putting this filth about?" he asked. His voice might have been one of the winter winds gusting outside.

"Filth? This is true, it is—" As it had so often in arguments with Quintus Glabrio, her voice began to rise. Heads all round the tavern turned toward her.

But Scaurus was not Glabrio. He cut in: "If the slime you wallow in spreads widely, it will be the worse for you. Do you understand?" The quiet, evenly spaced words reached her when a shouted threat might have been ignored. She nodded, a quick, frightened movement.

"Good enough," the tribune said. He finished his wine at leisure and held up his end of the conversation with Nepos. When they were both done, he pulled coppers from his belt-pouch, tossed them on the table, and strode out, Nepos at his side.

"That was well done," the priest said as they walked back toward the Roman camp. "No rancor matches a former lover's."

"Too true," Marcus agreed. A sudden, biting breeze blew snow into his face. "Damn, it's cold," he said, and pulled his cape up over his mouth and nose. He was not sorry for the excuse to keep still.

Once inside the ramparts of the camp, he separated from Nepos to attend to some business or other. He did not remember what it was five minutes later; he had other things on his mind.

He feared Damaris was not simply letting her spite run free, but had truth behind her slurs. Frightening her into silence was easier than quieting his own mind afterward. The charge she hissed out fit only too well with too much else he had noticed without thinking about.

The whole camp knew—thanks to Damaris and that shrill screech of hers—more about Glabrio's choice of pleasures than was anyone's business. In itself that might mean anything or nothing. But the junior centurion was sharing quarters with Gorgidas now, and the physician, as far as Scaurus knew, had no use for women. Recalling how nervous Gorgidas had seemed when he said he and Glabrio were joining forces, Marcus suddenly saw a new reason for the doctor's hesitancy.

The tribune's hands curled into fists. Of all his men, why these two, two of the ablest and sharpest, and two of his closest friends as well? He thought of the *fustuarium*, the Roman army's punishment for those who, in their full man-hood, bedded other men.

He had seen a *fustuarium* once in Gaul, on that occasion

for an inveterate thief. The culprit was dragged into the center of camp and tapped with an officer's staff. After that he was fair game; his comrades fell on him with clubs, stones, and fists. If lucky, condemned men died at once.

Marcus visualized Gorgidas and Quintus Glabrio suffering such a fate and flinched away in horror from his vision. Easiest, of course, would be to forget what he had heard from Damaris and trust her fear of him to keep her quiet. Or so he thought, until he tried to dismiss her words. The more he tried to shove them away, the louder they echoed, distracting him, putting a raw edge to everything around him. He barked at Gaius Philippus for nothing, swatted Malric when he would not stop singing the same song over and over. The tears which followed did nothing to sweeten Scaurus' disposition.

While Helvis comforted her son and looked angrily at the tribune, he snatched up a heavy cloak and went out into the night, muttering, "There are some things I have to deal with." He closed the door on her beginning protest.

Stars snapped in the blue-black winter sky. Marcus still found their patterns alien and still attached to the groupings the names his legionaries had given them more than a year ago. There was the Locust, there the Ballista, and there, low in the west now, the Pederasts. Scaurus shook his head and walked on, sandals soundless on snow and soft ground.

Like most cabins, the one Glabrio and Gorgidas shared was shut tight against the night's chill. Wooden shutters covered its windows, the spaces between their slats chinked tight with cloth to ward off the freezing wind. Only firefly gleams of lamplight peeped through to hint that the thatch-roofed hut was occupied.

The tribune stood in front of the door, his hand upraised to knock. He bethought himself of the Sacred Band of Thebes, of the hundred fifty pairs of lovers who had fought to their deaths at Chaeronea against Macedon's Philip and Alexander. His hand did not fall. These were not Thebans he led.

But he hesitated still, unable to bring his fist forward. Through the thin walls of the cabin, he heard the junior centurion and the physician talking. Though their words were muffled, they sounded altogether at ease with each other. Gorgidas said something short and sharp, and Glabrio laughed at him.

As Marcus stood in indecision, the image of Gaius Philippus rose unbidden to his mind. The senior centurion was talking to him just after he brought Helvis back to the barracks: "No one will care if you bed a woman, a boy, or a purple sheep, so long as you think with your head and not with your crotch."

Where dead Greek heroes had not stayed his hand, a Roman's homely advice did. If ever two men lived up to Gaius Philippus' standard, they were the two inside. Scaurus slowly walked back to his own hut, at peace with himself at last.

He heard a door open behind him, heard Quintus Glabrio call softly, "Is someone there?" By then the tribune was around the corner. The door closed again.

On his return, Scaurus took the scolding he got as one who deserves it, which only seemed to irk Helvis more; sometimes acceptance of blame is the last thing anger wants. But if absentminded, the tribune's apologies were genuine, and after a while Helvis subsided.

Malric took his undeserved punishment in stride, Marcus was thankful to see; he played with his adopted son until the boy grew drowsy.

The tribune was almost asleep himself when he happened to recall something he was sure he had forgotten: the name of the founder of Thebes' Sacred Band. It was Gorgidas.

During the winter, Aptos' sheltered valley learned but slowly what passed in the world outside. News of Amorion came, of all things, from a fugitive band of Yezda. The nomads, after a quick reconaissance, had decided the town was a tempting target. It had no wall, was empty of imperial troops, and should make easy meat.

The Yezda suffered a rude awakening. Zemarkhos' irregulars, blooded in the Vaspurakaner pogrom, sent the invaders reeling off in defeat—and what they did to the men they caught made it hard to choose between their savagery and the Yezda's.

After listening to the tale spun by the handful of half-frozen nomads, Gagik Bagratouni rumbled low in his throat, "Here is something in my life new: to tenderness feel toward Yezda. I would much give, to see Amorion burn, and Zemarkhos in it." His great, scarred hands gripped empty air; the brooding glow in his eyes gave him the aspect of a lion denied its prey.

Scaurus understood his vengefulness and took it as a good sign; time was beginning to heal the Vaspurakaner lord. Yet the tribune did not altogether agree with Bagratouni. In this winter of imperial weakness, any obstacle against the Yezda was worth something. Zemarkhos and his fanatics were a nasty boil on the body of Videssos, but the invaders were the plague.

Near midwinter day, an armed party of merchants made its way northwest from Amorion to Aptos, braving weather and the risk of attack in hope of reaping higher profits in a town where their kind seldom came. So it proved. Their stocks of spices, perfumes, fine brocades, and elaborately chased brasswork vessels from the capital sold at prices better than they could have realized in a city on a more traveled route.

Their leader, a muscular, craggy-faced fellow who looked more soldier than trader, contented himself with remarking, "Aye, we've done worse." Even with his double handful of guardsmen close by, he would not say more. Too many mercenary companies made a sport of robbing merchants.

He and his comrades were more forthcoming on other matters, sharing with anyone who cared to listen the news they had picked up on their travels. To his surprise, Marcus learned Baanes Onomagoulos still lived. The Videssian general had been badly wounded just before Maragha. Till now, Scaurus had assumed he'd perished, either of his wounds or in the pursuit after the battle.

But if rumor was to be trusted, Onomagoulos had escaped. Some sort of army under his command beat back a Yezda raid on the southern town of Kybistra, near the headwaters of the Arandos River.

"Good for him, if it's true," was Gaius Philippus' comment, "but the yarn came a long way before it ever got to us. Likely as not, he's ravens' meat himself, or else was a hundred miles away bedded down with something lively to keep the cold away. Good for him if that's true, too." He sounded wistful, as odd from him as diffidence from Gorgidas.

Like towns all through the Empire, Aptos celebrated the days after the winter solstice, when the sun at last turned north again. Bonfires burned in front of homes and shops; people jumped over them for luck. Men danced in the streets in women's clothing, and women dressed as men. The local abbot brought his monks down through the marketplace, wooden swords in hand, to burlesque soldiers. Tatikios Tornikes turned the tables by leading a dozen shopkeepers in a wicked parody of fat, drunken monks.

Aptos' celebration was rowdier than the one the Romans had seen the year before in Imbros. The latter was a real city and tried to ape the sophisticated ways of Videssos the capital. Aptos simply celebrated, and cared not a fig for the figure it cut.

The town had no theater or professional mime troupe. The locals put on skits in the streets, making up with exuberance what they lacked in polish. Like the ones at Imbros, their sketches were topical and irreverent. Tatikios did a quick change with one of the monks and came out dressed as a soldier. The rusty old mail shirt he had squeezed into was so tight it threatened to burst every time he moved. Marcus took a while to recognize his headgear. It might have been intended for a Roman helmet, but the crest ran from ear to ear instead of front to back—

Beside him, Viridovix chortled. Gaius Philippus' jaw was tightly clenched. "Oh, oh," Marcus muttered. The senior centurion wore a transversely crested helm to show his rank.

Tatikios had eyes only for a tall, fuzzy-bearded man who wore a fancy gown much like one Nerse Phorkaina was fond of. Every time the mock-noblewoman looked his way, though, he pulled his cloak over his eyes, shivering with fright.

"I'll kill that whoreson," Gaius Philippus ground out. His hand was on the hilt of his *gladius*; he did not sound as though he was joking.

"Nay, fool, 'tis all in fun," Viridovix said. "Last year at Imbros they were after scoffing at me for a tavern fight. The bards in Gaul do the same to a man. There's twice the disgrace in showing the taunting hurts."

"Is there?" Gaius Philippus said. After a while, to Marcus' relief, he let go of the sword, He stood watching till the playlet was done, but the tribune had seen his face less grim in battle.

The next skit, luckily, brought back his good humor. It showed what Aptos thought of Videssos' self-proclaimed Emperor. Posturing foolishly, a gorgeously dressed young man, plainly meant to be Ortaias, led a squad of monk-soldiers down Aptos' main street. Suddenly a six-year-old in nomad's furs leaped out from between two houses. The mock-Emperor shrieked and clutched at the seat of his robes. Throwing scepter one way and crown the other, he turned and fled, trampling half his men in the process.

"That's the way of it! Faster, faster, you spalpeen!" Viridovix shouted after him, doubled over with laughter.

"Aye, and give 'em a goldpiece each as you go," Gaius Philippus echoed. "No, don't, or they'll be after you themselves instead of leaving you for the Yezda!"

That crack drew cries of agreement from the townsfolk around him. As soon as he reached Videssos the city, Ortaias had set the mints churning out a flood of new coins to announce and, he hoped, popularize his reign. But his copper and silver pieces were thin and ill-shaped, his gold even more adulterated than his great-uncle Strobilos' had been. None of his tax collectors had yet been seen so far west, but rumor said even they would not accept his money, demanding instead older, purer coins.

Marcus found that the differing real values of coins nominally at par made gambling devilishly difficult. After more than a year in Videssos, though, he was used to the problem, and evening saw him in front of a table in the Dancing Bear, watching the little bone cubes roll.

"Ha! The suns!" exclaimed the leader of the merchant company, and scooped up the stake. The tribune gave the twin ones a sour look. Not only had they cost him three goldpieces —one of them a fine, pure coin minted by the Emperor Rhasios Akindynos a hundred twenty years ago—to his mind they were by rights a losing throw. When the Romans played at dice they used three, and reckoned the best roll a triple six. But to the Videssians, sixes lost. They called a double six "the demons"; it cost a gambler his bet and the dice both.

One of the other merchants was sitting at Scaurus' right. "He's hot tonight!" the trader crowed. "Three crowns says he makes it again!" He shoved the bright coins forward. They were not Videssian issue, but minted by some of the petty lords of mine-rich Vaspurakan. In the Empire's westlands they circulated widely, the more so because they were of purer gold than recent imperial money.

Marcus covered him with two more from his dwindling

store of old Videssian coins; he would have needed six or seven of Ortaias' wretched issue to match the stake. The merchant captain threw the dice. Three and five—that meant nothing. Nor did double fours. One and—Marcus had an anxious second until the other die stopped spinning. It was a two. "Whew!" he said.

More meaningless rolls followed, and still more. Side bets multiplied. At last the trader threw twelve and had to surrender the dice to the man at his left. Scaurus gathered in the other merchant's Vaspurakaner gold, along with the other bets he'd put down. As was true of the "princes'" other arts, the portraits on their money were executed in a strong, blocky style. Some coins bore square Vaspurakaner letters, others the more sinuous Videssian script.

Behind the tribune, a copper basin set on the tavern floor rang like a bell from a well-tossed dollop of wine. He heard cries of admiration, and the clink of money changing hands. Without looking, he was sure Gorgidas was winning the applause. When the Greek had found the Videssians played kottabos, his joy was undiluted. No one in the capital could match him, and surely no one in this country town. If the locals did not know it yet, they soon would.

The dice traveled slowly round the table. When they got to Marcus, he held them to his mouth to breathe life into them. The rational part of his mind insisted such superstitious foolishness would do no good. But it could not hurt, so he did it anyway.

His first several throws were meaningless; the Videssian game could be slow. Someone pulled the door of the Dancing Wolf open. "Shut that, will you?" Scaurus grunted without turning around as frigid air knifed into the tavern's warmth.

"So we will, and wine for everyone to make amends!" The tribune was on his feet even before a cheer rang through the Dancing Wolf. Snow melting on his jacket and in his beard, Senpat Sviodo grinned at him. Nevrat was right behind her husband.

Marcus rushed over to them, hugged them both, and pounded their backs. "What news?" he demanded.

"You might say hello first," Nevrat said, her dark eyes sparkling with mischief.

"Your pardon, hello. Now, what news?" They all laughed. But the tribune was not really joking. He had been waiting for the Vaspurakaners' return—and worrying over the word they would bring—too long for that.

"Are you going to throw or not?" an annoyed gambler called from the table where he had been sitting. "Give us the dice back if you aren't." Marcus flushed, realizing he was still holding them.

Nevrat pressed a coin into his hand; her fingers were still cold. "Here," she said. "Bet this."

He looked at the goldpiece. It was good money, not pale with silver or darkened by copper's blush—likely from a Vaspurakaner mint, he thought. But the inscription on the reverse was in Videssian letters: "By this right." Above the words stood a soldier brandishing a sword. Scaurus had not seen a coin like it before. He turned it over, curious to learn what lord had issued it.

The diemaker was skillful. The face on the obverse was no stylized portrait, but the picture of a living, breathing man. He was shaggy of hair and beard, with a proud nose, and a mouth bracketed by forceful lines. The tribune almost felt he knew him.

Scaurus stiffened. He did know this man, had seen his mouth wide with laughter and straight as a sword blade in wrath. The Roman looked up at the ceiling and whistled, soft and low.

He noticed the inscription under the portrait bust for the first time. "Avtokrator," it said, and then a name, but he needed no inscription to name Thorisin Gavras for him.

When the tribune got back to camp with his news, Helvis took it like any mercenary's woman. "This has to mean another round of civil war," she said. He nodded. She went on, "Both sides will be wild for troops—you can sell our swords at a good price."

"Civil war be damned," said Marcus, who remembered Rome's latest one from his childhood. "The only fight that counts is the one against Avshar and Yezd. Any others are distractions; the worse they get, the weaker the Empire becomes for the real test. With Thorisin as Emperor, Videssos may even have a prayer of winning; with Ortaias, I wouldn't give us six months."

"Us?" Helvis looked at him strangely. "Are you a Videssian? Do you think either Emperor would call you one? They hire swords—you have them. That's all you can hope to be to them: a tool, to be used and put aside when no longer needed. If Ortaias pays you more, you're a fool not to take his money."

The tribune had the uneasy feeling there was a good deal of truth in what she said. He thought of his men and goals as different from those of other troops Videssos hired, but did its overlords? Probably not. But the idea of serving a poltroon like young Sphrantzes was too much to stomach.

"If Ortaias melted down the golden globe atop the High Temple in Videssos and gave it all to me, I would not fight for him," he declared. "For that matter, I don't think my men would take his side either. They know him for the coward he is."

"Aye, courage speaks," Helvis admitted, but she added, "So does gold. And do you think Ortaias runs affairs in the city today? My guess is he has to ask his uncle's leave before he goes to the privy."

"That's worse, somehow," Scaurus muttered. Ortaias Sphrantzes was a fool and a craven; his uncle Vardanes, Marcus was sure, was neither. But try as he might to hide it, the elder Sphrantzes had a coldly ruthless streak his nephew lacked. The Roman would have trusted him further if he did not make such an effort to hide his true nature with an affable front. It was like perfume on a corpse, and made Marcus' hackles rise.

He made a clumsy botch of explaining, and knew it. But the feeling was still in his belly, and he did not think any weight of gold could make it leave.

He also knew he was far from convincing Helvis. The only principle the Namdaleni who fought for Videssos knew was expedience; the higher the pay and fewer the risks, the better.

She walked over to the small altar she'd lately installed on the cabin's eastern wall, lit a pinch of incense to thank. "However you decide," she said, "Phos deserves to be thanked." The sweet fumes quickly filled the small stuffy space.

When the tribune remained silent, she swung round to face him, really angry now. "You should be doing this, not me. Phos alone knows why he gives you such chances, when you repay him nothing. Here," she said, holding out the little alabaster jar of incense to him.

That peremptory, outthrust hand drove away the mild answer that might have kept peace between them. The tribune growled, "Probably because he's asleep, or more likely not there at all." Her horrified stare made him wish he'd held his tongue, but he had said too much to back away.

"If your precious Phos lets his people be smashed to bloody bits by a pack of devil-loving savages, what good is he? If you must have a god, pick one who earns his keep."

A skilled theologian could have come up with a number of answers to his blunt gibe: that Phos' evil counterpart Skotos was the power behind the success of the Yezda, or that from a Namdalener point of view the Videssians were misbelievers and therefore not entitled to their god's protection. But Helvis was challenged on a far more fundamental level. "Sacrilege!" she whispered, and slapped him in the face. An instant later she burst into tears.

Malric woke up and started to cry himself. "Go back to sleep," Scaurus snapped, but the tone that would have chilled a legionary's heart only frightened the three-year-old. He cried louder. Looking daggers at the tribune, Helvis stooped to comfort her son.

Marcus paced up and down, too upset to hold still. But his anger slowly cooled as Malric's wails shrank to whimpers and then to the raspy breathing of sleep. Helvis looked up at him, her eyes wary. "I'm sorry I hit you," she said tonelessly.

He rubbed his cheek. "Forget it. I was out of turn myself." They looked at each other like strangers; in too many ways they were, despite the child Helvis carried. What was I thinking, Scaurus asked himself, when I wanted her to share my life?

From the half-wondering, half-measuring way she studied him, he knew the same thought was in her mind.

He helped her to her feet; the warm contact of the flesh of her hand against his reminded him of one reason, at least, why the two of them were together. Though her pregnancy was nearly halfway through, it had yet to make much of a mark on her large-boned frame. There was a beginning bulge high on her belly, and her breasts were growing heavier, but someone who did not know her might have failed to notice her bigness.

But when Marcus tried to embrace her, she twisted free of his arms. "What good will that do?" she asked, her back to him. "It doesn't settle things, it doesn't change things, it just puts them off. And when we're angry, it's no good anyway."

The tribune bit down an angry retort. More times than one, troubles had dissolved in love's lazy aftermath. But her desire had grown fitful since pregnancy began; understanding that such things happened, Scaurus accepted it as best he could.

Tonight, though, he wanted her, and hoped it would help heal the rift between them. He moved forward, put the palms of his hands on her shoulders.

She wheeled, but not in desire. "You don't care about me or what I feel at all," she blazed. "All you can think of is your own pleasure."

"Ha!" It was anything but a laugh. "Were that so, I'd have looked elsewhere long before this."

Having swallowed his anger once, Marcus hit too hard when he finally loosed it. Helvis began to cry again, not with the noisy sobs she had used before but quietly, hopelessly, making no effort to wipe the tears from her face. They were running down her cheeks when she blew out the lamp and, as the wick's orange glow died, slid beneath the covers of the sleeping mat.

Scaurus stood in darkness some endless while, listening to the careful sobs that let out grief without disturbing the sleeping boy. At last he bent down to stroke her through the thick wool, not in want but to give what belated comfort he might.

She flinched away, as if from a blow. Careful not to touch her further, the tribune got under the blankets himself. The scent of incense was still in his nostrils, sweet as death.

He stared up at the low ceiling, though there was nothing to see in the darkness. Eventually he slept.

When he woke, the Roman felt wrung out and used up as after a day in battle. Helvis' face was puffed and blotchy from crying. They spoke to each other, moved around each other, with cautious courtesy, neither wanting to reopen last night's wound. But Scaurus knew it would be a long time healing, if it ever did.

He was glad of the excuse of seeing to his men to leave quickly, and Helvis seemed relieved to see him go. The soldiers, of course, were oblivious to their commander's private woes. They buzzed with excitement over the goldpiece he had come across. The tribune managed a wry smile at that; he had almost forgotten the coin and its meaning.

He soon found he had accurately gauged their mood. To a

man, they felt contempt for Ortaias Sphrantzes. "The mimes had the right of it," Minucius said. "With Thorisin Gavras alive, there'll hardly be a fight. The other'll run till he falls off the edge of the world."

"Aye, the Gavras is much better suited for kinging it," Viridovix agreed. "A fine talker he is, a rare good-looking wight to boot, and the stomach of him can hold a powerful lot of wine."

Gorgidas gave the Celt an exasperated look. "What does any of that have to do with kingship?" he demanded. "By your reckoning, Thorisin Gavras would make an excellent sophist, a pretty girl—" Marcus blinked at his choice of that figure, but had to admit its aptness. "—or a splendid sponge. But a king? Scarcely. What the state needs from a king is justice."

"Well be damned to you, you and your sponges," the Gaul said. "Forbye, be your would-be king never so just, if he talk like a sausage seller and look like a mouse turd, not a soul will pay him any mind at all. If you're a leader, ye maun fit the part." He preened ever so slightly, reminding his listeners he had been a noble with a large following himself.

"There's something to that," Gaius Philippus said. Reluctant as he was to go along with Viridovix on anything, he had led enough men to know how much of the art of leadership was style.

Gorgidas dipped his head in reluctant agreement. "I know there is. But it's too easy to look the part without having what's really needed to play it. Take Alkibiades, for instance." The name flew past centurion and Celt alike. Gorgidas sighed and tried another tack, asking Viridovix, "What good does it do a king to be able to outdrink his subjects?"

"Och, man, the veriest fool should be able to see that. After standing the yapping of nitpickers all the day—" Viridovix stared at Gorgidas until the doctor, reddening, urged him on with a rude gesture "—what better way to ease the sorrows than with sweet wine?" He smacked his lips.

"I must be going senile," Gorgidas muttered in Greek. "To be outargued by a red-mustached Celt . . ." He let the sentence trail off as he walked away.

Marcus left the discussion, too, walking out to the frozen fields to watch his soldiers exercise. Laon Pakhymer's Khatrishers darted here and there on horseback, wheeling, twisting, suddenly stopping short. Others practiced mounted archery, sending shafts slamming through heaped-up mounds of straw. For all their camaraderie with the Romans, they were still very much a separate command.

The foot soldiers, now, were something else again. The hundreds of stragglers who had joined the Romans after Maragha, as well as Gagik Bagratouni's refugees, were beginning to blend into the legionaries' ranks. Their beards and the sleeves on their mail shirts still gave Videssians and Vaspurakaners an exotic look, but constant practice was making them as adept with *pilum* and stabbing *gladius* as any son of Italy.

Phostis Apokavkos gave the tribune a wave and a leathery grin. Scaurus smiled back. He still felt good about taking the farmer-soldier out of the capital's slums and making a legionary of him. But then, Apokavkos had adopted the Romans as much as they him, shaving his face and picking up Latin to become as much like his new comrades as he could.

His tall, lean frame almost hid Doukitzes beside him. They were fast friends; Scaurus sometimes wondered why. Doukitzes was the sort of man Phostis had refused to become during his hungry time in Videssos the city: a small-time thief. The tribune had saved Doukitzes from losing his hand to Mavrikios' angry judgment not long before Maragha. Perhaps in gratitude, he had not plied his trade—or at least had not been caught—since joining the Romans after the battle. He waved, too, a little more hesitantly than Apokavkos.

Marcus watched their maniple let fly with a volley of practice-*pila*. He had a good little army, he thought with somber pride. That was as well; it would need to be good, soon enough.

Out of the corner of his eye he caught a motion decidedly not military. Arms round one another's waists, intent only on each other, Senpat Sviodo and Nevrat were making their slow, happy way to their cabin.

The sudden stab of envy was like a knife twisting in Scaurus' guts. The feeling's intensity was frightening, the more so because only weeks before he had been half of such a pair.

The world of the legions was simpler, he decided. Private life would not run by the brute simplicity of orders. He sighed, shook his head, and turned back to make what peace he could with Helvis.

IV

THE SWARTHY KHAMORTH SCOUT, WEARING GRAY-BROWN foxskins and mounted on a dun-colored shaggy pony, was like a lump of winter mud against the bright green of spring. Studying the plainsman closely, Marcus asked him, "How do I know you're from Thorisin Gavras? We've seen snares before."

The nomad gave back a contemptuous stare. He had no more use than his distant Yezda cousins for towns, plowed fields, or the folk who cherished them. But he had sworn loyalty to Gavras on his sword, and his clan-chief and the imperial contestant had drunk wine mixed with their two bloods.

Therefore he answered in his bad Videssian, "He bid me ask you what he say about excitable women, that morning in his tent."

"That they're great fun, but they wear," the tribune answered, instantly satisfied. He remembered the morning in question only too well, having been afraid Thorisin was about to arrest him for treason. He was surprised Gavras also recalled it. The then-Sevastokrator had been very drunk.

"You right," the Khamorth nodded. He grinned, a male grin that cut across all differences in way of life. "He right, too."

"There's something to it," Marcus agreed, and smiled back. By Thorisin's standards, though, Helvis hardly counted as excitable. The truce between her and Scaurus, brittle at first, had firmed as winter passed. If there were things they no longer spoke of, the tribune thought, surely that was a small enough price to pay for peace.

Any peace with a price on it, part of his mind said for the hundredth time, is too dearly bought. For the hundredth time, the rest of him shouted that part down.

The plainsman had said something while he was in his reverie. "I'm sorry?"

The disdain was back on the nomad's face; what good was this fellow, if he would not even listen? Scaurus felt himself flush. Speaking as if to an idiot child, the Khamorth repeated, "You be ready to break camp, three days' time? Thorisin, his men, so far behind me. I ride west meet them, bring here to you to join. You be ready?"

Excitement boiled in the tribune. Three days' time, and he would be cut off from the world no longer. Three days' time to break a camp that had housed his men for a season? If the Romans could not do it, they did not deserve their name.

"We'll be ready," he said.

The plainsmen swept a skeptical eye over ditch, palisade, and the townlet that had grown up inside them. To him and his, getting ready to leave a place was a matter of minutes, not hours or days. "Three days' time," he said once more. He made it sound like a warning.

Without waiting for an answer, he wheeled his little horse and trotted away. From his attitude, he had already wasted enough of this fine riding day on farmer folk.

A Khatrisher posted at the eastern end of Aptos' valley waved his fur cap over his head. Close by Marcus, Laon Pakhymer waved back to show the signal was understood. Thorisin Gavras' outriders were in sight. The picket came galloping back.

"Form up!" the tribune yelled. The buccinators' trumpets and cornets echoed his command. His foot soldiers, Romans and newcomers together, quick-marched to their positions behind the nine manipular standards, the *signa*. Even after a year and a half without it, Scaurus still missed the legionary eagle his detachment had not rated.

Beside the infantry assembled the Khatrisher horsemen. Pakhymer did not try to form them into neat ranks. They looked like what they were: irregulars, longer on toughness than order.

Most of Aptos' population lined the road into town. Fathers carried small boys and girls pickaback so they could see over the crowd—Phos alone knew when next an Emperor, even one with so uncertain a right to that title, would come this way.

From the talk he'd heard since the Khamorth scout appeared, Marcus knew half the rustics were wondering whether the hooves of Thorisin's horse would touch the ground. Those who knew better, like Phorkos' widow Nerse, were there, too.

"Ahhh!" said the townsmen. Still small in the distance, the first pair of Thorisin Gavras' cavalry came into view. They carried parasols, and Scaurus knew them for the Videssian equivalent of Rome's lictors with axes and bundles of fasces, the symbols that power resided here. Another pair followed, and another, until a dozen bright silk flowers bloomed ahead of Gavras' men—the full imperial number, right enough.

Straining his eyes, the tribune saw Thorisin himself close behind them, mounted on a fine bay horse. Only his scarlet boots made any personal claim to rank; the rest of his gear was good, but no more than that. Not even assuming the imperium could make him fond of its trappings.

His army rumbled down the road behind him, almost all cavalry, as was the Videssian way. Of all the nations the Empire knew, only the Halogai preferred to fight afoot; Roman infantry tactics had been an eye-opener here. Gavras' troops were about evenly divided between Videssians and Vaspurakaners—no wonder he had coined money to the "princes'" standard of weight.

"Good-looking men," Gaius Philippus remarked, and Scaurus nodded. The unconscious arrogance with which they rode said volumes about the confidence Thorisin had drilled into them. After the disaster in front of Maragha, that was no mean feat. Marcus' spirits rose.

He tried to gauge how many warriors accompanied Gavras as they came toward him. Maybe a thousand in the valley so far...now two...three thousand—no, probably not that many, for they had a good-sized baggage train in their midst. Say twenty-five hundred.

A good, solid first division, the tribune thought. In a moment the rest of the army would show itself, and then he would have a better idea of its real capabilities. Thorisin spotted him in front of his assembled troops and gave him quite an un-imperial wave. Warmed inside, he waved back.

It was certainly taking enough time for the next unit's van to appear. Marcus reached up to scratch his head, felt foolish as fingers rasped on the iron of his helmet.

"Hercules!" Gaius Philippus muttered under his breath. "I think that's all of them."

Marcus wanted to laugh or cry, or, better, both at once. This was Thorisin Gavras' all-conquering horde, with which he would reclaim Videssos from the usurper and drive the Yezda out of the Empire? Counting Pakhymer's few hundred, he had almost this many men himself.

Yet as Gavras' parasol bearers rode past the assembled inhabitants of Aptos, they bowed low to give honor to the Emperor. And as Thorisin brought his forces up to the troops Marcus had drawn up in review, Laon Pakhymer went to his knees and then to his belly in a full proskynesis, giving formal reverence as sovereign. So did Gagik Bagratouni and Zeprin the Red, who stood near Scaurus.

The Roman, true to his homeland's republican ways, had never prostrated himself for Mavrikios. He did not do so now, contenting himself with a deep bow. He remembered how furious the younger Gavras had been the first time he failed to bend the knee to the Emperor. Now Thorisin reined in his horse in front of the tribune and said with a dry chuckle, "Still stubborn as ever, aren't you?"

Directly addressed, Marcus lifted his head to study the Emperor at close range. Thorisin still sat his stallion with the same jauntiness that had endeared him to Videssos' citizenry when he was but Mavrikios' brother, still kept the ironic gleam in his eye that made one ever uncertain how seriously to take him. But there was a harder, somehow more finished look to him than the Roman remembered; it was very much like Mavrikios come again.

"Your Majesty, would you recognize me any other way?" Scaurus asked.

Thorisin smiled for a moment. His gaze traveled up and down the silent Roman ranks, estimating their numbers just as the tribune had reckoned his. "You give yourself too little credit," he said. "I'd know you by the wizardry that let you bring your troop out so near intact. You were there at the worst of it, weren't you?"

Scaurus shrugged. The worst of it had been where Mavrikios' Haloga bodyguard had fought for the Emperor to the last man and perished with him at the end. He said nothing of that, but Thorisin read it in his eyes. His smile slipped. "There will be a reckoning," he said quietly. "More than one, in fact."

The matter-of-fact promise in his voice almost made it possible to forget that Mavrikios had failed against the Yezda with an army of over fifty thousand men. His brother was undertaking that task, along with simultaneous civil war, and his forces, even adding in the Romans and their comrades, were less than a tenth as great.

"If you've a mind to," Thorisin said to Marcus, "you can dismiss your troopers. A little ceremonial takes me a long way. Gather your officers together, round up some wine, and we'll talk."

"So the pipsqueak really did start the rout?" Thorisin mused. "I'd heard it before, but it galled me to believe it, even of Ortaias." He shook his head. "One more reason for dealing with him—as if I needed another."

Bareheaded, a mug in his hand, his red-booted feet propped on a table, he looked like any long-time soldier taking his ease after travel. His commanders, Videssians and Vaspurakaners both, were as nonchalant. Mavrikios had used the elaborate imperial ceremonies to enhance his own dignity, though he thought them foolish. Thorisin simply could not be bothered.

He listened closely as Scaurus told of the Romans' wanderings, slapped his thigh with his left hand when the Roman explained how he had used Hannibal's trick to free himself from the Yezda. "Turning flocks back on the nomads, eh? A fine ploy and only just," he said.

The tribune did not mention Avshar's parting gift to him. As soon as the Khamorth scout let him know Thorisin was nearby, he had buried Mavrikios' head. With a real Gavras very much present, the risk of a false one seemed smaller.

"Enough of this chatter about us," Viridovix said to the Roman. He turned to Thorisin, asking him, "Where was it you disappeared to, man? For months not a one of us knew if you were alive or dead or off in fairyland to come back a hundred years from now, the which would be no use at all to anybody."

Thorisin took no offense, which was as well; Viridovix

curbed his tongue for no one. His tale was about what the tribune had expected. His mauled right wing of the great Videssian army had been pushed back into Vaspurakan's mountain fastnesses, terrain even more rugged than that which the Romans had crossed. There, much of the army had melted away, beaten soldiers slipping off singly or in small groups to try to make their way eastward.

Gaius Philippus nodded, commenting, "It's what I would have guessed, looking at the men you have with you. The peasant levies and fainthearts are long gone, dead or fled."

"That's the way of it," Thorisin agreed.

In one important respect, the younger Gavras' troops had had a harder time of it than the Romans. The Yezda made a real pursuit after them, and it took two or three bitter rearguard actions to shake free. "It was that cursed white-robed devil," one of the Videssian officers said. "He stuck tighter than a leech—aye, and sucked more blood, too."

Marcus and his entire party leaned forward, suddenly alert. "So Avshar was trailing you, then," the tribune said. "No wonder there was no sign of him in these parts—we had no idea what was keeping him out of Videssos."

"I still don't," Gavras admitted. "He disappeared a couple of weeks after the battle, and I have no idea where he is. As much as anything, his going saved us—without him the Yezda are fierce enough, but a rabble. With him—" Thorisin fell silent; from his expression, the words stuck in his mouth were not to his taste.

The officer who had mentioned Avshar—Indakos Skylitzes, his name was—asked Marcus, "Has Amorion gone mad? We sent a man there to proclaim Thorisin, and they horsewhipped him out of town—for a day, we thought he might not live. Phos' little suns, even in civil war, heralds have some rights." As a Videssian baron, Skylitzes knew whereof he spoke.

"It's Zemarkhos' city now, and his word is law there," Marcus said. He paused as a new thought struck him. "Was your envoy a Vaspurakaner, by any chance?"

Skylitzes looked uncertain, but Thorisin nodded. "Haik Amazasp? I should say so. What has that to do with—? Oh." His scowl deepened as he remembered how Amorion's fanatic priest had wanted to start his persecution of the "heretics" with imperial backing. "Ortaias is welcome to his support—not that he'll get much use from him."

"You'll avenge us?" Senpat Sviodo exclaimed eagerly. "You won't regret it—Amorion is a perfect place to push east. You know that as well as I." The young Vaspurakaner came halfway out of his seat in enthusiasm. Gagik Bagratouni began to rise, too, more slowly, but with a frightening sense of purpose.

Thorisin, though, waved them down once more. "No, we're after Videssos the city, nothing else. With it, the whole Empire falls to us; without it, none of the rest is truly ours."

Seeing their outraged disappointment, he went on, "If you don't mind your revenge at second hand, I think you'll get it. The Namdaleni are moving east out of Phanaskert, and I expect Amorion will be in their line of march. They'll bring the town down around Zemarkhos' ears if he squawks of heresy at them—and he will. He's bigot enough." Gavras contemplated the meeting with equanimity, even grim amusement. So, after a moment, did the Vaspurakaners.

Scaurus was ready to agree. Any trap that closed on the Namdaleni would be kicked open from the inside by six or seven thousand heavy-armed cavalry. So the men of the Duchy were on the move, too, were they? he thought. Armies were flowing like driblets from melting icicles after the winter freeze.

Something else occurred to him: the Namdaleni had a good many more soldiers hereabouts than Thorisin did. He asked, "What sort of understanding do you have with the easterners?"

"Mutual mistrust, as always," Gavras answered. "If they see their way clear, they'll go for our throats. I don't intend to give them the chance."

"Maybe Onomagoulos' men can come up from the south to help keep an eye on them," Marcus suggested.

It was the Emperor's turn to be startled. "What? Baanes is alive?"

"If traders' tales can be trusted," Gaius Philippus said, still doubting the merchants' rumor. He set it forth for Thorisin, who did not seem to find anything improbable in it.

"Well, well, good for the old fox. There's tricks left in him after all," Gavras murmured, but he did not sound overjoyed to Scaurus.

* * *

When Aptos disappeared behind a bend in the road, Gaius Philippus heaved a long sigh. "First time in full many a year I'm sorry to be on the move once more," he said.

"By the gods, why?" Marcus asked, surprised. Marching under a spring sky was one of the pleasures of a soldier's life. The last rains had given the foothills a carpet of new grass and were recent enough to keep Videssos' dirt roads from turning into choking ribbons of dust. The air was fine and mild, almost tasty, and sweetly clamorous with the calls of returning birds. Even the butterflies looked fresh, their bright wings not yet tattered and tarnished by time.

"Canna you tell?" Viridovix said to Scaurus. "The puir lad's heart is all broken in flinders—or would be, if he remembered where he mislaid it."

"Oh, be damned to you," Gaius Philippus said, the measure of his upset shown by his falling into the Celt's idiom.

For a moment Marcus honestly had no idea of what Viridovix was talking about, or why the senior centurion took the gibe seriously. When he stopped to think, though, an answer did occur to him. "Nerse?" he asked. "Phorkos' widow?"

"What if it is?" Gaius Philippus muttered, plainly sorry he'd said anything at all.

"Well, why didn't you court her, then?" the tribune burst out, but Gaius Philippus was doing no more talking. The veteran set his jaw and stared straight ahead as he marched, enduring Viridovix' teasing without snapping back. After a while the Celt grew bored of his unrewarding fun and went off to talk about swordplay with Minucius.

Studying Gaius Philippus' grim expression, Marcus came to his own conclusions. Strange that a man who was utterly fearless in battle, and who took fornication and rape as part of the warrior's trade, should be scared witless of paying suit to a woman for whom he felt something more than lust.

Thorisin Gavras' army hurried northeast toward the shore of the Videssian Sea. Gavras hoped to commandeer shipping and swoop down on Ortaias in the capital before the usurper could make ready to meet him. But at each port his troops approached, shipmasters hurried their vessels out to sea and sent them fleeing to bring young Sphrantzes word of his coming.

The third time that happened, at a fishing village called Tavas, Thorisin's short temper neared the snapping point. "For two coppers I'd sack the place," he snarled, pacing up and down like a caged tiger, watching a bulky merchantman's brightly dyed sails recede into sea mist as it drove north out of the Bay of Rhyax before turning east for the long run to Videssos.

He spat in disgust. "Bah! What's left here? Half a dozen fishing boats. Phos willing, I could put a good dozen men in each."

"You ought to pillage these faithless traders and peasants. Teach them to fear you," Komitta Rhangavve said, walking beside him. The fierce expression on her lean, aristocratic features made her resemble a hunting hawk, beautiful but deadly.

Alarmed at the bloodthirsty advice Gavras' lady gave, Scaurus said hastily, "Perhaps it's as well the merchant got away; Ortaias must be forewarned by now in any case. If the fleet in the city stands with him, he'd smash anything you could scrape together here."

Komitta Rhangavve glared at even this indirect disagreement, but Thorisin sighed, a heavy, frustrated sound. "You're probably right. If I could have brought it off at Prakana, though, four days ago—" He sighed again. "What was that thing poor Khoumnos used to say? 'If ifs and buts were candied nuts, then everyone would be fat.'" Nephon Khoumnos, though, was half a year dead, struck down by Avshar's sorcery at the battle before Maragha.

Neither Gavras nor Marcus found that a pleasant thought to dwell on. Returning rather more directly to rebutting Komitta, the tribune said, "At least the people hereabouts are for you, whatever the shipmasters do."

The Emperor's smile was still sour. "Of course they are— we've come far enough east that folk have had a good taste of Ortaias' taxmen; aye, and of his money, too, though they'd break teeth if they tried to bite it." Sphrantzes' wretched coinage was a standing joke in his opponent's army. As for his revenue agents, Scaurus had yet to see one. They ran from Thorisin even faster than the navarchs did.

Five days later came an envoy of Ortaias' who did not flee. Accompanied by a guard force of ten horsemen, he rode deliberately up to Thorisin's camp at evening. One of the troopers bore a white-painted shield on a spearstaff: a sign of truce.

"What can the henhearted wretch have to say to me?" Thorisin snapped, but let the emissary's party approach.

The soldiers with Sphrantzes' agents were nonentities— the hard shell of a nut, good only for protecting the kernel within. The envoy himself was something else again. Marcus recognized him as one of Vardanes Sphrantzes' henchmen, but could not recall his name.

Thorisin had no such difficulty. "Ah, Pikridios, how good to see you," he said, but there was venom in his voice.

Pikridios Goudeles affected not to notice. The bureaucrat dismounted with a sigh of relief. He'd sat his horse badly; from the look of his hands, the reins would have hurt them. They were soft and white, their only callus on the right middle finger. A pen-pusher right enough, Scaurus thought, feeling the aptness of the Videssian soldiery's contemptuous term for the Empire's civil servants.

Yet for all his unwarlike look, the small, dapper Goudeles was a man to be reckoned with. His dark eyes gleamed with ironic intelligence, and the quality of his nerve was adequately attested by his very presence in the rival Emperor's camp.

"Your Majesty," he said to Thorisin, and went to one knee, his head bowed—not a proskynesis, but the next thing to it.

Some of Gavras' soldiers cheered to see their lord so acclaimed by his foe's ambassador. Others growled because the acclamation was incomplete. Thorisin himself seemed taken aback. "Get up, get up," he said impatiently. Goudeles rose, brushing dust from the knee of his elegant riding breeches.

He made no move to speak further. The silence stretched. At last, conceding the point to him, Thorisin broke it: "Well, what now? Are you here to turn your worthless coat? What price do you want for it?"

Beneath the thin fringe of mustache, so like Vardanes', Scaurus noticed—perhaps irrelevantly, perhaps not—Goudeles' lip gave a delicate curl, as if to say he had noticed the insult but did not quite care to acknowledge it. "My lord Sevastokrator, I am merely here to help resolve the unfortunate misunderstanding between yourself and his Imperial Majesty the Avtokrator Ortaias Sphrantzes."

Every trooper who heard that shouted in outrage; hands tightened on sword hilts, reached for spears and bows. "String the little bastard up!" someone yelled. "Maybe after he's hung a while he'll know who the real Emperor is!" Three or four men sprang forward. Goudeles' self-control wavered; he shot an appealing glance at Thorisin Gavras.

Thorisin waved his soldiers back. They withdrew slowly, stiffly, like dogs whistled off a kill they think theirs by right. "What's going on?" Gaius Philippus whispered to Marcus. "If this rogue won't own Gavras as Emperor, by rights he's fair game."

"Your guess is as good as mine," the tribune answered. With Gavras' hot temper, Scaurus had expected him to deal roughly with Goudeles, ambassador or no—in civil war such niceties of usage were easy enough to cast aside. It was lucky Komitta was not in earshot of all this, he thought; she would already be heating pincers.

Yet Thorisin's manner remained mild. Though a warrior by choice, he had known his share of intrigue as well, and his years at his brother's right hand in the capital made him alert to subtleties less experienced men could miss. Voice still calm, he asked Goudeles, "So you do not reckon me rightful Avtokrator, eh?"

"Regrettably, I do not, my lord," Goudeles said, half-bowing, "nor does my principal." His glance at Thorisin was wary; they were fencing as surely as if they had sabers to hand.

"Just a damned rebel, am I?"

Goudeles spread his soft hands, gave a fastidious shrug.

"Then by Skotos' dung-splattered beard," Thorisin pounced, "why does your bloody principal—" He made the word an oath. "—still style me Sevastokrator? Is that his bribe to me, keeping a title he'll make sure is empty? Tell your precious Sphrantzes I am not so cheaply bought."

The envoy from the capital looked artfully pained at Gavras' crudity. "You fail to understand, my lord. Why should you not remain Sevastokrator? The title was yours during your deeply mourned brother's reign, and you are still close kin to the imperial house."

Thorisin stared at him as if he had started speaking some obscure foreign tongue. "Are you witstruck, man? The Sphrantzai are no kin of mine—I share no blood with jackals."

Once again, the insult failed to make an impression on

Goudeles. He said, "Then your Majesty has not yet heard the joyous news? How slowly it travels in these outlying districts!"

"What are you yapping of?" Gavras demanded, but his voice was suddenly tense.

His quarry vulnerable at last, Goudeles thrust home with suave precision. "Surely the Avtokrator will pay you all respect due a father-in-law, putting you in the late Emperor's place. Why, it must be more than a month now since his daughter Alypia and my lord Ortaias were united in wedlock."

Thorisin went white. Voice thick with rage, he choked out, "Flee now, while you still have breath in you!" And Goudeles and his guardsmen, with no ceremony whatever, leaped on their horses and rode for their lives.

Gaius Philippus took a characteristically pungent view of the marriage. "It'll do Ortaias less good than he thinks," he said. "If he's the same kind of lover as he is a general, he'll have to take a book to bed to know what to do with her."

Remembering the military tome constantly under Sphrantzes' arm, Scaurus had to smile. But alone in his tent with Helvis and the sleeping Malric later that evening, he burst out, "It was a filthy thing to do. As good as rape, joining Alypia to the house her father hated."

"Why so offended?" Helvis asked. She was very bulky now, uncomfortable, and often irritable. With a woman's bitter realism, she went on, "Are we ever anything but pawns in the game of power? Beyond the politics of it, why should you care?"

"The politics are bad enough." The marriage, forced or not, could only rob Thorisin Gavras of support and gain it for Ortaias and his uncle. Helvis was right, though: Marcus' anger was more personal than for his cause. "From the little I knew of her, I rather liked her," he confessed.

"What has that to do with the price of fish?" Helvis demanded. "Since the day you came to Videssos, you've known the contest you were in; aye, and played it well, I'll not deny. But it's not one with much room for things as small as likes."

Scaurus winced at that harsh picture of his career in his adopted homeland. In Videssos, scheming was natural as drawing breath. No one who hoped to advance could escape it altogether.

But Alypia Gavra, he thought, should not fall victim to it merely by accident of birth. Behind the schooled reserve with which she met the world, the tribune had felt a gentleness this unconsented marriage would mar forever. The image of her brought miserable and defenseless to Ortaias' bed made cold fury flash behind his eyes.

And how, he asked himself, am I going to say that to Helvis without lighting a suspicion in her better left unkindled? Not seeing any way, he kept his mouth shut.

Sentries' shouts woke Scaurus at earliest dawn. Stumbling to his feet, he threw on a heavy wool mantle and hurried out to see what the trouble was. Gaius Philippus was at the rampart before him, sword in hand, wearing only helmet and sandals.

Marcus followed the veteran's pointing finger. There was motion at the edge of sight in the east, visible at all only because silhouetted against the paling sky. "I give you two guesses," the senior centurion said.

"You can have the first one back—I know an army when I see it. Shows how sincere Goudeles' talk of Thorisin being an honored father-in-law was, doesn't it?"

"As if we needed showing. Well, let's be at it." The veteran's bellow made up for the cornets and trumpets of the still-sleeping buccinators. "Up, you weedy, worthless good-for-nothings, up! There's work to do today!"

Romans tumbled from their tents, pulling on corselets and tightening straps as they rushed to their places. Campfires banked during the night were fed to new life to light the running soldiers' paths.

Marcus and Gaius Philippus looked at each other and, in looking, realized they were hardly clad for battle. Gaius Philippus cursed. They dashed for their tents.

When the tribune emerged a couple of minutes later, he led his troops out to deploy in front of their fortified camp. Pakhymer's light cavalry screened their lines. The Khatrishers' winter-long association with the Romans made them as quick to be ready as the legionaries. The rest of Thorisin Gavras' forces were slower in emerging.

There was no time to plan elaborate strategies. Thorisin rode up on his highbred bay, grunted approval at the Romans' quiet steadiness. "You'll be on the right," he said. "Stay firm, and we'll smash them against you."

"Good enough," Marcus nodded. Less mobile than the mounted contingents of standard Videssian warfare, his infantry usually got a holding role. As Gavras' cavalry came into line, the tribune swung Pakhymer over to his own right to guard against outflanking moves from the foe.

"A rare lovely day it is for a shindy, isn't it now?" Viridovix said. His mail shirt was painted in squares of black and gold, imitating the checkered pattern of a Gallic tunic. A seven-spoked wheel crested his bronze helm. His sword, a twin to Scaurus', was still in its scabbard; his hand held nothing more menacing than a chunk of hard, dry bread. He took a healthy bite.

The tribune envied him his calm. The thought of food repelled him before combat, though afterwards he was always ravenous. It *was* a beautiful morning, still a bit crisp with night's chill. Squinting into the bright sunrise, Scaurus said, "Their general knows his business, whoever he is. An early morning fight puts the sun in our faces."

"Aye, so it does, doesn't it? What a rare sneaky thing to think of," the Celt said admiringly.

Ortaias' army was less than half a mile away now, coming on at a purposeful trot. It looked no larger than the one backing Thorisin, Marcus saw with relief. He wondered what part of the total force of the Sphrantzai it contained.

It was cavalry, as the tribune had known it would be. He felt the hoofbeats like approaching thunder.

Quintus Glabrio gave his maniple some last instructions: "When you use your *pila*, throw at their horses, not the men. They're bigger targets, less well armored, and if a horse goes down, he takes his rider with him." As always, the junior centurion's tone was measured and under firm control.

There was no time for more speechmaking than that; the enemy was very close. In the daybreak glare, it was still hard to see just what manner of men they were. Some had the scrubby look of nomads—Khamorth or even Yezda—while others . . . lanceheads gleamed briefly crimson as they swung down in a disciplined flurry. Namdaleni, Marcus thought grimly. The Sphrantzai hired the best.

"Drax! Drax! The great count Drax!" shouted the men of the Duchy, using their commander's name as war cry.

"At them!" Thorisin Gavras yelled, and his own horsemen galloped forward to meet the charge. Bowstrings snapped. A Namdalener tumbled from his saddle, unluckily hit below the eye at long range.

The enemy's light horse darted in front of the Namdaleni to volley back at Thorisin's men. But the field was now too tight for their hit-and-run tactics to be used to full effect. More sturdily mounted and more heavily armed, the Videssians and Vaspurakaners who followed Gavras hewed their way through the nomads toward the men of the Duchy who were the opposing army's core.

The count Drax was new-come from the Duchy. The only foot worth its pay he'd seen was that of the Halogai. Of Romans he knew nothing. He took them for peasant levies Thorisin had scraped up from Phos knew where. Crush them quickly, he decided, and then deal with Gavras' outnumbered cavalry at leisure. With a wave of his shield to give his men direction, he spurred his mount at the legionaries.

Dry-mouthed, Scaurus waited to receive the charge. The pounding hooves, the rhythmic shouting of the big men rushing toward him like armored boulders, the long lances that all seemed aimed at his chest . . . he could feel his calves tensing with the involuntary urge to flee. Longsword in hand, his right arm swung up.

Drax frowned in sudden doubt. If these were drafted farmers, why were they not running for their paltry lives?

"Loose!" the tribune shouted. A volley of *pila* flew forward, and another, and another. Horses screamed, swerved, and fell as they were hit, pitching riders headlong to the ground. Other beasts stumbled over the first ones down. Namdaleni who caught Roman javelins on their shields cursed and threw them away; the soft iron shanks of the *pila* bent with ease, fouling the shields beyond use.

Still, the legionaries sagged before the slowed charge's momentum. Trumpets blared, calling squads from the flank to hold the embattled center. The mounted surge staggered, stalled, turned to melee.

The knight who came at Scaurus was about forty, with a

cast in his right eye and a twisted little finger. Near immobile
in the press, he jabbed at the tribune with his lance. Marcus
parried, ducking under the thrust. His strong blade bit through
the wood below the lancehead, which flew spinning. Eyes
wide with fear, the Namdalener swung the ruined lance as he
might a club. Scaurus ducked again, stepped up and thrust,
felt his point pierce chain and flesh. Sphrantzes' mercenary
gave a shriek that ended in a bubbling moan. Scarlet foam on
his lips, he slid to the ground.

Close by, Zeprin the Red raised his long-hafted Haloga war
axe high above his helmet, to bring it crashing down on a
horse's head. Brains flew, pink-gray. The horse foundered like
a ship striking a jagged rock. Pinned under it, its Namdalener
rider screamed with a broken ankle, but not for long. A second stroke of the great axe silenced him for good.

An unhorsed mercenary slashed at Scaurus, who took the
blow on his shield. His *scutum* was bigger and heavier than
the horseman's lighter shield. Marcus shoved out with it. The
man of the Duchy stumbled backwards, tripped on a corpse's
upthrust foot. A legionary drove a stabbing-sword into his
throat.

Though the Namdalener charge was checked, they still
fought with the skill and fierceness Marcus had come to know.
Foul-mouthed Lucilius stood staring at his broken sword, the
hard steel snapped across by a cunning lance stroke. "Well,
fetch me a whole one!" he shouted, but before anybody could,
a man of the Duchy rode him down.

"By all the gods, why aren't these bastards on our side?
They're too bloody much work to fight," Gaius Philippus
panted. There was a great dent in the right side of his helmet,
and blood flowed down his face from a cut over one eye. The
tide of battle swept them apart before Scaurus could answer.

A Namdalener stabbed down at someone writhing on the
ground before him. He missed, swore, and brought his blade
back for another stroke. So intent was he on his kill that he
never noticed Marcus until the tribune's Gallic longsword
drank his life.

Marcus pulled the would-be victim up, then stared in disbelief. "Grace," said Nevrat Sviodo, and kissed him full on
the mouth. The shock was as great as if he'd taken a wound.
Slim saber in hand, she slipped back into battle, leaving him
gaping after her.

"Watch your left, sir!" someone cried. The tribune jerked up his shield in reflex response. A lancehead glanced off it; the Namdalener swept by without time for another blow. Marcus shook himself—surprise had almost cost him his neck.

With a banshee whoop, Viridovix leaped up behind a mounted mercenary and dragged him from his horse. He jerked up the luckless man's chin, drew sword across his throat like a bow over a viol's strings. Blood fountained. The Gaul shouted in triumph, sawed through windpipe and backbone. He lifted the dripping head and hurled it into the close-packed ranks of the Namdaleni, who cried out in horror as they recoiled from the grisly trophy.

The count Drax was not altogether sorry to see retreat begin. These foot soldiers of Thorisin's, whoever they were, fought like no foot he had met. They bent but would not break, rushing men from quiet spots along the line to meet threats so cleverly that no new points of weakness appeared. Quite professional, he thought with reluctant admiration.

From his left wing, the Khatrishers were spraying his bogged-down men with arrows and then darting away, just as he had hoped his hireling nomads would to Thorisin Gavras' heavy horse. But his clans of plainsmen were squeezed between his own men and the oncoming enemy. Soon they would break and run—to stand against this kind of punishment was not in them.

With a wry smile, Drax of Namdalen realized it was not in him, either. When Gavras' cavalry broke through the nomads and stormed into his stalled knights, the result would be unpleasant. And in the end, a mercenary captain's loyalty was to himself, not to his paymaster. Without men, he would have nothing to sell.

He reined in, tried to wheel his horse among his tight-packed countrymen. "Break off," he shouted, "and back to our camp! Keep your order, by the Wager!"

Marcus heard the count's shout to his men but was not sure he understood it; among themselves, the Namdaleni used a broad patois quite different from the Videssian spoken in the Empire. Yet he soon realized what Drax must have ordered, for pressure eased all along the line as the men of the Duchy broke off combat. It was skillfully done; the Namdaleni knew their business and left the legionaries few openings for mischief.

The tribune did not pursue them far. In part he was ruled by the same concern that governed Drax: not to spend his men unwisely. Moreover, the notion of infantry chasing horsemen did not appeal. If the Namdaleni spun round and counterattacked, they could cut off and destroy big chunks of his small force. In loose order the Romans would be horribly vulnerable to the tough mounted lancers.

Gavras' cavalry and the Khatrishers followed Sphrantzes' men for a mile or two, harassing their retreat, trying to turn it to rout. But when the Romans were not added in, the Namdaleni and their nomad outriders probably outnumbered the forces opposed to them. They withdrew in good order.

Scaurus looked up in the sky, amazed. The sun, which had but moments before—or so it seemed—blazed straight into his face as it rose, was well west of south. Marcus realized he was tired, hungry, dry as the Videssian plateau in summer, and in desperate need of easing himself. A slash on his sword hand he did not remember getting began to throb, the more so when sweat ran down his arm into it. He flexed his fingers. They all moved—no tendon was cut.

Legionaries were plundering the corpses of their fallen opponents. Others cut the throats of wounded horses, and of those Namdaleni so badly hurt as to be beyond hope of recovery. Foes with lesser injuries got the same rough medical treatment the Romans did—they could be ransomed later and hence were more valuable alive than dead.

Seriously wounded Romans were carried back into camp on litters for such healing as Gorgidas and Nepos could give. Marcus found the fat priest directing a double handful of women as they cleaned and bandaged wounds. Of Gorgidas there was no sign.

Surprised at that, Scaurus asked where the Greek doctor was. "Don't you know?" one of Nepos' helpers exclaimed, and began to giggle.

The tribune, worn out as he was, could make no sense of that. He stared foolishly. Nepos said gently, "You'll find him at your own tent, Scaurus."

"What? Why is he—? Oh!" Marcus said. He began to run,

though a moment before simply standing on his feet had been almost beyond him.

In fact Gorgidas was not in the tribune's tent, but coming back the way Scaurus was going. Dodging the tribune, he said, "Greetings. How went your stupid battle?"

"We won," Marcus answered automatically. "But—but—" he sputtered, and ran out of words. For once there were more urgent things than warfare.

"Rest easy, my friend. You have a son." His spare features alight, Gorgidas took the tribune's arm.

"Is Helvis all right?" Marcus demanded, though the smile on the physician's face told him nothing could be seriously amiss.

"As well as could be expected—better, I'd say. One of the easier births I've seen, less than half a day. She's a big-hipped girl, and it was not her first. Yes, she's fine."

"Thank you," Scaurus said, and would have hurried on, but Gorgidas kept the grip on his arm. The tribune turned round once more. Gorgidas was still smiling, but his eyes were pensive and far away. "I envy you," he said slowly. "It must be a marvelous feeling."

"It is," Marcus said, startled at the depth of sadness in the doctor's voice. He wondered if Gorgidas had meant to lay himself so bare, yet at the same time was touched by the physician's trust. "Thank you," he said again. Their eyes met in a moment of complete understanding.

It passed, and Gorgidas was his astringent self once more. "Go on with you," he said, lightly pushing the tribune forward. "I have enough to do, trying to patch the fools who'd sooner take life than give it." Shaking his head, he made his way down to the injured men not far away.

Minucius' companion Erene was with Helvis, her own daughter, scarcely two months old, asleep in the crook of her arm. The inside of the tribune's tent smelled of blood, the hot, rusty scent as thick as Scaurus had ever known it on the field. Truly, he thought, women fought battles of their own.

Perhaps expecting to see Gorgidas again, Erene started when Marcus, still sweating in his armor, pulled open the tentflap. She knew at once why he had come, but had her own concerns as well. "Is Minucius safe?" she asked anxiously.

"Yes, he's fine," Marcus answered, unconsciously echoing

Gorgidas a few minutes before. "Hardly a scratch—he's a clever fighter."

His voice woke Helvis, who had been dozing. Scaurus stooped beside her, kissed her gently. Erene, her fears at rest, slipped unnoticed from the tent.

The smile Helvis gave the tribune was a tired one. Her soft brown hair was all awry and still matted with sweat; purple circles were smudged under her eyes. But there was a triumph in them as she lifted the small blanket of soft lambswool and offered it to Scaurus.

"Yes, let me see him," Marcus said, carefully taking the light burden from her.

"'Him'? You've already seen Gorgidas," Helvis accused, but Marcus was not listening. He looked down at the face of his newborn son. "He looks like you," Helvis said softly.

"What? Nonsense." The baby was red, wrinkled, flat-nosed, and almost bald; he looked scarcely human, let alone like anyone in particular. His wide gray-blue eyes passed across the tribune's face, then returned and seemed to settle for a moment.

The baby wiggled. Scaurus, unaccustomed to such things, nearly dropped him. An arm came free of the swaddling blanket; a tiny fist waved in the air. Marcus cautiously extended a finger. The groping hand touched it, closed in a grasp of surprising strength. The tribune marveled at its miniature perfection—palm and wrist, pink-nailed fingers and thumb, all compressed into a space no longer than the first two joints of his middle finger.

Helvis misunderstood his examination. "He's complete," she said; "ten fingers, ten toes, all where they should be." They laughed together. The noise startled the baby, who began to cry. "Give him to me," Helvis said, and snuggled him against her. In her more knowing hold, the baby soon quieted.

"Do we name him as we planned?" she asked.

"I suppose so," the tribune sighed, not altogether happy with a bargain they'd made months before. He would have preferred a purely Roman name, with some good Latin praenomen ahead of the Aemilii Scauri's long-established nomen and cognomen. Helvis had argued, though, and with justice, that such a name slighted her side of their son's ancestry. Thus they decided the child's use-name would be Dosti, after her father; when heavier style was needed, he had a sonorous patronymic.

"Dosti the son of Aemilius Scaurus," Marcus said, rolling it off his tongue. He suddenly chuckled, looking at his tiny son. Helvis glanced up curiously. "For now," he explained, "the little fellow's name is longer than he is."

"You're out of your mind," she said, but she was smiling still.

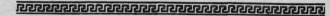

V

THE EARLY SUMMER SUN STOOD TALL IN THE SKY. THE CITY Videssos, capital and heart of the Empire that bore its name, gleamed under the bright gaze. White stucco and marble, tawny sandstone, brick the color of blood, the myriad golden globes on Phos' temples——all seemed close enough to reach out and touch, even when seen from the western shore of the strait the Videssians called the Cattle-Crossing.

But between the army on that western shore and the object of its desire swung an endlessly patrolling line of bronze-beaked warships. Ortaias Sphrantzes might have lost the transmarine suburbs of the capital, but when his forces pulled out they left behind few vessels larger than a fishing smack. Not even Thorisin Gavras' impetuosity made him eager to risk a crossing in the face of the enemy fleet.

Balked from advancing further, his frustration grew with his army. He summoned an officers' council to what had been the local governor's residence until that bureaucrat fled to Ortaias. An east-facing window of clear glass gave a splendid view of the Cattle-Crossing and Videssos the city beyond. Marcus suspected Gavras had chosen the meeting place as a goad to his generals.

Baanes Onomagoulos said, "Thorisin, without ships of our own, we'll stay here till we die of old age, and that's how it is. We could have ten times the men we do, and they wouldn't be worth a counterfeit copper to us. We have to get control of the sea."

He thumped his stick on the table; his wound had left his right leg shrunken and lame.

Thorisin glared at him, not so much for what he said but for the patronizing way he said it. Short, lean, and bald, Onomagoulos had a hard, big-nosed face; he had been Mavrikios Gavras' comrade since they were boys, but had never quite got the idea that the dead Emperor's little brother was now a man in his own right.

"I can't wish ships here," Thorisin snapped. "The Sphrantzai pay their captains well, if no one else. They know they're all that's keeping their heads from going up on the Milestone."

Privately, Marcus thought that an exaggeration. Along with Videssos' proud buildings and elegant gardens, its fortifications—the mightiest the Roman had ever seen—were visible from this seaside house. Even with the Cattle-Crossing somehow overleaped, an assault on that double line of frowning dun walls was enough to daunt any soldier. One problem at a time, he thought.

"Onomagoulos is right, I t'ink. Wit'out ships, you fail. Why not get dem from the Duchy?" Utprand Dagober's son entered the debate for the first time, his island accent almost thick enough to pass for that of the Namdaleni's Haloga cousins. His men were new-come to the seacoast, having marched and fought their way from Phanaskert clear across the Videssian westlands.

"Now there's a notion," Thorisin said dryly. Plainly he did not much like it, but Utprand's forces had swelled his own by a third. It behooved him to walk soft.

The Namdalener smiled a wintry smile; winter seemed at home in his eyes, the chill blue of the ice his northern ancestors left behind when they took Namdalen from the Empire two hundred years before. Matching Gavras irony for irony, he asked, "You cannot misdoubt our good fait'?"

"Surely not," Thorisin replied, and there were chuckles up and down the table. The Duchy of Namdalen had been a thorn in Videssos' flesh since its stormy birth. Its Haloga conquerors did not stay rude pirates long, but learned much from their more civilized subjects. That learning made their mixed-blooded descendants dangerous, subtle warriors. They fought for the Empire, aye, but they and their paymasters both knew they would seize it if they could.

"Well, what would you?" Soteric Dosti's son demanded of Gavras. Helvis' brother sat at Utprand's left hand; the young Namdalener had risen fast since the tribune last saw him. He went on, "Would you sooner win this war with our help, or lose without?"

Scaurus flinched; Soteric always presented choices so as to make yea unpalatable as nay. Save for a proud nose that bespoke partly Videssian ancestry, his features were much like his sister's, but his wide mouth habitually drew up in a thin, hard line.

Thorisin looked from him to the tribune and back again. Marcus' own lips compressed; he knew the Emperor still carried misgivings over the ties of friendship and blood between Romans and Namdaleni. But Gavras' answer was mild enough: "There still may be other alternatives than those."

His gaze swung back to Scaurus. "What say you?" he asked. "Not much, so far."

The tribune was glad of a question he could deal with dispassionately. "That ships are needed, no one can doubt. As to how to get them, others here know better than I. We Romans always took more naturally to fighting on land than on the sea. Put me on the other side of the Cattle-Crossing and you'll hear advice from me in plenty, never fear."

Thorisin smiled mirthlessly. "I believe that—the day you don't speak your mind is the day I begin to suspect you. And I grant you, silence is better than breaking wind by mouth when you've nothing useful to say."

But, having just disclaimed knowledge of naval warfare, Marcus thought back to his lost homeland's past. "My people fought wars with a country called Carthage, which at first had a strong fleet where we had none. We used a beached ship of theirs as a model for our own and soon we were challenging them on the sea. Could we not build our own here?"

The idea had not occurred to Gavras, whose thinking had dealt solely with ships already in existence. He rubbed his bearded chin as he thought; Marcus thought the white streaks on either side of his jaw were wider than they had been a year ago. Finally the Emperor asked, "How long did it take your folk to get their navy built?"

"Sixty days for the first ship, it's said."

"Too long, too long," Thorisin muttered, as much to himself as to his marshals. "I begrudge every day that passes. Phos alone knows what the Yezda are doing behind us."

"Not Phos alone," Soteric said, but so low Gavras could not hear. Few of the tales that the Namdaleni brought from their journey across Videssos were gladsome. Though they had no love for Thorisin Gavras, they agreed that the sooner he won his civil war—if he could—the better his hope of reclaiming the westlands for Videssos.

The Emperor refilled his wine cup from a shapely carafe of gilded silver—like the house in which the council sat, a possession of the recently departed governor. Gavras spat on the dark slate floor in rejection of Skotos and all his works, then raised his eyes and hands on high as he prayed to Phos—the same ritual over wine Scaurus had seen his first day in the Empire.

He realized with some surprise, though, that now he understood the prayer. What Gorgidas had said so long ago was true; little by little, Videssos was setting its mark on him.

Half an hour's ride south of the suburb the Videssians simply called "Across," citrus orchards came down to the sea, leaving only a thin strand of white beach to mark the coastline. Scaurus tethered his borrowed horse to the smooth gray branch of a lemon tree, then cursed softly when in the darkness he scraped his arm on one of the tree's protecting spines.

It was nearly midnight on a moonless night; the men dismounting near the Roman were but blacker shadows under Videssos' strange stars. The light from the great city on the eastern shore of the strait was of more use than their cold gleam, or would have been, had not a war galley's cruel silhouette blocked most of it from sight.

Gaius Philippus nearly tripped as he dismounted. "A pox on these stirrups," he muttered in Latin. "I knew I'd forget the bloody things."

"Quiet, there," Thorisin Gavras said, walking out onto the beach. The rest of his party followed. It was so dark the members were hard to recognize. What little light there was glistened off Nepos' smooth-shaved head and showed his short, tubby frame; Baanes Onomagoulos' painful rolling gait was also unmistakable. Most of the officers were simply tall shapes, one interchangeable with the next.

Gavras unhooded a tiny lantern, once, twice, three times. A cricket chirped in such perfect imitation of the signal that men jumped, laughing quick, nervous, almost silent laughs. But the insect call was not the response Thorisin awaited.

"There's too many of us here," Onomagoulos said nervously. A few seconds later he added, "Your precious fellow out there will get the wind up."

"Hush," Gavras said, making a gesture all but invisible in the dark. From the bow of the silent warship came one flash, then a second.

Thorisin gave a soft grunt of satisfaction, sent back a single answering flash. All was dark and silent for a few moments, then Marcus heard the soft slap of waves on wood as a boat was lowered from that lean, menacing shape ahead.

The tribune's right hand curled round his sword hilt. "Other alternatives"—he recalled Gavras' words of a week before only too well. This parley struck him as suicidally foolish; if the admiral aboard that bireme—drungarios of the fleet was his proper title, Marcus remembered—chose treachery and landed marines, the rebellion against the Sphrantzai would be short-lived indeed.

Thorisin had only laughed at him when he put his fears into words. "You never met Taron Leimmokheir, or you wouldn't speak such nonsense. If he promises a safe meeting, a safe meeting there will be. It's not in him to lie."

The boat was beyond its parent vessel's shadow now, and Scaurus saw Gavras had been right. There were but three men in it: a pair of rowers and a still figure at the stern who had to be the drungarios. The rowers feathered their oars so skillfully that they passed silently over the sea. Only the green-blue phosphorescence that foamed up at each stroke told of their passage.

The little rowboat beached, its keel scraping softly against sand. The rowers leaped out to pull it past waves' reach. When it was secured, Leimmokheir came striding toward the knot of men waiting for him by the trees. Either he was a lucky man or his night sight was very keen, for he unerringly picked out Thorisin Gavras from among his followers.

"Hello, Gavras," he said, clasping Thorisin's hand. "This skulking around by night is a dark business more ways than one, and I don't care for it a bit." His voice was deep and hoarse, roughened by years of shouting over wind and wave. Even at first hearing, Marcus understood why Thorisin Gavras trusted this man; it was not possible to imagine him deceitful.

"A dark business, aye," Gavras agreed, "but one which can lead toward the light. Help us pass the Cattle-Crossing and oust Ortaias the fool and his uncle the spider. Phos, man, you've had half a year now to see how the two of them run things—they aren't fit to clean the red boots, let alone to wear 'em."

Taron Leimmokheir drew in a slow, thoughtful breath. "I gave my oath to Ortaias Sphrantzes when it was not known if you were alive or dead. Would you forswear me? Skotos' ice is the final home for oathbreakers."

"Would you see the Empire dragged down to ruin by your scruples?" Thorisin shot back. There were times when he sounded all too much like Soteric, and Scaurus instinctively knew he was taking the wrong tack with this man.

"Why not work with them, not against?" Leimmokheir returned. "They freely offer you the title you bore under your brother, may good Phos shine upon his countenance, and declare their willingness to bind themselves by any oaths you name."

"Were it possible, I'd say I valued the oaths of the Sphrantzai less even than their coins."

That got home; Leimmokheir let out a bark of laughter before he could check himself. But he would not change his mind. "You've grown bitter and distrustful," he said. "If nothing else, the fact that you and they are now related by marriage will hold them to their pledges. Doubly damned are those who dare against kinsmen."

"You are an honest, pious man, Taron," Thorisin said regretfully. "Because you have no evil in you, you will not see it in others."

The drungarios half bowed. "That may be, but I, too, must try to do right as I see it. When next we meet, I will fight you."

"Seize him!" Soteric said urgently. At the edge of hearing, Leimmokheir's two sailors snapped to alertness.

But Gavras was shaking his head. "Would you make a Sphrantzes of me, Namdalener?" Close by, Utprand rumbled agreement. Thorisin ignored him, turning back to Taron Leimmokheir. "Go on, get out," he said. Marcus had never heard such bitter weariness in his voice.

The drungarios bowed once more, this time from the waist. He walked slowly down to his boat, turned as if to say something. Whatever it was, it did not pass his lips. He sat down at the boat's stern; his men pushed it out until they were waist-deep in the sea, then scrambled aboard themselves. Oars rose and fell; the rowboat turned in a tight circle, then moved steadily back to the galley.

Marcus heard a rope ladder creak as it took weight, the sound faint but clear across the water. Taron Leimmokheir's raspy bass rumbled a command. The bireme's quiet oars awoke, sending it gliding south like some monster centipede. It disappeared behind an outjutting point of land.

Thorisin watched it go, disappointment plain in every line of his body. He said softly to himself, "Honest and pious, yes, but too trusting by half. One day it will cost him."

"If it doesn't cost us first," Indakos Skylitzes exclaimed. "Look there!" From the north, a longboat was darting toward the lonely stretch of beach; no little ship's gig this, but a twenty-footer packed to the gunwales with armed men.

"Sold!" Gavras said, disbelief in his voice. He stood frozen for a moment as the longboat came ashore. "Phos curse that baseborn treacher for all eternity. Belike he landed marines south of us, too, just as soon as he was out of sight, to make it a good, thorough trap."

His sword rang free of scabbard. It glittered coldly in uncaring starlight. "Well, as friend Baanes said, there's more of us here than he reckoned on. We can give this lot a fight. Videssos!" he yelled, and charged the longboat, where soldiers were still climbing out onto the beach.

Scaurus among them, his officers pounded after him, sand spraying up as they ran. Only Nepos and Onomagoulos hung back—the one was no warrior, while the other could scarcely walk.

It was four to three against Gavras' party, or something close to that; there must have been twenty men in the grounded boat. But instead of using their numbers to any advantage, they stood surprised, waiting to receive their foes' onset.

"Ha, villains!" Thorisin cried. "Not the easy assassination you were promised, is it?" He cut at one of the men from the boat, who parried and slashed back. Lithe as a serpent, Thorisin twisted, cut again. The man groaned, dropped his blade to clutch at the spurting gash below his left shoulder. A last stroke, this one two-handed, ripped into his belly. He slumped to the sand, unmoving.

Marcus never wanted to know another fight like this battle in the darkness. To tell friend from foe was all but impossible, and it was not easy even to strike a blow. The beach sand was as treacherous as the combat, sliding and shifting so a man could hardly keep his feet planted under him.

An attacker slashed at Scaurus; his saber hissed past the tribune's ear. He stumbled back, wishing for a cuirass or shield. To hold the man off, he lunged out in a stop-thrust, and his opponent, intent on finishing an enemy he thought at his mercy, rushed forward to skewer himself on the blade he never saw. He grunted, coughed wetly, and died.

If none of Gavras' companions wore armor, the same seemed true of their assailants; few men who traveled by sea would risk its perilous weight. And Thorisin's followers were masters of war, soldiers who had come to their high ranks through years of honing their fighting skills. When coupled with their fury at this betrayal-caused battle, that balanced the advantage their enemies' numbers gave them.

Soon the would-be assassins sought escape, but they found no more than they would have granted. Three tried to launch the longboat once more, but they were cut down from behind.

Long legs churning through the sand, Soteric raced down the beach after the last of the fleeing bravoes. Finding flight useless, the warrior whirled to defend himself. Steel rang on steel. It was too black for Marcus to see much of that fight, but the Namdalener beat down his foe's guard with hammer-strokes of his sword and stretched him bleeding and lifeless on the soft white strand.

Scaurus' eyes jumped everywhere looking for more enemies, but there were none. A worse task began—seeing who among Thorisin's men had fallen. Indakos Skylitzes was down, as were two Vaspurakaner officers the tribune did not know well and a Namdalener who had accompanied Utprand and Soteric. The tribune wondered who would receive the dead man's sword, and what lives would suddenly be wrenched askew.

Gavras was jubilant. "Well fought, well fought!" he yelled, his glee filling the beach. "Thus always to murderers! They— here, stop that! What in Phos' holy name are you doing?"

Baanes Onomagoulos had been stumping up and down, methodically slitting the throats of those attackers who still moved. His hands gleamed, wet, black, and slick in the stars' pale light.

"What do you think?" Onomagoulos retorted. "That accursed Leimmokheir's marines will be here any time. Should I leave these whoresons to tell 'em where we've gone?"

"No," Thorisin admitted. "But you should have saved one for questioning."

"Too late now." Onomagoulos spread his bloody hands. "Nepos," he called, "make a light. I'd wager we'll have the answer to any questions soon enough."

The priest came up to Onomagoulos' side. His breathing grew deep and steady. Gavras' officers muttered in awe as a pale, golden radiance sprang into being round his hands. Marcus was less wonder-struck than some; this was a miracle he had seen before, from Apsimar the prelate of Imbros.

For all the amazement Baanes Onomagoulos showed, Nepos might have lit a torch. The half-crippled noble painfully bent by one of the fallen attackers. His knife snicked out to slit a belt-pouch. Goldpieces—a surprising number of goldpieces—spilled onto the sand. Onomagoulos scooped them up, held them close to Nepos' glowing palms. Thorisin's marshals crowded close to look.

"'Ort. the 1st Sphr., Avt. of Vid.,'" Onomagoulos read from a coin, not bothering to stretch the abbreviation full length. "Here's Ort. the first again—again." He turned a goldpiece over. "And again. Nothing but Phos-curse Ort. the first, in fact."

"Aye, ahnd ahll fresh-minted, too." That flat-voweled accent had to belong to Utprand Dagober's son.

"What else would Leimmokheir use to pay his hired killers?" Onomagoulos asked rhetorically.

"How could the Sphrantzai have infected him with their treachery?" Thorisin wondered. "Vardanes must be leagued with Skotos, to have suborned Taron Leimmokheir."

No one answered him; the crackle of brush pushed aside, loud in the midnight stillness, came from the south. Swords flew up instinctively. Nepos' light vanished as he took his concentration from it. "The son of a manurebag did land marines!" Onomagoulos growled.

"I don't think so," Gaius Philippus said. Woods-wise, he went on, "I think the noise was closer to us, made by something smaller than a man—a fox, maybe, or a badger."

"You are right, I think," Utprand said.

Not even the centurion of the Namdalener, though, seemed eager to wait and test their guess. With their comrades, they hurried back to their mounts. Soteric, Scaurus, and Nepos quickly lashed the bodies of Gavras' slain commanders to their horses. Moments later, they were trotting north through the orchard. Branches slapped at the tribune before he knew they were there.

If Leimmokheir's marines were behind the officers, they never caught them up. When Thorisin and his followers emerged from the fragrant rows of trees, the Emperor galloped his horse a quarter of a mile in sheer exuberance at being alive. He waited impatiently for his men to join him.

When they reached him at last, he had the air of a man who had come to a decision. "Very well, then," he declared. "If we cannot cross with Leimmokheir's let, we shall in his despite."

"'In his despite,'" Gorgidas echoed the next morning. "A ringing phrase, no doubt." The Roman camp was full of excitement as word of the night's adventure raced through Gavras' army. Viridovix, as was his way when left out of a fight, was wildly jealous and sulked for hours until Scaurus managed to jolly him from his sour mood.

The tribune's men bombarded him and Gaius Philippus with questions. Most were satisfied after one or two, but Gorgidas kept on, trying to pull from the Romans every detail of what had gone on. His cross-questioning was sharp as a jurist's, and he soon succeeded in annoying Gaius Philippus.

A more typical Roman than the thoughtful Scaurus, the senior centurion had little patience for anything without obvious practical use. "You don't want us," he complained to the doctor. "You want one of the buggers Onomagoulos let the air out of, to go at him with pincers and hot iron."

The Greek took no notice of his griping, but said, "Onomagoulos, eh? Thank you, that reminds me of something else I wanted to ask: how did he know he'd find Ortaias' monies in the dead men's pouches?"

"Great gods, that should be plain enough even to you." Gaius Philippus threw his hands in the air. "If their drungarios hired murderers, he'd have to pay in his master's coins." The centurion gave a short, hard laugh. "It's not likely he'd have any of Thorisin's. And don't think you can ignore me and have me go away," he went on. "You still haven't said the first thing about why you're flinging all these questions at us."

The usually voluble Greek stood mute. He arched one eyebrow and tried to stare Gaius Philippus down, but Marcus came in on the senior centurion's side. "Anyone would think you were writing a history," he told the physician.

A slow flush climbed Gorgidas' face. Scaurus saw that what he had meant for a joke was in grim earnest to the Greek. "Your pardon," he said, and meant it. "I did not know. How long have you been working on it?"

"Eh? Since I learned enough Videssian to ask for pen and parchment—you know as well as I there's no papyrus here."

"What language is it in?" the tribune asked.

"Hellenisti, ma Día! In Greek, by Zeus! What other tongue is there for serious thought?" Gorgidas slipped back into his native speech to answer.

Gaius Philippus stared at him in amazement. His own Greek consisted of a couple of dozen words, most of them foul, but he knew the name of the language when he heard it. "In Greek, you say? Of all the bootless things I've heard, that throws the triple six! Greek, in Videssos that's never heard the word, let alone the tongue? Why, man, you could be Homer or what's-his-name—the first history writer, I heard it once but I'm damned if I recall it—" He looked to Scaurus for help.

"Herodotos," the tribune supplied.

"Thanks; that's the name. As I say, Gorgidas, you could be either of those old bastards, or even both of 'em together, and who'd ever know it, here? Greek!" he repeated, half-contemptuous wonder in his voice.

The doctor's color deepened. "Yes, Greek, and why not?" he said tightly. "One day, maybe, I'll be easy enough in Videssian to write it, or I might have one of their scholars help translate what I write. Manetho the Egyptian and Berosos of Babylon wrote in Greek to teach us Hellenes of their nations' past glories; it wouldn't be the worst deed to make sure we are remembered in Videssos after the last of us has died."

He spoke with the same determination he might have shown when facing a difficult case, but Marcus saw he had not impressed Gaius Philippus. What happened after his own end was of no concern to the senior centurion. He sensed, however, that he had chaffed Gorgidas about as much as he could. In his rough way he was fond of the doctor, so he shrugged and gave up the argument, saying, "All this gabbing is a waste of time. I'd best go drill the men; they're fat and lazy enough as is." He strode off, still shaking his head.

"The Videssians will be interested in your work, I think," Marcus said to Gorgidas. "They have historians of their own; I remember Alypia Gavra saying she read them, and I think—though I'm not sure—she might have been taking notes for a book of her own. Why else would she have been at Mavrikios' council of war?" Something else occurred to the tribune. "She might be able to help you get yours translated."

He saw gratitude flicker in the doctor's eyes, but Gorgidas was prickly as always. "Aye, so she might—were she not on the far side of the Cattle-Crossing, married to the wrong Emperor. But who are we to boggle at such trivia?"

"All right, all right, your point's made. I tell you this, though—if Alypia were on the far side of the moon, I'd still want to see that history of yours."

"That's right, you read some Greek, don't you? I'd forgotten that." Gorgidas sighed, said ruefully, "Truly, Scaurus, one reason I started the thing in the first place was to keep myself from losing my letters. The gods know I'm no, ah, what's-his-name?" The physician's chuckle had a hollow ring. "But I find I can put together understandable sentences."

"I'd like to see what you've done," Scaurus said, and meant it. He had always found history, with its dispassionate approach, a more reliable guide to the conduct of affairs than the orators' high-flown rhetoric. Thucydides or Polybios was worth twenty of Demosthenes, who sold his tongue like a woman her virtue and sometimes composed speeches for prosecution and defense in the same case.

Gorgidas broke into his musing. "Speaking of Alypia and the Cattle-Crossing," he said, "did Gavras say anything of how he planned to pass it by? I'm not asking as a historian now, you understand, merely as someone with certain objections to being killed out of hand."

"I have a few of those myself," Marcus admitted. "No, I don't know what's in his mind." Still thinking in classical terms, he went on, "Whatever it is, it may well work. Thorisin is like Odysseus—he's *sophron.*"

"*Sophron*, eh?" Gorgidas said. "Well, let's hope you're right." The Greek word meant not so much having superior wits but getting the most distance from those one had. Gor-

gidas was not so sure it fit Gavras, but he thought it a fine
description for Scaurus himself.

Black-capped terns wheeled and dipped, screeching their
disapproval at the armed men scrambling down a splintery
ladder into the waist of a fishing boat that had seen better
days. "A pox on you, louse-bitten sea crows!" Viridovix
shouted up at them, shaking his fist. "I like the notion no
better than yourselves."

All along the docks and beaches of Videssos' western suburbs, troops were boarding by squads and platoons as motley a
fleet as Marcus had ever imagined. Three or four grain car-
riers, able to embark a whole company, formed the backbone
of Thorisin Gavras' makeshift armada. There were fishing
craft aplenty; those the eye could not pick out at once were
immediately obvious to the nose. There were smugglers'
boats, with great spreads of canvas and lines greyhound-lean.
There were little sponge-divers' vessels, some hardly more
than rowboats, with masts no thicker than a spearshaft. There
were keel-less barges taken from the river trade; how they
would act on the open sea was anyone's bet. And there were a
great many ships whose functions the tribune, no more nauti-
cal than most Romans, could not hope to guess.

He helped Nepos down onto the fishing boat's deck. "I
thank you," the priest said. Nepos sagged against the boat's
raised cabin. Timbers creaked under his weight, but he made
no move to stand free. "Merciful Phos, but I'm tired," he
said. His eyes were still merry, but there were dark circles
under them and his words came slowly, as if getting each one
out took effort.

"Well you might be," Scaurus answered. Aided by three
other sorcerers, the priest had spent the past two and a half
weeks weaving spells round the odd assortment of boats Thorisin had gathered from up and down the western coastlands.
Most of the work had fallen on Nepos' shoulders, for he held
a chair in sorcery at the Videssian Academy in the capital
while his colleagues were local wizards without outstanding
talent. At its easiest, sorcery was as exhausting as hard labor;
what the priest had accomplished was hardly sorcery at its
easiest.

Gorgidas descended, graceful as a cat; a moment later

Gaius Philippus came down beside him, planting himself on the gently rocking deck as if daring it to shake him.

"Viridovix!" It was a soft hail from the next boat down the dock, a lateen-rigged fishing craft even smaller and grubbier than the one the Celt was sharing with the Roman officers.

"Aye, Bagratouni?" Viridovix called. "Is your honor glad to be on the ocean, now?" Coming from landlocked Vaspurakan, Gagik Bagratouni had professed regret that he knew nothing of the sea.

The *nakharar's* leonine features were distinctly green. "Does always it move about so?" he asked.

"Bad cess to you for reminding me," Viridovix said, gulping.

"Use the rail, not my deck," warned the fishing boat's captain, a thin, dark, middle-aged man with hair and beard sun- and sea-bleached to the grayish-yellow color of his boat's planking. The Gaul's misery mystified him. How could a man be sick on an all but motionless boat?

"If my stomach decides to come up, now, I'll use whatever's underneath me, and that without a by-your-leave," Viridovix said, but in Latin, not Videssian.

"What now?" Marcus asked Nepos, waving out to the patrolling galleys, their broad sails like sharks' fins. "Shall we be invisible to them, like the Yezda for a few moments during the great battle?" He still sweat cold every time he thought of that, though Videssian sorcerers had quickly worked counterspells that brought the nomads back into sight.

"No, no." The priest managed to sound impatient and weary at the same time. "That spell is all very well against folk with no magic of their own, but if any opposing wizard is nearby one might just as well light a bonfire at the bow of the boat." The captain's head whipped round; he wanted no talk of bonfires aboard his ship.

Nepos continued, "Besides, the invisibility spell is easy to overcome, and if it were broken with us on the sea, the slaughter would be terrible. We are using a subtler measure, one crafted in the Academy last year. We will, in fact, be in full sight of the galleys all the way to the eastern shore of the Cattle-Crossing."

"Where's the magic in that?" Gaius Philippus demanded. "I could swim out there and accomplish as much, though I'd have little joy of it."

"Patience, I pray you," Nepos said. "Let me finish. Though we'll be in plain sight of the foe, he will not see us. That is the artistry; his eye will slide over us, look past us, but never light on us."

"I see," the senior centurion said approvingly. "It'll be like when I'm hunting partridges and walk past one without ever noticing it because its colors blend into the brush and woods where it's hiding."

"Something like that," Nepos nodded. "Though there's rather more to it. We don't blend into the ocean, you know. The eye, yes, and the ear as well, have to be tricked away from us by magic, not simple camouflage. But it's a gentler magic than the invisibility spell and nearly impossible to detect unless a wizard already knows it's there."

"There's the signal now," the fishing captain said. Thorisin Gavras' flagship, a rakish smugglers' vessel almost big enough to challenge one of Ortaias' warcraft, was flying the sky-blue Videssian imperial pennant. The steady northwesterly breeze whipped it out straight, showing Phos' sun bright in its center.

A sailor undid the mooring lines that held the fishing boat to the dock at stern and bow, tossed them aboard, and leaped nimbly down into the boat. At the captain's quick orders, his four-man crew unreefed the single square-rigged sail. The sailcloth was old, sagging, and much patched, but it held the wind. Pitching slightly in the light chop, the boat slid out into the Cattle-Crossing.

Scaurus led his companions to the bow, both to be out of the sailors' way and to see what lay ahead. The western part of the channel was as full of boats as an unwashed dog with fleas, but not one of the biremes ahead paid them the slightest heed. So far, at least, Nepos' magic held. "What will you do if your spell should fail in mid-crossing?" Marcus asked the priest.

"Pray," Nepos said shortly, "for we are undone." But seeing it was a question seriously meant and not asked only to vex him, he added, "There would be little else I could do; it's a complex magic, and not one easily laid on."

As always, Viridovix was lost in a private anguish from the moment the little fishing boat began to move. Knuckles white beneath freckles from the desperation of his grip, he clutched the boat's rail, leaning over it as far as he could. Gaius Philippus, who did not suffer from seasickness, said to Nepos, "Tell me, priest, is your conjuring proof against the sound of puking?"

On firm ground such sarcasm would have sparked a quarrel with the Celt, but he only moaned and held on tighter. Then he suddenly straightened, amazement ousting distress. "What was that, now?" he exclaimed, pointing down into the water. The others followed his finger, but there was nothing to see but the cyan-blue ocean with its tracing of lacy white foam.

"There's another!" Viridovix said. Not far from the boat, a smooth, silver-scaled shape flicked itself into the air, to glide for fifty yards before dropping back into the sea. "What manner of fairy might it be, and what's the meaning of it? Is the seeing of it a good omen, or foul?"

"You mean the flying fish?" Gorgidas asked in surprise. Children of the warm Mediterranean, he and the Romans took the little creatures for granted, but they were unknown in the cool waters of the northern ocean that was the only sea the Gaul knew.

And because they were so far removed from anything he had imagined, Viridovix would not believe his friends' insistence that these were but another kind of fish, not even when Nepos joined his assurances to theirs. "The lot of you are thinking to befool me," he said, "and rare cruel y'are, too, with me so sick and all." His bodily woes only served to make him ugly; his voice was petulant and full of hostility.

"Oh, for the—!" Gaius Philippus said in exasperation. "Bloody fool of a Celt!" Flying fish were skipping all around the boat now, perhaps fleeing some marauding albacore or tuna. One, more intrepid but less lucky than its fellows, landed on the deck almost at the centurion's feet. As it flopped on the planks, he took his dagger, still sheathed, from his belt and, reversing the weapon, struck the fish smartly behind the head with the pommel.

He picked up the foot-long, broken-backed fish and handed it to the Gaul. The broad gliding fins hung limply; already the golden eyes were dimming, the ocean-blue back and silver belly losing their living sheen and fading toward death's gray. "You killed it," Viridovix said in dismay, and threw it back into the sea.

"More foolishness," the centurion said. "They're fine eating, butterflied and fried." But Viridovix, still distressed, shook his head; he had seen a dream die, not a fish, and to think of it as food was beyond him.

"You should be grateful," Gorgidas observed. "With your interest in the flying fish, you've forgotten your seasickness."

"Why, indeed and I have," the Celt said, surprised. His quick-rising spirits brought a grin to his face. Just then a wave a trifle bigger than most slapped against the fishing boat's bow. The light craft rolled gently and Viridovix, eyes bulging and cheeks pale with nausea, had to seek the rail once more. "Be damned to you for making me remember," he choked out between heaves.

Some of Thorisin's boats were by the patrolling galleys now, and still no sign they had been seen. As it sailed toward the agreed-upon landing point a couple of miles south of the capital, the vessel Marcus rode passed within a hundred yards of a warship of the Sphrantzai.

Spell-protected or not, it was a nervous moment. The tribune could clearly read the name painted in gold on the ship's bow: *Corsair Breaker*. Her sharp bronze beak, greened by the sea, came in and out, in and out of view. There were white patches of barnacles on it and on those timbers usually below the waterline. A dart-throwing engine was on her foredeck, loaded and ready to shoot; the missile's steel head blurred in bright reflection.

Corsair Breaker's two banks of long oars rose and fell in smooth unison. Even a lubber like Scaurus could tell her rowers were a fine crew; indifferent to the wind, they drove her steadily north. Over the creak of oars in their locks and the slap of them in the sea came the bass roar of song they used to keep their rhythm:

> "Lit-tle bird with a yellow bill
> Sat outside my windowsill—"

The Videssian army sang that song, too, and the Romans with them as soon as they'd learned the words. There were, it was said, fifty-two verses to it, some witty, some brutal, some obscene, and most a mix of all three.

The hoarse ballad faded as *Corsair Breaker's* superior speed swept the bireme away on her patrolling path. Under-officers stood at the twin steering oars at her stern; a lookout was atop her mast to cry danger at anything untoward. Marcus swallowed a smile. If Nepos' magic suddenly disappeared, the poor fellow likely would have heart failure.

The tribune's smile returned—and not swallowed, either —as he watched his Emperor's mismatched excuse for a fleet sneak its way over the Cattle-Crossing under the nose of the imperial navy. Some of the faster boats were almost to the shore; even the slow, awkward barges were past the galleys loyal to Ortaias. With fortune, Videssos the city should be too much stunned at the sight of Gavras' army appeared from nowhere under its walls to put much thought to resistance.

"Aye, a splendid job," he said expansively to Nepos. "Puts the whole war in hailing distance of being won."

Like all of Phos' priests, Nepos was pledged to humility. He flushed under Scaurus' praise. "Thank you," he said shyly. He was academic as much as priest and so went on, "This success will take an important new charm out of the realm of theory and into the practical sphere. The research, of course, was the work of many; it's mere chance that makes me the one to execute it. It—"

The priest lurched and turned purple: no blush of modesty this, but a darkening as if strangler's hands were round his neck. Marcus and Gorgidas darted toward him, both afraid the fat little man's labor had brought on a fit of apoplexy.

But Nepos was suffering no fit, though tears rolled down his cheek to lose themselves in his thicket of beard. His hands moved in desperate passes; he whispered cantrips fast as his lips could shape them.

"What's toward?" Gaius Philippus barked. Doubly out of his reckoning on the sea and treating with magic, he nonetheless knew trouble when he saw it. His hand snaked to his sword hilt, but the familiar gesture brought him no comfort.

"Counterspell!" Nepos got out between his quickly repeated charms. He was shaking like a man with an ague. "A vicious one—aimed at me as much as my spell. And strong —Phos, who at the Academy can it be? I've never felt such strength—almost struck me down where I stood." He had been incanting between sentences, sometimes between words, and returned wholly to his sorcery once the gasped explanation was through.

The priest's skill was enough to save himself, but could not keep his spell intact. Still at his miserable perch over the rail,

Viridovix cried out, "Och, we're for it now! The cat's after kenning there's mice in the cupboard!"

Including *Corsair Breaker*, there were seven galleys in Marcus' sight. He could hardly imagine how Sphrantzes' ship captains and sailors must have felt, with the ocean full of their enemy's ships. Their reaction, though, was nothing like the palpitations the tribune had jokingly wished on them a few minutes before. They went charging against the small craft all around them like so many bulls rampaging through a herd of sheep.

Scaurus' heart leaped into his mouth to see one of the cruel-beaked ships bearing down on the rearmost barge, a craft that was, to his horror, filled with legionaries. But the bireme's captain, at least, was unnerved enough by his foes' apparition to make a fatal error of judgment. Instead of trusting to his vessel's ram, his port oars swept up and out of the way as he came gracefully alongside and demanded the barge's surrender.

In his pride, though, he forgot there was more to the bargain than his sleek ship against the slow-moving, clumsy river scow: there were men as well. Ropes snaked up to catch on belaying pins and the steering oar, binding ship to ship tight as a lover's embrace. And up those ropes and over the galley's low gunwales swarmed the Romans, whooping with wolfish glee. They pitched the handful of marines on board over the side; those splashes marked their end for, not true sailors, they wore cuirasses which now were fatal, not protecting.

Seeing his ship taken from under him, the captain fled to the high stern. He, too, wore armor: gilded, in token of his rank. It flashed brilliantly for a moment as he leaped into the sea to drown, too proud to outlive his folly.

That mattered little, as far as the outcome went. The Romans, no sailors themselves, laid hold of the bireme's pilot and put a sword against his throat. Thus encouraged, he bawled orders to the crew. Oars came raggedly to life; the sail spread and billowed. Like a race horse among carters' nags, the galley sprinted for the beach.

Elsewhere, things went not so well. Warned by their comrade's blunder, Ortaias' warships made no further unwise moves. A fishing boat kissed by their sharp bronze simply ceased to be, save as sodden canvas, splintered timbers, and men struggling in the warm blue waters of the strait. Worse still, alarm bells were ringing in the city, and through the boom of surf off sea walls Marcus could hear officers shouting their men aboard fresh galleys.

But all that needed time, and the Sphrantzai had little time to spend. Already Gavras' boats were beginning to beach, soldiers jumping from them as fast as they could scramble. And each attack run stole precious minutes from the warships, for their targets jinked and dodged with all the desperate skill their crews could summon. Even after a ram bit home, there was more delay as the triumphant bireme backed oars to pull itself free of its prey. Unspining was a delicate task, lest the warships, like bees, were to leave stings behind in their wounds, and with results as damaging to themselves.

Marcus shouted himself hoarse to see what seemed a surely fatal stroke go wide. He was so intent on the sprawling sea-fight that he almost did not hear the helmsman's frightened cry: "Phos have mercy! One o' the buggers is on our tail!"

"Come a point north," the captain ordered instantly, gauging wind, coast, and pursuer in one comprehensive glance.

"'Twill lose us some of our wind," the helmsman protested.

"Aye, but it's a shorter run to the beach. Steer so, damn you!" Pale beneath his sun-swarthied skin, the helmsman obeyed.

Scaurus bit his lip, not so much from fright but frustration. His fate was being decided here, and not a thing he could do but impotently wait. If that sea-bleached fishing captain knew his business, the boat might come safe through it; if not, surely not. But either way, there was nothing the tribune could do to help or hurt. His skills were worthless here, his opinions of no value.

The shore seemed nailed in place before him, while from behind the galley came rushing up, shark-sure and swift. Too fast, too fast, he thought; Achilles would surely catch this tortoise.

Gaius Philippus was making the same grim calculation. "He'll be up our arse before we ground," he said. "If we shed our mail shirts now, we have hope to swim it."

Abandoning armor was an admission of defeat, but that was not what set Marcus against it. There were archers on that cursed bireme; already a couple of shafts had whistled past, more swift and slender than any flying fish. To be shot swimming defenselessly in the sea was not an end he relished.

If the bireme was in arrow range the end of the chase could not be far away. With sick fascination, the tribune watched the imperial pennant stiff in the breeze at the warship's bow. Below it was another, this one crimson with five bronze bars, the drungarios' emblem. So, Marcus thought, it was Taron Leimmokheir himself who'd sink him. He would willingly have forgone the honor.

But another ship was racing up alongside the imperial vessel, not so big, but packed to the gunwales with armed men . . . and also flying the imperial banner. "Go on, Leimmokheir, go on, you sneaking filthy knife in the night!" Thorisin Gavras roared across the narrowing space of water, his furious bellow like song in Scaurus' ears. "Ram, and then you face me! You haven't the stones in your bag for it!"

No taunt, no insult could have moved the Videssian admiral from his chosen course, but hard reality did. If he sank the fishing boat ahead, Gavras would surely come alongside and board—and with so many soldiers crammed into his ship, that fight could have but one outcome. "Hard to port," Leimmokheir cried, and his ship heeled on its side as it twisted free from danger.

Thorisin and his men yelled derision after him: "Coward! Traitor!"

"No traitor I!" That was Leimmokheir's rough bass. "I said I would fight you if I met you again."

"You thought that would be never, you and your hired murderers!"

Wind and quickly growing distance swept away the admiral's reply. Thorisin shook his fist at the retreating galley and sent after it a volley of curses Leimmokheir never heard.

Marcus waved his thanks to the Emperor. "So it was you I rescued, was it?" Gavras shouted. "See, I must trust you after all—or maybe I didn't know who was in your boat!" The tribune wished Thorisin had not added that gibing postscript; all too likely it held a touch of truth.

"Shoaling, we are," one of the sailors warned, and grabbed the fishing boat's rail. Gorgidas and Nepos both had the wisdom to do the same. A moment later timbers groaned as the boat ran hard aground. Marcus and Gaius Philippus fell in a swearing heap; Viridovix, still leaning over the side, almost went overboard.

"This salt water'll play merry hell with my armor," Gaius

Philippus said mournfully as he splashed ashore. Marcus followed, carrying his sword above his head to keep it safe from rust.

A wave knocked Viridovix off his feet. He emerged from the sea looking like a drowned cat, his mustaches and long red locks plastered wetly across his face. But a grin flashed behind that hair. "It's one man jolly well out of a boat I am!" he cried. As soon as he got above the tideline, he carefully dried his blade in the white sand. He was careless in some things, but never with his weapons.

The whole fringe of beach was full of small units from Thorisin Gavras' army, all trying to form up into larger ones. A full maniple of Romans came marching toward the tribune from the captured Videssian bireme a quarter of a mile down the beach; Quintus Glabrio was their head.

"I thought you were done for when that whoreson came up on you," Marcus said, returning the junior centurion's salute. "'Well done' doesn't say enough."

As usual, Glabrio shrugged the praise aside. "If he hadn't made a mistake, it wouldn't have turned out so well."

Gavras' ship went aground next to the boat that had carried Scaurus and his companions. "Hurry, there!" the Emperor exhorted his men as they came up onto the land. "Form a perimeter! If the Sphrantzai have the wit to make a sally against us, we'll wish we were on the other shore again. Hurry!" he repeated.

He co-opted Glabrio's maniple as part of his guard force. Scaurus gave it to him without demur; he had been taking constant nervous glances at Videssos' frowning walls and great gates, wondering if the capital's masters would contest their rival's landing.

But rather than vomiting forth armed men, the city's gates were slamming shut to hold the newcomers out. The thunder of their closing was audible where Gavras' men stood. "Penpushers! Seal-stampers!" Thorisin said with contempt. "Ortaias and his snake of an uncle must think to win their war huddling behind the city's walls, hoping I'll grow bored and go away, or that their next assassination scheme won't miscarry, or suchlike foolishness. There can't be a real soldier among 'em, no one to tell them walls don't win sieges, not by themselves. That takes wit and gut both. The young Sphrantzes has neither, Phos knows; Vardanes I'll give credit for shrewdness, aye, but the only guts to him are the ones bulging over his belt."

Scaurus nodded at Gavras' assessment of his imperial foes, though he suspected there might be more to Vardanes Sphrantzes than Thorisin thought. But even after it was plain there would be no sally from Videssos, the tribune's eye kept drifting back to that double wall of dour brown stone. How much wit, he asked himself, would it take to keep men out, fighting from works like those?

He must have spoken his thoughts aloud, for Gaius Philippus commented soberly, "Close, but not quite on the mark. The real question is, how much wit will it take to get in?"

VI

TRUMPETS BLARED A FANFARE, THEN SKIRLED INTO A MARCH beat. Twelve parasols, the imperial number, popped open as one, bright flowers of red, blue, gold, and green silk. Thorisin Gavras' army, formed in a great long column, lifted weapons in salute of their overlord. A herald, a barrel-chested stentor of a man, roared out, "Forward—ho!" and, with the usual Videssian love of ostentatious ceremony, the column stamped into motion. It slowly paraded from south to north just out of missile range from the imperial capital's walls, a fierce spectacle intended to give the city's defenders second thoughts on their choice of masters.

"Behold Thorisin Gavras, his Imperial Majesty, rightful Avtokrator of the Videssians!" the herald bellowed from his place between Thorisin and his parasol bearers. The Emperor's bay stallion, his accustomed mount, was still on the other side of the Cattle-Crossing. He rode a black, its coat curried to dark luster.

Gavras waved to the city, doffing his helmet to let Sphrantzes' troops on the wall see his face. For the occasion he wore a golden circlet around the businesslike conical helm; his boots were a splash of blood against the horse's jet-black hide. Otherwise he was garbed as a common soldier—it was to soldiers he would appeal, and in any case he had no patience with the jewel-encrusted, gold-stitched vestments that were an Avtokrator's proper garb.

There were warriors aplenty to watch his progress before the city. They lined the lower, outer wall; the greatest numbers, as was natural, defended the gates. Except for gatehouse forces, the massive inner wall, fifty feet tall or even a bit more, was not so heavily garrisoned.

"Why serve pen-pushers?" the herald cried to the troops inside Videssos. "They'd sooner see you serfs than soldiers." That, Marcus knew, was only the truth. Bureaucratic Emperors had held sway in Videssos for most of the past half-century and, to break the power of their rivals, the provincial nobles, the pen-pushers systematically dismantled the native Videssian army and replaced it with mercenaries.

But that process was far-gone now, and the force defending Ortaias Sphrantzes and his uncle was itself largely made up of hired troops. They hooted and jeered at Gavras, crying, "All your people are serfs! That's why they need real men to fight for 'em!" The regiment of Namdaleni started its shout of "Drax! Drax! The great count Drax!" to drown out Gavras' herald's words.

One mercenary, a man with strong lungs and a practical turn of mind, shouted, "Why should we choose you over the Sphrantzai? They'll pay us and keep us on, and you'd send us home poor!" Thorisin's lips skinned back from his teeth in a humorless smile; his distrust of mercenaries was too well known, even though his own army was more than half hired troops.

Forgetting his herald, he yelled back, "Why prop up a worthless turntail rascal? For fierce Ortaias cost us everything in front of Maragha by running away like a frightened mouse, him and his talk of being 'ashamed to suffer not suffering.' Bah!"

On the last few words Thorisin's voice climbed to a squeaky tenor mockery of his foe's; he wickedly quoted young Sphrantzes' speech to his men just before the disastrous battle. His own soldiers were mostly survivors of that fight; they added their shouts to Gavras' derision: "Aye, give him to us, the coward!" "Send him to the amphitheater—he'd ride rings round your jockeys!" "You'd best be brave, you on the walls, if you have to fight after one of his speeches!" And Gaius Philippus, loud in Marcus' ear: "Give him over—we'll show him more than's in his book, I promise!"

The torrent of scorn that poured from Gavras' army seemed to have an effect on Ortaias' soldiers. They were men like any others, and sensitive to their fellow professionals' taunts.

When the army's abuse died away, there was thoughtful silence up on Videssos' walls.

But one of Sphrantzes' captains, a huge warrior who towered over his troops, roared out harsh, contemptuous laughter. "You ran, too, Gavras," he bellowed, "after your brother lost his head! How are you better than the lord we serve?"

Thorisin went red and then white. He dug spurs into his horse until it screamed and reared. "Attack!" he shouted. "Kill me that slime-tongued whore's get!" A few men took tentative steps toward the wall; most never moved from their places in column. Realistic with the stark good sense of men who risk their lives for pay, they knew such an impromptu assault on the city's works could only end in massacre.

While Gavras wrestled his stallion to stillness, Marcus hurried forward to try to calm the Emperor. Baanes Onomagoulos was already at his side, holding the horse's bridle and talking softly but urgently to the furious Gavras. Between them they brought his rage under control, but it did not abate for turning cold. He ground out, "The scum will pay for that, I vow." He shook his fist at the captain on the wall, who gave back a gesture herdsmen used when they talked of breeding stock.

The officer's cynical challenge gave spirit back to his comrades. They whooped at his obscene reply to Thorisin's fist and sent catcalls after Gavras as his military procession moved north.

As Scaurus returned to his place, he asked Baanes Onomagoulos, "Do you know that captain of Sphrantzes'? The bastard has his wits about him."

"So he does, worse luck for us. They were wavering up there until he opened his mouth." Onomagoulos shaded his eyes, peered at the wall. "Nay, I can't be sure, his helm is closed. But from the size of him, and that cursed wit, I'd guess he's the one calls himself Outis Rhavas. If it's him, he leads a real crew of cutthroats, they say. He's a new man, and I don't know much about him."

Marcus found that strange. By his name, Outis Rhavas was a Videssian, and the tribune thought Baanes, a fighting man of thirty years' experience, should be familiar with the Empire's leading soldiers. Still, he reminded himself, chaos was abroad in Videssos these days, and perhaps this Rhavas was a bandit chief doing his best to prosper in it.

Even as you are, he told himself, and shook his head, disliking the comparison.

Ortaias and his uncle seemed willing to stand siege, and Thorisin, after failing in his appeal at the city's walls, saw no choice but to undertake it. His men went to work building an earthen rampart to seal off the neck of Videssos' peninsula.

Some troops were almost useless for the task. Laon Pakhymer's Khatrishers dug and carried merrily for a couple of days, then grew bored and tired of the entire process. "Can't say I blame them," Pakhymer pointedly told Thorisin when the Emperor tried to order them back to their labor. "We came to fight the Yezda, not in your civil war. We can always go home again, you know—truth is, I miss my wife."

Gavras fumed, but he could hardly coerce the Khatrishers without starting a brand new civil war in his own army. Not wanting to lose the horsemen, he sent them out foraging with his Khamorth irregulars—he had not even tried to acquaint the nomads with the use of shovel and mattock.

Rather to his surprise, Marcus found he, too, missed Helvis, their storms notwithstanding. He was growing used to the idea that those would come from time to time, the inevitable result of attraction between two strong people, neither much disposed to change to suit the other's ways. Between them, though, they had much that was good, Malric and Dosti not least. The tribune had come late to fatherhood and found it more satisfying than anything else he had set his hand to.

In the first days of the siege of Videssos, he had scant time for loneliness. Unlike Pakhymer's troops, his Romans were men highly skilled in siege warfare. Spades and picks were part of their regular marching gear, and they erected field fortifications every night when they made camp.

Thorisin Gavras and Baanes Onomagoulos rode up to inspect the work. The Emperor wore a dissatisfied look, having just come from the amateurish barricade some of Onomagoulos' men were slowly throwing up. As ever since his wounding, Onomagoulos' face was set and tight, though less so now than Scaurus had sometimes seen him. Sitting a horse pained him less than the rocking hobble that was the ruin of his once-quick step.

Gavras' expression cleared as he surveyed the broad ditch and stake-topped earthwork the legionaries already had nearly done. The Romans held the southernmost half-mile of Thorisin's siege line. "Now here's something more like it," the Emperor said, more to Onomagoulos than Marcus. "A good deal better than your lads have turned out, Baanes."

"It looks well, yes," the older noble said shortly, not caring for the criticism. "What of it? Outlanders have some few skills: the Khamorth with the bow, the lance to the Namdaleni, and these fellows with their moles' tricks. A useful talent now, I grant."

He spoke offhandedly, not caring if the tribune heard, his unconscious assumption of superiority proof against embarrassment. Nettled, Marcus opened his mouth to make some hot reply. Before the words passed his lips, he remembered himself in a Roman tent in Gaul, listening to one of Caesar's legates saying, "Now, gentlemen, we all know the Celts are headstrong and rash. If we hold the high ground, we can surely lure them into charging uphill. . . ."

His mouth twisted into a brief, wry grin—so this was how it felt, to be reckoned a barbarian. Helvis was right again, it seemed.

But no, not altogether; catching the sour flicker on his face, Thorisin said quickly, "One day Baanes will choke, shoving that boot of his down his throat."

Scaurus shrugged. Thorisin's apology felt genuine, but at the same time the Emperor was using him to score a point off the powerful lord at his side. Nothing in this land ever wore but one face, the tribune thought with a moment's touch of despair.

He brought himself back to the business at hand. "We're properly dug in," he said, "from here to the sea." He waved to the walls of Videssos the city, their shadow in the late afternoon sun reaching almost to where he stood. "Next to that, though, all we've done is no more than a five-year-old playing at sand castles along the beach."

"True enough," Gavras said. "It matters not so much, though. They may have their castles, but they can't eat 'em, by Phos."

"As long as they rule the sea, they don't have to," Marcus said, letting his chief fret loose. "They can laugh at us while they ship in supplies. Ships are the key to cracking the city, and we don't have them."

"The key, aye," Thorisin murmured, his eyes far away.

Scaurus realized after a few seconds that the Emperor was not lost in contemplation. He was looking southeast into the Sailors' Sea, at the island lying on the misty edge of vision from Videssos. With abrupt quickening of interest, the Roman recalled the Videssian name for that island: it was called the Key.

But when he asked Gavras what was in his mind, the Emperor only said, "My plans are still foggy." He smiled, as if at some private joke. Onomagoulos, Marcus saw, had no more idea of what his overlord meant than did the tribune. Somehow, that reassured him.

By coincidence, that night was one of the misty ones common on the coast even in high summer, moon and stars swallowed up by the thick gray blanket rolling off the sea at sunset. Videssos' towers and crenelated walls disappeared as if they had never been. Torch-carrying sentries moved in hazy haloes of light; the taste of the ocean came with every indrawn breath.

Viridovix prowled along the earthwork, torch in his left hand and drawn sword in his right. "Sure and they can't be failing to take a whack at us in this porridge, can they?" he demanded when he ran into Scaurus and Gaius Philippus. "If that were me all shut up in there, I'd give the tails of the omadhauns outside a yank they'd remember awhile."

"So would I," Gaius Philippus said. His ideas of warfare rarely marched with the Gaul's, but this was such a time. He took the fog almost as a personal affront; it changed war from a game of skill, a professional's game, into one where any cabbagehead could make himself a genius with an hour's luck.

Marcus, though, saw what the centurion in his nervousness and the aggressive Celt missed: it was as foggy inside the city as out. "I'd bet Ortaias' marshals are pacing the walls themselves," he said, "waiting to hear scaling ladders shoved against them."

Viridovix blinked, then laughed. "Aye, belike that's the way of it," he said. "Two farmers, the each of 'em staying up of nights to watch his own henhouse for fear the other raid it. A sleepless, thankless job they both think it, too, and me along with 'em."

"It may be so," Gaius Philippus conceded. "The Sphrantzai haven't the imagination for anything risky. But what of

Gavras? This should be a night to suit him—he's a gambler born."

"There you have me," Scaurus said. "When the fog came down, I expected something lively would happen, but it seems I was wrong." He recounted the afternoon's conversation to the Roman and the Celt.

"There's deviltry somewhere, right enough," Gaius Philippus said. He yawned. "Whatever it is, it'll have to get along without me until morning. I'm turning in." His torch held waist-high so he could see the ground ahead, he headed for his tent; the Roman camp itself was set near the sea on the flat stretch of land that had been the Videssian army's exercise ground.

Scaurus followed him to bed a few minutes later and, to his annoyance, had trouble falling asleep. The gods knew it was peaceful almost to a fault without Dosti waking up several times a night. But the tribune missed Helvis warm on the sleeping-mat beside him. It was hardly fair, he thought as he turned restlessly: not so long ago he'd found it hard to sleep with a woman in his bed, and now as hard without one.

At the officers' conference the next morning Thorisin Gavras seemed pleased with himself, though Marcus had no idea why; as far as the Roman knew, nothing had changed since yesterday.

"He probably found himself a bouncy girl who'd say yes and not much more," was Soteric's guess after the meeting broke up. "Compared to poison-tongued Komitta, that'd be pleasure enough."

"I hadn't thought of that," Marcus laughed. "You may well be right."

Businesslike but slow, the siege proper got under way. A few of the military engineers who had accompanied Mavrikios Gavras' army still survived to follow his brother. Under their direction, Thorisin's men felled trees and knocked down a few houses to get timber for the engines and ladders they would presently need. The legionaries proved skilled help for the artisans, as they were used to aiding their own engineer platoons.

Save for the countermarching men visible on the walls, Videssos did its best to ignore the siege. Ships moved freely in and out of her harbors, bringing in supplies and men. Scaurus wanted to grind his teeth every time he saw one.

"Next thing you know, the Sphrantzai will try to stir up a storm behind us and use it to hammer us on the city's anvil. That's the way Vardanes thinks, and it's far from a bad plan," the tribune said to Gaius Philippus.

The senior centurion, though, was for once an optimist. "Let them try. We're getting more troops coming over to us than they are."

That, Marcus had to admit, was probably true. The nobles of Videssos' eastern dominions were not such great magnates as their counterparts in the westlands, but all the grandees, great or small, hated the bureaucrats who had seized the capital. They flocked to Thorisin's banner, this one leading seventy retainers, that one forty, the next a hundred and fifty.

"Of course," Gaius Philippus went on, following Scaurus' unspoken thought, "how useful such bumpkins will prove in the fighting remains to be seen."

After four or five clear nights the fog came again, if anything thicker than it had before. Again the tribune wondered whether the besieged Sphrantzai would try to sally under its cover, and doubled the sentries facing the capital.

It must have been near midnight when he heard shouts of alarm coming from the north. "Buccinators!" he shouted. The horns' bright music ripped through the murk. Cursing as they scrambled from their bedrolls, legionaries poured out of the tents in camp and, still buckling on armor, began to form up.

Hoofbeats pounded toward the camp. "Are all our lads up there asleep? Sure and the spalpeens're behind himself's rampart, and it so much trouble to make and all," Viridovix said.

"How would you know that?" Gaius Philippus said. "You didn't do a lick of work on it."

"And why should I, like some hod-toting serf? If you want to work like a kern, 'tis your own affair entirely, but you'll not see me at it. Give me a real fight, any day."

"I don't think those are Ortaias' men at all," Quintus Glabrio said suddenly, a statement startling enough to quell the brewing quarrel at once. "There's no sound of fighting and no more challenges from our sentries, either."

The young officer was proved right a few minutes later, when a troop of about a hundred of Thorisin Gavras' best Videssian cavalry rode south past the Roman camp. "Sorry about the start we gave you," their captain called to Scaurus as he went by. "We almost trampled one of your men up there in this Phos-cursed gloom." The tribune believed that; even with torches held high, the horsemen disappeared before they had gone another fifty yards.

"Blow 'stand down,'" Marcus ordered his trumpeters. The legionaries stood for a moment as if suspecting a trick, then, shaking their heads in annoyance, went back to their still-warm blankets.

"Wish he'd make up his bloody mind," grumbled one. And another: "A good night's sleep buggered right and proper." With a veteran's knack for making the best of things, a third said cheerily, "No matter. I had to get up to piss anyway."

The camp settled back into peace. Scaurus yawned. It was near high tide, and the boom of surf on the nearby beach was lulling as smooth wine, as soft deep drums in the distance.

The tribune paused, half-stooped, a hand on his tentflap. Why had he thought of drums, from the sound of sea meeting sand? He jerked upright as he recognized the noise for what it was: waves on wood. Ships offshore, and close!

The fear of treachery flooding through him, he shouted for the buccinators once more. This time his men came forth growling, as at any drill they disliked. He did not care; his alarm blazed brighter than the mist-shrouded torchlight.

"Peel me off two maniples, quick," he said to Gaius Philippus. "I think the Sphrantzai are landing on the beach. Set the rest of the men to defend here and send a runner to Gavras —I think we're betrayed. In fact, send Zeprin the Red— Thorisin's most likely to listen to him."

"I'll see to it he does," the burly Haloga promised, understanding Marcus' reasoning. Because of his former high rank in Mavrikios' Imperial Guards, he was well-known both to the younger Gavras and his men. Throwing a wolfskin cape over his mail shirt, he vanished into the mist.

The senior centurion was barking orders. As the legionaries rushed to the places they were assigned, he turned back to Scaurus. "Betrayed, is it? You think those dung-faced horse-boys are there for a welcoming party?"

"What better reason?"

"Not a one, worse luck. What's the plan—hold them until we get enough reinforcements to fling 'em back into the sea?"

"If we do. If we can." The tribune wished he knew more of

what he would face; ignorance's fog could be more dangerous than the gray clammy stuff billowing around him.

Viridovix hurried up. He leaned his shield against his hip to give himself two free hands with which to fasten his helmet strap under his chin. "You'll not get away with another shindy without me," he said to Scaurus.

"Well, come along then. From the way you talk, anyone would think I did it on purpose."

"So they would," Viridovix agreed darkly. But when Marcus looked to see if he was as serious as he sounded, the Celt was grinning at him.

The legionaries quick-marched south, following the Videssian cavalry. Marcus felt something soft squash under his sandal; even in the fog and dark he did not have to ask what it was. He heard Viridovix swear in Gaulish, caught the name of the Celtic horse-goddess Epona.

The tribune slid and almost fell as his feet went from dirt to shifting sand. The Videssians were still invisible in the swirling mist ahead, but he heard their captain call, "Come ashore!"

"Are you daft, landlubber?" a sailor's answer came thinly back. "My leadsmen near wet their breeches getting this close. We'll send boats!"

"Battle line!" the tribune said softly. Smooth as if on parade, the legionaries deployed from their marching column. "Yell 'Gavras' when we charge," Scaurus ordered. "Let the traitors know we know what they're at."

He feared he was come just too late. Already he could hear oars splashing toward shore, hear the scrape of light boats beaching. Well, no help for it. "Forward!" he said.

"Gavras!" The shout roared from two hundred throats. Swords drawn, *pila* ready to fling, the Romans slogged forward through the sand.

Down at the waterline there was a sudden chaos. Most of the Videssians were dismounted, walking up and down the beach holding torches to guide the boats in. Faintly through the fog, Scaurus saw some of those torches drop when his men bellowed out their war cry. A horse screamed off to one side; some Roman had seen movement in the mist and let fly with his javelin.

Full of asperity and command, an unseen voice demanded

of the Videssian cavalry leader, "What sort of welcome have you prepared for us, captain?"

"Hold up! Hold up! Hold up!" the tribune shouted frantically, and blessed the legionaries' good discipline for bringing them to a ragged halt.

"What now?" Gáius Philippus snarled. "So they've a bitch with them—what of it? Sometimes I think the imperials can't fight without their doxies alongside 'em."

The senior centurion's harsh voice ripped through the fog; Marcus thanked the gods whose existence he doubted that his comrade had spoken Latin. He answered in the same tongue; "Bitch she may well be, but that's Komitta Rhangavve out there, or I'm a Celt."

Gaius Philippus' teeth came together with an audible click. "Thorisin's woman? Oh, sweet Jupiter! Wait, though—she's on the other side of the Cattle-Crossing with all the other skirts and their brats . . . begging your pardon, sir," he added hastily.

Marcus waved the apology aside; in his confusion, he hardly heard the words that made it necessary. Those ships out there could not be Sphrantzes'—Komitta was a hellcat, but never a traitor. But they could not be Thorisin's, either. The boats in his makeshift flotilla had long since gone back to their usual tasks. That left nothing . . . except the reality just offshore.

Two torches bobbed toward the Romans. Marcus stepped out ahead of his men to meet them. The Videssian captain stumped along under one, a short, stocky, red-faced man with upsweeping eyebrows and an iron-gray beard. Carrying the other was indeed Komitta Rhangavve, her pale, narrow face beautiful and fierce as a falcon's.

The tribune gave them both his best courtier's bow, but then, to his mortification, he heard himself blurting, "Will one of you please tell me what in Skotos' name is going on?"

The captain frowned. He spat on the sand and looked through the fog toward heaven, his hands upraised. I've wounded his piety, Scaurus thought. Well, too bad for him.

Komitta looked down her elegant nose at the Roman. "The Emperor has decided it is time for his soldiers' companions and families to rejoin them," she said matter-of-factly. "Were you not informed of the move? A pity." She was the perfect aristocrat, asking a servant's pardon for some small oversight.

The tribune resisted an urge to take her by her sculpted shoulders and shake information out of her. It was the devout captain who came to his rescue: "The Key's ships have declared for Gavras, now that he's put the city under siege. They sailed up during the last fog; his Highness ordered them to stay hidden so they could take advantage of the next one to bring our kin across without interference from the Sphrantzai. Worked, too."

"The Key," Scaurus breathed. Now that someone had spelled it out for him in small simple words, he mentally kicked himself for his stupidity. The fleets of the island of the Key were second in importance in Videssos only to the capital's, something he had known for a year and more. But, land-oriented foreigner that he was, the fact had held no meaning for him, even after some broad hints from Thorisin Gavras.

Viridovix, subject to no discipline but his own, had been hanging back a couple of paces behind the Roman. Now he came forward to lay an indignant hand on Marcus' arm. "Is it that there's no fight here after all?" he said.

"So it would seem." The tribune nodded, still bemused.

"Isn't that the way of it?" the Gaul said loudly. "The first one his honor gives me a fair chance at, and it turns out there's not a fornicating thing for him to be giving, at all."

The Videssian captain, as much a professional at war as a Roman veteran, looked at the Celt as he would at any other dangerous madman. There was a smoldering interest in Komitta Rhangavve's eye, though, that Marcus hoped against hope Viridovix would not pick up.

Luck rode with him; the Gaul's noisy complaint had caught more ears than the ones close by. Guided by it, two of his lemans came running up the beach to smother him with hugs and squeals of, "Viridovix! Darling! We missed you so much!" Viridovix patted them as best he could with a torch in one hand and his shield in the other. To Scaurus' relief, Komitta's high-arched nostrils pinched as they might at a bad smell.

Turning back to his men, the tribune quickly explained what the real situation was. The Romans raised a cheer, excited both by the new strength the Key's fleet gave Gavras and, probably more, by the prospect of seeing their loved ones again. There was, Scaurus admitted reluctantly, something to this Videssian custom of keeping a soldier's family close by him, however much it went against the Roman way. The men stayed in better spirits and seemed to fight harder knowing that their families' fate as well as their own depended on their valor.

"We came for the wrong reason," he said to the legionaries, "but now that we're here we can be useful. Take your torches down to the shore and help guide those boats in."

That was a task they set to with a will, some of them even splashing out into the sea so the lights they carried would reach further. As the small boats beached, the Romans kept calling the names of their loved ones. A glad cry would ring out every few minutes as couples reunited. Scaurus saw some of these walk into the mist in search of privacy, but pretended not to notice; after the tension of a few minutes before, that sort of release was inevitable.

Then he heard a familiar contralto calling, "Marcus!" and forgot about Roman discipline himself. He folded Helvis into an embrace so tight that she squeaked and said, "Careful of the baby—and of me, too, you and your ironworks." Dosti was sound asleep in the crook of her right arm.

"Sorry," he lied; even through armor the feel of her roused him. She laughed, understanding him perfectly. She leaned against his shoulder, tilted her head up for a kiss.

Malric ran his hands over the tribune's mail. The excitement of the trip had kept him wide awake. "Papa," he said, "I was on the ship with the sailors and then on the little boat going through the waves with mama, and—"

"Good," Marcus said, absently ruffling his stepson's hair. Malric's adventures could wait. Scaurus' other hand was sliding to tease Helvis' breast, and she smiling up from eyes suddenly heavy-lidded and sensuous.

Out of the fog came a volley of discordant trumpet blasts, the metallic clatter of men running in mail, and loud shouts: "Gavras! Thorisin! The Emperor!"

"Ordure," muttered the tribune, all thoughts of love-making banished. He cursed himself for a fool. Somehow he had managed to forget the warning Zeprin the Red had taken to Thorisin. The Haloga had done his job only too well, it seemed; from the sound of them, hundreds of men were rushing the beach to meet the nonexistent invaders.

"Gavras!" he yelled at the top of his lungs, and the legionaries took up the cry, feeling at first hand the predicament in which they'd put the Videssian cavalry an hour before. An unpleasant prospect, being attacked by one's own army.

The Emperor's horsemen on the beach shouted as loudly as the Romans.

"Are you handling the traitors out there, Scaurus?" Thorisin was quite invisible, but the tribune could hear amusement struggling with concern in his voice.

"Quite well, thank you. We might have done better if we'd known they were coming." Gavras had known that. "My plans are foggy," Marcus remembered him saying. Foggy, forsooth! But he had not seen fit to tell his commanders. The jolt he must have got when Zeprin the Red stormed his tent shouting treachery served him right, Scaurus decided; he must have wondered if his scheme had turned in his hand to bite him.

The tribune gave him credit for taking nothing for granted; he had come ready to fight at need, and quickly, too. Now that they saw there was no danger, the troopers he had brought with him came running down to the seaside to help the boats in. It grew crowded and confused on the beach, but happy.

Komitta Rhangavve shrieked when Thorisin, mounted on his borrowed black, scooped her up and set her in front of his saddle like a prize of war. Gaius Philippus clucked in disapproval. "There's times when I wonder if he takes this war seriously enough to win," he said.

"Remember Caesar," Marcus said.

The senior centurion's eyes grew sad and fond, as at the mention of an old lover. "That bald whoremonger? Him and his Gallic tarts," he said, pure affection in his voice. "Aye, but you're right, he was a lion in the field. Caesar, eh?" he echoed musingly. "If the Gavras does half so well, we'll get our names in more histories than Gorgidas', and no mistake. Along with a copper, that'll buy you some wine."

"Scoffer," the tribune snorted, but knew he'd made his point.

Afterglow upon him, Marcus took some of his weight on his elbows. Helvis sighed, an animal sound of content. He listened to the ocean rhythm of his pulse, more compelling than the surf muttering to itself in the distance.

"Why isn't it always like this?" he said, more to some observer who was not there than to Helvis or himself.

He did not think she heard him. His fingers curious now in a new way, he touched her face, trying to bridge the gap between them. It was no good, of course; she remained the stubborn mystery anyone outside the self must always be, however closely bodies join. He looked down at her in the darkness inside their tent and could not read her eyes.

So he was startled when she shrugged beneath him, her sweat-slick skin slipping against his. Her voice was serious as she answered, "Much good can come from love, I think, but also much evil. Each time we begin, we make Phos' Wager again and bet on the good; this time we won."

He blinked there in the gloom; a thoughtful reply to his question was the last thing he had expected. The Namdaleni used their wager to justify right conduct in a world where they saw good and evil balanced. Though they were not sure Phos would triumph in the end, they staked their souls on acting as if his victory was certain. The comparison, Marcus had to admit, was apt.

And yet it did not bring Helvis closer to him, but only served to make plain their differences. She reached for her god in explanation as automatically as for a towel to dry her hands.

Then his nagging thoughts fell silent, for they were moving together again, her arms tightening round his back. Her breath warm in his ear, she whispered, "Too many never know the good at all, darling; be thankful we have it when we do."

For once he could not disagree. His lips came down on hers.

Once he had used the cover of fog to bring his soldiers' households over the Cattle-Crossing, Thorisin Gavras unleashed his new-found navy against the city's fleet. He hoped the sailors in the capital would follow those from the Key into rebellion against the Sphrantzai. Several captains did abandon the seal-stampers' cause for Gavras, bringing ships and crews with them.

But Taron Leimmokheir, more by his example and known integrity than any overt persuasion, held the bulk of the city's fleet to Ortaias and his uncle. The sea fight quickly grew more bitter than the stagnant siege before Videssos. Raid and counterraid saw galleys sunk and burned; pallid, bloated corpses would drift ashore days later, reminders that the naval war had horrors to match any the land could show.

The leader of the Key's fleets was a surprisingly young man, handsome and very much aware of it. Like most of the Videssian nobles Scaurus had come to know, this Elissaios Bouraphos was a touchy customer. "I thought we sailed to help you," he growled to Thorisin Gavras at an early morning officers' conference, "not to do all your bloody fighting for you." He ran his hands through hair that was beginning to thin at the temples, a habitual gesture; Marcus wondered if he was checking the day's losses.

"Well, what would you have me do?" Thorisin snapped back. "Storm the walls in a grand assault? I could spend five times the men I have on that, and well you know it. But with your ships aprowl, the seal-stampers can't bring a pound of olives or a dram of wine into Videssos. They'll get hungry in there by and by."

"So they will," Elissaios agreed sardonically. "But the Yezda will be fat, for they'll have eaten up the westlands while you sit here on your arse."

Silence fell round the table; Bouraphos had said aloud what everyone there thought in somber moments. In the civil war the Sphrantzai and Gavras both mustered what men they could round the capital, leaving the provinces to fend for themselves. Time enough to pick up the pieces after the victory was won . . . if any pieces were left.

"By Phos, he's right," Baanes Onomagoulos said to Thorisin. As was true of a good many of Gavras' officers, he had wide holdings in the westlands. "If I hear the wolves are outside Garsavra, Skotos strike me dead if I don't take my lads home to protect it."

The Emperor slowly rose to his feet. His eyes blazed, but his temper was under the rein of his will; each word he spoke might have been cut from steel. "Baanes, pull one man out of line without my leave and you will be struck dead, but not by Skotos. I'll do it myself, I vow. You gave me your oath and your proskynesis—you cannot take them back at a whim. Do you hear me, Baanes?"

Onomagoulos locked eyes with him; Thorisin stared back inflexibly. It was the marshal's eyes that broke away, flicking down the table to measure his support. "Aye, I hear you, Thorisin. Whatever you say, of course."

"Good. We'll speak no more about it, then," Gavras answered evenly, and went on with the business of the council.

"He's going to let him get away with that?" Gaius Philippus whispered incredulously to Marcus.

"It's just Onomagoulos' way of talking," the tribune whispered back, but he, too, was troubled. Baanes still had the habit of treating Thorisin Gavras as a boy; Scaurus wondered what it would take to make him lose that image of the Emperor in his mind.

Such nebulous concerns were swept away when the Romans returned to camp. Quintus Glabrio met them outside the palisade. "What's gone wrong?" Marcus asked at once, reading the junior centurion's tight-set features.

"I—you—" Glabrio started twice without being able to go forward; he could not control his voice as he did his face. He made a violent gesture of frustration and disgust, then spun on his heel and walked off, leaving his superiors to follow if they would.

Scaurus and Gaius Philippus exchanged mystified glances. Glabrio was as cool as they came; neither of them had seen him anything but quietly capable—until now.

He led them south past the camp, down along the earthwork the legionaries had thrown up to besiege Videssos. A knot of men had gathered at one of the sentry posts. As he came closer, Scaurus saw they all bore the same expression of mixed horror and rage that welled up through Quintus Glabrio's impassive mask.

The knot unraveled at the tribune's approach; the legionaries seemed glad of any excuse to get away. That left two men shielding what lay there, Gorgidas and Phostis Apokavkos.

"Are you sure you want to see this, Scaurus?" Gorgidas asked, turning to the tribune. His face was pale, though as legionary physician he had seen more pain and death than a dozen troopers rolled together.

"Stand aside," Marcus said harshly. The Greek and Apokavkos moved back to show him Doukitzes' corpse. He moaned. He could not stop himself. Was it for this, he thought, that I rescued the little sneak thief from Mavrikios' wrath? For this? The body there before him mutely answered yes.

Splayed now in death, Doukitzes was even smaller than

Scaurus remembered. He seemed more a doll cast aside by some vicious child than a man. But where would any child, no matter how vicious, have gained the horrendous skill for the deliberate, obscene mutilations that stole any semblance of dignity, of humanity, from the huddled corpse?

A pace behind him, he heard Gaius Philippus suck in a long, whistling breath of air. He did not notice his own hands clenching to fists until his nails bit into his palms.

"He must have died quickly," Gorgidas said, showing the tribune the neat slash that ran from under the little man's left ear to the center of his throat. A couple of purple-bellied flies buzzed indignantly away from his pointing finger. "He couldn't have been alive for the rest of—that. The whole camp—Asklepios, the whole whole city—would have heard him, and no one knew a thing until his relief came out and found him."

"A mercy for him, aye," Gaius Philippus grunted. "The only one he got, from the look of it."

"The Sphrantzai have Yezda fighting for them," Marcus said at last, groping for some sort of explanation. "This could be their work—they kill foully to terrify their enemies." But even as he spoke he doubted his own words. The Yezda were barbarians; they killed and tortured with savage gusto. The surgical precision of this butchery matched anything of theirs for brutality, but was far beyond it in cruel, cold malice.

Phostis Apokavkos said, "The Yezda had nothing to do with it, curse 'em. Almost wish they had—I'd come nearer understandin' then." The adopted Roman spoke Latin with the twang of Videssos' westlands; the accent only emphasized his grief. Though he shaved his face like his mates among the legionaries, he was still a Videssian in his heart of hearts. He and Doukitzes, two imperials making their way among the Romans, had been fast friends since the chaos after Maragha.

"You talk as if you know this wasn't sport for the nomads," Gaius Philippus said, "but at your folk's worst I can't imagine any of them doing it."

"For which I give you thanks," Apokavkos said, rubbing his long chin. More often than not he insisted on styling himself a Roman, but this once he accepted the Videssian label. "Don't have to imagine it, though—it's true. See here." He pointed to the dead man's forehead.

To Scaurus the wounds incised there had been just another

sample of the hideous virtuosity Doukitzes' killer had displayed. He looked again; this time his mind's eye stripped away the black dried blood and grasped the pattern the knife had cut. It was a word, or rather a Videssian name: Rhavas.

"Sure and the son of a sow's a natural-born turnip-head to be after doing such a thing," Viridovix said that evening by the Roman campfire. "He must ken we'll not be forgetting soon." He was eating lightly, bread and a few grapes; his stomach, always sensitive save in the heat of battle, had heaved itself up at the sight of Doukitzes' pathetic corpse.

"Aye," Gaius Philippus agreed, his square, hairy hands closing as if round an invisible neck. "And a fool twice in the bargain, for he's cooped up there in the city where getting away won't be so easy."

"One more reason to take it," Marcus said. He held out his apricot-glazed wine cup for a refill. Still shaken by what he had seen, he drank deep to dull the memory.

"The worst of it, sir, is what you said this morning," Quintus Glabrio said to Gaius Philippus, "though not quite the way you meant it. Doukitzes wasn't nomad's sport. To mutilate him so after he was dead—there's purpose in it, right enough, but may the gods spare me from too fine an understanding of such purposes." He put the heels of his hands to his eyes, as though they had betrayed him by looking on Doukitzes.

Scaurus drank again, stuck out his cup for yet another dollop of the sweet, syrupy Videssian wine. His companions matched him draught for draught, but their drinking brought no cheer. One by one they sought their beds, hoping sleep would prove a better anodyne than wine.

The tribune thrust the tent flap open, came out through it still arranging his mantle about him. He let his feet take him where they would; one path was good as the next, so long as it led away from the tent. Phos' Wager, or any other, could be lost as well as won.

Sentries gave Scaurus the clenched-fist Roman salute as he walked out the camp's north gate and into the darkness. He returned it absently, wishing no one at all had to see him; save for a few men coming and going to the latrines, the camp was quiet, its fires no more than embers.

Every legionary sentry post was double-manned now, both in camp and along Thorisin's besieging earthwork. The tribune saw torches glowing all the way down to the sea. Tonight, he knew, no man would sleep at his station.

The night was clear and cool, almost chilly. The moon had long since set behind Videssos' walls, leaving the sky to the distant stars. Glancing up at their still-strange patterns, Scaurus wondered if the Videssians used them to reckon destinies. It seemed a notion that would fit their beliefs, but he could not recall hearing of it in the Empire. Nepos would know.

The thought was gone almost as soon as it appeared, drowned in a fresh wave of resentment. The tribune wandered on, still going north; before long he was past the Roman section of line and coming up on the Namdalener camp. He gave that a wide berth, too, not much wanting to see any of the islanders right now.

He heard shouting in the distance ahead, a woman's voice. After a moment he recognized it as Komitta Rhangavve's. About now Thorisin was probably wishing she was back on the western side of the Cattle-Crossing. Scaurus let out a sour chuckle. It was a feeling he fully understood.

His laugh had startled someone nearby. He heard a sharp intake of breath, then a half-question, half-challenge: "Who is it?"

Another woman's voice, lower than Komitta's and more familiar, too, with a guttural trace of accent. Marcus peered into the night. "Nevrat? Is that you?"

"Who—?" she said again, but then, "Scaurus, yes?"

"Aye." The tribune briefly warmed to hear her. She and her husband no longer camped with the legionaries, having joined several of Senpat Sviodo's cousins among the Vaspurakaners who marched with Gavras. Marcus missed them both, Senpat for his blithe brashness, his wife for her clear thinking and courage, and the two of them together as a model of what a happy couple could be.

She walked slowly toward him, minding each step in the dark. As usual, she dressed mannishly in tunic and trousers; a swordbelt girded her waist. Her shining hair, blacker than the night, fell curling past her shoulders.

"What are you doing out and about?" Scaurus asked.

"Why not?" she retorted. "I feel like a cat prowling

through the darkness, looking for who knows what. And the night is very beautiful, don't you think?"

"Eh? I suppose it is," he answered; whatever beauties it held were lost on him.

"Are you all right?" she asked suddenly, lifting a hand to touch his shoulder.

He thought about it a moment. "No, not really," he said at last.

"Can I do anything?"

Crisp and direct as ever, he thought; Nevrat was not one to ask such a question unless she meant it to be taken seriously. Here, though, there could be only one answer. "Thank you, lady, no. This doesn't have that sort of cure, I fear."

He was afraid she would press him further, but she only nodded and said, "I hope you solve it soon, then." Her grip on his arm tightened for a second, then she was gone into the night.

Marcus kept walking, still without much goal. He was well among Gavras' Videssian contingents now. A couple of troopers passed within twenty feet of him, unaware of his presence. One was saying, "—and when his father asked him why he was crying, he said, 'This morning the baker came and ate the baby!'"

They both laughed loudly; they sounded a little drunk. Without the rest of the joke, the punchline was so much gibberish to Scaurus. Somehow that seemed to march very well with everything else that had happened that day.

A man on horseback trotted by, singing softly to himself. Caught up in his song, he, too, failed to notice the tribune.

An awkward footfall ahead, a muttered curse. As the woman approached, Marcus reflected there was scant need to ask her why she was walking through the night. Her slit skirt swung open with every step she took, giving glimpses of her white thighs.

Unlike the soldiers, she saw the tribune almost as soon as he knew she was there. She came boldly up to him. She was slim and dark and smelled of stale scent, wine, and sweat.

Her smile, half-seen in the darkness, was professionally inviting. "You're a tall one," she said, looking Marcus up and down. Her speech held the rhythm of the capital, quick and sharp, almost staccato. "Do you want to come with me? I'll make that scowl up and go, I promise." Scaurus had not known he was frowning. He smoothed his features as best he could.

The lacing of her blouse was undone; he could see her small breasts. He felt a tightness in his chest, as if he were trying to breathe deep in a too-tight cuirass. "Yes, I'll go with you," he said. "Is it far?"

"No, not very. Show me your money," she said, all business now.

That brought him up short. Save for the mantle he was naked, even his sandals left behind. But as he started to spread his hands regretfully, a glint of silver on his right index finger made him pause. He pulled the ring free, held it out to her. "Will this do?"

She hefted it, held it close to her face, then smiled again and reached for him with knowing fingers.

As she promised, her small tent was close by. Shrugging off his cloak, Scaurus wondered if she was what he sought. He doubted it, but lay down beside her nonetheless.

VII

"WHAT? RESAINA FALLEN TO THE YEZDA?" GAIUS PHI-
lippus was saying to Viridovix, astonishment in his voice.
"Where did you hear that?"

"One o' the sailor lads it was told me, last night over
knucklebones. Aye, it's certain sure, he says. What with their
moving around so much and all, those sailors get the news or
ever anyone else does."

"Yes, and it's always bad," Marcus said, spooning up a
mouthful of his morning porridge. "Kybistra in the far south
gone a couple of weeks ago, and now this." Resaina's loss
was a heavier blow. The town was perhaps two days' march
south of the Bay of Rhyax, well east of Amorion. If it had
truly fallen, the Yezda were getting past the roadblock the
latter city represented, in Zemarkhos' fanatic hands though it
was.

And while the westlands were falling town by town to the
invaders, the siege of Videssos dragged on. There were men
beginning to slip over the wall at night now, and others escaping in small boats. They brought tales of tightened belts inside
the city, of increasingly harsh and capricious rule.

Whatever the shortcomings of the regime of the Sphrantzai, though, the capital's double walls and tall towers were
always manned, its defenders ready to fight.

"All Thorisin's choices are bad," the tribune brooded. "He
can't go back over the Cattle-Crossing to fight the Yezda
without turning Ortaias and Vardanes loose behind him, but if
he doesn't, he won't have much of an empire left even if we
win here."

Gaius Philippus said, "What we need is to win here, and quickly. But that means storming the walls, and I shake in my shoes every time I think of trying."

"Och, such a pair for the glooms I never have seen," Viridovix said. "We canna go, we canna stay, and we canna be fighting either. Wellaway, we might as well the lot of us get drunk if nothing better's to be done."

"I've heard ideas I liked less," Gaius Philippus chuckled.

The Celt's casual dismissal of logic annoyed Marcus. Giving Viridovix an ironic dip of his head, he asked him, "What do you see left to us, now that you've disposed of all our choices?"

"I haven't done that at all, Roman dear," the Gaul retorted, his green eyes twinkling, "for you've left treachery out of the bargain, the which Gavras'll never do. Too honest by half, y'are."

"Hmp," Scaurus grunted—no denying Viridovix had a point. But he did not much care for the label the Celt gave him: "too credulous," it seemed to mean. Moreover, he did not feel he deserved it. He had not repeated that angry night with the whore, nor wanted to; even while she clawed his back, he knew she was not the answer to his troubles with Helvis. If anything, those had since grown worse. There were times when his guarded silence hung between them like a muffling cloak.

He was glad to have his unpleasant reverie broken by a tall Videssian he recognized as one of Gavras' messengers. He took a last pull of thin, sour beer; Videssian wine was too cloying for him to stomach in the early morning. To business, then. "What can I do for you?" he asked.

The soldier bowed as he would to any superior, but Scaurus caught his slightly raised eyebrow, his delicately curled lip—to aristocratic Videssians, beer was a peasant drink. "There will be an officers' conclave in his Majesty's quarters, to commence midway through the second hour."

Like the Romans, Videssos split day and night into twelve hours each, reckoned from sunrise and sunset. The tribune glanced at the sky; the sun was hardly yet well risen. "Plenty of time to make ready," he said. "I'll be there."

"Would your honor care for a wee drop of ale?" Viridovix asked the messenger, offering the little keg that held it.

Marcus saw the beginnings of a grin lurking under his flamered mustaches.

"Thank you, no," Thorisin's man replied, his face and voice now altogether expressionless. "I have others to inform." And with another bow he was gone, in almost unseemly haste.

As soon as he was out of sight, Gaius Philippus swatted Viridovix on the back. "'Thank you, no,'" mimicking the Videssian. Centurion and Celt broke up together, forgetting to snarl at each other.

"And would *your* honor care for a wee drop?" Viridovix asked him.

"Me? Gods, no! I hate the stuff."

"I'd best not waste it, then," Viridovix said, and swigged from the cask.

It was easy to divide the commanders in Thorisin's tent into two sets: those who knew of Resaina's fall, and the rest. A current of expectancy ran through the first group, though no one was sure what to look for. By contrast, the ignorant ones mostly wandered in late, as to any other meeting where nothing much was going to happen.

For a time it seemed they were going to be proved right. The first order of business was a fuzz-bearded Videssian lieutenant hauled in between a pair of burly guards. The youngster looked scared and a little sick.

"Well, what have we here?" Thorisin said impatiently, drumming his fingers on the table in front of him. He had more urgent things on his mind than whatever trouble this stripling had found for himself.

"Your Highness—" the lieutenant quavered, but Gavras silenced him with a look, turned his eyes questioningly to the senior guardsman.

"Sir, the prisoner, one Pastillas Monotes, last evening did most wickedly and profanely revile your Majesty in the hearing of his troops." The soldier's voice was an emotionless, memorized drone as he recited the charge against the luckless Monotes.

The Videssian officers at the table grew still, and Thorisin Gavras alert. To the Namdaleni, to the Khamorth, to the Romans, a free tongue was taken for granted, but this was the Empire, an ancient land steeped in ceremonial regard for the imperial person. Not even an Emperor so unconventional as Thorisin, perhaps, could take lèse-majesté lightly without forfeiting his respect among his own people. Marcus felt sympathy for the frightened young man before him, but knew he dared not interfere in this matter.

"In what way did this Monotes revile me?" the Emperor asked. His voice, too, took on the formal tone of a court.

"Sir," the guard repeated, still from memory, "the prisoner did state that, in failing to do more than blockade the city of Videssos, you were a spineless cur, a eunuch-hearted blockhead, and a man with a lion's roar but the hindquarters of a titmouse. Those were the prisoner's words, sir. In mitigation, sir," he went on, and humanity came into his voice at last, "the prisoner had consumed an excess of liquors."

Thorisin cocked his head quizzically at Monotes, who seemed to be doing his best to sink through the floor. "Like animals, don't you?" he remarked. Scaurus' hopes rose; the Emperor's comment was hardly one to precede a routine condemnation. Honest curiosity in his voice, Gavras asked, "Boy, did you really say all those things about me?"

"Yes, your Highness," the lieutenant whispered miserably, his face pale as undyed silk. He took a deep breath, then blurted, "I likely would've come up with worse, sir, if I'd had more wine."

"Disgraceful," Baanes Onomagoulos muttered, but Thorisin was grinning openly and coughing in his efforts not to snicker. After a moment he gave up and laughed out loud.

"Take him away," he said to the guards. "Run the wine-fumes out of him, and he'll do just fine. Titmouse, indeed!" he snorted, wiping his eyes. "Go on, get out," he said to Monotes, who was trying to splutter thanks, "or I'll make you wish I was one."

Monotes almost fell as the guards let him go; he scurried for the tent flap and was gone. Gavras' brief good humor disappeared with him. "Where is everyone?" he growled. Actually, only a few seats were still unfilled.

When the last Khamorth chieftain sauntered in, Thorisin glared him into his chair. The nomad was unperturbed—no farmer's anger could reach him, not even a king's.

"Good of you to join us," Gavras told him, but sarcasm was as wasted as wrath. The Emperor's next words, though, seized the attention of everyone up and down the long table.

Still taken with Pastillas Monotes' phrase, he said, "I propose to move my feathered hindquarters against the city's works at sunrise, two days hence."

There was a moment's silence, then a babble louder than any Scaurus had heard from Thorisin's marshals. Above it rose Soteric's cry: "Then you are a blockhead and you've lost whatever wits you had!"

Utprand Dagober's son echoed him a second later: "Ya, what brings on t'is madness?" Where Soteric sounded furious, a cold curiosity rode the older Namdalener's words. He gave Thorisin the same careful attention he would a difficult text in Phos' scriptures.

"Trust the islanders not to know what's going on," Gaius Philippus said to Marcus, the uproar covering his voice. It had faint contempt in it; to a professional, knowledge was worth lives. The Namdaleni, mercenaries by trade, were taken by surprise too often to measure up to the senior centurion's high standards.

Scaurus understood his lieutenant's disapproval, but, more sophisticated in the ways of intrigue than the blunt centurion, also understood why the men of the Duchy were sometimes caught short. Not only were they heretics in Videssian eyes, but also subjects of a duke who would fall upon the Empire himself if he thought the time right. No wonder news reached them slowly.

Thorisin Gavras waited till the tumult subsided; Marcus knew he was at his most dangerous when his anger was tightly checked. "Lost my wits, have I?" the Emperor said coldly, measuring Soteric as an eagle might a wolf cub on the ground below.

Soteric's eyes eventually flinched away from that confrontation, but the tribune still had to admire his brother-in-law's spirit, if not his sense. "By the Wager, yes," the Namdalener replied. "How many weeks is it of sitting on our behinds to starve the blackguards out? Now, out of the blue, it's up sword and at 'em. Idiocy, I call it."

"Watch your tongue, islander," Baanes Onomagoulos growled, his dislike for Namdaleni counting for more than his mixed feelings toward Thorisin. Other Videssian officers rumbled agreement.

Had Soteric spoken to Mavrikios Gavras thus in Thorisin's hearing, the younger of the brothers would have exploded.

When thorny speech came his own way, though, Thorisin met it straight on—just as his brother had, Marcus remembered.

"Not 'out of the blue,' Dosti's son," the Emperor said, and Soteric looked startled to hear his patronymic. Recalling the elder Gavras' use of his own full name, Scaurus knew Thorisin was borrowing another of Mavrikios' tricks.

"Listen," Thorisin went on, and in a few crisp sentences laid out his plight. He stared into Soteric's face once more. "So, hero of the age," he said at last, "what would you have me do?" He sounded very tired and finally out of patience.

The young Namdalener, sensitive to the mockery that made up so much of Videssian wit, bit his lip in anger and embarrassment. The words dragged from him: "Storm the city—if we can." He did not say—he did not need to say—that no one, Videssian or foreign foe, had taken those walls by assault. Everyone at the table knew that.

Utprand said to Thorisin, "Aye, storm t'city. You say that, and it sounds so easy. But we from t'Duchy, we pay the bill to win your Empire for you, and pay in blood." Scaurus could not help nodding; a mercenary captain who wasted his troops soon had nothing left to sell.

"To Skotos' frozen hell with you, then," Gavras snapped, his temper lost now. "Take your Namdaleni and go home, if you won't earn your keep. You say you pay in blood? I pay double, outlander—every man jack who falls on either side of this war diminishes me, friend and foe alike, for I am Avtokrator of all Videssos, and all its people are my subjects. Go on, get out—the sight of you sickens me."

After that tirade Marcus looked to see Utprand stalk from the tent. Indeed, Soteric pushed back his chair and began to rise, but a glance from the older Namdalener stopped him. In Thorisin's hot words was a truth that had not occurred to him before, and he paused to give it the thought it deserved. "Be it so, then," he said at last. "Two days hence." He sketched a salute and was gone, sweeping Soteric along in his wake.

The council broke up swiftly, officers leaving a few at a time, gabbling over what they had heard like so many washerwomen. As Marcus turned sideways to ease through the open tent flap, his eyes happened to meet those of Thorisin, who was still plotting strategy with Bouraphos the admiral. Thorisin's glance held unmistakable triumph in it. Scaurus suddenly wondered how angry the Emperor had really been and how much he had made the Namdaleni talk themselves into doing just what he had planned for them in the first place.

Gavras' army readied itself for the attack. Stone- and arrow-throwers moved forward, ready to give covering fire for the assault on the walls. Every archer's quiver was filled, to the same purpose. Inside sheds covered with green hides, rams swung on their chains.

"Very impressive," Gorgidas murmured, watching the bustle of military preparation. "And inside, I suppose, they're heating up their oil to give us the warm reception we deserve."

"*Absit omen*," Marcus said, but it was only too likely. Too much of the readying process was visible from the walls to leave Videssos' defenders in much doubt over what was about to happen, despite the army's best efforts at secrecy.

"If there was a commander in there with his wits about him and an ounce more guts than he needs to turn beans into wind, he'd sally now and set us back a week," Gaius Philippus said. He watched soldiers marching four abreast on the capital's battlements, insect-small in the distance.

Scaurus said, "I don't think it's likely. The pen-pushers inside must have their generals under their thumbs, or they'd've hit us long before this. Ortaias may play at being a warrior, but Vardanes' way of ruling is by taxes and tricks, not steel. He distrusts soldiers too much to turn them loose, I think."

"I hope you're right," the senior centurion said. Marcus noticed him doubling patrols and sentry postings all the same. He did not change the dispositions; watchfulness was seldom wasted.

The Romans, then, were not surprised when at twilight a raiding party came storming from a sally port all but hidden by one of the outer wall's towers. The marauders carried flaming brands, as well as swords and bows, and flung them at any pieces of matériel they saw. Flames clung and spread, unnaturally bright; the Videssians were skilled incendiary-makers.

Shouts of "Ortaias!" and "The Sphrantzai!" flew with the raiders' missiles. So did the sentries' cries of alarm, their answering yells of "Gavras!" and the first shrieks of the wounded. Another war cry was in the air, too, one that made

Scaurus, who normally faced battle without delight, jam his helmet down over his ears and rush to the fight: "Rhavas!" the marauders cheered, "Rhavas!"

Many of the attackers stopped short at the earthen breastwork that sealed the city Videssos from Videssos the Empire. These skirmished with the Roman pickets there, threw their torches and shot fire arrows, then fell back when they saw the defense ready for them. They fought, indeed, much like the bandits Outis Rhavas was said to lead: a brave onset, but no staying power.

One determined band, though, came scrambling over the chest-high rampart to trade swordstrokes with the Romans beyond and hack at their siege engines with axes, crowbars, and mauls. At their head was a tall, strongly built man who had to be Rhavas himself. With a cry of, "Stand and fight, murderer!" Marcus rushed at him.

To the tribune's disappointment, his foe wore a bascinet with its visor down; he wanted to see this man's eyes as he killed him. Whatever else he was, Rhavas was no coward. He loped toward Scaurus, his longsword held high. The two blades met with a ring of steel. Marcus felt the jolt clear to his shoulder. The druids' marks on his Gallic sword flared golden. They were hotter and brighter than he had seen them since his duel with Avshar the wizard-prince just after he came to the capital. His lips tightened—so Rhavas bore an enchanted blade, did he? It would do him no good.

But the fighting separated them after another inconclusive passage. Before the tribune could come to grips with Rhavas once more, Phostis Apokavkos attacked Ortaias' captain. In his fury to avenge Doukitzes, all the careful swordplay the legionaries had drilled into him was forgotten. He slashed and chopped with his *gladius*, a blade far too short for such work. Rhavas toyed with him like a cat with a baby squirrel, all the while laughing cruel and cold.

At length he tired of his sport and decided to make an end. His sword hurtled toward Apokavkos' helm. But the stroke was not quite true; Phostis reeled away, hand clapped to his head, but that head still rode his shoulders. With a bellow of fury, Rhavas leaped after him.

Gaius Philippus stepped deliberately into his path. "Stand aside, little man," Rhavas hissed, "or it will be the worse for you." Behind the senior centurion, Apokavkos was down on

his knees, blood running from one ear. Gaius Philippus
planted his feet to await the onslaught. He spat over the edge
of his shield.

A storm of blows rained down on him, furious as the fall
cloudbursts in the westland plateaus. The Roman, though,
was wiser by years of hard fighting than Phostis Apokavkos
and did not try to match Rhavas stroke for stroke. He stood on
the defensive, his own sword flicking out in counterattack
only when the thrusts brought no danger to himself.

Rhavas feinted, tried to spring around him. But the senior
centurion side-stepped quickly and kept himself between the
giant warrior and his prey. Then Marcus was hurrying forward
to give him aid, a dozen legionaries close behind. Viridovix,
as always an army in himself, stretched two of the skirmishers
in the dirt and bore in on Rhavas from another direction.

Still snarling curses, Rhavas had to retreat. He led the
rear-guard that held the Romans at bay while the rest of his
raiders made their way back over the besieging rampart. He
was the last to vault over it and, once on the other side, favored Scaurus with a mocking salute. "There will be other
times," he called, and the grim certainty in his voice sent a
thrill of danger down the tribune's back.

"Shall we give him a chase?" Gaius Philippus asked. The
bandit chieftain was standing there in no man's land, fairly
daring the Romans to pursue.

Marcus answered regretfully, "No, I think not. All he
wants to do is lure us into range of the engines on the walls."

"Aye, more lives than the whoreson's worth," Gaius Philippus conceded. He flexed his left shoulder, winced and said,
"He's strong as a bear, curse him. A couple of the ones he hit
me, I thought he broke my arm. This *scutum* will never be the
same again either." The bronze facing of the shield's upper
rim was all but hacked away, while the thick boards of the
frame beneath were chipped and split from the fierceness of
Rhavas' attack.

Water would not douse the fires the raiders had managed to
set; they had to be smothered with sand. Half a dozen dart-
throwers and one big stone-throwing engine were destroyed,
and several others had been wrecked by Rhavas' axemen and
crowbar swingers. Scaurus was surprised the damage was not
worse; luckily, the marauders had only had a few minutes to
carry out their assault.

Casualties were similarly light. Viridovix had accounted for half the enemy dead in his one brief flurry, a feat Marcus was sure he would not hear the last of for weeks to come. Of the Romans, it seemed no one had been killed, which gladdened the tribune's heart. Every legionary lost was one less link to the world he would never know again, one more man who shared his memories gone forever.

The worst-hurt man was Apokavkos. Gorgidas bent over him, easing his helmet off and palpating the left side of his head with skilled, gentle fingers. Apokavkos tried to speak, but produced only a confused, stammering sound.

Scaurus was alarmed at that, but the Greek doctor grunted in satisfaction, recognizing the symptom. "The blow he took threw his brain into commotion, as well it might," he told the tribune, "and so he's lost his voice for a time, but I think he'll recover. His skull is not broken, and he has full use of his limbs—don't you, Phostis?"

The Videssian moved them all to prove it. He tried to talk again, failed once more, and shook his head in annoyance, a motion immediately followed by a wince. "Head hurts," he scrawled in the dust.

"So you can write, can you? How interesting," Gorgidas said, ignoring what was written. For a moment he looked at Apokavkos more as a specimen than a man, but caught himself with an embarrassed chuckle. "I'll give you a draft of wine mixed with poppy juice. You'll sleep the day around, and when you wake the worst of your headache should be gone. You ought to have your voice back by then, too."

"Thanks," Apokavkos wrote. As with his last message, he used Videssian; while he spoke Latin, he could not write it. He climbed painfully to his feet and followed Gorgidas to his tent for the promised medicine.

"It's a good thing Drax's Namdaleni and the regular Videssian troops in the city didn't follow Rhavas' cutthroats out on sally," Marcus said to Gaius Philippus later that night. "They could have set things back as badly as you said, and we can't afford it with things in the westlands as they are."

The centurion carefully gnawed the last meat from a roasted chicken thigh, then tossed the bone into the fire. "Why should they follow Rhavas?" he said. "You know the Namdaleni, aye, and the imperials, too. Think they have any more stomach for his gang of roughs than we do? Probably hoping we'd kill the lot of 'em. There wouldn't be many a tear shed in there if we had, I'd bet."

Marcus stopped to consider that and decided Gaius Philippus was probably right. The men on the other side were most of them soldiers like any others and no doubt despised bandits the same way all regular troops did. It was their leaders who chose such instruments, not the rank and file. "The Sphrantzai," he said, the word sliding slimily off his tongue. Gaius Philippus nodded, understanding him perfectly.

The morning Thorisin Gavras had chosen for his assault dawned gray and foggy—not the porridge-thick blinding fog that had masked the arrival of the ships from the Key, but still a mist that cut visibility to less than a hundred paces. "Well, not *all* my prayers were wasted," Gaius Philippus said, drawing faint smiles from the legionaries who heard him. For the most part they went about their business grim-faced, knowing what was ahead of them.

"A big part of what we can do out there will depend on your men and the covering fire they can give us," Marcus was saying to Laon Pakhymer. The Khatrisher had brought his archers back from their foraging duties to join in the effort against the capital.

"I know," Pakhymer said. "Our quivers are full, and we've been driving the fletchers crazy with all the shafts we've asked for." He looked around, eyeing the murky weather with distaste. "We can't hit what we can't see, though, you know."

"Of course," Scaurus said, suddenly less glad of the fog than he had been. "But if you keep the top of the wall well-swept, it won't matter that your bowmen aren't aiming at anyone in particular."

"Of course," Pakhymer echoed ironically, and the tribune felt himself flush—a fine thing, him lecturing the Khatrisher on the tricks of the archer's trade, when Pakhymer had undoubtedly had a bow in his hand since the age of three. He changed the subject in some haste.

The voice of a trumpet rang out, high and thin in the early morning stillness. Marcus recognized the imperial fanfare, the signal for the attack. Much of his apprehension disappeared. No more waiting now. The event, whatever it held, was here.

The trumpet's last note was still in the air when the buccinator's horns blasted into life. The Romans, shouting,

"Gavras!" at the top of their lungs, rushed for the Silver Gate and the postern gate through which Rhavas' sally party had come. More legionaries flung hurdles, bundles of sticks, and spadesful of earth into the ditch that warded Videssos, trying to widen the front on which they could bring their arms to bear.

The first protection the capital's gates had was a chest-high work not much different from the one Gavras' men had thrown up, save that it was faced with stone. The few pickets manning it were quickly killed or captured; the Sphrantzai were not about to throw open the gates to rescue them, not with the enemy close behind.

High over the Silver Gate stood icons of Phos, reminders that Videssos was his holy city. They were being rudely treated now; buzzing over the Romans' heads like a swarm of angry gnats came the arrow barrage the Khatrishers were laying down, along with the more intermittent crack of dart-casting engines and the thump of the stone-throwers' hurling arms smacking into their rests.

"Reload there! Come on, wind 'em tight!" an artilleryman screamed to his crew—the perfect Videssian incarnation, Marcus thought, of Gaius Philippus. The senior centurion was crying the legionaries on, ordering the rams forward to pound at the Silver Gate's ironbound portals. The slope-sided sheds, covered with hides to foil fire, hot oil, and sand, ponderously advanced.

Looking up at the crenelated battlements over the gates, Scaurus felt a surge of hope. Much against his expectations, the missiles had briefly managed to drive the defenders from their posts. The rams took their positions unhindered. The passageway behind the gates echoed their first *boom*s like a great drum.

Gaius Philippus wore a wolfish grin. "The timbers may last forever," he said, "but the hinges can only take so much." *Boom-boom, boom-boom* went the rams.

But the Khatrishers could only keep up their murderous fire so long; arms tired, bowstrings weakened, and arrows began to run short. Soldiers appeared on the walls again. One of Bagratouni's Vaspurakaners shrieked as bubbling oil found its way through the joints of his armor to roast the flesh beneath. Another defender was about to tip his cauldron of sizzling fat down on the Romans when a Khatrisher shaft caught him in

he face. He staggered backward, spilling the blazing load
among his comrades. The Romans below cheered to hear their
cries of pain and fear.

Stones and missiles shot from the towers of the inner wall
were now beginning to fall on the legionaries. There were not
enough Khatrishers, nor could they shoot far enough, to si-
ence the snipers and catapults atop those towers.

Loud even through the din of fighting, the cry of "Ladders!
Ladders!" came from the north. Scaurus stole a glance that
way, saw men climbing for their lives and knowing they
would lose them if the enemy tipped those ladders into space
before they reached the top. The legionaries carried no scaling
adders—too risky by half, was the tribune's cold-blooded
appraisal.

The rams still pounded away. A chain with a hook on the
end snaked down to catch at one of the heads as it drove
forward, but the Romans, alert for such tricks, knocked it
aside. The huge iron clasps joining gate to wall creaked and
groaned at every stroke; the thick oak portals began to bend
inwards.

"Sure and we have 'em now!" Viridovix cried. His eyes
blazed with excitement. He waved his sword at the Videssians
on the walls, hot to come to grips with them at last. This
fighting at long range and the duel of ram and catapult were a
poor substitute for the hand-to-hand combat he craved.

Marcus was less eager, but still felt his confidence rising.
Ortaias' men were not putting up a strong defense. By rights,
he thought, the Romans should never have been able to get
their rams near the Silver Gate, let alone be on the point of
battering it down. He wondered how many men Elissaios
Bouraphos' ships were drawing off to ward the sea wall.
There were times when navies had their uses.

The fight at the sally port was not going so well for the
legionaries. A sharp dogleg in the wall protected it from engines and let the troops inside fire at the attackers' flanks. As
casualties mounted, Scaurus pulled most of his soldiers back,
leaving behind a couple of squads to keep the besieged Videssians from using the postern gate against them.

One last stroke of the rams, working in unison now, thudded into the battered timbers of the Silver Gate. They sagged
back like tired old men. The Romans surged past the rams'
protecting mantlets, shouting that the city was taken.

It was not. The passage between inner and outer portal was itself walled and roofed, and a stout portcullis barred the way. From behind it, archers poured death into the legionaries at point-blank range.

Brave as always, Laon Pakhymer's Khatrishers ran up to return their fire. In their light armor they suffered for it, Ortaias' bowmen on the walls taking a heavy toll. Watching his men fall, Pakhymer remained expressionless, but his pock-marks stood shadowy on a face gone pale. He sent his countrymen forward nonetheless.

More archers shot down at the Romans from the murder-holes above the passageway; unlike the ones at panicked Khliat the summer before, these were manned and deadly. *"Testudo!"* Gaius Philippus shouted, and *scuta* went up over the legionaries' heads to turn the hurtling darts. But worse than arrows rained down. Boiling water, sputtering oil, and red-hot sand poured through the death-holes, and the interlocked shields could not keep the soldiers beneath them altogether safe. Men cursed and screamed as they were burned.

Still more terrible were the flasks of vitriol the defenders cast down on the legionaries. The very facings of their shields bubbled and smoked, and whenever a drop touched flesh it seared it away to the bone.

Scaurus ground his teeth in an agony of frustration. Having forced the Silver Gate, his men were caught in a crueler trap than if they had failed at once. The rams, protected by their mantlets, were still inching forward and might yet batter down the portcullis, though, as he watched, a man inside the mantlet fell, pierced by an arrow that found its way over his shield.

But after the portcullis lay the second set of gates, stronger even than the ones already fallen. Could he ask his men to claw their way through that gauntlet and have any hope they could fight Ortaias' still-fresh troops afterward?

With unlimited manpower behind him, he might have tried it. His force, though, was anything but unlimited, and once gone, was gone for good. However much he wanted to aid Thorisin, the mercenary captain's creed came first: protect your men. Without them you can do nothing to help or hurt.

"Pull back," he ordered, and signaled the buccinators to blow retreat. It was a command the legionaries were not sorry to obey; they had charged to the attack in high excitement, but they recognized an impossibility when they saw one.

Again the Khatrishers did yeoman duty in covering the Romans, especially the withdrawal of the rams and their heavy shielding mantlets, of necessity a slow, painful business. Laon Pakhymer brushed thanks aside when Marcus tried to give them, saying only, "You did more for us, one day last year." He was silent for a moment, then said, "Could we beg use of your fractious doctor?"

"Of course," Scaurus said.

"Then I thank you. That arrow-pulling gadget of his is a clever whatsit, and his hands are soft, for all his sharp tongue."

"Gorgidas!" Marcus called, and the Greek physician came trotting up, a length of bandage flapping in his left hand.

"What do you want now, Scaurus? If you must put out a fire by throwing bodies on it, at least give me leave to cobble them back together. Don't waste my time with talk."

"Tend to the Khatrishers too, would you? The arrow-fire's hurt them worse than our men because they wear lighter panoplies, and Pakhymer here thinks well of your arrow-drawer."

"The spoon of Diokles? Aye, it's a useful tool." He pulled one from his belt; the smooth bronze was covered with blood. Gorgidas held the instrument up to the two officers. "Can either of you tell whose gore's been spilled on this—Roman, Khatrisher, or imperial for that matter?" He did not wait for an answer, but went on, "Well, neither can I; I haven't really stopped to look—nor will I. I'm a busy man, thanks to you two, so kindly let me ply my trade."

Pakhymer stared at his retreating back. "Did that mean yes?"

"It meant he has been tending them all along. I should have known."

"There are demons on that man's trail," Pakhymer said slowly. His eyes held a certain superstitious awe; he intended his words to be taken literally. "Demons everywhere today," he murmured, "pulling the Balance down against us." In Videssian eyes, the Khatrishers were sunk deeper in heresy than even the Namdaleni. Where the men of the Duchy spoke of Phos' Wager with at least the hope that Phos would at last overcome Skotos, Pakhymer's people held the struggle between good and evil to be an even one, its ultimate winner impossible to know.

Scaurus was too tired and too full of disappointment to

exercise himself over the fine points of a theology he did not share. With some surprise, he realized the sky was bright and blue—where had the fog gone? His shadow was pointing away from Videssos' works; the sun was in his eyes as he looked toward them. The assault had lasted most of the day. For all it had accomplished, it might as well not have been made.

Jeers flew from the wall as the Romans retreated, loudest among them the booming, scorn-filled laugh of Outis Rhavas. "Go back to your mothers, little boys," the bandit chieftain roared, his voice loaded with hateful mirth. "You've played where you don't belong and got a spanking for your trouble. Go home and be good and you won't get hurt again!"

Marcus swallowed hard. He had thought he was beyond feeling worse, but found he was wrong. Defeat was five times more bitter at the hands of Rhavas. His head hung as he led the weary, painful trudge back to camp.

Inside Videssos the soldiers of the Sphrantzai celebrated their defense far into the night. They had reason to rejoice; none of Thorisin's other attacks had come as close to success as the Romans', and Scaurus knew how far from victory the legionaries had been.

The sound of the revels only made Gavras' defeated army more sullen as it licked its wounds back behind its rampart. The tribune heard angry talk round the Roman campfires and did not blame his soldiers for it. They had fought as well as men could fight; but stone, brick, and iron were stronger than flesh and blood.

When the Namdalener came up to the Roman camp, nervous sentries almost speared him before he could convince them he was friendly. He asked for Scaurus, saying he would speak to no one else. The tribune's sword was drawn as he walked to the north gate; apart from his own troops, he was not prepared to take anyone on trust.

But the islander proved to be a man he knew, a veteran mercenary named Fayard who had once been under the command of Helvis' dead husband Hemond. He stepped forward out of the darkness to take the tribune's hand between his two, the usual Namdalener clasp. "Soteric asks you to share a cup of wine with him at our camp," he said. Years in the Empire had left his Videssian almost accent-free.

"This is a message you were bidden to give to me alone?" Scaurus asked in surprise.

"I had my orders," Fayard shrugged. He had the resigned air of a soldier used to carrying them out whether or not he found sense in them.

"Of course I'll come. Give me a moment, though." Marcus quickly found Gaius Philippus, told him of Soteric's request. The senior centurion's eyes narrowed. He stroked his chin in thought.

"He wants something from us," was his first comment, echoing Scaurus' guess. Gaius Philippus followed it a moment later with, "He's not very good at these games, is he? By now the whole camp'll know you're off on some secret meeting, where if his man had just sung out what he wanted to the gate crew, nobody would have thought twice about it."

"Maybe I should take you off combat duty," Marcus said. "You're getting to be a fine intriguer yourself, you know."

Gaius Philippus snorted, knowing the tribune's threat was empty. "Ha! You don't need to be a cow to know where milk comes from."

Scaurus fought temptation and lost. "You're right—that would be udderly ridiculous." He walked off whistling, somehow feeling better than he had since the ill-fated attack began.

He and Fayard drew three challenges in the ten-minute trip to the Namdalener camp and another at its palisade. Guardsmen who would have ignored a platoon the night before now reached for spear or bow at the smallest movement. Defeat, Marcus thought, made men jump at shadows.

Yet another sentry stood, armed, in front of Soteric's tent. A trifle shortsighted, he peered closely into the tribune's face before standing aside to let him pass. Fayard ceremoniously held the tent flap open. "You aren't coming, too?" Marcus said.

"Me? By the Wager, no," the man of the Duchy answered. "Soteric pulled me out of a game of dice to fetch you, and just when I was starting to win. So by your leave—" He was gone before the sentence was complete.

"Come in, Scaurus, or at least let the flap drop," Soteric called. "The wind will put out the candles."

If Marcus had had any doubts that Soteric's invitation was not merely social, the company Helvis' brother kept would have erased them. A bandage on his forearm, Utprand Dagober's son sat on the sleeping mat by Soteric, his bearing and his cold eyes wolfish as always. Next to him were a pair of Namdaleni the tribune did not know, save by name: Clozart Leatherbreeches and Turgot of Sotevag, whose native town was on the eastern shore of the island Duchy. The four of them together spoke for most of the islanders who followed Gavras.

They shifted to give Scaurus room to sit. Turgot swore softly as he moved. "My arse is bandaged," he explained to the Roman. "Took an arrow right in the cheek, I did."

"He doesn't care a moldy grape for your arse," Clozart rumbled. Marcus thought he looked foolish in the tight leather trousers he affected—he was nearing fifty, and his belly bulged over their fastening—but his square face was hard and capable, the face of a man who acts and lets consequences sort themselves out afterward.

"Have some wine," Turgot said, pouring from a squat pitcher. "We wouldn't want Fayard forsworn, would we?" Marcus shook his head, sipped politely. For all their ostentatious contempt for Videssian ways, some Namdaleni played the game of indirection even more maddeningly than the imperials who had taught it to them.

Soteric, though, was not one of those. Tossing his own cup back at a gulp, he demanded bluntly, "Well, what did you think of today's fiasco?"

"About what I thought before," the tribune answered. "With those walls, a handful of lame old men could hold off an army, so long as they weren't too old to remember to keep dropping rocks on its head."

"Ha! Well said, t'at," Utprand said, baring his teeth in the grimace that served him for a chuckle. "But t'question has more behind it. Gavras sent us forward to be killed, against works he had no hope of taking. Why should we serve such a man as that?"

"So you're thinking of going over to the Sphrantzai?" Marcus asked carefully. If their answer was aye, he knew he would have to use all his guile to leave the islanders' camp, for that was a choice he could never make. And if guile failed . . . He shifted his weight, bringing his sword to a position where it would be easier to seize.

But Clozart spat in fine contempt. "I fart in Ortaias Sphrantzes' face," he said.

"A pox on the twit," Soteric nodded. "The seal-stamping

fop's a worse bargain than Gavras ever would be, him and his pot-metal 'goldpieces.'"

"What then?" Scaurus said, puzzled. "What other choice is there?"

"Home," Turgot said at once, and longing filled his eyes at the word. "The lads have had a bellyful, and so have I. Let the damned imperials bake in their own oven, and may both sides burn. Give me cool Sotevag again and the long waves rolling off the endless gray ocean, and if the Empire's recruiters come my way again I'll set the hounds to 'em like your Vaspura-kaner friend did to the Videssian priest."

The tribune felt no longing, only a jealousy that by now itself was tired. In this world he and his had no home, nor were they likely to. "You make it sound simple," he said dryly. "But what do you propose to do, march through the Empire's eastlands until you come to your own country?"

His intended sarcasm fell on deaf ears. "Aye," Clozart said, "or rather the sea across from it. Why not? What do the imperials have between here and there to stop us?"

"It should be easy," Utprand agreed. "T'Empire stripped t'garrisons bare to fight the Yezda, and then again for t'is civil war. Once we get clear of Videssos, there would be no army dare come near us. And T'orisin has to let us go—if he tries to hold us, the Sphrantzai come out and eat him up."

The chilly logic was convincing, as was Utprand himself; if the bleak Namdalener said a thing could be done, it very likely could. The only question Marcus could find was, "Why tell me now?"

"We want you and yours to come with us," Soteric answered.

The tribune stared, surprised past speech. The Namdelener rushed on, "Duke Tomond, Phos love him, would be proud to have such fighters take service with him. There's room and to spare in the Duchy, enough to make your troops yeoman farmers, each with his own plot, and you, I'd guess, a count. How's the sound of that? 'Scaurus, Scaurus, the great count Scaurus!' if ever you chose to go on campaign again."

Soteric's tickling at his vanity left Marcus unmoved; he had more influence as a general in the Empire than he would with a fancy title of nobility in Namdalen. But for the first time since the Romans were swept to this world, he found himself tempted to cast aside his allegiance to Videssos. Here, freely offered, was the thing he had thought impossible: a home, a place of their own in which they could belong.

The offer of land alone would seem like a miracle to his troops. Civil wars had been fought in Rome to get discharged veterans the allotments their generals promised. "Room and to spare . . ."

"Aye, outlander, it's a lovely country we have," Turgot said, still sentimental over the motherland he missed. "Sotevag sits on the coast, between oak woods and croplands, and I spend much of my time there, I will say. But I have a steading up in the moors as well—the high hills, all covered with heather and gorse, and flocks of sheep on 'em. The sky's a different color from what it is here, a deeper blue, almost makes you think you can see *through* it. And the wind carries music on its breath, not the smell of horseshit and dust."

The Roman sat silent, all but overwhelmed by his own memories of Mediolanum lost forever, of the snow-mantled Alps seen from a safe, warm house, of tart, pungent Italian wine, of speaking his mind in Latin instead of picking through this painfully learned other tongue . . .

All four Namdaleni were watching him closely. Clozart saw his struggle for decision but, mistrusting everyone not of his island nation, mistook its meaning. Dropping into the thick patois the men of the Duchy used among themselves, he said to his comrades, "I told you we never should have started this. Look at him there, figuring whether to sell us out or no."

He did not think Scaurus could follow his speech; few Videssians would have been able to. But more than a year's time with Helvis had given the tribune a grasp of the island dialect. His quick-sprung optimism faded. He and his were as alien to the Namdaleni as to the imperials.

Soteric knew him better than the other three and saw he had understood. Giving Clozart a venomous glare, he apologized as handsomely as he could.

"We know your worth," Utprand agreed. "You would not be here else."

Marcus nodded his thanks; praise from a soldier like this one was praise to be cherished. "I'll put what you've said to my men," he said. Clozart's hard face reflected only disbelief, but the tribune meant it. There was no point in keeping the Namdalener offer from the legionaries, and no way to do so short of shutting them all in camp and killing any islander who came within hailing distance. Better by far to lead events than be led by them.

When the tribune emerged from his brother-in-law's tent, Fayard was nowhere to be seen. The dice spoke loudly to Namdaleni, and he doubtless decided Scaurus knew the way back to his own quarters.

His mind was spinning as he walked back to the Roman camp. His first feeling at Soteric's proposal still held true: after a Roman upbringing and almost two years in the Empire of Videssos, being a count in the Duchy seemed rather like being a large wolf in a small pack. Nor was he eager to abandon the Empire. The Yezda were foes who needed fighting once the civil war was won—if it could be won.

On the other hand, when thinking only of the Romans' best interests, Namdalen looked attractive indeed. He still had a hard time believing there could be land to offer freely to soldiers. In Rome the Senate kept a jealous grip on it; in the Empire it was in the hands of the nobles, with small freeholders taxed to the wall. Land—it would draw his men, right enough.

And on another level altogether, Helvis would surely leave him if he said Soteric nay, and that he did not want. What was between them refused to die, batter it about as they would. And they had a son . . . Was nothing ever simple?

Gaius Philippus waited just inside the north gate, edgily pacing back and forth. His saturnine features lit as he saw Scaurus. "About time," he said. "Another hour and I'd have come after you, and brought friends with me."

"No need for that," Marcus said. "We have some talking to do, though. Fetch Glabrio and Gorgidas and meet me back here—we'll take a stroll outside the palisade. Bring the Celt, while you're at it; this affects him, too."

"Viridovix? Is it a talk you want, or a brawl?" Gaius Philippus chuckled, but he hurried away to do what the tribune asked. Marcus saw how the Romans followed him with their eyes; they knew something was afoot. Damn Soteric and his amateur theatrics, he thought.

It was only a couple of minutes before the men whose judgment he most trusted and respected were gathered round him, curiosity on their faces. He led them into the night, talking all the while of little things, doing his futile best to make the conference seem ordinary to his men.

Out of earshot of the camp, though, he dropped the façade and gave a bald recounting of what had passed. A thoughtful silence followed as his comrades began to work the thing through, much as he had on his way back from Soteric's tent.

Gaius Philippus was the first to break it. "Were it up to me, I'd tell 'em no. I haven't a thing against the islanders—they're brave men and fine friends to drink with, but I don't want to spend the rest of my days living among barbarians." The senior centurion had in full measure the sense of superiority the Romans felt for all other peoples save Greeks. In this world Videssos was the standard by which such things were gauged, and he identified himself with the imperial folk here, forgetting they reckoned him as barbarous as the Namdaleni.

Gorgidas understood that perfectly well, but his choice was the same. He said, "I left Elis for Rome years ago because I knew my home was a backwater. Am I to reverse that course now? I think not—here I stay. There's too much I have yet to learn, too much the men of the Duchy don't know themselves."

The other two were slower to answer. Viridovix said, "Sure and it's not an easy choice you set us, Scaurus dear, but I think I'm for the change, belike for all the reasons the last two were against it. I'm easier with the islanders than with these sly, haughty imperials, where you never know the thought in a man's head until one day there's a hired dagger between your ribs because he misliked the cut of your tunic. Aye, I'll go."

That left only Quintus Glabrio; to judge by the pain on his face, his was the hardest choice of all. "And I," he said finally. Gorgidas' sharp intake of breath only made him seem more miserable, but he went on, "It's the land, more than anything else. The hope of it was the only reason I took service in the legions; it was the chance to be my own man one day, not a slave to someone else's wages. Without land, no one really has anything."

"You're a worse slave to land than to any human master," Gaius Philippus retorted. "I joined the eagles to keep from starving at the miserable little stone-bound plot where I was born. You *want* to walk behind an ox's arse from sunup to sundown, boy? You must be daft."

But Glabrio only shook his head; his dream was proof against the senior centurion's harsh memories, proof even against his bond with Gorgidas. The physician looked like a soldier doggedly not showing a wound pained him, but he made no complaint against his companion's decision, whatever his eyes might say. Marcus admired him the more, thinking of his own private fears and wondering how much they would sway his course.

The centurions were too well-disciplined and Gorgidas too polite to ask the obvious question, but Viridovix put it squarely: "And what does your honor intend to do?"

Scaurus had hoped some consensus might show itself in his comrades' answers, but they were as divided among themselves as he was in himself. He stood silent a long while, feeling his inner balance sway now one way, now the other.

At last he said, "With this attack gone for nothing, I don't think Gavras has any real chance to take the city, and without it he'll lose the civil war. I'll go to Namdalen, I think; under the Sphrantzai the Empire will fall, and in any case I would not serve them. The Yezda, almost, are better, for they wear no mask of virtue."

Even with the decision made, he was far from sure it was right. He said, "In this I will give no man orders. Let each one do as he will. Gaius, my friend, my teacher, I know you'll do gallantly with the men who feel as you do." They embraced; Scaurus was shocked to see tears on the veteran's cheeks.

"A man does what he thinks is right," Gaius Philippus said. "A long time ago, when I was hardly more than a boy, I fought on Marius' side in the civil war, while my closest friend chose Sulla. While the war lasted I would have killed him if I could, but years later I happened to meet him in a tavern, and we drank the place dry between us. May it be so with you and me one day."

"May it be so," Marcus whispered, and his own face was wet.

Viridovix was hugging Gaius Philippus now, saying, "The crows take me if I won't miss you, you hard-shell runt!"

"And I you, you great hulking savage!"

With their long habit of discretion, what Gorgidas and Quintus Glabrio thought they kept to themselves.

"There's no point in throwing the camp into an uproar tonight," Marcus said. "Morning muster will be the right time to let the men know their choice; keep it to yourselves until then."

There were nods all around. They walked slowly back to the palisade, not one picking up the pace, all thinking this might be the last time they were together. The raucous noises from behind the city's walls were an intrusion on their thoughts. Things sounded as much like a riot as a celebration, the tribune thought bitterly. He cursed the Sphrantzai yet again, for forcing him to a decision he did not want to make.

The sentries drooped like flowers in a drought when their officers passed them by without a hint of what they had discussed. All through the camp, men stared toward them.

"Be damned to you!" Viridovix shouted. "I've not grown a second head, nor a crest of purple feathers either, so dinna be dragging your eyes over me so!" The Celt's short temper was reassuringly normal; legionaries turned back to their food, their talk, or their endless games of chance.

Gorgidas said, "You'll forgive me, I hope, but I have wounded to attend to, crude as my methods are." Much to his own dismay, he still fought hurts with styptics and ointments, tourniquets and sutures. Nepos maintained he had the skill to learn Videssian healing arts, but his efforts bore no fruit. Scaurus suspected that was one reason, and not the least, he had decided to stay in Videssos.

Quintus Glabrio followed the physician, talking in a voice too low for Scaurus to hear; he saw Gorgidas dip his head in a Greek affirmative.

Someone hefted a skin of wine. Viridovix ambled toward it, drawn as surely as nails by a lodestone.

Helvis was sleeping when the tribune ducked into their tent. He touched her cheek, felt her stir. She sat up, careful not to wake Malric or Dosti. "It's late," she said, a sleepy complaint. "What do you want?"

Scaurus told her of her brother's plan, speaking as tersely as he had to his officers. She said nothing for a full minute when he was through, then asked, "What will you do?" It was a curiously uninflected question, all emotion waiting on the answer.

He said only, "I'll go." Reasons did not matter now; the essence of the thing was the choice itself.

Even in the darkness he saw her eyes go wide. She had been braced for a no and for the explosion that would follow it. "You will? We will?" she said foolishly. Then she laughed in absolute delight, forgetting her sleeping children. She flung her arms around the tribune's neck, planted a lopsided kiss on his mouth.

Her joy did not make him any easier over his decision; somehow it only brought into sharper focus the doubts he felt. Caught up in that joy, she did not notice his somber mood. "When will we leave?" she asked, eager and practical at the same time.

"In three or four days, I'd guess." Marcus answered with reluctance; putting a date to the departure made it painfully real.

Malric woke up, and crossly. "Stop talking so much," he said. "I want to go back to sleep."

Helvis scooped him up and hugged him. "We're talking so much because we're happy. We're going home soon."

Her words meant nothing to her son, who had been born in Videssos and known no life save that of the camp. "How can we go home?" he asked. "We *are* home."

The tribune had to smile. "How do you propose to explain that to him?"

"Hush," Helvis said, rocking the sleepy boy back and forth. "Phos be thanked, he'll learn what the word really means. And thank you, my very dear, for giving him the chance. I love you for it."

Scaurus nodded, a short, abrupt motion. He was still fighting his internal battle, and praise seemed suspect. But with his choice made, what need was there to load his qualms on her? Better, he thought, to hold them to himself.

He slid under the blanket; this day had drained him, and in another way the one upcoming would be worse. But it was a long time before he slept.

Turmoil outside woke him at first light of day. He knuckled his eyes, cursed groggily, and then sat bolt upright. The first cause for the uproar that crossed his mind was his men's somehow learning what was afoot. He scrambled into his cloak and dashed out of the tent. It would be all too easy for hubbub to turn to riot.

But there was no sign of riot, though the legionaries were not standing to muster in front of their eight-man tents. Instead they were packed in a shoving, shouting mass against the western wall of the camp, peering and pointing over the palisade in high excitement. More kept coming as the camp awakened.

The tribune pushed through the crowd; his men gave way with salutes as they recognized him. They were jammed so close together, though, that he took several minutes to work his way up to the palisade.

He did not have to be right by it—his inches let him see over the last couple of ranks of men. Someone next to him pounded him on the back: Minucius. The trooper's eyes were alight with triumph, his strong features stretched in a grin. "Will you look at that, sir?" he exclaimed. "Will you just look at that?"

For a moment Marcus still did not know what he meant. There ahead was Thorisin's earthwork and, beyond it, the capital's fortifications, silently indomitable as always.

That sentence had no sooner taken shape than it echoed like a gong inside him. No wonder the great double walls seemed silent in the dawn—not a defender was on them.

He felt giddy, as if he had gulped down a jug of neat wine. "Step aside! Make room!" he cried, ramming his way to the very front—he had to see as much as he could, be as close as he could. Normally he would have been ashamed to use his rank so, but in his excitement he did not give it a second thought.

There were the Silver Gates straight ahead, the works that had beaten back everything his men could throw at them. They were wide open now, and in them stood three men with torches, almost hopping in their eagerness to wave the besiegers into Videssos. Their shouts came thinly across the no man's land between the city and the siege-works: "Hurrah for Thorisin Gavras, Avtokrator of the Videssians!"

VIII

THE TORCH-WAVERS AND THEIR FRIENDS BEHIND THEM WERE as unsavory a lot of ruffians as the tribune had ever seen. Gaudy in street finery—baggy tunics with wide, flopping sleeves and tights dyed in an eye-searing rainbow of colors—they swarmed around the orderly Roman ranks, flourishing cudgels and shortswords and shouting at the top of their lungs.

No matter who they were, though, their cries were what Scaurus most wanted to hear: "Gavras the Emperor!" "Dig up Ortaias' bones!" "To the Milestone with the Sphrantzai, the dung-munching Skotos-lovers!"

As he looked north along the wall, the tribune saw Thorisin's army loping by squads and companies through every wide-flung gate. The Namdaleni were moving up from their stretch of siege line along with all the rest. If Gavras was a winner after all, withdrawal suddenly looked foolish.

"Reprieve," Gaius Philippus said, and Marcus nodded, feeling relief like a cool wind in his mind. He blessed the mixed emotions that had made him hesitate before announcing the pullout to his men. Never had he come to a decision more reluctantly and never was he gladder to see events overturn it.

Helvis would be disappointed, but victory paid all debts. She would get over it, he told himself.

The news grew wilder with every step he took into the city, until he had no idea what to believe. Ortaias had abdicated, taken refuge in the High Temple, fled the city, been overthrown, been killed, been torn into seven hundred pieces so even his ghost would never find rest. The rebellion had started because of food riots, treachery among Ortaias'

167

backers, and anger at the excesses of Outis Rhavas' men, of the great count Drax, or of the Khamorth. Its leader was Rhavas, Mertikes Zigabenos—whom Scaurus vaguely remembered as Nephon Khoumnos' aide—the Princess Empress Alypia, Balsamon the patriarch, or no one.

"They don't know what's happening any more than we do," Gaius Philippus said in disgust as he listened to the umpteenth contradictory tale, all of them told with passionate conviction. "You might as well shut your ears."

That was not quite true. On one thing, at least, all rumors came together—though the rest of Videssos had slipped from their hands, the Sphrantzai still held the palace quarter. Unlike much of what he heard, that made sense to Scaurus. Many buildings in the palace complex were fortresses in their own right, perfect refuges for a faction beaten elsewhere.

It also decided Scaurus' course of action. The Silver Gate opened onto Middle Street, the capital's main thoroughfare, which ran directly to the palaces with but a single dogleg. The tribune told the buccinators, "Blow double-time!" Above the blare of horns he shouted, "Come on, boys! We've waited long enough for this!" The legionaries raised a cheer and quickstepped down the slate-paved street at a pace that soon left most of the rowdies gasping far behind them.

The tribune remembered the Romans' parade along Middle Street the day they first came to the capital. Then it had been slow march, with a herald in front of them crying, "Make way for the valiant Romans, brave defenders of the Empire!" The street had cleared like magic. Today pedestrians got no more warning than the clatter of iron-spiked sandals on the flagstones and, if Phos was with them, a shouted "Gangway!" After that it was their own lookout, and more than one was flung aside or simply run down and trampled.

Just as they had on that first day, the sidewalks filled to watch the troops go by; to Videssos' fickle, jaded populace, even civil war could become entertainment. Farmers and tradesmen, monks and students, whores and thieves, fat merchants and sore-covered beggars, all came rushing out to see what the new spectacle might be. Some cheered, some called down curses on the Sphrantzai, but most just stood and stared, delighted the morning had brought them this diversion.

Marcus saw an elderly woman point at the legionaries, heard her screech, "It's the Gamblers, come to sack Videssos!" She used city slang for the Namdaleni; even in the language of insult, theology came into play.

Curse the ignorant harridan, thought Scaurus. The crowds had just left off being a mob; they could become one again in an instant. But the leader of the street toughs, a thick-shouldered bear of a man named Arsaber, was still jogging along beside the legionaries and came to their rescue now. "Shut it, you scrawny old bitch!" he bellowed. "These here ain't Gamblers, they're our friends the Ronams, so don't you give 'em any trouble, hear?"

He turned back to the tribune, grinning a rotten-toothed grin. "You Ronams, you're all right. I remember during the riots last summer, you put things down without enjoying it too much." He spoke of riots and the quelling thereof with the expert knowledge someone else might show on wine.

Thanks to a bungling herald's slip at the imperial reception just after the Romans came to Videssos, much of the city still mispronounced their name. Marcus did not think the moment ripe for correcting Arsaber, though. "Well, thanks," he said.

The plaza of Stavrakios, the coppersmiths' district—already full of the sound of hammering—the plaza of the Ox, the red-granite imperial office building that doubled as archives and jail, and a double handful of Phos' temples, large and small, all flashed quickly by as the legionaries stormed toward the palaces.

Then Middle Street opened out into the plaza of Palamas, the greatest forum in the city. Scaurus flicked a glance at the Milestone, a column of the same red granite as the imperial offices. There must have been a score of heads mounted on pikes at its base, like so many gruesome fruit. Nearly all were fresh, but terror had not been enough to keep the Sphrantzai on the throne.

The plaza market stalls were open, but Thorisin Gavras' blockade had cut deeply into their trade. Bakers, oil sellers, butchers, and wine merchants had little to sell, and that rationed and supervised by government inspectors. Ironically, it was commerce in luxuries that flourished under the siege. Jewels and precious metals, rare drugs, amulets, silks and brocades found customers galore. These were the things that could always be exchanged for food, so long as there was food.

The eruption of more than a thousand armed men into the

plaza of Palamas sent the rich merchants flying for their lives,
stuffing their goods into pockets or pouches and kicking over
their stalls in their panic to be gone. "Will you look at the loot
getting away," Viridovix said wistfully.

"Shut up," Gaius Philippus growled. "Don't give the lads
more ideas than they have already." His vine-stave staff of
office thwacked down on the corseleted shoulder of a legionary who had started to stray. "Come on, Paterculus—the
fight's this way! Besides, you bonehead, the pickings'll be
better yet in the palaces." That prediction was plenty to keep
the men in line—the troopers who heard him fairly purred in
anticipation.

They thundered past the great oval of the Amphitheater, the
southern flank of Palamas' plaza. Then they were into the
quarter of the palaces, its elegant buildings set off from one
another by artfully placed gardens and groves and wide
stretches of close-trimmed emerald lawn.

A Roman swore and dropped his *scutum* to clutch at his
right shoulder with his left hand. High overhead, an archer in
a cypress tree whooped and nocked another shaft. His triumph
was short-lived. Zeprin the Red's great two-handed axe was
made for hewing heads, not timber, but the muscular Haloga
proved no mean woodsman. The axe bit, jerked free, bit
again. Chips flew at every stroke. The cypress swayed, tot-
tered, fell; the sniper's scream of terror cut off abruptly as he
was crushed beneath the trunk.

"The gardeners will be angry at me," Zeprin said. A longtime veteran of the Imperial Guard, he thought of the palace
complex as his home and mourned the damage he had done it.
For the dead enemy he showed no remorse.

"Dinna fash yoursel', Haloga dear," Viridovix told him
dryly. "They'll be after having other things on their minds."

He waved ahead—a barricade of logs, broken benches,
and levered-up paving flags scarred the smooth expanse of
lawn. There were helmeted soldiers behind it and bodies in
front—the high-water mark, it seemed, of the mob's attack on
the palaces.

The makeshift works might have been strong enough to
hold off rioters, but Scaurus' troops were another matter—and
a second look told him the defenders were not many. "Battle
line!" he ordered. His men shook themselves out into

place, their hobnailed *caligae* ripping the smooth turf. His eyes caught Gaius Philippus'; they nodded together. "Charge!" the tribune shouted, and the Romans rolled down on the barricade.

A few arrows snapped toward them, but only a few. With cries of "Gavras!" and "Thorisin!" they hit the waist-high rampart and started scrambling over. Some of the warriors on the other side stayed to fight with saber and spear, but most, seeing themselves hopelessly outnumbered, turned to flee.

"Don't follow too close! Let 'em run!" Gaius Philippus roared out—in Latin, so the enemy could not understand. "They'll show us where their mates are lurking!"

The command tested Roman obedience to the utmost, for their foes used not only "The Sphrantzai!" and "Ortaias!" as war cries, but also "Rhavas!" It was all the senior centurion could do to hold his men in check. The battle-heat was on them, fanned hotter by lust for vengeance.

But Gaius Philippus' levelheaded order proved its worth. The enemy fell back, not on the barracks where Scaurus had expected them to make their stand, but through the ceremonial buildings of the palace complex and past the Hall of the Nineteen Couches to the Grand Courtroom itself, after Phos' High Temple the most splendid edifice in all Videssos.

The Hall of the Nineteen Couches had walls of green-shot marble and gilded bronze double doors that would have done credit to a keep. It was useless as a strongpoint, though, for a dozen low, wide windows made it impossible to hold against assault.

Marcus wished the same was true of the Grand Courtroom. It was a small compound in its own right, with outsweeping wings of offices making three sides of a square. Archers stood on the domed roof of the courtroom proper; others, looking for targets, peered through windows in the wings. Those windows were few, small, and high—the architect who designed the thickset building of golden sandstone had made sure it could double as a citadel.

"Zeprin!" Scaurus shouted, and the Haloga appeared before him, axe at port arms. The tribune said, "Since you've already turned logger, hack me down a couple of tall straight ones for rams."

"Rams against the Grand Gates?" Zeprin the Red sounded horrified.

"I know they're treasures," Marcus said with what patience he could. "But do you think those whoresons'll come out by themselves?"

After a moment the Haloga sighed and shrugged. "Aye, there are times when it's what must be done, not what should be." His thick muscles bunched under his mail shirt; he attacked the stately pines with a ferocity that told something of his dismay. The Romans were at the foot-and-a-half thick trunks as fast as they fell, chopping branches away and then tugging the trimmed logs up.

"All right, at 'em!" Gaius Philippus said. The men at the rams clumsily swung their heavy burdens toward the Grand Gates. Shieldmen leaped out on either side of them to cover them from arrow-fire. The makeshift batterers, of course, had no mantlets; Marcus hoped the enemy trapped inside the Grand Courtroom had not had time to bring anything more lethal than bowmen up to the roof.

The ram crews lumbered forward, warded by their comrades' upraised *scuta*. The Grand Gates groaned at the impact, as if in pain. The logs jolted from the Romans' hands. Men tumbled, writhing as they fell to keep from being crushed. They scrambled to their feet, lifted the rams once more, and drew back for another blow.

More legionaries fanned out to deal with the few dozen men who had fled to the Grand Courtroom too late to take shelter inside. Soon only Romans stood erect in the courtyard. Not one of Rhavas' men had asked for quarter—in that, at least, they perfectly understood the temper of their foes.

Out of the corner of his eye Marcus noticed the upper stories of the nearby Hall of Ambassadors. They were crowded with faces watching the fighting. The tribune had several friends among the foreign envoys. He hoped they were safe. This, he thought, was a closer view of Videssos' government in action than they were likely to want.

Rhavas' archers were hitting back. One sharpshooter high on the courtroom dome scored again and again. Then he crumpled, sliding down over the orange-red tiles to fall like so many limp rags to the greenery far below.

The range and upward angle had made him a nearly impossible mark. "Well shot!" Marcus cried, looking round to find out who had picked off the bowman. He saw Viridovix pounding a skinny, swarthy man on the back: Arigh Arghun's son, the envoy of the Arshaum to Videssos' court. His nomadic people dwelt on the steppe west of the Khamorth, and he carried a plainsman's short, horn-reinforced bow. Bitter experience against the Yezda had taught Scaurus how marvelously long and flat those bows shot; the dead sharpshooter was but another proof.

"Isn't he the finest little fellow now?" Viridovix crowed, gleefully thumping Arigh again. The big ruddy Celt and slight, flat-faced, black-haired nomad made a strange pair, but they had often roistered together when the Romans were stationed in the city. Each owned a fierce, uncomplicated view of life that appealed to the other, the more so in the wordly-wise capital.

The tribune's brief musing was snapped by a scream within the Grand Courtroom, a woman's shriek of mortal anguish that sent the hairs on his arms and at the nape of his neck bristling upright. Hardened though they were, the Romans and their foes both stood frozen in horror for a moment before returning to their business of murdering one another.

Marcus' first thought after his wits began to work again was that Alypia Gavra might well be in the besieged courtroom. If that scream had been hers— "Harder, damn you!" he shouted to the men at the rams and shoved sword in scabbard so he could take hold of a log.

The ram crews needed no urging; the cry had put fresh spirit in them as well. They rushed forward. The Grand Gates tolled like a sub-bass bell. Scaurus fell, scraping elbows and knees and feeling the wind half knocked from him, almost as if he had run full-tilt into the gates himself.

He leaped to his feet and ran back to the log, never noticing the fist-sized stone that smashed into the grass where he had sprawled. Then it was back and forward again, and yet again. The rough bark drew blood from even the most callused hands.

Twice as tall as a man, the burnished gates were leaning drunkenly back against the bar that held them upright. Quintus Glabrio's clear voice rang out, "Once more! This one pays for all." The rams crashed home. With the desperate sound a great plank makes on breaking, the bar gave way. The Grand Gates flew open, as if kicked. Cheering, the Romans surged forward.

A fierce volley met them, but Scaurus, expecting such, had

put shieldmen in front of the ram crews to hold off the arrows. Then it was savage fighting at the breached gate. The small opening kept the Romans from bringing their full number into play, and Rhavas' bandits fought with the reckless fury of men who knew themselves trapped. Even so, the legionaries were better armed and better trained; step by bitter step they pushed their foes back from the entrance and into the court room.

As he fought his way past the Grand Gates, Marcus felt the dismay Zeprin the Red had known when the tribune ordered rams brought to bear against them. The high reliefs on them were exquisite, a wordless chronicle of the Emperor Stavrakios' conquest of Agder in the far northeast eleven hundred years before. Here the imperial troops led back prisoners, the bowed heads of the captive women agonizing portraits of despair. A little higher, engineers carved a road along the side of a cliff so the army could advance; a pack mule's hoof skittered on the edge of disaster. At the join of the gates Stavrakios led a counterattack against the Halogai. And over all stood the Miracle of Phos, when hot sun in midwinter melted a frozen river and trapped the barbarians without retreat. The Videssian god appeared in brooding majesty above his chosen folk.

But Agder was lost to the Empire these last eight long centuries, and now, the reliefs that showed its overthrow themselves met war. The rams had flattened mountains and crushed faces with impartial brutality. A tiny twisted bronze ear was trampled in the grass at the tribune's feet. Nothing can come into being without change, he told himself, but the maxim did little to console him.

He shouldered past one of Rhavas' bravoes, thrust home under the arm where his mail shirt was weak. The man groaned and twisted away, enlarging his own wound. As he fell, Scaurus tore his small round shield from him to replace the *scutum* left outside the courtroom.

Marcus' eyes took a few seconds to adjust to the relative gloom within. He had expected to face Outis Rhavas at the entrance—had Ortaias Sphrantzes' foul captain fled? No, there he was, by a seething iron cauldron in the very center of the porphyry floor; the rude log fire kindled on that perfect surface was a desecration in itself. A knot of men around him jostled one another, each trying to dip a surcoat sleeve into whatever mixture bubbled in the kettle.

By it sprawled a gutted corpse, naked, female. The druids' stamps on Marcus' blade flared into light, but he did not need them to warn him of magic.

The fight was not the well-planned, carefully orchestrated engagement in which Gaius Philippus could take pride. The Romans perforce broke ranks to battle through the Grand Gates; inside the courtroom it was a vicious sprawl of fighting, one on one, three against two, up and down the broad center aisle and around the tall columns of light-drinking basalt. A hanging of cloth of gold and scarlet silk came tumbling down to enfold a handful of warriors in its precious web.

Marcus fought his way toward Rhavas. He moved cautiously; his hobnailed *caligae* would not bite on the glass-smooth flooring, and he felt as if he were walking on ice.

When one of Rhavas' men stumbled against him, they both fell heavily. They grappled, so closely locked together Scaurus could smell his enemy's fear. He could not stab with his sword; it was too long. He smashed the pommel into the brigand's face until the clutching arms around him relaxed their grip.

The tribune staggered to his feet. There were shouts outside—more of Thorisin's men reaching the palace complex at last through Videssos' maze of streets. Scaurus had no time for them. Outis Rhavas loomed over him, a tower of enameled steel from closed helm to mailed boots.

Most Videssians fought by choice from horseback and thus preferred sabers. But as he had in the brush at the rampart, Rhavas swung a heavy longsword. His giant frame made it a wickedly effective weapon; even the tall Scaurus gave away inches of reach.

"A pity you scrape your face bare," Rhavas hissed, his voice full of venom. "It ruins the pleasure of shaving your corpse."

The tribune did not answer; he knew the taunt was only meant to enrage and distract him. Their blades rang together. As Marcus had already found, Outis Rhavas was as skilled as he was strong. Stroke by stroke, he drove the Roman back; it was all Scaurus could do to parry the storm of blows. After the protection of his lost *scutum*, the small shield he carried seemed no more useful than a lady's powder puff.

But for all their fell captain's might, Rhavas' band was falling back around him. They fought as bandits do, furiously but without order. Though the legionaries' maniples were in disarray, long training had drilled into them the notion that they were parts of a greater whole. Like a constricting snake's coils, they pressed constantly, never yielding an advantage once gained.

Thus when Rhavas threatened Marcus, he was alone, while Viridovix and half a dozen Romans leaped to the tribune's defense. Balked of his prey, Rhavas cursed horribly. But he gave ground, falling back until he was one of the last defenders of the cauldron that still boiled and steamed in the center of the courtroom.

Even through woodsmoke, Marcus caught its contents' sick-sweet carrion reek, but a score of Rhavas' soldiers had already wet their sleeves in the liquid. And not soldiers alone; the sleeve that went into the pot now was purple satin shot through with thread of silver and gold.

"Vardanes!" the tribune shouted, and at the cry the elder Sphrantzes jerked as if jabbed with a pin. Scaurus had rarely seen Ortaias' uncle other than perfectly composed or known that round, ruddy face with its fringe of neat black beard to reflect anything but what the Sevastos wanted seen. But now he wore the furtive, guilty look of a man surprised at a perversion.

The battle stiffened. Some of Rhavas' bandits, it seemed, would not fall, no matter what blows landed on them. Marcus heard Gaius Philippus snarl, "Go down, you bastard, go down!", heard the soft, meaty sound of a blade driven home.

But the senior centurion's foe only grinned like a snake. Scaurus saw the yellowish stain on his surcoat sleeve. He slashed back at the Roman, a clumsy stroke Gaius Philippus turned with his shield. But doubt clouded the veteran's eyes —how was he to beat a man he could not wound?

That same doubt appeared on more and more Roman faces. As Rhavas' anointed gained confidence in their invulnerability to steel, they began running risks no warrior would have thought sane, taking ten blows to land one. They taunted the legionaries, as boys will taunt a savage dog when safely behind a high fence. And, inevitably, they took their share of victims. The Roman advance stumbled.

Smiling wickedly, a tall, jackal-lean Videssian engaged Viridovix. The cutthroat swung his sword two-handed—what need had he of shield? The big Gaul slid to one side, light on

is feet as a great hunting cat. His blade, twin to Scaurus'
own, sang through the air, druids' marks flashing gold.

It bit through flesh and windpipe and bone. Before the
expression of horrified surprise could form on the brigand's
face, his head leaped from his shoulders, hitting the ground
with a warm, splattery thud. The spouting corpse collapsed,
its limbs thrashing, for a moment not realizing they were
dead.

Viridovix's banshee howl of triumph filled the courtroom.
He leaped forward. Another muck-sleeved ruffian fell, clutching at the guts the Celt's sword laid out into his hands, neat as
an anatomical demonstration.

Marcus went hunting stained surcoats, too, realizing that,
as had always been true in Videssos, his good Gallic blade
was proof against sorcery. Like Viridovix, he killed his first
man with ridiculous ease. Not knowing the weapon he faced,
the bandit scarcely bothered to protect himself. He gasped as
the tribune's sword found his heart, then tried to breathe, but
coughed blood instead.

"Liar!" he whispered, slumping to the floor; his eyes were
on Rhavas.

The harsh captain's men wavered in their attack, new-
found confidence faltering as they watched their comrades die
so in surprise. Then Arsaber, the hulking street ruffian, felled
yet another of their number, his heavy club making a shattered
ruin of the left side of his opponent's face.

Gaius Philippus was no scholar, but in battle he missed
nothing. "It's only iron won't hurt 'em!" he shouted to the
legionaries. He snatched a *pilum* from one of the Romans,
grabbing the shank to wield it clubwise. He shouted in fierce
delight as the blow sent one of Rhavas' warriors spinning
back, sword flying from nerveless fingers. Marcus did not
think that man would rise again; the senior centurion had ex-
orcised all his fear of magic in one prodigious swing.

"Stand, you ball-less rabbits!" Rhavas bellowed, and Vardanes Sphrantzes' well-trained baritone rose in exhortation:
"Hold fast! Hold fast!" But they were shouting against a gale
of fear roaring through their followers—sword and spear had
not held the Romans, and now sorcery failed as well.

One desperate band cut its way clean through the legionaries; its handful of survivors dashed through the Grand Gates,
intent only on escape. Marcus heard their cries of despair as

they ran headlong into more of Thorisin Gavras' troops outside. With agility born of desperation, bandits clawed their way up wall hangings to insecure refuges in window niches ten feet above the floor. Others tried to surrender, but not many of Scaurus' men would let them yield. Quintus Glabrio kept more than one from being killed out of hand, but he could not be everywhere.

Outis Rhavas cut down a bolting man from behind, and then another, his own way of encouraging his bandits to stand and fight. But even with the hardiest of his irregulars at his side, the surging Romans at last drove him from his wizard's cauldron. He fell back toward the imperial throne.

Marcus traded swordstrokes with one of his lieutenants. The man was fast as a striking viper; he pinked Scaurus twice in quick succession, and a vicious slash just missed the tribune's eye. But the cutthroat's heel slipped in the great pool of blood that had gushed from the serving wench his master had killed. Before he could recover, Scaurus' blade tore out his throat. He fell across the girl's outraged corpse.

As the tribune pushed forward, he glanced down into the iron pot Rhavas had defended with such ferocity and found himself looking at horror. Floating in the boiling, scum-filled water was a dead baby, the soft flesh beginning to fall away from its bones. No, he corrected himself, not even a baby— the tiny body was no longer than the distance between the tips of his outstretched thumb and little finger.

His eyes slipped to the serving wench's opened belly, back in disbelief to the cauldron, and he was sick where he stood. He spat again and again to clear his mouth of the taste and wished he might somehow wipe his vision clear so easily.

Cold in him was the knowledge that there were, after all, worse evils than Doukitzes' tortured death. He was tempted to follow the creed of Videssos, for in Outis Rhavas surely Skotos walked on earth.

That thought led to another, and sudden dreadful certainty gripped him. "Rhavas!" he shouted; the name was putrid as the vomit on his tongue. Then he solved the other's anagram, his monstrous joke, and cried another name: "Avshar!"

It grew very still within the Grand Courtroom; blows hung in the air, unstruck. Outis Rhavas' name brought with it rage and hatred, but the wizard-prince of Yezd had struck cold terror into Videssos' heart for a generation. Inside the ranks of

Rhavas' men, Marcus saw Vardanes Sphrantzes' red cheeks go pale as he understood his state's greatest foe had been a chief upholder of his rule.

Across the thirty feet that separated them, Rhavas—no, Avshar—dipped his head to the tribune in derisive acknowledgement of his astuteness. "Very good," he chuckled, and Scaurus wondered how he had not known that fell voice at first hearing. "You have more wit than these dogs, it seems—much good will it do you."

After that moment of stunned dismay, the legionaries hurled themselves with redoubled fury at the backers of him who had styled himself Outis Rhavas. The men they faced threw down their swords in scores. Rhavas the brigand chief was a captain they had followed in hope of blood and plunder, but few were the Videssians who would willingly serve Avshar.

A bandit leaped at his longtime master's back, saber upraised to cut him down. But Avshar whirled with the speed of a wolf; his heavy longsword smashed through helm and skull alike. "A dog indeed," he cried, "nipping at the heels he followed! Are there more?"

The men who had been his flinched away in fright, all save a black handful who still clove to him, who would have happily fought for him had they thought him Skotos enfleshed—the worst of his band, but far from the weakest. Almost all wore surcoats stained with his protective brew—no qualm of conscience had kept them from dipping their sleeves in that horrid pot.

Vardanes Sphrantzes stood in indecision, a spider caught in a greater spider's web. He did not think of himself as an evil man, merely a practical one, and he feared Avshar with the sincere fear a far from perfect man can have for one truly wicked. But the Sevastos was more afraid to yield himself to Scaurus and, through him, to Thorisin Gavras. He knew too well the common fate of losers in Videssos' civil wars and also knew his actions in raising his nephew to the throne—and since—were sure to doom him in the victor's eyes.

The wizard-prince saw Sphrantzes waver; he flayed him into motion with the whip of his voice: "Come, worm, do you think you can do without me now?" And Vardanes, who had felt only contempt for soldiers, looked once more at the Romans' crested helms and at their stabbing swords and long spears. It seemed they were all bearing down on him alone. His will failed him, and he fled with Avshar.

The way they chose—the only way they could have chosen—was a narrow spiral stair that opened out into the Grand Courtroom just to the right of the imperial throne's gold and sapphire brilliance. It had not been part of the throne room's original design, for it brutally abridged a delicate wall mosaic. Marcus wondered what ancient treason caused some cautious Emperor to put safety above beauty.

Once Avshar's few partisans had gained the stair, the legionaries' advance was easy no more. Those steps had been made so one man could hold back an army, and the wizard-prince himself was rear guard, a cork not to be lightly pulled from the bottle.

The tribune and Viridovix attacked by turns; not only were they nearest Avshar in size and strength, but theirs were blades to stand against his sorcery. At every stroke the druids' marks incised upon them flashed golden, turning aside the banes locked within his brand.

Legionaries, crowding close behind their champions, jabbed spears over them at Avshar. Warded as he was, the thrusts could not hurt him, but spoiled his swordstrokes and threatened to trip him up. His heavy blade hewed clear through more than one soft iron *pilum*-shank; nevertheless he was forced back, step by slow step.

"Let's the both of us fight him at the same time," Viridovix panted. Marcus shook his head. The stairway was so narrow two men abreast would only foul each other, but he would have refused had it been wider. The first time his sword had met the Gaul's, they were whirled here; were they to touch again, only the gods knew what might befall.

The spiral wound through three complete turns. Then Avshar's massive frame was silhouetted against a background lighter than the stairway's oppressive gloom. The wizard-prince drew back away from the topmost step, as if inviting his pursuers to come on.

That Marcus did, but warily, expecting deviltry. He remembered Avshar's escape from Videssos the year before—the sea-wall arsenal's sudden-slammed door, the corpse of the wizard's servant speaking with his master's voice, the swords and spears that flew to the attack with no man wielding them.

Avshar was never more dangerous than when seeming to give way.

A blade slammed against his upraised shield, but there was a ruffian back of it, a red-faced man with a great mat of greasy black beard. Scaurus parried, countered. The thrust was clumsy, but his reach and long blade made his stocky foe give back a pace. He stepped up quickly, Viridovix only a single stair behind him, legionaries jamming the stairway behind.

The suite above the throne room had to be the Emperor's disrobing chamber, a private retreat from the ceremonial of the Grand Courtroom. There had been, Marcus saw, six or eight well-stuffed chairs and a couch set up in the outer room; Avshar's men had flung them against the seascape-painted walls to gain fighting room. The rough treatment had burst one, and gray feathers whirled in the air.

Even as he fenced with the black-bearded highbinder, Scaurus wondered why Avshar had yielded the stair so easily there at the end, why for the moment he was leaving the battle to his henchmen. Where was he? Hardly time to see, with this cutthroat hacking away like a berserker.

The tribune let his foe's slash hiss past, stepped forward inside the saber's arc, and ran him through the throat. Aye, there was Avshar, in front of a closed door with Vardanes Sphrantzes. He bent low to say something to the Sevastos, who shook his head. Avshar smashed him in the face with his gauntleted hand.

Vardanes, strong-willed in this ruin of all his hopes, still would not do the wizard's bidding. With cold deliberation, Avshar hit him again. Marcus saw something crumple inside the proud Sevastos. All his life the bureaucrat had upheld his faction by circumventing brute force, by bringing Videssos' proud soldiers to heel without violence. Now at last he had to confront it with no buffers, and found he could not. He pulled a brass key from his belt, worked the lock, and slipped into the room beyond.

Marcus forgot him almost as soon as he disappeared. Fighting back to back, the tribune and Viridovix cleared enough space to let the legionaries emerge, a couple at a time, from the stairwell. Even with reinforcements constantly added, the fight was savage. Save for Scaurus' sword and the Celt's, Roman blades would not wound Avshar's men. They had to be clubbed into submission with spearshafts and other makeshift bludgeons, or else disarmed by a clever sword-stroke and then wrestled to the floor and dispatched with bare hands. They made the Romans pay dearly for each life.

The price would have been higher yet, but Avshar, as if conceding all was lost, stood aloof from the struggle, watching his men die one by one. Only when a legionary drew too near the door he was guarding did his blade flash forth, wielded as always with skill and might to daunt a hero. There was no shame in seeking easier prey, and so in the end the wizard-prince stood all alone before that doorway.

Facing a lesser foe, the Romans would have rolled over him and after Vardanes Sphrantzes. But Avshar was like a lion brought to bay; the debased majesty in him carried awe mingled with the dread. Push forward, Scaurus thought—make an end. But Avshar's gaze came baleful through visor slits, and the tribune could not move. Even Viridovix, a stranger to intimidation, stood frozen.

A strange silence fell, broken only by the legionaries' panting and the moans of the injured. Without turning, Avshar rapped on the door behind him. His iron-knuckled hand made it jump on its hinges. Only silence answered him. He hit it again, saying, "Come out, fool, lest I stand aside and let them have you."

There was another pause, but as Avshar began to slide away from the door, Vardanes Sphrantzes drew it open. The Sevastos clutched a dagger in his right hand. His left cruelly prisoned the wrist of a young girl; she wore only a short shift of transparent golden silk that served but to accent her nakedness beneath.

For all its paint, her face was not a palace tart's; the knowledge on it was of a different kind. But not until her calm greeting, "Well met, Marcus Aemilius Scaurus," did the tribune know her for Alypia Gavra.

Caught by surprise, he took an involuntary step forward. Sphrantzes' dagger leaped for her throat. Light glinted off the mirror-bright sliver of steel. The stiletto was only a noble's jewel-encrusted toy, but it could let her life river out before any man could stop it. Alypia stood motionless under its cold caress.

Scaurus also froze, two paces away. "Let her go, Vardanes," he urged, watching Sphrantzes closely. Vardanes' plump face was unnaturally pale, save for two spots of red that marked the impact of Avshar's hand. A thin trickle of blood ran from his left nostril into his beard. His pearl-bedecked Sevastos' coronet sat awry on his head—for the dandy Sphrantzes was, a telling sign of disintegration. His eyes were wide and staring, trapped eyes.

"Let her go," Marcus repeated softly. "She won't buy your escape—you know that." The Sevastos shook his head, but the dagger fell—not much, but an inch or two.

Avshar chuckled, his mirth more terrible than a shriek of hate. "Aye, let her go, Vardanes," he said. "Let her go, just as you let Videssos go when it was in your hands. You took your pleasure from it as from her, and then watched with drool dribbling down your chin as it slipped through your fingers. Of course, let her go. What better way to end your bungling life? Even as a puppet you were worthless."

Marcus never knew whether Avshar's contempt was more than the Sevastos could endure or whether, in some last calculation of his own, Vardanes decided—and perhaps rightly— the wizard-prince's death might be the one coin to buy his safety from Thorisin Gavras. Whatever his reasons, he suddenly shoved Alypia forward, sending her stumbling into the tribune's arms, then whirled and drove his dagger into Avshar's armored breast.

The thin steel needle was the perfect weapon to pierce a cuirass, and Sphrantzes' desperate stab was backed by all the power his well-fed frame could give. Scaurus had always thought there was muscle under that fat. Now he knew it, for when Vardanes' hand came away, the stiletto was driven home hilt-deep.

But Avshar did not crumple. "Ah, Vardanes," he said, laughing a laugh jagged as broken glass. "Futile to the very end. My magics proofed you against cold iron's bite. Did you think they would do less for me, their maker? See now, it should be done this way."

Swift as a serpent's strike, he seized the Sevastos, lifted him off his feet, and flung him against the wall. Marcus heard his skull shatter—the exact sound, he thought, of a dropped crock of porridge. Blood sprayed over the painted waves; Vardanes was dead before he slid to the floor.

Avshar drew the dagger from his chest, tucked it into his belt. "A very good day to you all," he said with a last mocking bow, and darted into the farther chamber.

His flight freed the Romans from the paralysis with which they had watched the past minutes' drama. They rushed to the door; but though the locks were on the outside, they would not open. The Romans attacked the door with swords and their armored shoulders, but the apartment over the throne room was, among other things, a redoubt, and the portal did not yield.

Through the noise of their pounding came Avshar's voice, loudly chanting in some harsh tongue that was not Videssian. More magic, Marcus thought with a twist of fear in his guts. "Zeprin!" he shouted, and then cursed the confused pushing and shoving that followed as the Haloga bulled his way up the crowded spiral stair.

He burst puffing out of the stair well; the climb had left his normally ruddy features almost purple. His head swiveled till he spied Scaurus' tall horsehair plume. The tribune stabbed his thumb at the door. "Avshar's on the other side. He—"

Marcus had been about to warn the Haloga that Avshar was brewing sorcery, but found himself ignored. Zeprin the Red had nursed his hatred and lust for vengeance since Mavrikios fell at Maragha; now they exploded. He hurled himself at the doorway, roaring, "Where will you run now, wizard?"

Legionaries scattered as his great axe came down. It was as well they did; in his berserk fury the Haloga paid them no heed. Timbers split under his hammerstrokes—no wood, no matter how thick or seasoned, could stand up to such an assault for long.

Scaurus realized his arms were still tight around Alypia Gavra; her skin was warm through the thin negligee. "Your pardon, my lady," he said. "Here." He wrapped her in his scarlet cape of rank.

"Thank you," she said, stepping free of him to draw it around her. Her green eyes carried gratitude, but only as a thin crust over pain. "I've known worse than the touch of a friend," she added quietly.

Before Marcus could find a suitable reply, Zeprin shouted in triumph as the door's boards and bolts gave up the unequal struggle. Axe held high, he shouldered his way past the riven timbers, followed close by Scaurus and Viridovix, each with his strong blade at the ready. Gaius Philippus and more Romans pushed in after them.

The tribune had not got much of a glimpse beyond the

shattered door when Vardanes opened it, nor again when Avshar took refuge behind it. He stared now in amazement. It was a chamber straight from an expensive brothel: the ceiling mirror of polished bronze, the obscene but beautifully executed wall frescoes, the scattered bright silks that were donned only to be taken off, the soft, wide bed with its coverlets pulled down in invitation.

And he stared for another reason, the same which brought Zeprin's rush to a stumbling, confused halt a couple of paces into the room—save for the invaders, it was empty. The Haloga's knuckles were white round the haft of his axe. Primed to kill, he found himself without a target. His breath came in sobbing gasps as he fought to bring his body back under the control of his will.

Marcus' eyes flicked to the windows, tall, narrow slits through which a cat could not have crawled, let alone a man. Viridovix rammed his sword into its scabbard, a gesture eloquent in its disgust. "The cullion's gone and magicked us again," he said, and swore in Gaulish.

For all the sinking feeling in his stomach, the tribune would not yet let himself believe that. He ordered the soldiers behind him, "Turn this place inside out. For all we know, Avshar's hiding under the bed or lurking in that closet there." They stepped past him; one suspicious legionary jabbed his *gladius* into the mattress again and again, thinking Avshar might somehow have got inside it.

"Nay, it's magic sure enough," Viridovix said dolorously as the search went on without success.

"Shut up," Marcus said, but he was not paying much attention to the Celt. He had just noticed the gilded manacles set into the bedposts and reflected that Vardanes Sphrantzes' death, perhaps, had been too easy.

"There's magic and magic," Gaius Philippus said. "Remember the whole Yezda battle line winked out for a second until the Videssian wizards matched their spell? Maybe that's the trick the whoreson's using here."

That had not occurred to the tribune. Though he had scant hope in it, he sent runners through the palace complex and others to Phos' High Temple, all seeking Nepos the mage. He also posted legionaries shoulder to shoulder in the broken doorway, saying, "If Avshar can make himself impalpable as well as invisible, he deserves to get away."

"No he doesn't," Gaius Philippus growled.

The sound of more fighting pierced the slit windows. Scaurus went over for a look, but their field of view was too narrow to show him anything but a brief glimpse of running men. They were Videssians, but whether Thorisin's troops advancing or followers of the Sphrantzai counterattacking, he could not tell.

Worried, he decided to go downstairs to make sure the legionaries were in position to defend the Grand Courtroom at need. Their discipline should have been enough to make such precautions automatic, but better safe; what with Avshar's magic and the fight up the stairs, usual patterns could slip.

He left the doorway full of guards and put others in front of the stairwell. Their eyes told him they thought their posts absurd, but they did not question him; like Fayard the Namdalener, they carried out their orders without complaint.

Alypia Gavra accompanied the tribune down the spiral stair. "So now you have seen my shame," she said, still outwardly as self-possessed as ever. But Marcus saw how tightly she held his cape closed round her neck, how she tugged at its hem with her other hand, trying to make it cover more of her.

He knew she meant more than the wisp of yellow silk beneath that cape. He spoke slowly, choosing his words with care, "What does not corrupt a man's heart cannot corrupt his life, or do him any lasting harm."

In Rome it would have been a Stoic commonplace; but to the Videssians, deeds spoke louder than intentions, as suited a folk who saw the universe as a war between good and evil. Thus Alypia searched Marcus' face in the gloom of the stair well, suspecting mockery. Finding none, she said at last, very low, "If I can ever come to believe that, you will have given me back myself. No thanks could be enough."

She stared straight ahead the rest of the way down the steps. Scaurus studied the stair well's rough stonework, giving her what privacy he could.

Alypia gasped in dismay as they came down into the throne room. It no longer had the semblance of the Empire's solemn ceremonial heart, but only of any battlefield after the fighting is done. Bodies and debris littered the polished floor, which was further marred by drying pools of blood. Wounded men cursed, groaned, or lay silent, according to how badly they were hurt. Gorgidas went from one to the next, giving the aid he could.

A glance told Marcus there would be no trouble at the Grand Gates. Unobtrusively effective as always, Quintus Glabrio had a double squad of legionaries ready to hold off an attack. But they were standing at ease now, their *pila* grounded and swords sheathed. The junior centurion waved to his commander. "Everything under control," he said, and Scaurus nodded.

Avshar's accursed kettle still steamed in the center of the hall, though the fire under it had gone out. The tribune tried to lead Alypia by as quickly as he could, but she stopped dead at the sight of the pathetic mutilated corpse beside it.

"Oh, my poor, dear Kalline," she whispered, making Phos' circular sun-sign over her breast. "I feared it was so when I heard your cry. So this is your reward for loyalty to your mistress?"

She somehow kept her features impassive, but two tears slid down her cheeks. Then her eyes rolled up in her head, and she crumpled to the floor, her strong spirit at last overwhelmed by the day's series of shocks. The borrowed cape came open as she fell, leaving her almost bare.

"One of Vardanes' trollops, is she?" a Roman asked the tribune, leering down at her. "I've seen prettier faces, maybe, but by Venus' cleft there'd be a lively time with those long smooth legs wrapped around me."

"She's Alypia Gavra, Thorisin's niece, so shut your filth-filled mouth," Scaurus grated. The legionary fell back a pace in fright, then darted off to find something, anything, to do somewhere else. Marcus watched him go, surprised at his own fury. The trooper had jumped to a natural enough conclusion.

At the tribune's call, Gorgidas hurried over to see to Alypia. He put her in as comfortable a position as he could, then folded Scaurus' cape around her again. That finished, he stood and started to go to the next injured legionary. "Aren't you going to do anything more?" Marcus demanded.

"What do you recommend?" Gorgidas said. "I could probably rouse her, but it wouldn't be doing her any favor. As far as I can see, the poor lass has had enough jolts to last any six people a lifetime—can you blame her for fainting? I say let her, if that's what she needs. Rest is the best medicine the body knows, and I'm damned if I'll tamper with it."

"Well, all right," Scaurus said mildly, reminding himself for the hundredth time how touchy the Greek was when anyone interfered with his medical judgment.

Alypia was stirring and muttering to herself when Nepos came bustling in behind one of Marcus' runners. Despite a remorseful cluck at the damage the Grand Gates had taken, the fat priest was in high good spirits as he entered the throne room. He scattered blessings on everyone around him. Most Romans ignored him, but some of the legionaries had come to worship Phos; they and the Videssians who had taken service with them bowed as Nepos went past.

He saw Scaurus and bobbed his head in greeting, smiling broadly as he approached. But he was less than halfway to the tribune when he staggered, as at some physical blow. "Phos have mercy!" he whispered. "What has been done here?" He moved forward again, but slowly; Marcus thought of a man pushing his way into a heavy gale.

He looked into the cauldron with a cry of disgust, a deeper loathing even than Scaurus' own. The tribune saw the torture's wanton viciousness; but as priest and mage, Nepos understood the malignance of the sorcery it powered and recoiled in horror from his understanding.

"You did right to summon me," he said, visibly gathering himself. "That the Sphrantzai opposed us is one thing, but this—this—" At a loss for words, he paused. "I never imagined they could fall to these depths. Ortaias Sphrantzes, from all I know of him, is but a silly young man, while Vardanes—"

"Is lying dead upstairs," Scaurus finished for him. Nepos gaped at the tribune, who went on, "The wizardry we dealt with, but the wizard, now—" In a few quick sentences he set out what had passed. "We may have him besieged up there," he finished.

"Avshar trapped? Trapped?" Nepos burst out when he was through. "Why are you wasting my time with talk?"

"He may be," Marcus repeated, but Nepos was no longer listening. The priest turned and ran for the stairway, his blue robe flapping about his ankles. Marcus heard his sandals clatter on the stairs, heard him run into a descending Roman.

"Get out of my way, you rattlebrained, slouching gowk!" Nepos shouted, his voice squeaking up into high tenor in his agitation. There were brief shuffling sounds as he and the trooper jockeyed for position, then he was past and dashing upward again.

When the legionary emerged from the stairwell he was still shaking his head. "Who stuck a pin in *him*?" he asked plaintively, but got no answer.

Alypia Gavra's eyes came open. Nepos had hardly spared her a second glance; Avshar's foul sorcery and Scaurus' news that the wizard-prince might still be taken drove from his mind such trivia as the Emperor's niece.

She sat slowly and carefully. Marcus was ready to help support her, but she waved him away. Though she was still very pale, her mouth twisted in annoyance. "I thought better of myself than this," she said.

"It doesn't matter," the tribune answered. "The important thing is that you're safe and the city's in Thorisin's hands." Why, so it is, he thought rather dazedly. He had been too caught up in the fighting to realize this was victory at last. Excitement flooded through him.

"Oh, yes, I'm perfectly safe." Alypia's voice carried a weary, cynical undertone Marcus had not heard in it before. "My uncle will no doubt welcome me with open arms—me, the wife of his rival Avtokrator and plaything of—" She broke off, unwilling to bring even the thought to light.

"We all knew the marriage was forced," Scaurus said stoutly. Alypia managed a wan smile, but more at his vehemence than for what he said. Some of his elation trickled away. There could be an uncomfortable amount of truth in Alypia's worries.

He was distracted by the sound of Nepos coming down the spiral stairway. It was easy to recognize the priest by his footfalls; his sandals slapped the stone steps instead of clicking off them as did the Romans' hobnailed footgear. It was also easy to guess his mood, for his descending steps were slow and heavy, altogether unlike his excited dash upwards.

The first glimpse of him confirmed the tribune's fears; the light was gone from his eyes, while his shoulders slumped as if bearing the world's weight. "Gone?" Marcus asked rhetorically.

"Gone!" Nepos echoed. "The stink of magic will linger for days, but its author is escaped to torment us further. Skotos drag him straight to hell, is there no limit to his strength? A spell of apportation is known to us of the Academy, but it requires long preparation and will not let the caster carry chattels. Yet Avshar cast it in seconds and vanished, armor, sword, and all. Phos grant that in his haste he blundered and projected himself into a volcano's heart or out over the open sea, there to sink under the weight of his iron."

But the priest's forlorn tone told how likely he judged that, nor could Scaurus make himself imagine so simple an end for Avshar. The wizard-prince, he was sure, had gone where he wanted to go and nowhere else—whatever spot his malice chose as the one that would harm Videssos worst. And with that thought, what was left of the taste of triumph turned sour in the tribune's mouth.

IX

VIRIDOVIX SAID, "IT ONLY GOES TO SHOW WHAT I'VE SAID all along—there's no trust to be put in these Videssians. The city folk stand by the Sphrantzai all through the siege and then turn on 'em after they'd gone and won it."

"Things are hardly as simple as that," Marcus replied, leaning back in his chair. The Romans had returned to the barracks they occupied last year before Mavrikios set out on campaign against the Yezda. The sweet scent of orange blossoms drifted in through wide-flung shutters; fine mesh kept nocturnal pests outside.

Gaius Philippus bit into a hard roll, part of the iron rations every legionary carried, as supplies inside the city were very short. He chewed deliberately, reached out to the low table in front of him for a mug of wine to wash the bite down. "Aye, the bloody fools brought it on themselves," he agreed. "If Rhavas'—no, Avshar's, I should say—brigands hadn't been off plundering to celebrate beating us back, Zigabenos' coup wouldn't have had a prayer."

"His and Alypia Gavra's," Marcus corrected.

A pail dropped with a crash and made Gaius Philippus jump. "Have a care there, you thumb-fingered oafs!" he shouted. The barracks were not in the same tidy shape the Romans had left them. During the siege they had held Khamorth and, from the smell and mess, their horses as well. Legionaries swept, scrubbed, and hauled garbage away; others made up fresh straw pallets to replace the filthy ones that had satisfied the nomads.

Reluctantly, the senior centurion returned to the topic at

191

hand. "Well, yes," he said grudgingly to Scaurus, slow as usual to give a woman credit for wit and pluck.

But here credit was due, Marcus thought. Rumors still flew through Videssos; like cheese, they had ripened through the day and now at evening some were truly bizarre. But unlike most of the city, Scaurus had talked with some of the people involved in events and he had a fair notion of what had actually gone on.

"Lucky for us Alypia realized Thorisin would never take the city from outside," he insisted. "The timing was hers, and it could hardly have been better."

The princess and Mertikes Zigabenos—who had kept his post as an officer of the Imperial Guard—were plotting against the Sphrantzai before Thorisin's siege even began. Alypia's handmaiden Kalline made the perfect go-between; her pregnancy protected her from suspicion and, as it had resulted from a rape by one of Rhavas' roughs, bound her to the plotters' cause. But as long as it seemed Thorisin might capture Videssos, the conspiracy remained one of words alone.

After his assault failed, though, assault from inside the city suddenly became urgent. Alypia managed to get word to Zigabenos that Ortaias had closeted himself away in the isolation of the private imperial chambers to compose a victory address to his troops.

Gaius Philippus knew that part of the story, too. His comment was, "The lady could have sat tight one day more. If there wouldn't have been a mutiny after that speech, I don't know soldiers." The senior centurion had endured more than one of Ortais Sphrantzes' orations and exaggerated only slightly.

Most of the regiments of the Imperial Guard had been lost at Maragha. Though Mertikes Zigabenos kept his title, Outis Rhavas' troopers actually warded the Sphrantzai. But the Romans had given them a hard tussle at the walls, and afterward most of them went on a drinking spree which quickly led to fist-fights and looting. Their victims, naturally, fought back, which brought more of them out of the palace complex to reinforce their mates—and gave Zigabenos his chance.

He only commanded three squads of men, but at the head of one of them he descended on Ortaias' secluded retreat, seized the feckless Avtokrator at his desk, and spirited him away to the High Temple of Phos; Balsamon the patriarch had long been well inclined toward the Gavrai.

The other two squads attacked the Grand Courtroom to rescue Alypia and use her as a rallying point for rebellion. Their luck did not match their commander's. Kalline had been caught returning to her mistress. Rhavas himself questioned her; he soon tore through her protests of innocence.

"She started to scream an hour before midnight," Marcus remembered Alypia saying, "and when she stopped, I knew the secret was lost. I never thought Rhavas was Avshar, but I was sure he was not one to let her die under torture till it suited him." The princess' would-be rescuers walked into ambush. None walked out again.

But Zigabenos was either a student of past coups or had a gift for sedition. From the High Temple he sent criers to every quarter of the city with a single message: "Come hear the patriarch!"

Everyone who claimed to be quoting Balsamon's speech for Scaurus gave a different version. The tribune thought that a great pity. He could all but see Balsamon on the High Temple's steps, probably wearing the shabby monk's robe he preferred to his patriarchal regalia. The moment's drama would have brought out the best in the old prelate—torches held high against the night, a sea of expectant faces waiting for what he would say.

Whatever his exact words were, they swung the city toward Thorisin Gavras in a quarter of an hour's time. Marcus was sure the sight of Ortaias Sphrantzes trussed up and shivering at the patriarch's feet had a good deal to do with that swing, as did Rhavas' thieving band rampaging through the shops of Videssos' merchants. Once given focus by Balsamon, the city mob was plenty capable of taking matters into its own hands.

"Almost you could feel sorry for Vardanes," Viridovix said, wiping grease from his chin with the back of his hand; from somewhere or other in the hungry city he had managed to come up with a fat roast partridge. "The puppet master found he couldn't be doing without his puppet after all."

After what he had seen in the bedchamber over the throne room, there was no room in Marcus for pity over Vardanes

Sphrantzes, but the Celt's observation was astute. Much like the Videssian army, the citizens of the capital found Ortaias' foppish, foolish pedantry more amusing than annoying, and so his uncle had no trouble ruling through him. But the elder Sphrantzes, though a far more able man than his nephew, was himself quite cordially despised throughout the city. Once Ortaias was overthrown, Vardanes found no one would obey him when he gave orders in his own name.

His messengers had hurried out of the palace with orders for the regiments on the walls to put down the rising. But some of those messengers deserted as soon as they were out of sight, others were waylaid by the mob, and those who carried out their missions found themselves ignored. The Sevastos' Videssian troops liked him no better than did their civilian cousins, and his mercenaries thought of their own safety before his—Gavras would likely pay them, too, if he sat on the throne.

In the end, only Rhavas' bandits and murderers stood by Sphrantzes. All hands were raised against them, just as they were against him; neither they nor he could afford fussiness.

"Vardanes got what he deserved," the tribune said. "There at the last he was more Avshar's puppet than even Ortaias had been his." Fish on a hook might be a better comparison yet, he thought.

Gorgidas said, "If Rhavas and Avshar are one and the same, we probably know why Doukitzes met the end he did."

"Eh? Why?" Marcus said foolishly, stifling a yawn. Two days of hard fighting left him too tired to follow the doctor's reasoning.

Gorgidas gave him a disdainful look; to the Greek, wits were for use. "As a threat, of course, or more likely a promise. You know the wizard has hated you since you bested him at swords that night in the Hall of the Nineteen Couches. He must have wished that were you under his knife, not just one of your men."

"Avshar hates everyone," Scaurus said, but Gorgidas' words carried an unpleasant ring of truth in them. The tribune had had the same thought himself and did not care for it; to be a viciously skilled mage's personal enemy was daunting. He was suddenly glad of his exhaustion; it left him numb to worry.

* * *

Despite the reassurances he had given himself that morning, Marcus was not eager to confront Helvis with the obvious fact that they were staying in Videssos. He put off the evil moment as long as he could, talking with his friends until his eyelids began gluing themselves shut.

The cool night air did little to rouse him as he walked to the barracks hall he had assigned to partnered legionaries. It was not the same one of the Romans' four they had used the year before. That hall, with its partitions for couples' privacy, had been primarily a stable to the Khamorth, and the tribune wished Hercules were here to run a river through it.

Though the hall he had chosen for partnered men was tidier than that, he found Helvis busily cleaning, not satisfied with the job the legionaries had done. "Hello," she said, pecking him on the cheek as she swept. "On campaign I don't mind dirt, but when we're settled, I can't abide it."

Under other circumstances that speech might have gladdened Scaurus, who was fairly fastidious himself when he had the time. But Helvis' voice was full of challenge. "We *are* going to be settled here, aren't we?" she pursued.

The tribune wished he had fallen asleep where he sat. Worn out as he was, he did not want a quarrel. He spread his hands placatingly. "Yes, for the time—"

"All right," Helvis said, so abruptly that he blinked. "I'm not blind; I can see it would be madness to leave Videssos now."

Marcus almost shouted in relief. He had hoped her years as a soldier's woman would make her understand how the land lay, but hadn't dared believe it.

She was not finished, though. The blue of her eyes reminded Scaurus of steel as she went on, "This time, well enough. But the next, we do what we must."

There was no doubt in the tribune's mind what she meant by that, but he was content to let it go. The issue was dead anyway, he thought; with the civil war done, defection would not come up again. He stripped off his armor and was asleep in seconds.

Thorisin Gavras was Avtokrator self-proclaimed for nearly a year; with Ortaias Sphrantzes beaten, no one disputed his claim. Yet he remained a pretender in the eyes of Videssian law until his formal coronation.

As with any other aspect of imperial life, formality implied ceremony. Gavras was hardly inside the city before the chamberlains took charge of him; the Empire's topsy-turvy politics had made them experts at preparing coronations on short notice. Thorisin, for once, did not squabble with them—his legitimacy as Emperor was too important to risk.

Thus Scaurus found himself routed from bed far earlier than would have suited him, given hasty instructions on his rôle in the upcoming ceremonial by a self-important eunuch, and placed at the head of a maniple of Romans close behind the sedan chair that would carry Thorisin from the palace compound to the High Temple of Phos, where Balsamon was to anoint and crown him Emperor of the Videssians.

Thorisin emerged, stiff-faced, from the Hall of the Nineteen Couches and walked slowly past his assembled troop contingents to the litter. By custom, the procession should have begun at the Grand Courtroom, but that building was already in the hands of a swarm of craftsmen repairing the damage it had suffered in the previous day's fighting.

In all other respects, though, the new Avtokrator followed traditional usage. On this day he put aside the soldier's garb he favored for Videssos' splendid imperial raiment. Above the red boots, his calves were covered by blue-dyed woolen leggings; his bejeweled belt was of links of gold, while the silken kilt hanging from it was again blue, with a border of white. His scabbard was similarly magnificent, but Marcus noticed that the sword in it was his usual saber, its leather grip dark with sweat stains. His tunic was scarlet, shot through with cloth of gold. Over it he wore a cape of pure white wool, closed at the throat with a golden fibula. His head was bare.

Namdaleni, Videssian soldiers, Videssian sailors, Khatrishers, more Videssians—as Thorisin Gavras strode by each company, the troops went to their knees and then to their bellies in the proskynēsis, acknowledging him their master. That was still a custom Marcus, used to Rome's republican ways, could not bring himself to follow. He and his men bowed deeply from the waist, but did not abase themselves before the Emperor.

For a moment Thorisin the man peeped through the imperial façade. "Stiff-necked bastard," he murmured out of the side of his mouth, so low only the tribune heard. Then he was past, settling himself into the blue and gilt sedan chair that was used only for the coronation journey.

Mertikes Zigabenos and seven of his men were the imperial bearers, their pride of place earned by the coup that had toppled Ortaias. Zigabenos himself stood at the front right, a thin-faced, lantern-jawed young man who wore his beard in the bushy Vaspurakaner style. Slung over his back he bore a large, bronze-faced oval shield. It was nothing like any a present-day Videssian would carry into battle, but Marcus had been briefed on the rôle it would soon play.

"Are we ready?" Gavras asked. Zigabenos gave a curt nod. "Then let's be at it," the Emperor said.

A dozen bright silk parasols popped open ahead of the traveling chair, further tokens—as if those were needed—of the imperial dignity. Zigabenos' men bent to the handles at their commander's signal, then straightened, raising Thorisin to their shoulders. Their pace a slow march, they followed the parasol bearers and Thorisin's strong-lunged herald out through the gardens of the palace compound toward the plaza of Palamas.

"Behold Thorisin Gavras, Avtokrator of the Videssians!" the herald roared to the multitude assembled there. The citizens of the capital, like the court functionaries, knew their role in the coronation. "Thou conquerest, Thorisin!" they cried: the traditional acclamation for new Emperors, delivered in the archaic Videssian of Phos' liturgy.

"Thou conquerest! Thou conquerest!" they thundered as the imperial procession made its way through the square. Marcus was surprised at their enthusiasm. From what he knew of the city's populace, they would turn out for any sort of spectacle, but would almost rather face the rack than admit they were impressed.

He understood a few seconds later, when palace servants began throwing handfuls of gold and silver coins into the crowd. The Videssians knew the largess to which they were entitled on a change of Emperors, whether the tribune did or not.

"Hey, the money's real gold! Hurrah for Thorisin Gavras!" someone yelled, startled out of formal responses by the quality of Thorisin's coinage. The cheers redoubled. But Scaurus knew the Vaspurakaner mines from which Thorisin had taken that gold were now in Yezda hands, and wondered how long it would be before the currency was cheapened again.

Still, this was no time for such gloomy thoughts, not with the applause of thousands ringing in his ears. "Hurrah for the Ronams!" he heard, and caught a glimpse of Arsaber standing tall in the middle of a knot of prosperous-looking merchants. One or more of them, he suspected, would go home lighter by a purse.

More cheering crowds lined Middle Street; every window of the three-story government office building had two or three faces peering from it. "Look at all the damned pen-pushers, wondering if Gavras'll have 'em for lunch," Gaius Philippus said. "Me, I hope he does."

A few blocks past the offices, the imperial procession turned north toward Phos' High Temple. The golden globes atop its spires gleamed in the bright morning sun.

The High Temple's great enclosed courtyard was, if anything, even more packed then the plaza of Palamas had been. Priests and soldiers held a lane open in the crush and kept the throng from flowing onto the broad stairs leading up to the shrine.

At the top of the stairs, somehow not dwarfed by the looming magnificence of the temple behind him, stood Balsamon. The partriarch was a fat, balding old man with a mischievous wit, but it suddenly struck Scaurus how great his power was in Videssos. Ortaias Sphrantzes was not the first Emperor he had helped cast down, and Thorisin Gavras would be—what? the third? the fifth?—over whose accession he had presided.

But his time was not quite come. Mertikes Zigabenos and his guardsmen carried Gavras through the crowd, which grew quiet, knowing what to expect. Followed by the ceremonial contingents, the Emperor's litter climbed the stairs. It halted two steps below the patriarch. The bearers lowered the chair to the ground. Thorisin climbed out and waited while his troops arranged themselves on the lower stairs.

Zigabenos unslung his shield and laid it, face up, before the Emperor. Thorisin stepped up onto it; it took his weight without buckling. Marcus was already marching up toward him, as were the other commanders of the units he had chosen to honor: the admiral Elissaios Bouraphos, Baanes Onomagoulos, Laon Pakhymer, Utprand Dagober's son, and a Namdalener the tribune did not know, a tall, dour man with pale eyes that showed nothing of the thoughts behind them. Scaurus guessed he had to be the great count Drax, perhaps included here to show that his mercenaries were still wanted by the Empire, even under its new master.

Once again, though, Zigabenos had precedence. He took from his belt a circlet of gold, which he offered to Thorisin Gavras. Following custom, Thorisin refused. Zigabenos offered it a second time and was again refused. At the third offering, Gavras bowed in acceptance. Zigabenos placed it on his head, declaring in a loud voice, "Thorisin Gavras, I confer on you the title of Avtokrator!"

That was the cue Scaurus and Gavras' other officers had awaited. They stooped and lifted the ceremonial shield to shoulder height, exalting the Emperor atop it. The waiting, expectantly silent crowd below burst into cries of "Thou conquerest, Thorisin! Thou conquerest!"

Baanes Onomagoulos' lame leg almost gave way beneath him as the officers lowered Thorisin to the ground once more, but Drax and Marcus, who stood on either side of the Videssian, took up the weight so smoothly the shield barely wavered.

"Steady, old boy. It's all done now," Gavras said as he stepped off it. Onomagoulos whispered an apology. Scaurus was glad to see the two men, usually so edgy in each other's company, behave graciously now. It seemed a good omen.

No sooner had Gavras descended from the shield than Balsamon, clad in vestments little less splendid than the Emperor's, came down to meet him. The patriarch performed no proskynesis; in the precinct of the Temple, his authority was second only to the Avtokrator's. He bowed low before Thorisin, the wispy gray strands of his beard curling over the imperial crown which he held on a blue silk cushion.

As the patriarch straightened, his eyes, lively beneath bushy, still-black brows, flicked over Thorisin's companions. That half-amused, half-ironic gaze settled on Scaurus for a moment. The tribune blinked—had Balsamon winked at him? He'd wondered that once before, inside the Temple last year. Surely not, and yet—

Again, as before, he was never sure. Balsamon's glance was elsewhere before he could make up his mind. The patriarch fumbled, produced a small silver flask. "Not the least of

Phos' inventions, pockets," he remarked. The top rank of soldiers might have heard him; the second one surely did not.

Then his reedy tenor expanded to fill the wide enclosure. A younger priest stood close by to relay what he said, but there was no need. "Bow your head," Balsamon said to Gavras, and the Avtokrator of the Videssians obeyed.

The patriarch unstoppered the little flask, poured its contents over Thorisin's head. The oil was golden in the morning sunlight; Scaurus caught myrrh's sweet, musky fragrance and the more bitter but still pleasing scent of aloes. "As Phos' light shines on us all," Balsamon declared, "so may his blessings pour down on you with this anointing."

"May it be so," Thorisin responded soberly.

Still holding the crown in his left hand, Balsamon used his right to rub the oil over Thorisin's head. As he did so, he spoke the Videssians' most basic prayer, the assembled multitude echoing his words: "We bless thee, Phos, Lord with the great and good mind, by thy grace our protector, watchful beforehand that the great test of life may be decided in our favor."

"Amen," the crown finished. Marcus heard the Namdaleni add their own closing to the Videssian creed: "On this we stake our very souls." Utprand spoke the addition firmly, but Drax, closer yet, was silent. Scaurus' head turned in surprise —had the great count adopted the Empire's usage? He saw Drax's lips soundlessly shaping the Namdalener clause and wondered whether courtesy or expedience caused his discretion.

The "Amens," fortunately, were loud enough to drown out most of the sound of heresy; it would have been a fine thing, Marcus thought, to have the coronation interrupted by a religious riot.

Balsamon took the crown, a low dome of gold inset with pearls, sapphires, and rubies, and placed it firmly on Thorisin Gavras' lowered head. The throng below let out a soft sigh. It was done; a new Avtokrator ruled Videssos. The murmuring died away quickly, for the crowd was waiting for the patriarch to speak.

He paused a moment in thought before beginning, "Well, my friends, we have been disabused of a mistake and abused by it as well. A throne is only a few sticks, plated with gold and covered by velvet, but it's said to enoble whatever funda-

ment rests on it, by some magic subtler even than they work in
the Academy. Having a throne of my own, I've always suspected that was nonsense, you know—" One bushy eyebrow
raised just enough to show his listeners they were not to take
this last too seriously. "—but sometimes the choice is not
between bad and good but rather bad and worse."

"Without an Avtokrator we would have perished, like a
body without its head." Marcus thought of Mavrikios' end and
shivered to himself. Coming from republican Rome, he had
doubts about that statement as well, but Videssos, he reflected, had been an empire so long it was likely true for her.

Balsamon went on, "There is always hope when a new
Emperor sits the throne, no matter how graceless he may
seem, and a new sovereign's advisers may serve him as a
man's brains do his face, that is, to give form to what would
otherwise be blank."

Someone shouted, "Phos knows Ortaias has no brains of
his own!" and drew a laugh. Marcus joined it, but at the same
time he recognized the fine line Balsamon was treading, trying
to justify his actions to the crowd and, more important, to
Thorisin Gavras.

The patriarch returned to his analogy. "But there was a
canker eating at those brains, one whose nature I learned late,
but not too late. And so I made what amends I could, as you
see here." He bowed low once more; Marcus heard him stage-
whisper to Gavras, "Your turn now."

With a curt nod, the Emperor looked out over the throng.
"For all his fancy talk, Ortaias Sphrantzes knows no more of
war than how to run from it and no more of rule than stealing
it when the rightful holder's away. Given five years, he'd have
made old Strobilos look good to you—unless the damned
Yezda took the city first, which is likely."

Thorisin was no polished rhetorician; like Mavrikios, he
had a straightforward style, adapted from the battlefield. To
the sophisticated listeners of the capital, it was novel but effective.

"There're not a lot of promises to make," he went on.
"We're in a mess, and I'll do my best to get us out the other
side in one piece. I will say this—Phos willing, you won't
want to curse my face every time you see it on a goldpiece."

That pledge earned real applause; Ortaias' debased coinage
had won him no love. Scaurus, though, still wondered how

Thorisin planned to carry it out. If Videssos' pen-pushers with all their bureaucratic sleights of hand, could not keep up the quality of the Empire's money, could a soldier like Gavras?

"One last thing," the Emperor said. "I know the city followed Ortaias at first for lack of anything better, and then perforce, because his troops held it. Well and good; I'll hear no slanders over who backed whom or who said what about me before yesterday morning, so rest easy there." A low mutter of approval and relief ran through the crowd. Marcus had heard of the informers who had flourished in Rome during the civil war between the Marians and Sulla, and of the purges and counterpurges. He gave Gavras credit for magnanimous good sense and waited for the Emperor's warning against future plots.

Thorisin, however, said only, "You'll not get more talk from me now. I said that was the last thing and I meant it. If all you wanted was empty words, you might as well have kept Ortaias."

Watching the crowd slowly disperse, a dissatisfied Gaius Philippus said, "He should have put the fear of their Phos in 'em."

But the tribune was coming to understand the Videssians better than his lieutenant, and realized the armored ranks of soldiers on the High Temple's steps were a stronger precaution against conspiracy than any words. An overt threat from the new Avtokrator would have roused contempt. Gavras was wise enough to see that. There was more subtlety to him than showed at first, Scaurus thought, and was rather glad of it.

"What should we do with him?" That was Komitta Rhangavve's voice, merciless and a little shrill with anger. She answered her own question: "We should make him such an example that no one would dare rebel for the next fifty years. Put out his eyes with hot irons, lop off his ears and then his hands and feet, and burn what's left in the plaza of the Ox."

Thorisin Gavras, still in full imperial regalia, whistled in half-horrified respect for his mistress' savagery. "Well, Ortaias, how does that program sound to you? You'd be the one most affected by it, after all." His chuckle could not have been pleasant in his defeated rival's ears.

Ortaias' arms were bound behind him; one of Zigabenos'

troopers sat on either side of him on the couch in the patriarch's library. He looked as if he would sooner be hiding under it. In Scaurus' mind the young noble had never cut a prepossessing figure: he was tall, skinny, and awkward, with a patchy excuse for a beard. Clad only in a thin linen shift, his hair awry and his face filthy and frightened, at the moment he seemed to the tribune more a pitiful figure than a wicked one or one to inspire hatred.

There was a tremor in his high voice as he answered, "Had I won, I would not have treated you so."

"No, probably not," Gavras admitted. "You haven't the stomach for it. A safe, quiet poison in the night would suit you better."

A rumble of agreement ran around the heavy elm table that filled most of the floor space in the library—from Komitta, from Onomagoulos and Elissaios Bouraphos, from Drax and Utprand Dagober's son, from Mertikes Zigabenos. Nor could Marcus deny that Thorisin likely spoke the truth. He could not help noticing, though, the patriarch's silence and, perhaps more surprisingly, Alypia Gavras's.

In a somber tunic and skirt of dark green, the paint scrubbed from her face, the princess seemed once more to be as Scaurus had known her in the past: cool, competent, almost forbidding. He was pleased to see her at this council, a sign that, contrary to her fears, Thorisin still had confidence in her. But she kept her eyes downcast and would not look at Ortaias Sphrantzes. The silver wine cup in her hand shook ever so slightly.

Balsamon leaned back in his chair until it teetered on its hind legs, reached over his shoulder to pluck a volume from a half-empty shelf. Scaurus knew his audience chamber, on the other hand, was so full of books it was nearly useless for its intended function. But then, the patriarch enjoyed confounding expectations, in small things as well as great.

Thus the tribune was unsurprised to see him put the slim leather-bound text in his lap without opening it. Balsamon said to Komitta, "You know, my dear, imitating the Yezda is not the way to best them."

The reproof was mild, but she bristled. "What have they to do with this? An aristocrat deals with his foes so they can harm him no further." Her voice rose. "And a true aristocrat pays no heed to such milksop counsels as yours, priest, though as your father was a fuller I would not expect you to know such things."

"Komitta, will you—" Thorisin tried, too late, to cut off his hot-tempered mistress. Onomagoulos and Zigabenos stared at her in dismay; even Drax and Utprand, to whom Balsamon was no more than a heretic, were not used to hearing clerics reviled.

But the patriarch's wit was a sharper weapon than outrage. "Aye, it's true I grew up with the stench of piss, but then, at least, we got pure bleached cloth from it. Now—" He wrinkled up his nose and looked sidelong at Komitta.

She spluttered furiously, but Gavras overrode her: "Quiet, there. You had that coming." She sat in stiff, rebellious silence. Not for the first time, Marcus admired the Emperor for being able to bring her to heel—sometimes, at any rate. Thorisin went on, "I wasn't going to do as you said anyway. I tell you frankly I can't brook it, not for this sniveling wretch."

"Be so good as not to waste my time with such meetings henceforth, then, if you have no intention of listening to my advice." Komitta rose, graceful with anger, and stalked out of the room, a procession of one.

Gavras swung round on Marcus. "Well, sirrah, what say you? I sometimes think I have to pull your thoughts like teeth. Shall I send him to the Kynegion and have done?" A small hunting-park near the High Temple, the Kynegion was also Videssos' chief execution grounds.

In Rome capital punishment was an extraordinary sentence, but, thought Scaurus, it had been meted out to Catiline, who aimed at overthrowing the state. He answered slowly, "Yes, I think so, if it can be done without turning all the seal-stampers against you."

"Bugger the seal-stampers," Bouraphos ground out. "They're good for nothing but telling you why you can't have the gold for the refits you need."

"Aye, they're rabbity little men, the lot of 'em," Baanes Onomagoulos said. "Shorten him and put fear in all their livers."

But Thorisin, rubbing his chin as he considered, was watching the tribune in reluctant admiration. "You have a habit of pointing out unpleasant facts, don't you? I'm too much a soldier to like taking the bureaucrats seriously, but there's no denying they have power—too much, by Phos."

"Who says there's no denying it?" Onomagoulos growled. He jabbed a scornful thumb at Ortaias Sphrantzes. "Look at this uprooted weed here. This is what the pen-pushers have for a leader."

"What about Vardanes?" That was Zigabenos, who had been in the city while Ortaias reigned and his uncle ruled.

Onomagoulos blinked, but said, "Well, what about him? Another coward, if ever there was one. Shove steel in a pen-pusher's face, and he's yours to do with as you will."

"Which is, of course, why there have been bureaucrats or men backed by bureaucrats on the imperial throne for forty-five of the last fifty-one years," Alypia Gavra said, her measured tones more effective than open mockery. "It's why the bureaucrats and their mercenaries broke—how many? two dozen? three?—rebellions by provincial nobles in that time, and why they converted almost all the peasant militia in Videssos to tax-bound serfs during that stretch of time. Clear proof they're walkovers, is it not?"

Onomagoulos flushed right up to the bald crown of his head. He opened his mouth, closed it without saying anything. Thorisin was taken by a sudden coughing fit. Ortaias Sphrantzes, with nothing at all to lose, burst into a sudden giggle to see his captors quarrel among themselves.

Still beaming at his niece, the Emperor asked her, "What do you want us to do with the scapegrace, then?"

For the first time since the meeting began, she turned her eyes toward the man whose Empress, at least in name, she had been. For all the emotion she betrayed, she might have been examining a carcass of beef. At last she said, "I don't think he could be put to death without stirring up enmities better left unraised. For my part, I have no burning need to see him dead. He in his way was as much his uncle's prisoner as was I, and no more in control of his fate or actions."

From his wretched seat on the couch, Ortaias said softly, "Thank you, Alypia," and, quite uncharacteristically, fell silent again. The princess gave no notice that she heard him.

Baanes Onomagoulos, still smarting from her sarcasm, saw a chance for revenge. He said, "Thorisin, of course she will speak for him. And why should she not? The two of them, after all, are man and wife, their concerns bound together by a shared couch."

"Now you wait one minute—" Scaurus began hotly, but

Alypia needed no one to defend her. Moving with the icy control she showed on most occasions, she rose from her seat and dashed her wine cup in Onomagoulos' face. Coughing and cursing, he rubbed at his stinging eyes. The thick red wine dripped from his pointed beard onto his embroidered silk tunic, plastering it to his chest.

His hand started to seek his sword hilt, but he thought better of that even before Elissaios Bouraphos grabbed his wrist. Through eyelids already swelling shut, he looked to Thorisin Gavras, but found nothing to satisfy him on the Emperor's face. Muttering, "No one uses me thus," he climbed from his chair and limped toward the door, his painful gait an unintentioned parody of Komitta Rhangavve's lithe exit a few minutes before.

"You may be interested in knowing," Balsamon's voice pursued him, "that last night I declared annulled the marriage, if such it may be called, between Sphrantzes and Alypia Gavra—at the princess' urgent request. You may also be interested in knowing that the priest who performed that marriage is at a monastery on the southern bank of the Astris River, a stone's throw from the steppe—and I ordered that the day I learned of the wedding, not last night."

But Onomagoulos only snarled, "Bah!" and slammed the heavy door behind him.

An ivory figurine wobbled and fell to the floor. Balsamon, more distressed than he had been at any time during the meeting, leaped to his feet with a cry of alarm and hurried over to it. He wheezed as he bent to retrieve it, peered anxiously at the palm-high statuette.

"No harm, Phos be praised," he said, setting it carefully back on its stand. Marcus remembered his passion for ivories from Makuran, the kingdom that had been Videssos' western neighbor and rival until the Yezda came down off the steppe and conquered it less than a lifetime ago. More to himself than anyone else, the patriarch complained, "Things haven't been where they ought to be since Gennadios left."

The dour priest had been as much Balsamon's watchdog as companion, Scaurus knew, and there were times when the patriarch took unecclesiastical glee in baiting him. Now that he was gone, it seemed Balsamon missed him. "What became of him?" the tribune asked, idly curious.

"Eh? I told you," Balsamon answered peevishly. "He's

spending his time by the Astris, praying the Khamorth don't decide to swim over and raid the henhouse."

"Oh," Marcus said. The patriarch had not named the priest who married Alypia to Ortaias, but he was not surprised Gennadios was the man. He had been the creature of Mavrikios' predecessor Strobilos Sphrantzes and doubtless stayed loyal to the clan. It would have been commendable, Scaurus thought, in a better cause; he could not work up much regret at the priest's exile.

"Are we quite through shilly-shallying about?" Thorisin asked with ill-concealed impatience.

"Shilly-shallying?" Balsamon exclaimed, mock-indignant. "Nonsense! We've trimmed this council by a fifth in a half hour's time. May you do as well with the pen-pushers!"

"Hmp," the Emperor said. He plucked a hair from his beard, crossed his eyes to examine it closely. It was white. He threw it away. Turning back to Alypia, he asked, "You say you don't want his head?"

"No, not really," she replied. "He's a foolish puppy, not as brave as he should be, and a dreadful bore." Indignation struggled for a moment with the fright on Ortaias Sphrantzes' face. "But you'd soon run short of subjects, uncle, if you did to death everyone who fit those bills. Were Vardanes here, now—" Her voice did not rise, but a sort of grim eagerness made it frightening to hear.

"Aye." Thorisin's right hand curled into a fist. "Well," he resumed, "suppose we let the losel live." Ortaias leaned forward in sudden hope; his guards pushed him back onto the couch. The Emperor ignored him, growling, "Skotos can pull me down to hell before I just turn him loose. He'd be plotting again before the rope marks faded. He has to know—and the people have to know—what a complete and utter idiot he's been, and he'll pay the price for it."

"Of course," Alypia nodded; she was at least as good a practical politician as her uncle. "How does this sound . . . ?"

Almost all the units which accompanied Thorisin Gavras on his coronation march had been dismissed to their barracks while the Emperor and his councilors debated Ortaias Sphrantzes' fate. Only a couple of squads of Videssian body-guards waited for the Emperor outside the patriarchal residence, along with the dozen parasol bearers who were an Avtokrator's inevitable public companions.

The streets were nearly empty of spectators, too. A few Videssians stood and gawped at the shrunken imperial party as it made its way back toward the palaces, but most of the city folk had already found other things to amuse them.

Thus Marcus saw the tall man pushing his way toward them at a good distance, but thought nothing much of him— just another Videssian with a bit of a seaman's roll in his walk. In the great port the capital was, that hardly rated notice.

Even when the fellow waved to Thorisin Gavras, Scaurus all but ignored him. So many people had done so much cheering and greeting that the tribune was numb to it. But when the man shouted, "Hail to your Imperial Majesty!" ice walked up Scaurus' spine. That raspy bass, better suited to cutting through wind and wave than to the city, could only belong to Taron Leimmokheir.

The tribune had met Ortaias' drungarios of the fleet but twice, once on a pitch-dark beach and the other time when being chased by his galley. Neither occasion had been ideal for marking Leimmokheir's features. Nor were those remarkable: perhaps forty-five, the admiral had a rawboned look to him, his face lined and tanned by the sun, his hair and beard too gray to show much of their own sun bleaching.

If Marcus, then, had an excuse for not recognizing Leimmokheir at sight, the same could not be said for Thorisin Gavras, who had dealt with the drungarios almost daily when his brother was Emperor. Yet Thorisin was more taken aback by Leimmokheir's appearance than was the tribune. He stopped in his tracks, gaping as at a ghost.

His halt let the admiral elbow his way through the remaining guardsmen. Exclaiming, "Congratulations to you, Gavras! Well done!" Leimmokheir went to his knees and then to his belly in the middle of the street.

He was still down in the proskynesis when Thorisin finally found his voice. "Of all the colossal effrontery, this takes the prize," he whispered. Then, with a sudden full-throated bellow of rage, "Guards! Seize me the treacherous rogue!"

"Here, what's this? Take your hands off me!" Leimmokheir struck out against his assailants, but they were many to his one—and there could hardly be a worse position for self-defense than the proskynesis. In seconds he was hauled upright, his arms pinned painfully behind him—almost exactly, Marcus thought irrelevantly, as Vardanes Sphrantzes had held Alypia.

The drungarios glared at Thorisin Gavras. "What's all this in aid of?" he shouted, still trying to twist free. "Is this the thanks you give everyone who wouldn't fall at your knees and worship? If it is, what's that snake of a Namdalener doing beside you? He'd sell his mother for two coppers, if he thought she'd bring so much."

The count Drax snarled and took a step forward, but Thorisin stopped him with a gesture. "You're a fine one to talk of serpents, Leimmokheir, you and your treachery, you and your hired assassins after a pledge of safe-conduct."

Taron Leimmokheir's tufted eyebrows—almost a match for Balsamon's—crawled halfway up his forehead like a pair of gray caterpillars. Amazingly, he threw back his head and laughed. "I don't know what you drink these days, boy." Gavras reddened dangerously, but Leimmokheir did not notice. "But pass me the bottle if there's any left when you're done. Whatever's in it makes you see the strangest things." He spoke as he might to any equal, ignoring the guardsmen clinging to him.

Scaurus remembered what he'd thought the first time he heard the drungarios' voice—that there was no guile in him. That first impression returned now, as strong as before. His two years in the Empire, though, had taught him that deceit was everywhere, all too often artfully disguised as candor.

That was how the Emperor saw it. If anything, his anger was hotter at seeing himself betrayed by a man he had thought trustworthy. He said, "You can lie till you drop, Leimmokheir, but you're a tomfool to try. There's no testimony for you to argue away. I was there, you know, and saw your hired manslayers with my own eyes—"

"That's more than I did," Leimmokheir shot back, but Gavras stormed on.

"Aye, and fleshed my blade in a couple as well." The Emperor turned to the guards. "Take this fine, upstanding gentleman to gaol. We'll give him a nice, quiet place to think until I decide what to do with him. Go on, get him out of my sight." Holding the drungarios as they were, the troopers could not salute, but they nodded and hauled him away.

Only then did Leimmokheir really seem to understand this was not some practical joke. "Gavras, you bloody nincompoop, I still don't know what in Skotos' frozen hell you think I did, but I didn't do it, whatever it was. Phos have mercy on you for tormenting an innocent man. Watch that, you clumsy oafs!" he shouted to his captors as they dragged him through a puddle. His protests faded in the distance.

Matters pertaining to Ortaias Sphrantzes had been scheduled for two days later, but it was pelting down rain, and they had to be postponed. It rained again the next day, and the next. Watching the dirty gray clouds rolling out of the north, Scaurus realized the storm was but the first harbinger of the long fall rains. Where had the year gone? he asked himself; that question never had an answer.

At last the weather relented. The north wind still blew moist and cool, but the sun was bright; it flashed dazzlingly off still-wet walls and made every lingering drop of water into a rainbow. And if it had not had enough time to dry every seat in Videssos' huge Amphitheater, the people whose bottoms were dampened did not complain. The spectacle they were anticipating made up for such minor inconveniences.

"Sure and there's enough people," Viridovix said, his eyes traveling from the legionaries' central spine up and up the sides of the great limestone bowl. "The poor omadhauns in the last row won't be after seeing what's happening today till next week, so far away they are."

"More Celtic nonsense," Gaius Philippus said with a snort. "I'll grant you, though, we won't be much bigger than bugs to them." His own practiced gaze slid over the crowd. "Worthless, most of 'em, like the fat ones back home——" He meant Rome, and Marcus winced to be reminded. "——who come out on the feast days to watch the gladiators kill each other."

The tribune agreed with that assessment; the buzz of conversation floating out of the stands had a cruel undercurrent, and on the faces in the first few rows, the ones close enough to see clearly, the air of vulpine avidity was all too plain.

He caught a glimpse of Gorgidas in the contingent of foreign envoys some little distance down the spine. As an aspiring historian, the Greek had wanted a close-up view of this day's festivities, and preferred the ambassadors' company to disguising himself as a legionary. He was listening to some tale from Arigh Arghun's son and scribbling quick notes on a three-leafed wax tablet. Two more hung at his belt.

Taso Vones, the ambassador from Khatrish, waved cheerily to the tribune, who grinned back. He liked the little Khatrisher, whose sharp, jolly wits belied his mousy appearance.

Horns filled the Amphitheater with bronzen music. The crowd's noise rose expectantly. Preceded by his retinue of parasol bearers, Thorisin Gavras strode into the arena. The applause was loud as he mounted the dozen steps that led up to the spine, but it fell short of the deafening tumult Scaurus had heard before in the Amphitheater. The Emperor, for once, was not what the populace had turned out to see.

Each unit of troops Gavras passed presented arms as he went by; at Gaius Philippus' barked command the Romans held their *pila* out at arm's length ahead of them. Gavras nodded slightly. He and the senior centurion, both lifelong soldiers, understood each other very well.

Not so the bureaucrats Thorisin passed on his way to the throne. They looked nervous as they bowed to their new sovereign; Goudeles, for one, was pale against his robe of dark blue silk. But Gavras paid them no more attention than he did to the clutter of a millenium and a half of heroic art that he passed: statues bronze, statues marble—some painted, some not—statues chryselephantine, even an obelisk of gilded granite long ago taken as booty from Makuran.

The Emperor grew animated once more when he came to the foreign dignitaries. He paused for a moment to say something to Gawtruz of Thatagush, at which the squat, swarthy envoy nodded. Then Gavras included Taso Vones in the conversation, whatever it was. The Khatrisher laughed and gave a rueful tug at his beard, as unkempt as Gawtruz'.

Even without hearing the words, Marcus understood the byplay. He, too, thought the fuzzy beard looked foolish on Vones, who could have passed for a Videssian without it. But his ruler still enforced a few Khamorth ways, in memory of his ancestors who had carved the state from Videssos' eastern provinces centuries before, and so the little envoy was doomed to wear the shaggy whiskers he despised.

Thorisin seated himself on a high stool at the center of the Amphitheater's spine; the chair was backless so all the spectators could see him. His parasol bearers grouped themselves around him. He raised his right hand in a gesture of command;

the crowd grew quiet and leaned forward in their seats, craning their necks for a better view.

They all knew where to look. The gate that came open was the one through which, on most days, race horses entered the Amphitheater. Today the procession was much shorter: Thorisin Gavras' deep-chested herald, two Videssian guardsmen gorgeous in gilded cuirasses, and a groom leading a single donkey.

Ortaias Sphrantzes rode the beast, but it needed a guide nonetheless, for its saddle was reversed, and he sat facing its tail. Long familiar with their own idiom of humiliation, the watching Videssians burst into gaffaws. An overripe fruit came sailing out of the stands, to squash at the donkey's feet. Others followed, but the barrage was mercifully short; Videssos had been under siege too recently for there to be much food to waste.

The herald, nimbly sidestepping a hurtling melon, cried out, "Behold Ortaias Sphrantzes, who thought to rebel against the rightful Avtokrator of the Videssians, his Imperial Majesty Thorisin Gavras!" The crowd shouted back, "Thou conquerest, Gavras! Thou conquerest!"—as heartily, Marcus thought, as if they had forgotten that a week before they called Ortaias their lord.

Accompanied by the crowd's jeers, Ortaias and his guardians made a slow circuit of the Amphitheater, the herald all the while booming out his condemnation. Marcus heard more fruit splattering around Sphrantzes; the breeze brought him a rotten egg's gagging stench.

Some of the hurled refuse found its target. By the time Ortaias Sphrantzes came back into the tribune's sight, his robe was dyed with bright splashes of pulp and juice. The donkey he rode, Scaurus decided, had to be drugged. It ambled on placidly, pausing only to dip its head to nibble at a fragment of apple in its path. Its leader jerked on the long guide rope, and it abandoned the tidbit to move ahead once more.

At last it completed the course and halted in front of the gate through which it had entered. The two guards came back and lifted Ortaias off his mount, then led him up before Thorisin Gavras.

When they released his arms, he went to the ground in a proskynesis. The Emperor rose from his stool. "We see your submission," he said, speaking for the first time, and such were the acoustics of the Amphitheater that his words, though spoken in the tone of ordinary conversation, could be heard in the arena's uppermost rows. "Do you then renounce, now and forever, all claim upon the sovereignty of our Empire, protected by Phos?"

"Indeed yes, I yield the throne to you. I—" The moment the answer Thorisin Gavras required was complete, he cut Ortaias off with the same imperious gesture he had used to summon him forth.

Gaius Philippus gave the ghost of a chuckle. "Some things never change. I'd bet the scrawny bastard just had a two-hour abdication speech nipped in the bud—and a good thing, too, says I."

Thorisin spoke again. "Receive now the reward for your treachery."

The guardsmen raised Ortaias to his feet. They quickly pulled the robe off over his head. The crowd whooped; Gaius Philippus muttered "Scrawny" again. One of the guards, the larger and more muscular of the pair, stepped behind the luckless Sphrantzes and delivered a tremendous kick to his bare backside. Ortaias yelped and fell to his knees.

Viridovix clucked in disappointment. "The Gavras is too soft by half," he said. "He should be packing a wickerwork all full of this spalpeen and howsoever many followed him, and then lighting it off. There'd been a spectacle for the people to remember, now."

"You and Komitta Rhangavve," Marcus said to himself, slightly aghast at the Gaul's straightforward savagery.

"'Tis what the holy druids would do," Viridovix said righteously. That, Scaurus knew, was only too true. The Celtic priests appeased their gods by sacrificing criminals to them . . . or innocent folk, if no criminals were handy.

As Ortaias Sphrantzes, rubbing the bruised part, rose to his feet, one of Phos' priests descended from the Amphitheater's spine and approached him, carrying scissors and a long, gleaming razor. The crowd fell silent; religion was always respected in Videssos. But Marcus knew no blood sacrifice was in the offing here. Another priest followed the first, this one bearing a plain blue robe and a copy of Phos' sacred scriptures, glorious in its binding of enameled bronze.

Ortaias bowed his head to the first priest. The scissors flashed in the autumn sun. A lock of stringy brown hair fell at the deposed Emperor's feet, then another and another, until only a short stubble remained. Then the razor came into play; Sphrantzes' scalp was soon shiny bare.

The second priest stepped forward. Folding the monk's robe over the crook of his arm, he held out the sacred writings to Ortaias and said, "Behold the law under which you shall live if you choose. If in your heart you feel you can observe it, enter the monastic life; if not, speak now."

But Ortaias, with everyone else, was aware of the penalty for balking. "I will observe it," he said. The great-voiced herald relayed his words to the crowd. There was a collective sigh. The creation of a monk was always a serious business, even when the reasons for it were blatantly political. Nor could faith and politics be neatly separated in the Empire; Scaurus thought of Zemarkhos in Amorion and felt his mouth compress in a thin, hard line.

The priest repeated the offer of admission twice more, received the same response each time. He handed the holy book to his colleague, then robed the new monk in his monastic garb, saying, "As the garment of Phos' blue covers your naked body, so may his righteousness enfold your heart and preserve it from all evil." Again the herald boomed out the petition.

"So may it be," Ortaias replied, but his voice was lost in the thousands echoing his prayer. Despite himself Marcus was moved, marveling at Videssos' force of faith. Almost there were times he wished he shared it, but, like Gorgidas, he was too well rooted in the perceptible world to feel comfortable in that of the spirit.

Ortaias Sphrantzes left the Amphitheater through the same gate he had entered, arm in arm with the two priests who had made him part of their fellowship. Well satisfied with the day's show, the crowd began to disperse. Venders took up their calls: "Wine! Sweet wine!" "Spiced cakes!" "Holy images to protect your beloved!" "Raiii—sins!"

Unhappy to the end, Gausi Philippus grumbled, "And now he'll spend the rest of his stupid days living the high life here in the city, but with a bald head and a blue robe to make it all right."

"Not exactly," Marcus chuckled; Thorisin might be blunt, but he was hardly as naïve as that. The tribune thought it altogether fitting that Gennadios should gain some company in his monastery at Videssos' distant frontier. He and the new Brother Ortaias, no doubt, would have a great deal to talk about.

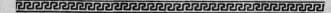

X

"WHAT DO YOU MEAN, NO FUNDS ARE AVAILABLE?" THORI-
sin Gavras asked, his voice dangerously calm. His gaze
speared the logothete as if that financial official were an
enemy to be ridden down.

The Hall of the Nineteen Couches grew still. Marcus could
hear the torches crackling, hear the wind sighing outside. If he
turned his head, he knew he would see snowflakes kissing the
Hall's wide windows; winter in the capital was not as harsh as
in the westland plateaus, but it was bad enough. He pulled his
cloak tighter round himself.

The logothete gulped. He was about thirty, thin, pale, and
precise. His name, Scaurus remembered, was Addaios
Vourtzes; he was some sort of distant cousin to the city governor of the northeastern town of Imbros. He had to gather himself before going on in the face of the Emperor's hostility.

But go on he did, at first haltingly and then with more
animation as his courage returned. "Your Majesty, you expect
too much from the tax-gathering facilities available to us. That
any revenues whatsoever have been collected should be
praised as one of Phos' special miracles. The recent unpleas-
antness—" Now there, thought the tribune, was a fine, bureaucratic euphemism for civil war. "—and, worse, the
presence of large numbers of unauthorized interlopers—" By
which he meant the Yezda, Marcus knew. "—on imperial soil,
have made any accrual of surplusage a manifest impossibility."

What was he talking about? the tribune wondered irritably.

His Videssian was fluent by now, but this jargon left him floundering.

Baanes Onomagoulos' translation was rough but serviceable. "By which you're saying that your precious dues-takers pissed themselves whenever they thought they saw a nomad, and turned tail before they could find out if they were right." The noble gave a coarse laugh.

"That's the way of it," Drax the Namdalener agreed. He turned a calculating eye on Vourtzes. "From what I've seen of you pen-pushers, any excuse not to pay is a good one. By the Wager, you'd think the money came out of your purse, not the peasants'."

"Well said," Thorisin exclaimed, his usual distrust for the islanders quenched when Drax echoed a sentiment he heartily shared. The count nodded his thanks.

Vourtzes proffered a thick roll of parchment. "Here are the figures to support the position I have outlined—"

Numbers in a ledger, though, meant little to the soldiers he faced. Thorisin slapped the scroll aside, snarling, "To the crows with this gibberish! It's gold I need, not excuses."

Elissaios Bouraphos said, "These fornicating seal-stampers think paper will patch anything. That was why I put in with you, your Highness—I kept getting reports instead of repairs —and sick I got of them, too."

"If you will examine the returns I have presented to you," Vourtzes said with rather desperate determination, "you will reach the inescapable conclusion that—"

"—The bureaucrats are out to bugger honest men," Onomagoulos finished for him. "Everyone knows that, and has since my grandfather's day. All you ever wanted was to keep the power in your own slimy hands. And if a soldier reached the throne despite you, you starved him with tricks like this."

"There is no trickery!" Vourtzes wailed, his distress wringing a simple declarative sentence from him.

Marcus had no love for the harried logothete, but he recognized sincerity when he heard it. "I think there may be something in what this fellow claims," he said.

Thorisin and his marshals stared at the Roman as if disbelieving their ears. "Whose side are you on?" the Emperor demanded. Even Addaios Vourtzes' look of gratitude was wary. He seemed to suspect some trap that would only lead to deeper trouble for him.

But Alypia Gavra watched the tribune alertly; her expression was masked as usual, but Scaurus could read no disapproval in it. And unlike the Videssian military men, he had had civilian as well as warlike experience, and knew how much easier it was to spend money than to collect it.

Ignoring Thorisin's half-accusation, he persisted, "Gathering taxes could hardly have been easy this past year. For one thing, sir, your men and Ortaias' both must have gone into some parts of the westlands, with neither side getting all it should. And Baanes has to be partly right—with the Yezda loose, parts of the Empire aren't safe for tax collectors. But even where there are no Yezda at any given moment, the lands they've ravaged still yield no cash—you can't get wool from a bald sheep."

"A mercenary with comprehension of basic fiscal realities," Vourtzes said to himself. "How extraordinary." Almost as an afterthought, he added, "Thank you," to the tribune.

The Emperor looked thoughtful, but Baanes Onomagoulos' face grew stormy; Scaurus, watching the noble's bare scalp go red, suddenly regretted his chance-chosen metaphor.

Alypia took another jab at Baanes. "Not all arrears are the tax collectors' fault," she said. "If big landowners paid what they owed, the treasury would be better off."

"That is very definitely the case," Vourtzes said. "Legitimately credentialed agents of the fisc have been assaulted, on occasion even killed, in the attempt to assess payments due on prominent estates, some of them properties of clans represented in this very chamber." While he named no names, he, too, was looking at Onomagoulos.

The noble's glare was hot enough to roast the bureaucrat, Marcus, and Alypia Gavra all together. The tribune, seeing Alypia's eyebrows arch, nodded almost imperceptibly in recognition of a common danger.

As he had in Balsamon's library, Elissaios Bouraphos tried to ease Onomagoulos' wrath, putting a hand on his shoulder and talking to him in a low voice. But the admiral was himself a possessor of wide estates, and said to Thorisin, "You know why we held back payments to the pen-pushers—aye, you did the same on your lands before your brother threw Strobilos out. Why should we give them the rope to hang us by?"

"I won't say you're wrong there," the Emperor admitted with a chuckle. "Since I'm not a pen-pusher, though, Elissaios, surely you'll pay in everything you owe without a whimper?"

"Surely," Bouraphos said. Then he whimpered, so convincingly that everyone at the table burst into laughter. Even Addaios Vourtzes' mouth twitched. Marcus revised his estimate of the admiral, which had not included a sense of humor.

Utprand Dagober's son spoke up for the first time, and the somber warning in his voice snuffed out the mirth. "You can wrangle all you like over who pays w'at. W'at needs to be settled is who pays me."

"Rest easy," Thorisin said. "I don't see your lads on the streets begging for pennies."

"No," Utprand said, "nor will you." That was not warning, but unmistakable threat. The great count Drax looked pained at his countryman's plain speaking, but Utprand ignored him. They did not care much for each other; Scaurus suspected the Namdaleni were not immune to the disease of faction.

Gavras, for his part, was one to appreciate frankness. "You'll have your money, outlander," he said. Seeing Addaios Vourtzes purse his lips to protest, he turned to the logothete. "Let me guess," he said sourly. "You haven't got it."

"Essentially, that is correct. As I have attempted to indicate, the precise situation is outlined—"

The Emperor cut him off as brusquely as he had Ortaias Sphrantzes in the Amphitheater. "Can you bring in enough to keep everyone happy till spring?"

Faced with a problem whose answer was not to his precious accounts scroll, Vourtzes grew cautious. His lips moved silently as he reckoned to himself. "That is dependent upon a variety of factors not subject to my ministry's control: the condition of roads, quality of harvest, ability of agents to penetrate areas subject to disturbances . . ." From the way the bureaucrat avoided it, Marcus began to think the word "Yezda" made him break out in hives.

"There's something he's leaving out," Baanes Onomagoulos said, "and that's the likelihood the damned sealstampers are pocketing one goldpiece in three for their own schemes. Oh, yes, they show us this pile of turds." He pointed contemptuously at Vourtzes' assessment document. "But who can make heads or tails of it? That's how they've kept their power, because no one who hasn't grown up in their way of cheating knows he's swindled until it's too late for him to do anything about it."

Vourtzes sputtered denials, but Thorisin gave him a long, measuring stare. Even Alypia Gavra nodded, however reluctantly; she might despise Onomagoulos, but she did not make the mistake of thinking him a fool.

"What's needed then," Marcus said, "is someone to watch over these functionaries, to make sure they're doing what they say they are."

"Brilliant—you should join the Academy," Elissaios Bouraphos said sardonically. "Who's to do it, though? Who can, among the men to be trusted? We're the lot of us soldiers. What do we know about the clerks' tricks the pen-pushers use? I keep more records than most of us, I'd bet, having to keep track of ships' stores and such, but I'd founder in a week in the chancery, to say nothing of being bored out of my wits."

"You're right," the Emperor said. "None of us has the knowledge for the job, worse luck, for it's one that needs doing." His voice grew musing; his eyes, speculation in them, swung toward the tribune. "Or is that so indeed? When you came to Videssos from your other world, Scaurus, do I remember your saying you had held some sort of civil post as well as commanding your troops?"

"Yes, that's so; I was one of the praetors at Mediolanum." Marcus realized that meant nothing to Gavras, and explained, "I held one of the magistracies in my home town, responsible for hearing suits, publishing edicts, and collecting tribute to send on to Rome, our capital."

"So you know something of this sharpers' business, then?" Thorisin pressed.

"Something, yes."

The Emperor looked from one of his officers to the next. Their smirks said more plainly than words that they were thinking along with him. Few things are more pleasant than seeing someone else handed a task one would hate to do oneself. Thorisin turned to Scaurus again. "I'd say you just talked your way into a job." And to Vourtzes he added, "Ha, penpusher, what do you think of that? Try your number-juggling now and see what it gets you!"

"Whatever pleases your Imperial Majesty, of course," the logothete murmured, but he did not sound pleased.

Scaurus said quickly, "It's not something I'll put full time into; I have to pay heed to my men."

"Of course, of course," the Emperor agreed; Marcus saw Drax, Utprand, and Onomagoulos nodding with him. Thorisin continued, "That lieutenant of yours is a sound man, though, and more than up to handling a lot of the day-to-day things. Give it as much time as you can. I'll see if I can't come up with some fancy title for the job and a raise in pay to go with it. You'll earn the money, I think."

"Fair enough," the tribune said. Thorisin's marshals made sympathetic noises; Marcus accepted their condolences and countered their bad jokes with his own.

In fact, he was not nearly so displeased as one of them would have been. A moderately ambitious man, he had long since realized there were definite limits to how high an outlander infantry commander could rise in Videssos on the strength of his troops alone. And his plans at Rome had been ultimately political, not soldierly; the military tribunate was a step aspiring young men took, but not one to stand on forever.

So he had made his suggestion; if Thorisin Gavras did not act on it, nothing whatever was lost. But he had acted, and now the tribune would see what came of that. Anticipation flowered in him. Regardless of the contempt the soldier-nobles had for the palace bureaucracy, it maintained Videssos no less than they. Nor, as Alypia Gavra had pointed out, was it necessarily the weaker party.

He saw her watching him with an expression of ironic amusement and had the uneasy feeling that all his half-formed, murky plans were quite transparent to her.

"I am extremely sorry, sir," Pandhelis the secretary was saying to someone outside the office Marcus had taken as his own, "but I have specific instructions that the *epoptes* is to be disturbed on no account whatever." As promised, Thorisin had conferred an impressively vague title on the Roman, meaning approximately "inspector."

"Och, a pox take you and your instructions both." The door flew open. Viridovix stomped into the little room, Helvis just behind him. Seeing Scaurus, the Gaul clapped a dramatic hand to his forehead. "I've seen that face before, indeed and I have. Don't be telling me, now, the name'll come back to me in a minute, I'm sure it will." He wrinkled his brow in mock concentration.

Wringing his hands, Pandhelis said to the tribune, "I'm sorry, sir, they would not listen to me——"

"Never mind. I'm glad to see them." Marcus threw down his pen with a sigh of relief; a new callus was forming on his right index finger. Shoving tax rolls and reckoning beads to one side of the untidy desk, he looked up at his visitors. "What needs doing?"

"Nothing needs doing. We're here to collect you," Helvis said firmly. "It's Midwinter's Day, in case you've forgotten—time for rejoicing, not chaining yourself up like some slave."

"But——" Marcus started to protest. Then he rubbed his eyes, red-lined and scratchy from staring at an endless procession of numbers. Enough is enough, he thought, and stood up, stretching till his joints creaked. "All right, I'm your man."

"I should hope so," she said, a sudden smoky glow in her blue eyes. "I've started wondering if you remembered."

"Ho-ho!" Viridovix said with a wink. His brawny arm propelled Scaurus out from around the desk, out of the cubicle, and into the corridor, giving the tribune no chance to change his mind. "Come along with you, Roman dear. There's a party laid on to make even a stodgy spalpeen like you frolic."

As always, the first breath of frigid outside air made the tribune cough. His own breath sighed out in a great steaming cloud. Whatever one could say against them, the bureaucrats kept their wing of Grand Courtroom offices heated almost summery-warm. It made the winter outside twice as hard to endure. He shivered in his cloak.

Ice glittered on bare-branched trees; the smooth-rolled lawns that were the palace gardeners' emerald delight in summer now were patchy and brown. Somewhere high overhead a gull screeched. Most birds were long gone to the warm lands of the unknown south, but the gulls stayed. Scavengers and thieves, they were birds that fit the capital.

"And how's that bairn of yours?" Viridovix asked as they walked back toward the Roman barracks.

"Dosti? He couldn't be better," Marcus answered proudly. "He has four teeth now, two top and two bottom. He likes to use 'em, too—he bit my finger the other day."

"Your finger?" Helvis said. "Don't complain of fingers, my dear—high time the boy was weaned."

"Oww," Viridovix sympathized.

The big Gaul waved as soon as he was in sight of the barracks; Scaurus saw a Roman wave back from a window. "What sort of ambush are you leading me into?" he asked.

"You'll see soon enough," Viridovix said. The moment they walked into the barracks hall, he shouted, "Pay up the goldpiece you owe me, Soteric, for here's himself in the flesh of him!"

The Namdalener flipped him the coin. "It's not a bet I'm sorry to lose," he said. "I thought he was too in love with his inks and parchments to recall how the common folk celebrate."

"To the crows with you," Marcus said to the man he counted his brother-in-law, aiming a lazy punch that Soteric dodged.

Viridovix was biting the goldpiece he'd won. "It's not of the best, but then it's not of the worst either," he said philosophically and tucked it into his belt-pouch.

The tribune was not paying much attention to the Celt, looking instead from face to grinning face around him. "This is the crew you've gathered to carouse with?" he said to Viridovix. Grinning too, the Celt nodded.

"Then the gods look to Videssos tonight!" Marcus exclaimed, and drew a cheer from everyone.

There was Taso Vones, arm in arm with a buxom Videssian woman several inches taller than he was. Gawtruz of Thatagush stood beside him, working hard on a wineskin. "How about some for the rest of us?" Gaius Philippus said pointedly.

"What's a skin of wine, among one man?" Gawtruz retorted, and kept drinking. He lowered the skin again a moment later, but only to belch.

Soteric had brought Fayard and Turgot of Sotevag with him. Turgot needed no help from Gawtruz's wineskin; he was already unsteady on his feet. His companion was a very blond Namdalener girl named Mavia. Scaurus doubted she was out of her teens. In a dark-haired land, her bright tresses gleamed like a goldpiece among old coppers.

Fayard greeted Helvis in the island dialect; her dead husband had been his captain. She smiled and answered in the same speech.

Arigh Arghun's son was in the middle of telling a dirty story to all three of Viridovix' lemans. Marcus wondered again how the Celt kept them from catfights. Probably the happy-go-lucky Gaul's own lack of jealousy, he thought. Viridovix seemed altogether unconcerned when they exploded into laughter at the end of Arigh's tale.

Quintus Glabrio said something low-voiced to Gorgidas, who smiled and nodded. Next to them, Katakolon Kekaumenos of Agder stirred impatiently. "Are we then assembled?" he asked. "An it be so, let's to the revels." His accent was almost as archaic as the sacred liturgy; Agder, though once part of the Empire, had been severed from Videssos' more quickly changing currents of speech for many years. Kekaumenos himself was a solidly built, saturnine man whose jacket of creamy snow-leopard pelts was worth a small fortune in the capital.

Marcus also thought him something of a prig; as the party trooped out of the barracks hall, he asked Taso Vones, "Who invited the dog in the manger?"

Aesop meant nothing to the Khatrisher, as Scaurus should have known. He sighed. There were times, most often brought on by such trivial things, when he was sure he would never fit this world. He explained himself *sans* metaphor.

"As a matter of fact, *I* invited him," Vones said. The Roman's embarrassment seemed to amuse him; he shared with Balsamon a fondness for discomfiting people. "I have my reasons. Agder's a far northern land, you know, and the turn of the sun at midwinter means more to them than to the Videssians or me—they're always half afraid it won't come back. When they see it start north again they wassail hard, believe me."

Videssos might not have feared for the sun's return, but it celebrated all the same. The two midwinter fests Marcus had seen before were in provincial towns. The captial's holiday was perhaps less boisterous than their uninhibited rejoicing, but made up for it with more polish. And the city's sheer size let the tribune imagine himself in the middle of a world bent solely on pleasure.

Winter's early night was falling fast, but torches and candles everywhere gave plenty of light. Bonfires blazed on many street corners; it was reckoned lucky to jump through them.

Helvis slid free of Marcus' arm round her waist. She ran for one of the fires, jumped. Her hair flew out around her head like a dark halo; despite the hand she kept by her side, her

skirt billowed away from her legs. Someone on the far side of
the fire cheered. The tribune's pulse quickened, too. She came
back to him flushed from the run and the cold, her eyes bright.
When he put his arm around her again, she pressed his hand
tight against the top of her hip.

Nothing escaped Taso Vones' birdlike gaze. With a smile
up at his own lady—whose name, Scaurus learned, was Plakidia Teletze—he said, "Better than crawling through co-
dices, isn't it?"

"You'd best believe it," the tribune answered, and tipped
Helvis' chin up for a quick kiss. Her lips were warm and alive
against his.

"It's a public disgrace you'll make of yourselves," Viridovix complained. To show how serious he was, he planted
good, thorough kisses on all his lady friends. They seemed
perfectly content with his gallant impartiality. From long practice, it had almost a polish to it, like a conjuror plucking his
ten-thousandth gold ring out of the air.

Waves of laughter came rolling out of the Amphitheater, a
sound like a god's mirth. Videssos' mime troupes, naturally,
were the best the Empire could offer. Eyeing the failing day,
Gorgidas said, "It's probably too dark for them to squeeze in
another show. What say we find an eatery now, before the
crowd coming out fills them all to overflowing?"

"Always is a good idea, food," Gawtruz said in the heavy
Khamorth-flavored accent he affected most of the time. The
envoy from Thatagush slapped his thick belly. His appetite
was real, but Scaurus knew the boorishness was an act to lull
the unwary. A clever diplomat hid beneath that piggish exterior.

Gorgidas' good sense got his comrades into an inn a few
blocks off the plaza of Palamas while the establishment was
still only half full. The proprietor and a serving girl shoved
two tables together for them. Before they had finished their
first round of wine—Soteric, Fayard, and Katakolon Kekaumenos chose ale—the room was packed. The owner hauled a
couple of battered tables from the kitchens out into the street
to serve a few more customers, planting fat candles on them to
give his guests light. "I wish I'd bought that bigger place,"
Marcus heard him say to himself as he bustled back and forth.

Delicious odors wafted out of the kitchen. Scaurus and his
friends nibbled on sweetmeats and drank, waiting for their

dinner to cook. At last a servingmaid, staggering a little under its weight, fetched a fat, roast goose to the table. Steel flashed in the torchlight as she expertly carved the bird.

The tribune liked most Videssian cooking, and when the eatery's owner proclaimed goose "our specialty" he had gone along without a qualm. His first bite gave him second thoughts. The goose was smothered in a sauce of cinnamon and sharp cheese, a combination piquant enough to bring tears to his eyes. There were times when the Empire's sophisticated striving for pleasure through contrasting tastes went beyond what his palate could tolerate.

Gaius Philippus seemed similarly nonplussed, but the rest ate with every sign of enjoyment. Stifling a sigh, the tribune took a handful of shelled almonds from a dish by the half-demolished goose. They were sprinkled with garlic powder. The sigh became a groan; why hadn't the garlic gone on the meat instead?

"You're not eating much," Hevis said.

"No." Perhaps it was just as well. Being chairbound day in and day out had made him gain weight. And, he thought, raising his cup to his lips, he had more room for wine.

"Here, pretty one, would you care to sit by me?" That was Gauis Philippus, greeting a courtesan in a clinging dress of thin yellow stuffs. He stole a chair from a nearby table; its owner had gotten up to go to the jakes. The fellow's companions glowered at the senior centurion. He stared them down; long years of command gave him a presence none of the city men could match.

The woman saw that, too. There was real interest on her face as she sat, not just a whore's counterfeit passion. She helped herself to food and drink. A pretty thing, Marcus thought, and was glad for Gaius Philippus, whose luck in such matters was usually poor.

The shade of yellow she wore reminded the tribune of the diaphanous silk gown Vardanes Sphrantzes had forced on Alypia Gavra, and of her slim body unconcealed beneath it. The thought warmed and annoyed him at the same time. There should have been no room for it with Helvis beside him, her fingers teasing the nape of his neck.

Turgot stretched across the table to reach for the dish of almonds. He popped a handful into his mouth, then tried to curse around them. "Stinking garlic!" he said, washing out the taste with a hefty swig of wine. "Back in the Duchy we wouldn't foul good food with the stuff." He drank again, his face losing its soldier's hardness as he thought of his home.

"Well, I like it," Mavia said with a flip of her head. Her hair flashed gold-red in the torchlight, almost the color of flame itself. To prove the truth of her words, she ate an almond, then another one. Marcus guessed she'd come to the Empire long ago as a mercenary's small daughter and learned Videssian tastes as well as the Duchy's. Turgot, sitting hunched over his wine cup, suddenly seemed sad and tired and old.

The Videssian whose chair Gaius Philippus had annexed returned. He stood in confusion for a moment, while his friends explained what had happened. He turned toward the Roman—an unsteady turn, for he had considerable wine on board. "Now you shee—*see*—here, sir—" he began.

"Go home and sober up," the senior centurion said, not unkindly. He had other things on his mind than fighting. His eyes kept slipping hungrily to the courtesan's dark nipples, plainly visible through the fabric of her dress.

Viridovix's admiring gaze followed his. Only when the drunken Videssian started a further protest did the Celt seem to notice him. He burst out laughing, saying to Gaius Philippus, "Sure and the poor sot's clean forgotten a prick's good for more things than pissing through."

He spoke in the Empire's language so everyone round the party's two tables could share the joke. They laughed with him, but the man he'd insulted understood him, too. With a grunt of sodden rage the fellow swung at him, a wild haymaking right that came nowhere near the Gaul.

Viridovix sprang to his feet, quick as a cat despite all he'd drunk himself. His green eyes glowed with amusement of a new sort. "Your honor shouldn't ought to have done that, now," he said. He grabbed the luckless Videssian, lifted him off his feet, and hurled him down *splash!* into the great tureen of sea-turtle stew that stood as the centerpiece of his comrades' table.

The sturdy table did not collapse, but greasy greenish stew and bits of white meat splattered in all directions. The drunk feebly kicked his legs as he tried to right himself; his friends, drenched by their dinners, swore and spluttered and wiped at their faces.

"What are you doing, you loose fish, you clapped-out poxy blackguard, you beggarly, lousy, beetle-headed knave!" Gaius Philippus' courtesan screeched as she daubed futilely at herself. A good-sized chunk of meat was stuck in her hair above the gold hoop she wore in her right ear, but she did not notice it.

Nor did the Celt pay her bravura curses any mind. The men he'd swashed were coming at him, with determination if no great skill. Viridovix flattened the first of them, but the next one dashed a cup of wine in his face. While he choked and gasped, the fellow jumped on him, followed a second later by a companion.

Gaius Philippus and Gawtruz of Thatagush hauled them off. "Two against one's not fair," the senior centurion said, still mildly, flinging his man in one direction. Gawtruz wasted no words on his, but tossed him in the other. If they had hoped to quell the fight, they could hardly have done a worse job of it. The hurled men went careening into tables, bowling over two men seated at one and a woman at the other. Food flew. What had been a private quarrel instantly became general.

Viridovix's banshee howl of fighting glee rose over the anguished cries of the inn's owner and the sound of smashing crockery. The two tables were a bastion under siege, and it seemed everyone else in the eatery was trying to storm them.

Marcus had heard reports of Viridovix's tavern brawling, but until now had never been caught up in it himself. A mug whizzed past his head, to shatter against the wall. A fat Videssian punched him in the belly. "Oof!" he said, and doubled over. He swung back, felt his fist sink into flab.

"You will excuse me, I pray," Taso Vones said, and dove under the table, pulling Plakidia Teletze with him. She let out an unladylike squawk of protest as she disappeared.

It was, Marcus thought, the most good-natured fight he had been in. Perhaps all the battlers were in holiday spirits, or was it simply that Viridovix, at heart a good-natured soul, had set the stamp of his character on the brawl he'd started? Whatever it was, none of the scrappers showed the slightest desire to reach for the knives that hung at most of their belts. They pounded each other with high gusto, but no serious blood was spilled.

"Yipe!" said Scaurus, thrashing frantically. Someone had pulled open his tunic and poured a bowlful of syrup-sweetened snow down his back. It felt like a million frozen, crawling ants.

The eatery's owner ran from one little knot of fighting to the next, shouting, "Stop this! Stop this at once, I tell you!" No one paid him any mind until the fat Videssian, annoyed at his noise, hit him in the side of the head. He stumbled out into the night. "The guard! The guard!" His cries faded as he ran down the street.

A city man, fists flailing, charged Arigh Arghun's son, who was not much more than half as big. There was a flurry of arms and legs—Marcus could not see all that went on, because he was trading punches with a man who reeked of wine—and the Videssian thudded to the ground. He lay still; whatever Arigh's handfighting technique was, it worked well.

A plate broke, almost in the tribune's ear. He whirled round to see a Videssian stagger away clutching his head. Helvis still had a piece of the plate in her hand. "Thank you, dear," he said. She smiled and nodded.

Nor was she the only Namdalener woman able to handle herself in a ruction. Mavia and Gaius Philippus' tart were going at it hammer and tongs, screeching and clawing and pulling hair, and it was easy to see the blonde was getting the better of the battle. But her foe was still game; when the senior centurion tried to drag her out of the fray she raked her nails down his cheek, missing his eye by no more than an inch. "Stay and fight, then, you mangy trollop!" he yelled, all vestiges of chivalry forgotten.

Katakolon Kekaumenos sat sipping his wine, a bubble of calm in the brabble around him. One of the brawlers was rash enough to mistake his quiet for cowardice and started to tip his chair over backward. Kakaumenos was on his feet and spinning toward the Videssian almost before it began to move. He punched him once in the face and once in the belly, then lifted his sagging body over his head and threw him through a window. That done, he straightened the chair and returned to his wine, quiet as a snow leopard just after it has fed.

"That'll teach you to be trifling with an honest man, won't it now?" Viridovix yelled after the Videssian. He got no answer.

The tribune took a punch over the ear. He saw brief stars, but his assailant howled and clutched his left fist round a broken knuckle. Scaurus, too experienced to throw that kind of punch, hit him in the pit of the stomach. He doubled over and fell, gasping for air. Turgot and Gawtruz both jumped on him.

"All right in there, enough now!" an accented tenor called from the doorway. "Break it up, or we'll use our spearshafts on you!" The mail-shirted Vaspurakaners pushed into the shambles that had been the inn's common room. "Break it up, I said!" their officer repeated, and someone yelped as one of the troopers carried out the threat.

"Hullo, Senpat," Marcus said indistinctly. One of his hands was in his mouth, trying to find out if a back tooth was loose. It was. Spitting redly, he asked, "How's your lady?"

"Nevrat? She's fine—" The young Vaspurakaner noble broke off in mid-sentence, a comic expression of surprise on his handsome features. "You, Scaurus, of all people, tavern brawling? You, the sensible, sober fellow who keeps everyone else out of trouble? By Vaspur the Firstborn, I'd not have believed it without the seeing."

"Heresy," someone muttered, but softly; fifteen Vaspurakaners crowded the room, every one of them armed.

Embarrassed, the tribune so far forgot his Stoic principles as to cast the blame elsewhere. "It's Viridovix' fault. He started the thing."

"Don't listen to him for even a second, Sviodo dear," the Celt said to Senpat. "He was enjoying himself as much as the rest of us." And Marcus, wine and battle both still firing his blood, could not say him nay.

The taverner, staring in horrified dismay at overturned tables, broken chairs, assorted potshards, and half a dozen of his kitchen creations splashed everywhere, let out a baritone shriek of despair. Not only was his eatery wrecked, but this Phos-despised foreign guard captain turned out to be friends with the wreckers! "Who's going to pay for all this?" he moaned.

Abrupt silence fell. The men still standing looked at each other, at their comrades unconscious on the floor, at the door —which was full of Vaspurakaners. "Someone had better pay," the innkeeper went on, his tone moving from despondence to threat, "or the whole city'll know why, and then—"

"Shut up," Scaurus said; he'd seen enough anti-foreign riots in Videssos never to want to see another. He reached for his belt. The taverner's eyes widened in alarm, but he was seeking his purse, not his sword. "We share and share alike," he said, his gaze including his own party and everyone else in the inn.

"Why add me in?" Gorgidas demanded. "I didn't help break up the place." That was true enough; the Greek, not caring for fighting of any sort, had stayed on the sidelines.

"Then call it your fine for a liver full of milk," Viridovix hooted. "If you're after talking your way free, what's to stop the rest of these omadhauns from doing the same?"

Gorgidas glared at him and opened his mouth to argue further, but Quintus Glabrio touched his arm. The junior centurion was another who did not brawl for sport, but a swollen lip and a bruise on his cheek said he had not been idle. He murmured something. Gorgidas dipped his head in acquiescence, the Greek gesture giving his exasperation perfect expression.

There were no other arguments. Scaurus turned back to the inn-keeper. "All right, what do you say this stuff is worth?" Seeing an ignorant outland mercenary in front of him, the man doubled the fair price. But the tribune laughed scornfully; it was folly to think of gulling someone with his nose fresh out of the tax rolls. At his counteroffer the taverner flinched and called on Phos, but grew much more reasonable. They settled quickly.

"Don't forget the fellow lying out there in the snow," Senpat Sviodo said helpfully. "The more shares, the less each one pays." Three of his Vaspurakaners dragged the fellow back and flipped water in his face until he revived. It took several minutes; Marcus was glad Kekaumenos was a friend.

"Is that everyone?" he asked, scanning the battered room.

"Should be," Gaius Philippus said, but Gawtruz broke in, "Vones, where is he?" His fat face was smug; he loved to score points off his fellow envoy.

Heads turned. No one saw the little Khatrisher. Then Viridovix remembered, "Dove clear out of the shindy, he did," the Celt said, and lifted a tablecloth. Plakidia Teletze screamed. Vones, quicker thinking, snatched the cloth out of Viridovix's hand and yanked it down.

"Begging your honor's pardon, I'm sure," Viridovix said, suave as any ambassador himself, "but when you're finished the rest of us would be glad for a word with ye." Then the effort of holding himself back was too much, and he doubled over with a guffaw.

Vones emerged a moment later, urbane as ever. "Wasn't

what it seemed," he said blandly. "Merely a coincidence, you understand, the way we happened to fall."

Grinning, Arigh interrupted, "Your breeches are unbuttoned, Taso."

"Why, so they are." Not a bit nonplussed, Vones did them up again. "Now then, gentlemen, what do I owe you for my share in the festivities?" Plakidia scrambled out while he was talking. She bolted away from him; at Senpat Sviodo's gesture his men stood aside to let her pass.

"It's not us you should be after paying at all, at all," Viridovix chuckled, and Vones got off free. Scaurus dug in his pouch, filled his free hand with silver. He counted out seventeen coins. It took twenty-four to equal a goldpiece of pure metal, but the tribune saw a couple of the city men spend two of Ortaias' debased coins to pay their shares, and even then the innkeeper looked unhappy.

Gaius Philippus saw that, too, and narrowed his eyes in disgust. "You could be getting steel, not gold," he pointed out, toying with the hilt of his shortsword. He had the look of a man who had scores of taproom fights behind him and had ended some of them just that way. The taverner wet his lips nervously as he counted the coins and pronounced himself satisfied. In fact he was hardly lying; too often threats were all he got after a brawl.

"Come by the barracks when you have the chance," Marcus urged Senpat Sviodo as they left the inn. "We haven't seen much of you lately."

"I'll do that," the young noble answered. "I know I should have long ago, but there's so much to see here in the city. It's like another world." Scaurus nodded his understanding; next to Videssos, Vaspurakan's towns were but backwoods villages.

The courtesan in yellow tried to make up to Gaius Philippus but, his cheek still smarting, he rounded on her with advice more pungent than he'd had for the innkeeper. She answered with a two-fingered gesture every Videssian knew, and cast sheep's eyes at the fat man who'd hit Marcus in the stomach. They strolled off arm in arm.

The senior centurion stared glumly after her. Viridovix clucked. "Foosh, it's a rare wasteful man y'are," he said. "That was a lass with fire in her; a rare ride she would have given you." Scaurus thought that an odd sentiment, coming from the Gaul—his own companions were all of them lovely, but none had any spirit to speak of.

"Women," Gaius Philippus said, as if the word was enough to explain everything.

"Only take the time to know 'em, Roman dear, and you'll find 'em not so strange," Viridovix retorted. "And they're great fun besides—isn't that right, my dears, my darlings?" He swept all three of them into his arms; the way they snuggled close spoke louder than any words of agreement.

Gaius Philippus did his best to stay impassive; Marcus was probably the only one who noticed his jaw jet, saw his eyes narrow and grow hard. The Celt's teasing, this time, had struck deep, though Viridovix himself did not realize it. When the Celt opened his mouth for another sally, the tribune stepped on his foot.

"Ow! Bad cess to you, you hulking looby!" Viridovix exclaimed, hopping. "What was the point o' that?"

Scaurus apologized and meant it; in his hurry, he'd trod harder than he intended.

"Well, all right then," the Gaul said. He stretched luxuriantly. "Indeed and the shindy was not a bad way to be starting the evening, if a bit tame. Let's be off to another tavern and do it ag—och, you black spalpeen, that was no accident!" The tribune had stepped on his other foot.

Viridovix bent down and flung a handful of snow in his face. Cheeks stinging and eyebrows frosted white, Marcus retaliated in kind—as did Helvis, who had taken some of the snow that missed the Roman. In an instant everyone was pelting everyone else, laughing and shouting and cheering each other on. Marcus was just as well pleased; a snowfight was safer than most things Viridovix reckoned entertainment.

Sitting secure in Videssos, it was easy to imagine the Empire still master of all its lands—or it would have been, had Scaurus not been wrestling with the imperial tax rolls. In his office he had a map of the westlands showing the districts from which revenues had been collected. Most towns and villages in the coastal lowlands had little bronze pins stabbed through them, indicating that imperial agents had taken what was due from them. The central plateau, though, the natural settling ground for nomads like the Yezda, showed virtually a blank expanse of parchment. Worse, a finger of that same ominous blankness pushed east down the Arandos River valley toward Garsavra. If the town fell, it opened the way for the invaders to burst forward all the way to the shore of the Sailors' Sea.

Baanes Onomagoulos was as well aware of the somber truth as the imperial finance ministry. The noble's estates were hard by Garsavra, and his patience with Thorisin, never long, grew shorter with every report of a new Yezda advance.

The Emperor knew the reason for Onomagoulos' constant reproaches and knew there was some justice to them. He bore them with more self-control than Marcus had thought he owned. He committed such aid as he could to the Arandos valley; more, in Scaurus' eyes, than Videssos, threatened all through the westlands, could readily afford to spend there. But at every session of the imperial council Onomagoulos' cry was always for more men.

Thorisin's patience finally wore thin. About six weeks after the midwinter fest, he told his captious marshal, "Baanes, I am not made of soldiers, and Garsavra is not Videssos' only weak point. The nomads are pushing out of Vaspurakan toward Pityos and they're raiding in the westlands' south as well. And the winter's cold enough to freeze the Astris, so the Khamorth'll likely poke south across it to see if we poke back. The company I sent west ten days ago will have to be the last."

Onomagoulos ran his fingers up over the crown of his head, a gesture, Marcus guessed, born when hair still covered it. "Two hundred seventy-five men! Huzzah!" he said sourly. "How many Namdaleni, aye, and these other damned outlanders, too," he added with a glance at Scaurus, "are sitting here in the city, eating like so many hogs?"

Drax answered with the cool mercenary's logic Marcus had come to expect from the great count: "Why should his Majesty throw my men away in a fight they're not suited for? We're heavier-armed than you Videssians care to be. Most times we find it useful, but in deep snow we're slow and floundering, easy meat for the nomads' light horse."

"The same is true of my men, but more so, for we aren't mounted," Marcus echoed.

The quarrel might have been smoothed over there, for Onomagoulos was a soldier and recognized the point the others made. But Soteric happened to be at the council instead of

Utprand, who was ill with a coughing fever. Scaurus' head-strong brother-in-law took offense at Baanes' gibe at the Namdaleni and gave it back in kind. "Hogs, is it? You bloody cocksure snake, if you knew anything about nomads you wouldn't have let yourself get trapped in front of Maragha. Then you wouldn't be sitting here carping about the upshot of your own stupidity!"

"Barbarian bastard!" Onomagoulos shouted. His chair crashed over backward as he tried to leap to his feet; his hand darted for his sword hilt. But his crippled leg buckled, and he had to grab for the council table to keep from falling. He had taken the laming wound in the fight Soteric named, and the Namdalener laughed at him for it.

"Will you watch that polluted tongue of yours?" Scaurus hissed at him. Drax, too, put a warning hand on his arm, but Soteric shook it off. He and Utprand bore the count no love.

Onomagoulos regained his feet. His saber rasped free. "Come on, baseborn!" he yelled, almost beside himself with rage. "One leg's plenty to deal with scum like you!"

Soteric surged up. Marcus and Drax, sitting on either side of him, started to grab his shoulders to haul him down again, but it was Thorisin's battlefield roar of "Enough!" that froze everyone in place, Roman and great count no less than the combatants.

"Enough!" the Emperor yelled again, barely softer. "Phos' light, the two of you are worse than a couple of brats fratching over who lost the candy. Mertikes, get Baanes' chair—he seems to have mislaid it." Zigabenos jumped to obey. "Now, the both of you sit down and keep still unless you've something useful to say." Under his glower they did, Soteric a bit shamefaced but Onomagoulos still furious and making only the barest effort to hide it.

Speaking to Gavras as if to a small boy, the Videssian noble persisted, "Garsavra must have more troops, Thorisin. It is a very important city, both of itself and for its location."

The Emperor bridled at that tone, which he had heard from Onomagoulos for too many years. But he still tried for patience as he answered, "Baanes, I have given Garsavra twenty-five hundred men, at least. Along with the retainers you muster on your estates, surely enough warriors are there to hold back the Yezda till spring. They don't fly over the snow themselves, you know; they slog through it like anyone else. When spring comes I intend to hit them hard, and I won't piddle away my striking force a squad here and a company there until I have nothing left."

Onomagoulos stuck out his chin; his pointed beard jutted toward Gavras. "The men are needed, I tell you. Will you not listen to plain sense?"

No one at the table wanted to meet Thorisin's eye while he was being hectored so, but all gazes slid his way regardless. He said only, "You may not have them," but there was iron in his voice.

Everyone heard the warning except Onomagoulos, whose angry frustration made him exclaim, "Your brother would have given them to me."

Marcus wanted to disappear; had Baanes searched for a year, he could not have found a worse thing to say. Thorisin's jealousy of the friendship between Mavrikios and Onomagoulos was painfully obvious. Imperial dignity forgotten, Gavras leaned forward, bellowing, "He'd have given you the back of his hand for your insolence, you toplofty runt!"

"Unweaned pup, your eyes aren't open to see the world in front of your face!" Baanes was not yelling at the Avtokrator of the Videssians, but at his comrade's tag-along little brother.

"Clod from a dungheap! You think your precious estates are worth more than the whole Empire!"

"I changed your diapers, puling moppet!" They shouted insults and curses at each other for a good minute, oblivious to anyone else's presence. Finally Onomagoulos rose once more, crying, "There's one more man Garsavra will have, by Phos! I won't stay in the same city with you—the stench of you curdles my nose!"

"It's big enough," Thorisin retorted. "Good riddance; Videssos is well shut of you."

By now, Scaurus thought, I should be used to the sight of people stalking out of Thorisin's councils. Baanes Onomagoulos' stalk was in fact a limp, but the effect remained the same. As he reached the polished bronze doors of the Hall of the Nineteen Couches, he turned round for a final scowl at the Emperor, who replied with an obscene gesture. Onomagoulos spat on the floor, as Videssians did before wine and food to show their rejection of Skotos. He hobbled out into the snow.

"Where were we?" the Emperor said.

* * *

Marcus expected Baanes to be restored to Thorisin's good graces; the Emperor's temper ran high at flood but quickly ebbed. Onomagoulos' anger, though, was of a more lasting sort. Two days after the stormy council he kept the promise he'd made there, sailing over the Cattle-Crossing and setting out for Garsavra.

"I mislike this," the tribune said when he heard the news. "He's flying in the face of the Emperor's authority." Though he was in the Roman barracks, he looked round before he spoke and then was low-voiced—the price of living in the Empire, he thought discontentedly.

"You're right, I fear," Gaius Philippus said. "If I were Gavras, I'd haul him back in chains."

"The two of you make no sense," Viridovix complained. "It was the Gavras who gave him leave to go—or ordered him, more like."

"Ordered him to drop dead, perhaps," Gorgidas said, "but not to go off and fight his own private war." He lifted an ironic eyebrow at the Gaul. "When will you learn words can say one thing and mean another?"

"Och, you think you're such a tricksy Greek. This I'll tell you, though—if it was my home in danger, I'd go see to it, and be damned to any who tried to stop me, himself included." The Gaul folded his arms across his chest, as if daring the doctor to disagree.

It was Gaius Philippus, though, who snorted at him. "Likely you would, and maybe lose your home and all your neighbors' in the bargain. Think of yourself first and your mates last and that's what happens. Why else do you think Caesar's been able to fight one clan of Celts at a time?"

Viridovix gnawed at his drooping mustache; the senior centurion's gibe was to the point. But he replied, "'Twon't matter a bit in the end. Divided or no, we'll be whipping the lot of you back home with your tails tucked into their grooves."

"Not a chance," Gaius Philippus said, and the old dispute began again. Ever since the Romans came to Videssos, he and Viridovix had been arguing over who would win the fighting in Gaul. They both took the question seriously, although—or perhaps because—they could never answer it.

Not much caring to listen, Marcus left for his desk in the

pen-pushers' wing of the Grand Courtroom. The problems there were new ones, but they did not seem to have solutions more definite than his friends' debating topic.

Pandhelis fetched him ledgers and reports in an unending stream. They further confused issues about as often as they settled them. Videssian bureaucrats, with their rhetorical training, took pride in making their meaning as obscure as possible. Trying to thread his way through a thicket of allusions he barely understood, Scaurus wondered why he had ever wanted a political career.

He slept at his desk that night, stupefied by a pile of assessment documents written in a hand so tiny as to defy the eye. The legionaries were already at the practice field when he got back to the barracks. He walked down Middle Street to join them, breakfasting on a hard, square rye-flour roll dipped in honey, that he bought in the plaza of Palamas.

It was another chilly day, with little flurries of snow blowing through the streets. When the tribune came up to a bathhouse with an imposing façade of golden sandstone and white marble, his enthusiasm for practice abruptly disappeared. He wrestled his conscience to the mat and went in. Falling asleep to the press of work, he told himself, was enough to make anyone feel grimy.

The bathhouse's owner took his copper at the door with a broad smile, waving him forward into the undressing chamber. He gave another copper to the boy there to make sure his clothes would not be stolen while he was bathing, then shed his sheepskin coat, tunic, and trousers with a sigh of relief.

The sounds of the bath drew him on. As was true at Rome, Videssian baths were as much social places as ones devoted to cleanliness. Hawkers of sausages, wine, and pastries were crying their wares; so was the hair-remover, for those men who affected such fastidiousness. He fell silent for a moment, then Scaurus heard his client yelp as he began to pluck an armpit.

Usually the tribune, with Stoic abstemiousness, limited himself to a cold bath, but after coming in out of the snow that was intolerable. He sweated for a while in the steam bath, baking the winter out. Then the cold plunge seemed attractive rather than self-tormenting. He climbed out of the pool when the icy water began to bite, stretching himself on the tiles to relax for a few minutes before going on to soak in the pleasantly warm pool beyond.

"Scrape you off, sir?" asked a youth with a curved strigil in his hand.

"Thank you, yes," the tribune said; he'd brought along a little money for small luxuries like this, as it was next to impossible for a bather to scrape all of himself. He sighed at the pleasant roughness of the strigil sliding back and forth over his flesh.

Around him plump middle-aged men puffed as they exercised with weights. Masseurs pummeled grunting victims, now clapping hands down on their shoulders, now cupping them to produce an almost drumlike beat. Three young men played the Videssian game called *trigon*, throwing a ball unexpectedly from one to the next. They feinted and shouted; whenever one dropped the ball the other two would cry out as he lost a point. Off in a corner, a handful of more sedentary types diced the morning away.

There was a tremendous splash as someone leaped into the warm pool in the hall beyond, followed closely by cries of annoyance from the nearby people whom he'd drenched. The splasher came up not a whit dismayed. After blowing the water out of his mouth and nose, he started to sing in a resonant baritone.

"Everyone thinks he sounds wonderful in the baths," the youth with the strigil said, cocking his head critically. He fancied himself a connoiseur of bathhouse music. "He's not bad, I must say, for all his funny accent."

"No, he isn't," Marcus agreed, though his ear was so poor he could hardly tell good singing from bad. But only one man in Videssos owned that brogue. Tipping the youth a final copper, he got up and went in to say hello to Viridovix.

The Celt was facing the entranceway and broke off his tune in mid-note when he saw the tribune. "If it's not himself, come to wash the ink off him!" he cried. "And a good deal of himself there is to wash, too!"

Scaurus looked down. He'd felt his middle thickening from days in a chair without exercise, but hadn't realized the result was so plain to see. Annoyed, he ran three steps forward and dove into the warm water a good deal more neatly than Viridovix had. It was a shallow dive; the pool was no more than chest-deep.

He swam over to the Celt. The two of them were strange fish among the olive-skinned, dark-haired Videssians: Marcus dark blond, his face, arms, and lower legs permanently tanned from his time in the field but the rest of him paler; and Viridovix, fair with the pink-white Gallic fairness that refused to take the sun, his burnished copper hair sodden against his head and curling in bright ringlets on his chest and belly and at his groin.

"Shirking again," they both said at the same time, and laughed together. Neither was in any hurry to get out. The pool was heated to that perfect temperature where the water does not register against the skin. Marcus thought of the sharp wind outside, then chose not to.

A small boy, drawn perhaps by the Celt's strangeness, splashed him from behind. Viridovix spun round, saw his laughing foe. "Do that to me, will you now?" he roared, mock-ferocious, and splashed back. They pelted each other with water until the youngster's father had to go and take his son, unwilling, from the pool. Viridovix waved to them both as they left. "A fine lad, and a fine time, too," he said to Scaurus.

"From the look of you, you had your fine time last night," the tribune retorted. He had been staring at Viridovix's back and shoulders when the Gaul turned them during the water fight. They were covered with scratches that surely came from a woman's nails. One or two of them, Scaurus thought, must have drawn blood; they were still red and angry.

Viridovix smoothed down his mustaches, fairly dripping smugness. He said a couple of sentences in his own Celtic tongue before dropping back into Latin, which he still preferred to Videssian. "A wildcat she was, all right," he said, smiling at the memory. "You canna see it under my hair, but she fair bit the ear off me, too, there at the end."

He was in so expansive a mood that Marcus asked, "Which one was it?" He was hard pressed to imagine any of the Celt's three women showing such ferocity. They seemed too docile for it.

"Och, none o' them," Viridovix answered, understanding the question and not put out by it: plainly he felt like boasting. "They're well enough, I'll not deny; still, the time comes when so much sweetness starts to pall. The new one, now!

She's slim, so she is, but wild and shameless as a wolf bitch in heat."

"Good for you, then," Scaurus said. Viridovix, he thought, would likely jolly this new wench into joining the rest. He had a gift in such matters.

"Aye, she's all I hoped she would be," the Gaul said happily. "Ever since she gave me her eye, bold as you please down there on the foggy beach, I've known she'd not be hard for me to lure under the sheets."

"Good for—" the tribune started to repeat, and then stopped in horrified amazement as the full meaning of Viridovix' words sank in. His head whipped round to see who might be listening before he remembered they had been speaking Latin. One small thing to be grateful for, he thought—probably the only one. "Do you mean to tell me it's Komitta Rhangavve's skirt you're lifting?"

"Aren't you the clever one, now? But it's herself lifts it, I assure you—as greedy a cleft as any I've known."

"Are you witstruck all of a sudden, man? It's the Emperor's mistress you're diddling, not some tavern drab."

"And what o' that? A Celtic noble is entitled to better than such trollops," Viridovix said proudly. "Forbye, if Thorisin doesn't want me diddling his lady, then let him diddle her his own self and not stay up till dead of night kinging it. He'll get himself no sons that way."

"Will you give him a red-headed one, then? If no other way, he'll know the cuckoo by its feathers."

Viridovix chuckled at that, but nothing the Roman said would make him change his mind. He was enjoying himself, and was not a man to think of tomorrow till it came. He started singing again, a bouncy love song. Half a dozen Videssians joined in, filling the chamber with music. Marcus tried to decide whether drowning him now would make things better or worse.

XI

"PANDHELIS, WHERE HAVE YOU HIDDEN LAST YEAR'S TAX register for Kybistra?" Scaurus asked. The clerk shuffled through rolls of parchment, spread his hands regretfully. Muttering a curse, Scaurus stood up from his desk and walked down the hall to see if Pikridios Goudeles had the document he needed.

The dapper bureaucrat looked up from his work as the tribune came in. He and Scaurus had learned wary respect for each other since the latter began overseeing the bureaucrats for Thorisin Gavras. "What peculations have you unearthed now?" Goudeles asked. As always, a current of mockery flowed just below the surface of his words.

When Marcus told him what he wanted, Goudeles grew brisk. "It should be around here someplace," he said. He went from pigeonhole to pigeonhole, unrolling the first few inches of the scrolls in them to see what they contained. When the search failed to turn up anything, his mobile eyebrows came down in irritation. He shouted for a couple of clerks to look in nearby rooms, but they returned equally unsuccessful. His frown deepened. "Ask the silverfish and the mice," he suggested.

"No, you probably trained them to lie for you," Marcus said. When the Roman first started the job the Emperor had set him, Goudeles tested him with doctored records. The tribune returned them without comment and got what looked to be real cooperation thereafter. He wondered if this was another, subtler snare.

But Goudeles was rubbing his neatly bearded chin in

thought. "That cadaster might not be here at all," he said slowly. "It might already be stored in the archives building down on Middle Street. It shouldn't be—it's too new—but you never can tell. I don't have it, at any rate."

"All right, I'll try there. If nothing else, I'll get to stretch my legs. Thanks, Pikridios." Goudeles gave a languid wave of acknowledgment. A strange character, Scaurus thought, looking and acting the effete seal-stamper almost to the point of self-parody, but with the grit to confront Thorisin Gavras in his own camp for the Sphrantzai. Well, he told himself, only in the comedies is a man all of a piece.

The brown slate flags of the path from the Grand Courtroom to the forum of Palamas were wet and slippery; most of the snow that had blanketed the palace complex' lawns was gone. The sun was almost hot in a bright blue sky. The tribune eyed it suspiciously. There had been another of these spells a couple of weeks before, followed close by the worst blizzard of the winter. This one, though, might be spring after all.

The tribune had a good idea of the reception he would get at the imperial offices that housed the archives—nor was he disappointed. Functionaries herded him from file to musty file until he began to hate the smell of old parchment. There was no sign of the document he sought, or of any less than three years old. Some were much older than that; he turned up one that seemed to speak of Namdalen as still part of the Empire, though fading ink and strange, archaic script made it impossible to be sure.

When he showed the ancient scroll to the secretary in charge of those files, that worthy said, "You needn't look as if you're blaming me. What would you expect to find in the archives but old papers?" He seemed scandalized that anyone could expect him to produce a recent document.

"I have been through all three floors of this building," Scaurus said, fighting to hold his patience. "Is there any other place the scurvy thing might be lurking?"

"I suppose it might be in the sub-basement," the secretary answered, his tone saying he was sure it wasn't. "That's where the real antiques get stowed, below the prisons."

"I may as well try, as long as I'm here."

"Take a lamp with you," the secretary advised, "and keep your sword drawn. The rats down there aren't often bothered and they can be fierce."

"Splendid," the tribune muttered. It was useful information all the same; though he had known the imperial offices held a jail, he had not been aware there was anything beneath it. He made sure the lamp he chose was full of oil.

He was glad of the lamp as soon as he started down the stairway to the prison, for even that was below the level of the street and had no light save what came from the torches flickering in their iron brackets every few feet along the walls. The rough-hewn blocks of stone above them were thick with soot that had not been cleaned away for years.

It was time for the prisoners' daily meal. A pair of bored guards pushed a squeaking handcart down the central aisleway. Two more, almost equally bored, covered them with drawn bows as they passed out loaves of coarse, husk-filled bread, small bowls of fish stew that smelled none too fresh, and squat earthen jugs of water. The fare was miserable, but the inmates crowded to the front of their cells to get it. One made a face as he tasted the stew. "You washed your feet in it again, Podopagouros," he said.

"Aye, well, they needed it," the guard answered, unperturbed.

The tribune had to ask his way down to the sub-basement. He walked past the rows of cells to a small door whose hinges creaked rustily as he opened it. As with many doorways in the imperial offices, an image of the Emperor was set above this one. But Scaurus blinked at the portrait: a roundfaced old man with a short white beard. Who—? He held up his lamp to read the accompanying text: "Phos preserve the Avtokrator Strobilos Sphrantzes." It had been more than five years now since Strobilos was Emperor.

Long before he reached the bottom of the stairway, Marcus knew he would never find the taxroll, even if it was here. The little clay lamp in his hand was not very bright, but it shed enough light for him to see boxes of records haphazardly piled on one another. Some were overturned, their contents half-buried in the dust and mold on the floor. The air tasted dead.

The lamp flickered. Scaurus felt his heart jump with it. There could be no worse fate than to be lost down here, alone in the blackness. No, not altogether alone; as the flame blazed up again, its glow came back greenly from scores of gleaming eyes. Some of them, the tribune thought nervously, were higher off the ground than a rat's eyes had any right to be.

He retreated, making very sure that little door was bolted. Strobilos stared incuriously down at him; even the imperial artist had had trouble portraying him as anything but a dullard.

Its torches bright and cheerful, the prison level seemed almost attractive compared to what was below it. The guards with their handcart had not moved ahead more than six or seven cells. Their rhythm was slow, nearly hypnotic—a loaf to the left, a bowl of stew to the right; a bowl of stew to the left, a loaf to the right; a water jar to either side; creak forward and repeat.

"You, there!" someone called from one of the cells. "Yes, you, outlander!" Marcus had been about to go on, sure no one down here could be talking to him, but that second call stopped him. He looked round curiously.

He had not recognized Taron Leimmokheir in his shabby linen prison robe. The ex-admiral had lost weight, and his hair and beard were long and shaggy; months in this sunless place had robbed him of his sailor's tan. But as Scaurus walked over to his cell, he saw Leimmokheir still bore himself with military erectness. The cell itself was neat and clean as it could be, cleaner, in fact, than the passageway outside.

"What is it, Leimmokheir?" the tribune asked, not very kindly. The man on the other side of those rust-flaked bars had come too close to killing him and was condemned to be here for planning the murder of the Emperor the Roman supported.

"I'd have you take a message to Gavras, if you would." The words were a request, but Leimmokheir's deep hoarse voice somehow kept its tone of command, prisoner though he was. Marcus waited.

Leimmokheir read his face. "Oh, I'm not such a fool as to ask to be set free. I know the odds of that. But by Phos, outlander, tell him he holds an innocent man. By Phos and his light, by the hope of heaven and the fear of Skotos' ice below, I swear it." He drew the sun-sign over his breast, repeating harshly, "He holds an innocent man!"

The convict in the next cell, a sallow man with a weasel's narrow wicked face, leered at Scaurus. "Aye, we're all innocent here," he said. "That's why they keep us here, you know, to save us from the guilty ones outside. Innocent!" His laugh made the word a filthy joke.

The Roman, though, paused in some uncertainty. Barefoot and unkempt Leimmokheir might be, but his speech still had the oddly compelling quality Marcus had noted when he first heard it on that midnight beach, still carried the conviction that here was a man who would not, or could not, lie. His eyes bored into the tribune's, and Scaurus lowered his first.

The food cart came groaning up. The tribune made his decision. "I'll do what I can," he said. Leimmokheir acknowledged him not with a nod, but with lowered head and right hand on heart——the imperial soldier's salute to a superior. If this was acting, Scaurus thought, it deserved a prize.

He began to regret his promise before he got back to the palace compound. As if he didn't have troubles enough, without trying to convince Gavras he might have made a mistake. Thorisin was much more mistrustful of his aides than Mavrikios had been——with reason, Marcus had to admit. If he ever learned the tribune had planned to defect . . . ! It did not bear thinking about.

If, on the other hand, he approached the Emperor through Alypia Gavra, that might blunt Thorisin's suspicions, the more so if she took his side. At least he could learn what she thought of Leimmokheir, which would give better perspective on how far to credit the ex-admiral. He smacked fist into open palm, pleased with his own cleverness.

She might even know where that fornicating tax roll was, he thought.

The eunuch steward Mizizios rapped lightly at the handsome door. Like most of those in the small secluded building that was the imperial family's private household, it was ornamented with inlays of ebony and red cedar. "Yes, bring him in, of course," Scaurus heard the princess say. Mizizios bowed as he worked the silver latch.

He followed the tribune into the chamber, but Alypia waved him away. "Let us talk in peace." Seeing the eunuch hesitate, she added, "Go on; my virtue's safe with him." It was, Marcus thought, as much the bitterness in her voice as the order itself that made Mizizios flee.

But she was gracious again as she offered the Roman a chair, urged him to take wine and cakes. "Thank you, your Majesty," he said. "It's kind of you to see me on such short notice." He bit into one of the little cakes with enjoyment. They were stuffed with raisins and nuts and dusted lightly with cinnamon; better here than over goose, he thought. That midwinter meal still rankled.

"My uncle has made it plain to both of us that the pen-pushers' iniquities are of the highest importance, has he not?" she said, raising her eyebrows slightly. Was that surprise at his thanks, Scaurus wondered, or lurking sarcasm? He could not read Alypia at all and did not think the reverse was true; he felt at a disadvantage.

"If I'm interrupting anything . . ." he said, and let the sentence drop.

"Nothing that won't keep," she said, waving to a desk as overloaded with scrolls and books as his own. He could read the title picked out in gold leaf on a leather-bound volume's spine: the *Chronicle of Seven Reigns*. She followed his eye, nodded. "History is a business that takes its own time."

The desk itself was plain pine, no finer than the one Marcus used. The rest of the furnishings, including the chairs on which he and Alypia sat, were as austere. The only ornament was an icon of Phos above the desk, an image stern in judgment.

At first glance, the princess seemed almost equally severe. She wore blouse and skirt of plain dark brown, unrelieved by jewelry; her hair was pulled back into a small, tight bun at the nape of her neck. But her green eyes—rare for a Videssian—held just enough ironic amusement to temper the harshness she tried to project. "To what pen-pushers' inquities are we referring?" she asked, and Scaurus heard it in her voice as well.

"None," he admitted, "unless you happen to know where they've spirited away Kybistra's tax records."

"I don't," she said at once, "but surely you could have a mage find them for you."

"Why, so I could," Scaurus said, amazed. The notion had never entered his mind. For all his time in Videssos, down deep he still did not accept magic, and it rarely occurred to him to use it. He wondered how much sorcery went on around him, unnoticed, every day among folk who took it as much for granted as a cloak against the cold.

Such musings vanished as he remembered his chief reason for seeing the princess. "I'm not here on account of the pen-pushers, actually," he began, and set out the story of how

Taron Leimmokheir had recognized him and insisted on his own innocence.

Alypia grew serious as she listened, alert and intent. The expression suited her face perfectly; Marcus thought of the goddess Minerva as he watched her. She was silent for several moments after he finished, then asked at last, "What do you make of what he said?"

"I don't know what to believe. The evidence against him is strong, and yet I thought the first time I heard his voice that he was a man whose word was good. It troubles me."

"Well it might. I've known Leimmokheir five years now, since my father won the throne, and never seen him do anything dishonorable or base." Her mouth twitched in a mirthless smile. "He even treated me as if I were really Empress. He may have been artless enough to think I was."

Scaurus rested his chin on the back of his hand, looked down at the floor. "Then I'd best see your uncle, hadn't I?" He did not relish the prospect; Thorisin was anything but reasonable on the matter of Leimmokheir.

Alypia understood that, too. "I'll come with you, if you like."

"I'd be grateful," he said frankly. "It would make me less likely to be taken for a traitor."

She smiled. "Hardly that. Shall we find him now?"

The bare-branched trees' shadows were long outside. "Tomorrow will do well enough. I'd like to see to my men with what's left of today; as is, I don't get as much chance as I should."

"All right. My uncle likes to ride in the early morning, so I'll meet you at midday outside the Grand Courtroom." She stood, a sign the audience was at an end.

"Thanks," he said, rising too.

He took another little cake from the enamelwork tray, then smiled himself as the memory came back. He'd had these cakes before and knew who baked them. "They're as good as I remembered," he said.

For the first time he saw Alypia's reserve crack. Her eyes widened slightly, her hand fluttered as if to brush the compliment away. "Tomorrow, then," she said quietly.

"Tomorrow."

* * *

When the tribune got back to the barracks he found an argument in full swing. Gorgidas had made the mistake of trying to explain the Greek notion of democracy to Viridovix and succeeded only in horrifying the Celtic noble.

"It's fair unnatural," Viridovix said. "'Twas the gods themselves set some folk above the rest." Arigh Arghun's son, who was there visiting the Gaul and soaking up some wine, nodded vigorously.

"Nonsense," Scaurus said. The Roman patricians had tried to put that one over on the rest of the people, too. It had been centuries since it worked.

But Gorgidas turned on him, snapping, "What makes you think I need *your* help? Your precious Roman republic has its nobles, too, though they buy their way to the rôle instead of being born into it. Why is a Crassus a man worth hearing, if not for his moneybags?"

"What are you yattering about?" Arigh said impatiently; the allusion meant nothing to him and hardly more to Viridovix. The Arshaum was a chieftain's son, though, and knew what he thought of the Greek's idea. "A clan has nobles for the same reason an army has generals—so when trouble comes, people know whom to follow."

Gorgidas shot back, "Why follow anyone simply because of birth? Wisdom would be a better guide."

"Be a man never so wise, if he comes dung-footed from the fields and speaks like the clodhopper born, no one'll be after hearing his widsom regardless," Viridovix said.

Arigh's flat features showed his contempt for all farmers, noble and peasant alike, but he followed the principle the Celt was laying down. In his harsh, clipped speech he said to Gorgidas, "Here, outlander, let me tell you a story to show you what I mean."

"A story, is it? Wait a moment, will you?" The physician trotted off, to return with tablet and stylus. If anything could ease him out of an argumentative mood, it was the prospect of learning more about the world in which he found himself. He poised stylus over wax. "All right, carry on."

"This happened a few years back, you'll understand," Arigh began, "among the Arshaum who fellow the standard of the Black Sheep—near neighbors to my father's clan. One of their war leaders was a baseborn man named Kuyuk, and he had a yen for power. He toppled the clan-chief neat as you please, but because he was a nobody's son, the nobles were touchy about doing what he told them. He was clever, though, was Kuyuk, and had himself a scheme.

"One of the things the clan-chief left behind when he ran was a golden foot-bath. The nobles washed their feet in it, aye, and pissed in it, too, sometimes. Now Kuyuk had a goldsmith melt it down and recast it in the shape of a wind spirit. He set it up among the tents, and all the clansmen of the Black Sheep made sacrifice to it."

"Sounds like something out of Herodotos," Gorgidas said, little translucent spirals of wax curling up from his darting stylus.

"Out of what? Anyway, Kuyuk let this go on for a while and then called in his factious nobles. He told them where the image came from, and said, 'You used to wash your feet in that basin, and piddle in it, and even puke. Now you sacrifice to it, because it's in a spirit's shape. The same holds true for me: when I was a commoner you could revile me all you liked, but as clan-chief I deserve the honor of my station.'"

"Och, what a tricksy man!" Viridovix exclaimed in admiration. "That should have taught them respect."

"Not likely! The chief noble, whose name was Mutugen, stuck a knife into Kuyuk. Then all the nobles gathered round and pissed on his corpse. As Mutugen said, 'Gold is gold no matter what the shape, and a baseborn man's still baseborn with a crown on his head.' Mutugen's son Tutukan is chief of the Black Sheep to this day—they wouldn't follow a nobody."

"True, your nobles wouldn't," Marcus said, "but what of the rest of the clan? Were they sorry to see Kuyuk killed?"

"Who knows? What difference does it make?" Arigh answered, honestly confused. Viridovix slapped him on the back in agreement.

Gorgidas threw his hands in the air. Now, put in a more dispassionate frame of mind by his ethnographic jotting, he was willing to admit Scaurus to his side. He said, "Don't let them reach you, Roman. They haven't experienced it, and understand no more than a blind man does a painting."

"Honh!" said Viridovix. "Arigh, what say you the two of us find a nice aristocratic tavern and have a jar or two o' the noble grape?" Tall Celt and short wiry plainsman strode out of the barracks side by side.

Gorgidas' note-taking and his own visit to Alypia Gavra reminded Marcus of the Greek doctor's other interest. "How is that history of yours doing?" he asked.

"It comes, Scaurus, a bit at a time, but it comes."

"May I see it?" the Roman asked, suddenly curious. "My Greek was never of the finest, I know, and it's the worse for rust, but I'd like to try, if you'd let me."

Gorgidas hesitated. "I have only the one copy." But unless he wrote for himself alone, the tribune was his only possible audience for his work in the original, and no Videssian translation, even if somehow made, could be the same. "Mind you care for it, now—don't let your brat be gumming it."

"Of course not," Scaurus soothed him.

"Well all right, then, I'll fetch it, or such of it as is fit to see. No, no stay there, don't trouble yourself. I'll get it." The Greek went off to his billet in the next barracks hall. He returned with a pair of parchment scrolls, which he defiantly handed to Marcus.

"Thank you," the tribune said, but Gorgidas brushed the amenities aside with an impatient wave of his hand. Marcus knew better than to push him; the physician was a large-hearted man, but disliked admitting it even to himself.

Scaurus took the scrolls back to his own quarters, lit a lamp, and settled down on the bedroll to read. As twilight deepened, he realized how poor and flickering the light was. He thought of the priest Apsimar back at Imbros and the aura of pearly radiance the ascetic cleric could project at will. Sometimes magic was very handy, though Apsimar would cry blasphemy if asked to be a reading lamp . . .

Concentration on Gorgidas' history drove such trivia from his mind. The going was slow at first. Scaurus had not read Greek for several years—it was distressing to see how much of his painfully built vocabulary had fallen by the wayside. The farther he went, though, the more he realized the physician had created—what was that phrase of Thucydides'?—a *ktema es aei*, a possession for all time.

Gorgidas' style was pleasingly straightforward; he wrote a smooth *koine* Greek, with only a few unusual spellings to remind one he came from Elis, a city that used the Doric dialect. But the history had more to offer than an agreeable style. There was real thought behind it. Gorgidas constantly strove to reach beyond mere events to illuminate the principles they illustrated. Marcus wondered if his physician's training had a hand in that. A doctor had to recognize a disease's true nature rather than treating only its symptoms.

Thus when speaking of anti-Namdalener riots in Videssos, Gorgidas gave an account of what had happened in the particular case he had observed, but went on to remark, "A city mob is a thing that loves trouble and is rash by nature; the civil strife it causes may be more dangerous and harder to put down than warfare with foreign foes." It was a truth not limited to the Empire alone.

Helvis came in, breaking Marcus' train of thought. She had Dosti in the crook of her arm and led Malric by the hand. Her son by Hemond broke free from his mother and jumped on Scaurus' stomach. "We went walking on the sea wall," he said with a five-year-old's frightening enthusiasm, "and mama bought me a sausage, and we watched the ships sailing away—"

Marcus lifted a questioning eyebrow. "Bouraphos," Helvis said. The tribune nodded. It was about time Thorisin sent Pityos help against the Yezda, and the drungarios of the fleet could reach the port on the Videssian Sea long before any force got there by land.

Malric burbled on; Scaurus listened with half an ear. Helvis set Dosti down. He tried to stand, fell over, and crawled toward his father. "Da!" he announced. "Da-da-da!" He reached for the roll of parchment the tribune had set down. Remembering Gorgidas' half-serious warning, Marcus snatched it away. The baby's face clouded over. Marcus grabbed him and tossed him up and down, which seemed to please him well enough.

"Me, too," Malric said, tugging at his arm.

Scaurus tried hard not to favor Dosti over his stepson. "All right, hero, but you're a bit big for me to handle lying down." The tribune climbed to his feet. He gave Dosti back to Helvis, then swung Malric through the air until the boy shrieked with glee.

"Enough," Helvis warned practically, "or he won't keep that sausage down." To her son she added, "And enough for you, too, young man. Get ready to go to bed." After the usual protests, Malric slipped out of shirt and breeches and slid under the covers. He fell asleep at once.

"What did you rescue from this one?" Helvis asked, hefting Dosti. "Are you bringing your taxes to bed now?"

"I should hope not," Marcus exclaimed; there was a perversion not even Vardanes Sphrantzes could enjoy. The tribune showed Helvis Gorgidas' history. The strange script made her frown. Though she could read only a few words of Videssian, she knew what the signs were supposed to look like, and was taken aback that a different system could represent sounds.

Something almost like fear was in her eyes as she said to Scaurus, "There are times when I nearly forget from how far away you come, dear, and then something like this reminds me. This is your Latin, then?"

"Not quite," the tribune said, but he could see his explanation left her confused. Nor did she understand his interest in the past.

"It's gone, and gone forever. What could be more useless?" she said.

"How can you hope to understand what will come without knowing what's come before?"

"What comes will come, whether I understand it or not. Now is plenty for me."

Marcus shook his head. "There's more than a little barbarian in you, I fear," he said, but fondly.

"And what if there is?" Her stare challenged him. She put Dosti in his crib.

He took her in his arms. "I wasn't complaining," he said.

It always amused Scaurus how students and masters of the Videssian Academy turned to watch him as he made his way through the gray sandstone building's corridors. They could be priest or noble, graybeard scholar or ropemaker's gifted son, but the sight of a mercenary captain in the halls never failed to make heads swing.

He was glad Nepos kept early hours. With luck, the chubby little priest could find his missing tax roll for him before he was due to meet Alypia Gavra. At first it seemed he would have that luck, for Nepos' hours were even earlier than he'd thought; when he peered into the refectory a drowsy-looking student told him, "Aye, he was here, but he's already gone to lecture. Where, you say? I think in one of the chambers on the third floor, I'm not sure which." The young man went back to his honey-sweetened barley porridge.

Marcus trudged up the stairs, then walked past open doors until he found his man. He slid into an empty seat at the back of the room. Nepos beamed at him but kept on teaching. His dozen or so students scribbled notes as they tried to keep pace.

Now and then a student would ask a question; Nepos dealt with them effortlessly but patiently, always asking at the end of his explanation, "Now do you understand?" To that Scaurus would have had to answer no. As near as he could gather, the priest's subject matter was somewhere on the border between theology and sorcery, and decidedly too abstruse for the uninitiated. Still, the tribune judged him a fine speaker, witty, thoughtful, self-possessed.

"That will do for today," Nepos said as Marcus was beginning to fidget. Most of the students trooped out; a couple stayed behind to ask questions too complex to interrupt the flow of the lecture. They, too, looked curiously at Scaurus as they left.

So did Nepos. "Well, well," he chuckled, pumping the tribune's hand. "What brings you here? Surely not a profound interest in the relation between the ubiquity of Phos' grace and proper application of the law of contact."

"Uh, no," Scaurus said. But when he explained why he had come, Nepos laughed until his round cheeks reddened. The tribune did not see the joke, and said so.

"Your pardon, I pray. I have a twofold reason for mirth." He ticked them off his fingers. "First, for something so trivial you hardly need the services of a chairholder in theoretical thaumaturgy. Any street-corner wizard could find your lost register for a fee of a couple of silver bits."

"Oh." Marcus felt his face grow hot. "But I don't know any street-corner wizards, and I do know you."

"Quite right, quite right. Don't take me wrong; I'm happy to help. But a mage of my power is no more *needed* for so simple a spell than a sledgehammer to push a pin through gauze. It struck me funny."

"I never claimed to know anything of magic. What else amuses you?" Feeling foolish, the tribune tried to hide it with gruffness.

"Only that today's lecture topic turns out to be relevant to you after all. Thanks to Phos' all-pervading goodness, things once conjoined are ever after so related that contact between them can be restored. Would you have, perhaps, a tax roll from a city close by Kybistra?"

Scaurus thought. "Yes, back at my offices I was working on the receipts from Doxon. I don't know that part of the Empire well, but from my maps the two towns are only a day's journey apart."

"Excellent! Using one roll to seek another will strengthen the spell, for, of course, it's also true that like acts most powerfully on like. Lead on, my friend—no, don't be foolish, I have no plans till the afternoon, and this shan't take long, I promise."

As they walked through the palace compound, the priest kept up a stream of chatter on his students, on the weather, on bits of Academy gossip that meant little to Scaurus, and on whatever else popped into his mind. He loved to talk. The Roman gave him a better audience than most of his countrymen, who were also fond of listening to themselves.

Marcus thought the two of them made a pair as strange as Viridovix and Arigh: a fat little shave-pate priest with a fuzzy black beard and a tall blond mercenary-turned-bureaucrat.

"Do you prefer this to the field?" Nepos asked as the tribune ushered him into his office. Pandhelis the secretary looked up in surprise as he saw the priest's blue robe out of the corner of his eye. He jumped to his feet, making the sun-sign over his breast. Nepos returned it.

Scaurus considered. "I thought I would when I started. These days I often wonder—answers are so much less clear-cut here." He didn't want to say much more than that, not with Pandhelis listening. He returned to the business at hand. Doxon's cadaster was where he'd left it, shoved to one corner of his desk. "Will you need any special gear for your spell?" he asked Nepos.

"No, not a thing. Merely a few pinches of dust, to serve as a symbolic link between that which is lost and that which seeks it. Dust, I think, will not be hard to come by in these surroundings." The priest chuckled. Marcus did, too; Pandhelis, a bureaucrat born, sniffed audibly.

Nepos got his dust from the windowsill, carefully put it down in the center of a clean square of parchment. "The manifestations of the spell vary," he explained to Scaurus. "If the missing object is close by, the dust may shape itself into an arrow pointing it out, or may leave its resting point and guide the seeker directly. If the distance is greater, though, it will form a word or image to show him the location of what he's looking for."

In Rome the tribune would have thought that so much hogwash, but he knew better here. Nepos began a chant in the archaic Videssian dialect. He held Doxon's tax roll in his right hand, while the stubby fingers of his left moved in quick passes, amazingly sure and precise. The priest wore a smile of simple pleasure; Marcus thought of a master musician amusing himself with a children's tune.

Nepos called out a last word in a commanding tone of voice, then stabbed his left forefinger down at the dust. But though it roiled briefly, as if breathed upon, it showed no pattern.

Nepos frowned, as Scaurus' imaginary musician might have at a lute string suddenly out of tune. He scratched his chin, looked at the Roman in some embarrassment. "My apologies. I must have done something wrong, though I don't know what. Let me try again." His second effort was no more successful than the first. The dust stirred, then settled meaninglessly.

The priest studied his hands, seemingly wondering if they had betrayed him for some reason of their own. "How curious," he murmured. "Your book is not destroyed, of that I'm sure, else the dust would not have moved at all. But are you certain it's in the city?"

"Where else would it be?" Scaurus retorted, unable to imagine anyone wanting to spirit off such a stupefying document.

"Shall we try to find out?" The question was rhetorical; Nepos was already examining the contents of his belt-pouch to see if he had what he needed. He grunted in satisfaction as he produced a small stoppered glass vial in the shape of a flower's seed-capsule. He put a couple of drops of the liquid within on his tongue, making a face at the taste. "Now this not every wizard will know, so you did well coming to me after all. It clears the mind of doubts and lets it see further, thus increasing the power of the spell."

"What is it?" Scaurus asked.

Nepos hesitated; he did not like to reveal his craft's secrets. But the drug was already having its way with him. "Poppy juice and henbane," he said drowsily. The pupils of his eyes shrank down almost to nothing. But his voice and hands, drilled by years of the wizard's art, went through the incantation without faltering.

Again the finger darted at the dust. Marcus' eyes widened as he watched the pinches of dead stuff writhe like a tiny snake and shape themselves into a word. Successful magic never failed to raise his hackles.

"How interesting," Nepos said, though his decoction dulled the interest in his voice. "Even aided, I did not think the cantrip could reach to Garsavra."

"Fair enough," Scaurus answered, "because I didn't think the tax roll could be there either." He scratched his head, wondering why it was. No matter, he decided; Onomagoulos could always send it back.

The tribune dispatched Pandhelis to take Nepos to the Roman barracks and put him to bed. The priest went without demur. The potion he had swallowed left his legs rubbery and his usually lively spirit as muffled as a drum beaten through several thicknesses of cloth. "No, don't worry for me. It will wear off soon," he reassured Scaurus, fighting back an enormous yawn. He lurched off on Pandhelis' arm.

Marcus looked out the window, then quickly followed the secretary and priest downstairs. By the shortness of the shadows it was nearly noon, and it would not do to keep Alypia Gavra waiting.

To his dismay, he found her already standing by the Grand Gates. She did not seem angry, though. In fact, she was deep in conversation with the four Romans on sentry duty for her uncle.

"Aye, your god's well enough, my lady," Minucius was saying, "but I miss the legion's eagle. That old bird watched over us a lot of times." The legionary's companions nodded soberly. So did Alypia. She frowned, as if trying to fix Minucius' remark in her memory. Marcus could not help smiling. He'd seen that expression on Gorgidas too often not to recognize it now—the mark of a historian at work.

Spotting his commander, Minucius came to attention, grounding his spear with a sharp thud. He and his comrades gave Scaurus the clenched-fist Roman salute. "As you were. I'm outranked here," the tribune said easily. He bowed to Alypia.

"Don't let me interfere between your men and you," she said.

"You weren't." Back in his days with Caesar in Gaul, the least breach of order would have disturbed him mightily. Two and a half years as a mercenary captain had taught him the difference between spit and polish for their own sake and the real discipline that was needed to survive.

The chamberlain inside the Grand Gates clicked his tongue between his teeth. "Your Highness, where are your attendants?" he asked.

"Doing whatever they do, I imagine. I have no use for them," she answered curtly, and ignored the functionary's indignant look. Scaurus noted the edge in her voice; her natural leaning toward privacy could only have been exaggerated by the time she spent as Vardanes Sphrantzes' captive.

The court attendant gave an eloquent shrug, but bowed and conducted them forward. As the tribune walked up the colonnaded central hall toward the imperial throne, he saw the damage of the previous summer's fight had been repaired. Tapestries hung untorn, while tiny bits of matching stone were cemented into chipped columns.

Then Scaurus realized not all the injuries had been healed. He strode over a patch of slightly discolored porphyry flooring, a patch whose polish did not quite match the mirrorlike perfection of the rest. It would have been about here, he thought, that Avshar's fire blazed. He wondered again where the wizard-prince's sorcery had snatched him; through all the winter there had been no report of him.

Alypia's eyes were fathomless, but the closer she drew to the throne—and to the passageway beside it—the tighter her mouth became, until Marcus saw her bite her lip.

Another chamberlain led Katakolon Kekaumenos back from his audience with the Emperor. The legate from Agder gave Scaurus his wintry smile, inclined his head to Alypia Gavra. Once he was out of earshot, she murmured, "You'd think he paid for every word he spoke."

Their guide fell in the proskynesis before the throne. From his belly he called up to Thorisin, "Her Highness the Princess Alypia Gavra! The *epoptes* and commander Scaurus the

Ronam!" Marcus stifled the urge to kick him in his upraised backside.

"Phos' light, fool, I know who they are," the Emperor growled, still with no use for court ceremonial. The attendant rose. He gaped to see the tribune still on his feet. Alypia was of royal blood, but why was this outlander so privileged? "Never mind, Kabasilas," Thorisin said. "My brother made allowances for him, and I do, too. He earns them, mostly." Kabasilas bowed and withdrew, but his curled lip spoke volumes.

Gavras cocked an eyebrow at the tribune. "So, *epoptes* and commander Scaurus, what now? Are the seal-stampers siphoning off goldpieces to buy themselves counting-boards with beads of ruby and silver?"

"As for that," Marcus said, "I'm having some trouble finding out." He told the Emperor of the missing tax register, thinking to slide from an easy matter to the harder one that was his main purpose here.

"I thought you know better than to come to me with such twaddle," Thorisin said impatiently. "Send to Baanes if you will, but you have no need to bother me about it."

Scaurus accepted the rebuke; like Mavrikios, the younger Gavras appreciated directness. But when the Roman began his plea for Taron Leimmokheir, the Emperor did not let him get past the ex-admiral's name before he roared, "No, by Skotos' filth-filled beard! Are you turned treacher, too?"

His bellow filled the Grand Courtroom. Courtiers froze in mid-step; a chamberlain almost dropped the fat red candle he was carrying. It went out. His curse, a eunuch's contralto, echoed Gavras'. Minucius poked his head into the throne room to see what had happened.

"You were the one who told me it wasn't in the man to lie," Marcus said, persisting where a man born in the Empire might well quail.

"Aye, so I did, and came near paying my life for my stupidity," Thorisin retorted. "Now you tell me to put the wasp back in my tunic for another sting. Let him stay mured up till he rots, and gabble out his prayers lest worse befall him."

"Uncle, I think you're wrong," Alypia said. "What little decency came my way while the Sphrantzai reigned came from Leimmokheir. Away from his precious ships he's a child, with no more skill at politics than Marcus' foster son."

The tribune blinked, first at her mentioning Malric and then at her calling him by his own praenomen. When used alone, it was normally a mark of close personal ties. He wondered whether she knew the Roman custom.

She was going on, "You know I'm telling you the truth, uncle. How many years, now, have you known Leimmokheir? More than a handful, surely. You know the man he is. Do you really think that man could play you false?"

The Emperor's fist slammed down on the gold-sheathed arm of his throne. The ancient seat was not made for such treatment; it gave a painful creak of protest. Thorisin leaned forward to emphasize his words. "The man I knew would not break faith. But Leimmokheir did, and thus I knew him not at all. Who does worse evil, the man who shows his wickedness for the whole world to see or the one who stores it up to loose against those who trust him?"

"A good question for a priest," Alypia said, "but not one with much meaning if Leimmokheir is innocent."

"I was there, girl. I saw what was done, saw the new-minted goldpieces of the Sphrantzai in the murderers' pouches. Let Leimmokheir explain them away—that might earn his freedom." The Emperor laughed, but it was a sound of hurt. Marcus knew it was futile to argue further; feeling betrayed by a man he had thought honest, Gavras would not, could not, yield to argument.

"Thank you for hearing me, at least," the tribune said. "I gave my word to put the case to you once more."

"Then you misgave it."

"No, I think not."

"There are times, outlander, when you try my patience," the Emperor said dangerously. Scaurus met his eye, hiding the twinge of fear he felt. Much of the position he had built for himself in Videssos was based on not letting the sheer weight of imperial authority coerce him. That, for a man of republican Rome, was easy. Facing an angry Thorisin Gavras was something else again.

Gavras made a dissatisfied sound deep in his throat. "Kabasilas!" he called, and the chamberlain was at his elbow as the last syllable of his name still echoed in the high-ceilinged throne room. Marcus expected some sonorous formula of dismissal, but that was not Thorisin's way. He jerked his head toward his niece and the tribune and left Kabasilas to put such formality in the gesture as he might.

The steward did his best, but his bows and flourishes seemed all the more artificial next to the Emperor's unvarnished rudeness. The other court functionaries craned their necks at Scaurus and Alypia as he led them away, wondering how much favor they had lost. That would be as it was, Marcus thought. He laughed at himself—a piece of fatalism worthy of the Halogai.

When they came out to the Grand Gates once more, Alypia stopped to talk a few minutes longer with the Roman sentries there, then departed for the imperial residence. Scaurus went up to his offices to dictate a letter to Baanes Onomagoulos; Pandhelis' script was far more legible than his own. That accomplished, he basked in a pleasant glow of self-satisfaction as he started back to the barracks.

It did not last long. Viridovix was coming toward him, a jar of wine in his hand and an anticipatory grin on his face. The Gaul threw him a cheery wave and ducked into a small doorway in the other wing of the Grand Courtroom.

Maybe I should have drowned him, Marcus thought angrily. Had Viridovix no idea what he was playing at? There was no more caution in him than guile in Taron Leimmokheir. What would he do next, ask Thorisin for the loan of a bedroom? The tribune warned himself not to suggest that—Viridovix might take him up on it.

With the Celt gone, Scaurus was surprised to see Arigh at the barracks. The Arshaum was talking to Gorgidas again while the Greek took notes. Gorgidas was asking, "Who sees to your sick, then?"

The question seemed to bore Arigh, who scratched beneath his tunic of sueded leather. At last he said indifferently, "The shamans drive out evil spirits, of course, and for smaller ills the old women know of herbs, I suppose. Ask me of war, where I can talk of what I know." He slapped the curved sword that hung at his side.

Quintus Glabrio came in; he smiled and waved to Gorgidas without interrupting the physician's jottings. Instead he said to Marcus, "I'm glad to see you here, sir. A couple of my men have a running quarrel I can't seem to get to the bottom of. Maybe they'll heed you."

"I doubt that, if you can't solve it," the tribune said, but he went with Glabrio anyhow. The legionaries stood stiff-faced as he warned them not to let their dislike for each other affect their soldiering. They nodded at the correct times. Scaurus was not deceived; anything the able junior centurion could not cure over the course of time would not yield to his brief intercession. The men were on formal notice now, so perhaps something was accomplished.

Arigh had gone when he returned. Gorgidas was working up his notes, rubbing out a word here, a phrase there with the blunt end of his stylus, then reversing it to put his changes on the wax. "Viridovix will think you're trying to steal his friend away," the tribune said.

"What do I care what that long-shanked Gaul thinks?" Gorgidas asked, but could not quite keep amusement from his voice. Sometimes Viridovix made his friends want to wring his neck, but they remained his friends in spite of it. Less pleased, the doctor went on, "At least I can learn what the plainsman has to teach me."

There was no mistaking his bitterness. Marcus knew he was still seeing Nepos and other healer-priests, still trying to master their arts, and still falling short. No wonder he was putting more energy into his history these days. Medicine could not be satisfying to him right now.

Scaurus yawned, cozily warm under the thick wool blanket. Helvis' steady breathing beside him said she had already dropped off; so did her arm flung carelessly across his chest. Malric was asleep on her other side, while Dosti's breath came raspy from his crib. The baby was getting over a minor fever; Marcus drowsily hoped he would not catch it.

But an itchy something in the back of his mind kept him from following them into slumber. He rehashed the day's events, trying to track it down. Was it his failure to gain Taron Leimmokheir's release? Close, he thought, but not on the mark. He had not expected to win that one.

Why close, then? He heard Alypia Gavra's voice once more as she talked with the legionaries outside the Grand Courtroom. Whatever else she knew about their ways, he realized, she was perfectly familiar with the proper use of Roman names.

He was a long time sleeping.

XII

THE TRIBUNE SNEEZED. GAIUS PHILIPPUS LOOKED AT HIM IN disgust. "Aren't you through with that bloody thing yet?"

"It hangs on and on," Marcus said dolefully, wiping his nose. His eyes were watery, too, and his head seemed three times its proper size. "What is it, two weeks now?"

"At least. That's what you get for having your brat." Revoltingly healthy himself, Gaius Philippus spooned up his breakfast porridge, took a great gulp of wine. "That's good!" He patted his belly. Scaurus had scant appetite, which was as well, for his sense of taste had disappeared.

Viridovix strode into the barracks, splendid in his cape of crimson skins. He helped himself to peppery lamb sausage, porridge, and wine, then sank into a chair by the tribune and senior centurion. "The top o' the day t'ye!" he said, lifting his mug in salute.

"And to you," Marcus returned. He looked the Celt up and down. "Why such finery so early in the morning?"

"Early in the morning it may be for some, Scaurus dear, but I'm thinking of it as night's end. And a rare fine night it was, too." He winked at the two Romans.

"Mmph," Marcus said, as noncommittal a noise as he could muster. Normally he enjoyed Viridovix in a bragging mood, but since the Gaul had taken up with Komitta Rhangavve the less he heard the better. Nor did Gaius Philippus' incurious expression offer Viridovix any encouragement; the senior centurion, Marcus was sure, was jealous of the Celt, but would sooner have been racked than admit it.

Irrepressible as always, Viridovix needed scant prompting.

After a long, noisy pull at his wine, he remarked, "Would your honor believe it, the wench had the brass to tell me to put all my other lassies to one side and have her only. Not ask, mind you, but tell! And me sharing her with himself without so much as a peep. The cheek of it all!" He bit into the sausage, made a face at its spiciness, and drank again.

"Sharing who with whom?" Gaius Philippus asked, confused by pronouns.

"Never mind," Marcus said quickly. The fewer people who knew of Viridovix's trysting, the longer word of it would take to get back to Thorisin Gavras. Even Viridovix saw that, for he suddenly looked sly. But his report of what Komitta had said worried the tribune enough to make him ask, "What did you tell the lady?"

"What any Celtic noble and gentleman would, of course: to go futter the moon. No colleen bespeaks me so."

"Oh, no." Scaurus wanted to hold his aching head in his hands. With Komitta's savage temper and great sense of her own rank, it was a wonder Viridovix was here to tell the tale. In fact— "What did she say to that?"

"Och, she carried on somewhat, sure and she did, but I horned it out of her." Viridovix stretched complacently. The tribune looked at him in awe. If that was true, the Gaul was a mighty lanceman indeed.

Viridovix routed a piece of gristle out from between his teeth with a fingernail, then belched. "Still and all," he said, "if ye maun play the tomcat of evenings, then the day's the time for lying up. A bit o' sleep'd be welcome now, so by your leaves—" He rose, finished his wine, and walked out, whistling cheerily.

"Enough of your 'never minds,'" Gaius Philippus said as soon as the Celt was gone. "You don't go fish-belly color over trifles. What's toward?"

So Marcus, his hand forced, told him and had the remote pleasure of watching his jaw drop to his chest. "Almighty Jove," the senior centurion said at last. "The lad doesn't think small, does he now?"

He thought another minute, then added, "He's welcome to her, too, for my silver. I'd sooner strop my tool on a sword blade than go near that one. All in all, it's safer." The tribune winced at the image, but slowly nodded; down deep inside he felt the same way.

* * *

As spring drew on, Scaurus spent less time at tax records. Most of the receipts had come in after the fall harvest, and he was through most of the backlog by the time the days began to grow longer once more. He knew he had done an imperfect job of overseeing the Videssian bureaucracy. It was too large, too complex, and too well entrenched for any one man, let alone an outsider, to control it fully. But he did think he had done some good and kept more revenue flowing into the imperial treasury than it would have got without him.

He was only too aware of some of his failures. One afternoon Pikridios Goudeles had mortified him by coming into the offices with a massy golden ring set with an enormous emerald. The minister wore it with great ostentation and flashed it at the tribune so openly that Marcus was sure its price came from diverted funds. Indeed, Goudeles hardly bothered to deny it, only smiling a superior smile. Yet try as Scaurus would, he could find no errors in the books.

Goudeles let him stew for several days, then, still with that condescending air, showed the Roman the sly bit of jugglery he'd used. "For," he said, "having used it myself, I see no point in letting just anyone slide it past you. That would reflect on my own skill."

More or less sincerely, Marcus thanked him and said nothing further about the ring; he had fairly lost this contest of wit with the bureaucrat, just as he had won the one before. They remained not-quite-friends, each with a healthy regard for the other's competence. As Scaurus came less often to his desk in the Grand Courtroom wing, he sometimes missed the seal-stamper's dry, delicate wit, his exquisite sense of where to place a dart.

Before long, only one major item was outstanding on the tribune's list: the tax roll for Kybistra. Onomagoulos ignored his first request for it; he sent out another, more strongly worded. "That echo will be a long time returning, I think," Goudeles told him.

"Eh? Why?" Marcus asked irritably.

The bureaucrat's eyebrow could not have lifted by the thickness of a hair, but he contrived to make the Roman feel like a small, stupid child. "Ah, well," Goudeles murmured, "it was a disorderly time for everyone."

Scaurus thumped his forehead with the heel of his hand,

annoyed with himself for missing what was obvious, once pointed out. Onomagoulos had taken refuge at Kybistra after Maragha; the tribune wondered what part of his accounts would not bear close inspection. Thorisin, he thought, would be interested in that question, too.

So it proved. The imperial rescript that went out to Garsavra all but crackled off its parchment. By that time Marcus cared less than he had. He was working hard with his troops as they readied themselves for the coming summer campaign. As he sweated on the practice field, he was gratified to see the beginning potbelly he had grown during the winter's inactivity start to fade away.

Roman training techniques were enough to melt the fat off anyone. The Videssians, Vaspurakaners, and other locals who had taken service with the legionaries grumbled constantly, as soldiers will over any exercises. Gaius Philippus, naturally, worked them all the harder for their complaints. As for Scaurus, he threw himself into the drills with an enthusiasm he had not felt when he first joined the legions.

The troops exercised with double-weight weapons of wood, and fought at pells until their arms ached, thrusting now at the dummy posts' faces, now at their flanks, and again at thigh level. They used heavy wicker shields, too, and practiced advancing and retreating from their imaginary foes.

"Hard work, this," Gagik Bagratouni said. The Vaspurakaner *nakharar* still led his countrymen and had learned to swear in broken Latin as foully as in his hardly more fluent Videssian. "By the time comes real battle, a relief it will be."

"That's the idea," Gaius Philippus said. Bagratouni groaned and shook his head, sending sweat flying everywhere. He was well into his forties, and the drill came hard for him. He worked at it with the fierce concentration of a man trying to forget past shadows, and his countrymen showed a spirit and discipline that won the Romans' admiration.

The only thing that horrified the mountaineers was having to learn to swim. The streams in their homeland were trickles most of the year, floods the rest. Learn they did, but they never came to enjoy the water legionary-style, as a pleasant way to end a day's exercises.

The Videssians among the legionaries were not quite at

their high pitch. A dozen times a day Marcus would hear some Roman yelling, "The point, damn it, the point! A pox on the bloody edge! It isn't good for anything anyway!" The imperials always promised to mend their swordplay and always slipped back. Most were ex-cavalrymen, used to the saber's sweet slash. Thrusting with the short *gladius* went against their instincts.

More patient than most of his fellows, Quintus Glabrio would explain, "No matter how hard you cut, armor and bones both shield your foe's vitals, but even a poorly delivered stab may kill. Besides, with the stabbing stroke you don't expose your own body and often you can kill your man before he knows you've delivered the stroke." Having nodded in solemn agreement, the Videssians would do as they were ordered—for a while.

Then there were those to whom Roman discipline meant nothing at all. Viridovix was as deadly a fighter as Scaurus had seen, but utterly out of place in the orderly lines of the legionaries' maniples. Even Gaius Philippus acknowledged the hopelessness of making him keep rank. "I'm just glad he's on our side," was the senior centurion's comment.

Zeprin the Red was another lone wolf. His great axe unsuited him for action among the legionaries' spears and swords, as did his temperament. Where Viridovix saw battle as high sport, the Haloga looked on it as his cold gods' testing place. "Their shield-maidens guide upwards the souls of those who fall bravely. With my enemy's blood I will buy my stairway to heaven," he rumbled, testing the edge of his doublebitted weapon with his thumb. No one seemed inclined to argue, though to Videssian ears that was pagan superstition of the rankest sort.

Drax of Namdalen and his captains came out to the practice field several times to watch the Romans work. Their smart drill impressed the great count, who told Scaurus, "By the Wager, I wish that son of a pimp Goudeles had warned me what sort of men you had. I thought my knights would ride right through you so we could roll up Thorisin's horse like a pair of leggings." He shook his head ruefully. "Didn't quite work that way."

"You gave us a bad time, too," the tribune returned the compliment. Drax remained a mystery to him—a skilled warrior, certainly, but a man who showed little of himself to the world outside. Though unfailingly courteous, he had a stiff face a horse trader would envy.

"He reminds me of Vardanes Sphrantzes with the back of his head shaved," Gaius Philippus said after the islander left, but that far Marcus would not go. Whatever Drax's mask concealed, he did not think it was the unmourned Sevastos' cruelty.

However much the Namdaleni admired the legionaries, the senior centurion remained dissatisfied. "They're soft," he mourned. "They need a couple of days of real marching to get the winter laziness out of 'em once for all."

"Let's do it, then," Marcus said, though he felt a twinge of trepidation. If the troopers needed work, what of him?

"Full kits tomorrow," he heard Gaius Philippus order, and listened to the chorus of donkey brays that followed. The full Roman pack ran to more than a third of a man's weight; along with weapons and iron rations, it included a mess kit, cup, spare clothes in a small wicker hamper, a tent section, palisade stakes or firewood, and either a saw, pick, spade, or sickle for camping and foraging. Small wonder the legionaries called themselves mules.

Dawn was only a promise when they tramped out of the city, northward bound. The Videssian gate crew shook their heads in sympathy as they watched the soldiers march past. "Make way, there!" Gaius Philippus rasped, and waggoners hastily got their produce-filled wains out of the roadway. Like most of the Empire's civilians, they distrusted what little they knew about mercenaries and were not anxious to learn more.

Marcus pulled a round, ruddy apple from one of the wagons. He tossed the driver a small copper coin to pay for it and had to laugh at the disbelief on the man's face. "Belike their puir spalpeen was after thinking you'd breakfast on him instead of his fruit," Viridovix said.

There was less room for good cheer as the day wore along. The military step was something the Romans fell into with unthinking ease, each of them automatically holding his place in his maniple's formation. The men who had taken service since they came to Videssos did their best to imitate them but, here as in so many small ways, practice told. And because the newcomers were less orderly, they tired quicker.

Still, almost no one dropped from the line of march, no matter how footsore he became. Blistered toes were nothing to the blistering Gaius Philippus gave fallers-out, nor was any trooper eager to face his fellows' jeers.

Phostis Apokavkos, first of all the Videssians to become a legionary, strode along between two Romans, hunching forward a little under the weight of his pack. His long face crinkled into a smile as he flipped Scaurus a salute.

The tribune returned it. He hardly reckoned Apokavkos a Videssian any more. Like any son of Italy's, the ex-farmer's hands were branded with the mark of the legions. When he learned the mark's significance, Apokavkos had insisted on receiving it, but Scaurus had not asked it of any of the other recruits, nor had they volunteered.

By afternoon the tribune was feeling pleased with himself. There seemed to be a band of hot iron around his chest, and his legs ached at every forward step, but he kept up with his men without much trouble. He did not think they would make the twenty miles that was a good day's march, but they were not far from it.

Already they were past the band of suburbs that huddled under Videssos' walls and out into the countryside. Wheatfields, forests, and vineyards were all glad with new leaf. There were newly returned birds overhead, too. A blackcap swooped low. "Churr! Tak-tak-tak!" it scolded the legionaries, then darted off on its endless pursuit of insects. A small flock of linnets, scarlet heads and breasts bright, twittered as they winged their way toward a gorse-covered hilltop.

Gaius Philippus began eyeing likely looking fields for a place to camp. At last he found one that suited him, with a fine view of the surrounding area and a swift clear stream running by. Woods at the edge of the field promised fuel for campfires. The senior centurion looked a question toward Scaurus, who nodded. "Perfect," he said. Even though this was but a drill, from skill and habit Gaius Philippus was incapable of picking a bad site.

The buccinators' horns blared out the order to halt. The legionaries pulled tools from their packs and fell to work on the square ditch and rampart that would shelter them for the night. Stakes sprouted atop the earthwork wall. Inside, eight-man tents went up in neat rows that left streets running at right angles and a good-sized open central forum. By the time the sun was down, Marcus would have trusted the camp to hold against three or four times his fifteen hundred men.

Some of the farmers hereabout must have reported the Romans' arrival to the local lord, for it had just grown dark when he rode up to investigate with a double handful of armed retainers. Marcus courteously showed him around the camp; he seemed a bit unnerved to be surrounded by so much orderly force.

"Be gone again tomorrow, you say?" he asked for the third time. "Well, good, good. Have a pleasant night of it, now." And he and his men rode away, looking back over their shoulders until the night swallowed them.

"What was all that in aid of?" Gaius Philippus demanded. "Why didn't you just tell him to bugger off?"

"You'd never make a politician," Marcus answered. "After he saw what we had, he didn't have the nerve to ask for the price of the firewood we cut, and I didn't have to embarrass him by telling him no right out loud. Face got saved all around."

"Hmm." It was plain Gaius Philippus did not give a counterfeit copper for the noble's feelings. The tribune, though, found it easier to avoid antagonizing anyone gratuitously. With the touchy Videssians, even that little was not always easy.

He settled down by a campfire to gnaw journeybread, smoked meat, and an onion, and emptied his canteen of the last of the wine it held. When he started to get up to rinse it out, he discovered he could barely stagger to the stream. The break—the first he'd had from marching all day—gave his legs a chance to stiffen, and they'd taken it with a vengeance.

Many legionaries were in the same plight. Gorgidas went from one to the next, kneading life into cramped calves and thighs. The spare Greek, loose-limbed himself after the hard march, spotted Marcus hobbling back to the fireside. "*Kai su, teknon?*" he said in his own tongue. "You too, son? Stretch out there, and I'll see what I can do for you."

Scaurus obediently lay back. He gasped as the doctor's fingers dug into his legs. "I think I'd rather have the aches," he said, but he and Gorgidas both knew he was lying. When the Greek was done, the tribune found he could walk again, more or less as he always had.

"Don't be too proud of yourself," Gorgidas advised, watching his efforts like a parent with a toddler. "You'll still feel it come morning."

The physician, as usual, was right. Marcus shambled down to the stream to splash water on his face, unable to assume any better pace or gait. His sole consolation was that he was far from alone; about one legionary in three looked to have had his legs age thirty years overnight.

"Come on, you lazy sods! It's no further back than it was out!" Gaius Philippus shouted unsympathetically. One of the oldest men in the camp, he showed no visible sign of strain.

"Och, to the crows with you!" That was Viridovix; not being under Roman discipline, he could say what the legionaries felt. The march had been hard on the Gaul. Though larger and stronger than almost all the Romans, he lacked their stamina.

However much Gaius Philippus pressed as the legionaries started back, he did not get the speed he wanted. It took a good deal of marching for the men to work their muscles loose. To the senior centurion's eloquent disgust, they were still a couple of miles short of Videssos when night fell.

"We'll camp here," he growled, again choosing a prime defensive position in pastureland between two suburbs. "I won't have us sneaking in after dark like so many footpads, and you whoresons don't deserve the sweets of the city anyway. Loafing good-for-naughts! Caesar'd be ashamed of the lot of you." That meant little to the Videssians and Vaspurakaners, but it was enough to make the Romans hang their heads in shame. Mention of their old commander was almost too painful to bear.

When Marcus woke the next morning, he found to his surprise that he was much less sore than he had been the day before. "I feel the same way," Quintus Glabrio said with one of his rare smiles. "We're likely just numb from the waist down."

There were quite a few bright sails in the Cattle-Crossing; probably a grain convoy from the westlands' southern coast, thought Scaurus. A city the size of Videssos was far too big for the local countryside to feed.

Less than an hour brought the legionaries to the capital's mighty walls. "Have yourselves a good hike?" one of the gatecrew asked as he waved them through. He grinned at the abuse he got by way of reply.

It was hardly past dawn; Videssos' streets, soon to be swarming with life, as yet were nearly deserted. A few early risers were wandering into Phos' temples for the sunrise liturgy. Here and there people of the night—whores, thieves, gamblers—still strutted or skulked. A cat darted away from the legionaries, a fishtail hanging from the corner of its mouth.

The whole city was sweet with the smell of baking bread. The bakers were at their ovens before the sun was up and stayed till it was dark once more, sweating their lives away to keep Videssos fed. Marcus smiled as he felt his nostrils dilate, heard his stomach growl. Journeybread fought hunger, but the mere thought of a fresh, soft, steaming loaf teased the appetite to new life.

The legionaries entered the palace compound from the north, marching past the Videssian Academy. The sun gleamed off the golden dome on its high spire. Though the season was still early spring, the day already gave promise of being hot and muggy. Marcus was glad for a granite colonnade's long, cool shadow.

Hoofbeats rang round a bend in the path, loud in the morning stillness. The tribune's eyebrows rose. Who was galloping a horse down the palace compound's twisting ways? A typical Roman, Scaurus did not know that much of horses, but it hardly took an equestrian to realize the rider was asking for a broken neck.

The great bay stallion thundered round the bend in the track. Marcus felt alarm stab into his guts—that was the Emperor's horse! But Thorisin was not in the saddle; instead Alypia Gavra bestrode the beast, barely in control. She fought it to a halt just in front of the Romans, whose first ranks were giving back from the seeming runaway.

Not liking the check, the stallion snorted and tossed its head, eager to be given free rein once more. Alypia ignored it. She stared down the long Roman column, despair on her face. "So you've come to betray us, too!" she cried.

Glabrio stepped forward and seized the horse's head. Scaurus said, "Betray you? With a training march?"

The princess and the Roman shared a long, confusion-filled look. Then Alypia exclaimed, "Oh, Phos be praised! Come at once, then—a band of assassins is attacking the private chambers!"

"What?" Marcus said foolishly, but even as he was filling

his lungs to order the legionaries forward he heard Gaius Philippus below, "Battle stations! Forward at double-time!"

Scaurus envied the senior centurion's immunity to surprise. "Shout 'Gavras!' as you come," he added. "Let both sides know help's on the way!"

The legionaries reached back over their shoulders for *pila*, tugged swords free from brass scabbards. "Gavras!" they roared. The Emperor's horse whinnied in alarm and reared, pulling free of Quintus Galbrio's grasp. Alypia held her seat. She could ride, as befitted a onetime provincial noble's daughter. Though Thorisin's frightened charger would have been a handful for anyone, she wheeled it and cantered forward at the Romans' head.

"Get back, my lady!" Marcus called to her. When she would not, he told off half a dozen men to hold her horse and keep her out of the fighting. They ignored her protests and did as they were ordered.

Nestled in the copse of cherry trees just now beginning to come into fragrant bloom, the private imperial residence was a dwelling made for peace. But its outer doors gaped open, and before them a sentry lay unmoving in a pool of blood. "Surround the place!" Marcus snapped, maniples peeled off to right and left.

For all his hurry, he was horribly afraid he had come too late. But as he rushed toward the yawning doorway, he heard fighting within. "It's a rescue, not revenge!" he yelled. The legionaries cheered behind him: "Gavras! Gavras!"

An archer leaped out into the doorway and let fly. Close behind Scaurus, a Roman clutched at his face, then skidded down on his belly. No time to see who had fallen, nor could the Videssian get off a second shot. He threw his bow to one side and drew saber.

He must have known it was hopeless, with hundreds of men thundering toward him. He set his feet and waited nonetheless. The tribune had a moment to admire his courage before their swords met. Then it was all automatic response: thrust, parry, slash, riposte, parry—thrust! Marcus felt his blade bite, twisted his wrist to make sure it was a killing blow. His foe groaned and slowly crumpled.

The Romans spilled down the hallway, their hobnailed *caligae* clattering on the mosaic floor. The light streaming through the alabaster ceiling panels was pale and calm, not the right sort of light at all to shine on battle. And battle there had already been aplenty: the corpses of sentries and eunuch servants sprawled together with those of their assailants. The red tesserae of hunting mosaics were overlain by true blood's brighter crimson; it spattered precious icons and portrait busts of Avtokrators centuries forgotten.

Marcus saw Mizizios lying dead. The eunuch had a sword in his hand and wore an ancient helmet of strange design, loot from a Videssian triumph of long ago. He had been a quick thinker to clap it on his head, but it had not saved him. A great saber cut opened his belly and spilled his entrails out on the floor.

Shouts and the pounding of axes against a barricaded door led the legionaries on. They rounded a last corner, only to be halted by a savage counterattack from the squadron of assassins. In the narrow corridor numbers were of scant advantage. Men pushed and cursed and struck, gasping when they were hit.

The assassins' captain was a burly man of about forty in a much-battered chain-mail shirt. He carried a torch in his right hand, and shouted through the door to Thorisin, "Your bullyboys are here too late, Gavras! You'll be roast meat before they do you any good!"

"Not so!" cried Zeprin the Red, who was fighting in the first rank of legionaries. He still blamed himself for Mavrikios Gavras' death, and would not let a second Emperor weigh on his conscience. The thick-muscled Haloga flung his great war axe at the torch-carrier. The throw was not good; quarters were too close for that. Instead of one of the gleaming steel bits burying itself in the Videssian's chest, it was the end of the axe handle that caught him in the pit of the stomach. Mail shirt or no, he doubled over as if kicked by a steer. The smoking torch fell to the floor and went out.

Snarling an oath, one of the trapped attackers sprang at Zeprin, who stood for a second weaponless. The Haloga did not—could not—retreat. He ducked under a furious slash, came up to seize his foe and crush him against his armored chest. The tendons stood out on his massive arms; his opponent's hands scrabbled uselessly at his back. Scaurus heard bones crack even through the din of combat. Zeprin threw the lifeless corpse aside.

At the same moment Viridovix, with an enormous two-handed slash, sent another assassin's head springing from his shoulders. The tribune could feel the enemy's spirit drain away. A quiet bit of murder was one thing, but facing these berserkers was something else again. Nor were the Romans themselves idle. Their shortswords stabbed past the Vides-sians' defenses, while their large *scuta* turned blow after blow. "Gavras!" they shouted, and pushed their foes back and back.

Then the blocked door flew open, and Thorisin Gavras and his four or five surviving guards charged at the enemy's backs, crying, "The Romans! The Romans!" It was more gal-lant than sensible, but Thorisin had an un-Videssian fondness for battle.

Some of the attackers spun round against him, still trying to complete their mission. Gaius Philippus cut one down from behind. "You bloody stupid bastard," he said, jerking his *gla-dius* free.

Marcus swore as a saber gashed his forearm. He tightened his fingers on his sword hilt. They all answered—no tendon was cut—but blood made the sword slippery in his hand.

Thorisin killed the man he was facing. The Emperor, not one to relish having to flee even before overpowering numbers, fought now with savage ferocity to try to ease the discredit only he felt. When he had been Sevastokrator he probably would have let his fury run away with him, but the imperial office was tempering him as it had his brother. See-ing only a handful of his assailants on their feet, he cried, "Take them alive! I'll have answers for this!"

Most of the assassins, knowing what fate held for them, battled all the harder, trying to make the legionaries kill them outright. One ran himself through. But a couple were borne to the floor and trussed up like dressed carcasses. So was their leader, who still could hardly breathe, let alone fight back.

"Very timely," Thorisin said, looking Marcus up and down. He started to offer his hand to clasp, stopped when he saw the tribune's wound.

Scaurus did not really feel it yet. He answered, "Thank your niece, not me. She lathered your horse for you, but I don't think you'll complain."

The Emperor smiled thinly. "No, I suppose not. Took the beast, did she?" He listened as the Roman explained how he had encountered Alypia.

Thorisin's smile grew wider. He said, "I never have cared for her scribbling away behind closed doors, but I won't complain of that any more, either. She must have gone out the window when the barney started, and run for the stables. Firefoot's usually saddled by dawn." Marcus remembered Gavras' fondness for a morning gallop.

Thorisin prodded a dead body with his foot. "Good thing these lice were too stupid to throw a cordon round the building." He slapped Scaurus on the back. "Enough talk—get that arm seen to. You're losing blood."

The tribune tore a strip of cloth from the corpse's surcoat; Gavras helped him tie the rude dressing. His arm, numb a few minutes before, began to throb fiercely. He went looking for Gorgidas.

The doctor, Marcus thought with annoyance, did not seem to be anywhere within the rambling imperial residence. However much the legionaries outnumbered the twoscore or so assassins, they had not beaten them down without harm to themselves. Five men were dead—two of them irreplaceable Romans—and a good many more were wounded, more or less severely. Grumbling and clenching his fist against the hurt, the tribune went outside.

He saw Gorgidas kneeling over a man in the pathway—a Roman, from his armor—but had no chance to approach the physician. Alypia Gavra came rushing up to him. "Is my uncle—" she began, and then stopped, unwilling even to complete the question.

"Unscratched, thanks to you," Scaurus told her.

"Phos be thanked," she whispered, and then, to the tribune's glad confusion, threw her arms round his neck and kissed him. The legionaries who had kept her from the residence whooped. At the sound she jerked away in alarm, as if just realizing what she had done.

He reached out to her, but reluctantly held back when he saw her shy away. However brief, her show of warmth pleased him more, perhaps, then he was ready to admit. He told himself it was but pleasure at seeing her wounded spirit healing, and knew he was lying.

"You're hurt!" she exclaimed, spying the oozing bandage for the first time.

"It's not too bad." He opened and closed his hand to show her he could, though the proof cost him some pain. True to his Stoic training, he tried not to let it show on his face, but the princess saw sweat spring out on his forehead.

"Get it looked at," she said firmly, seeming relieved to be able to give advice that was sensible and impersonal at the same time. Scaurus hesitated, wishing this once for some of Viridovix' brass. He did not have it, and the moment passed. Anything he said would too likely be wrong.

He slowly walked over to Gorgidas. The doctor did not notice him. He was still bent low over the fallen legionary, his hands pressed against the soldier's face—the attitude, Marcus realized, of a Videssian healer-priest. The Greek's shoulders quivered with the effort he was making. "Live, damn you, live!" he said over and over in his native tongue.

But the legionary would never live again, not with that green-feathered arrow jutting up from between the doctor's fingers. Marcus could not tell whether Gorgidas had finally mastered the healing force, nor did it matter now; not even the Videssians could raise the dead.

At last the Greek felt Scaurus' presence. He raised his head, and the tribune gave back a pace from the grief and self-tormenting, impotent anger in his face. "It's no use," Gorgidas said, more to himself than to Scaurus. "Nothing is any use." He sagged in defeat, and his hands, red-black with blood beginning to dry, slid away from the dead man's face.

Marcus suddenly forgot his wound. "Jupiter Best and Greatest," he said softly, an oath he had not sworn since the days in his teens when he still believed in the gods. Quintus Glabrio lay tumbled in death. His features were already loosening into the vacant mask of the dead. The arrow stood just below his right eye and must have killed him instantly. A fly lit on the fletching, felt the perch give under its weight, and darted away.

"Let me see to that," Gorgidas said dully. Like an automaton, the tribune held out his arm. The doctor washed the cut with a sponge soaked in vinegar. Stunned or no, Scaurus had all he could do to keep from crying out. Gorgidas pinned the gash closed, snipping off the tip of each *fibula* as he pushed it through. With his arm shrieking from the wound and the vinegar wash, Marcus hardly felt the pins go in. Tears began streaming down the Greek's face as he dressed the cut; he had to try three times before he could close the catch on the complex *fibula* that secured the end of the bandage.

"Are there more hurt?" he asked Scaurus. "There must be."

"Yes, a few." The doctor turned to go; Marcus stopped him

with his good arm. "I'm sorrier than I know how to tell you," he said awkwardly. "To me he was a fine officer, a good man, and a friend, but—" He broke off, unsure how to continue.

"I've known you know, for all your discretion, Scaurus," Gorgidas said tiredly. "That doesn't matter any longer either, does it? Now let me be about my business, will you?"

Marcus still hesitated. "Can I do anything to help?"

"The gods curse you, Roman; you're a decent blockhead, but a blockhead all the same. There he lies, all I hold dear in this worthless world, and me with all my training and skill in healing the hurt, and what good is it? What can I do with it? Feel him grow cold under my hands."

He shook free of the tribune. "Let me go, and we'll see what miracles of medicine I work for these other poor sods." He walked through the open doorway of the imperial residence, a lean, lonely man wearing anguish like a cloak.

"What ails your healer?" Alypia Garva asked.

Scaurus jumped; lost in his own thoughts, he had not heard her come up. "This is his close friend," he said shortly, nodding at Glabrio, "and mine as well." Hearing the rebuff, the princess drew back. Marcus chose not to care; the taste of triumph was bitter in his mouth.

"Lovely, isn't it?" Thorisin said to Marcus late that afternoon. He was speaking ironically; the little reception room in the imperial chambers had seen its share of fighting. There was a sword cut in the upholstery of the couch on which the tribune sat; horsehair stuffing leaked through it. A bloodstain marred the marble floor.

The Emperor went on, "When I set you over the cadasters, outlander, I thought you would be watching the pen-pushers, but it seems you flushed a noble instead."

Scaurus grew alert. "So they were Onomagoulos' men, then?" The assassins had fought in grim silence; for all the tribune knew, Ortaias Sphrantzes might have hired them.

Gavras, though, seemed to think he was being stupid. "Of course they're Baanes'. I hardly needed to question them to find that out, did I?"

"I don't understand," Scaurus said.

"Why else would that fornicating, polluted, pox-ridden son of a two-copper whore Elissaios Bouraphos have brought his bloody collection of boats back from Pityos? For a pleasure cruise? Phos' light, man, he's not hiding out there. You must have seen the galleys' sails as you marched in this morning."

Marcus felt his face grow warm. "I thought it was a grain convoy."

"Landsmen!" Gavras muttered, rolling his eyes. "It bloody well isn't, as anyone with eyes in his head should know. The plan was simple enough—as soon as I'm dealt with, across comes Baanes to take over, smooth as you like," Thorisin spat in vast contempt. "As if he could—that bald pimple hasn't the wit to break wind and piddle at the same time. And while he tries to murder me and I settle him, who gains? The Yezda, of course. I wonder if he's not in their pay."

The Emperor, Scaurus thought, had a dangerous habit of underestimating his foes. He had done so with the Sphrantzai, and now again with Onomagoulos, who, loyal or not, was a capable, if arrogant, soldier. Marcus started to warn Gavras of that, but remembered how the conversation had opened and asked instead, "Why credit—" That seemed a safer word than *blame*. "—me with Baanes' plot?"

"Because you kept hounding him for Kybistra's tax roll. There were things in it he'd have done better not to write down."

"Ah?" Marcus made an interested noise to draw the Emperor out.

"Oh, truly, truly. Your friend Nepos filled the assassins so full of some potion of his that they spewed up everything they knew. Their captain, Skotos take him, knew plenty, too. Did you ever wonder why friend Baanes did so careful a job of slitting throats when we were waylaid last year after the parley?"

"Ah?" Marcus said again. He jumped as several men in heavy-soled boots tramped down the hallway, but they were only workmen coming to set things to rights once more. Live long enough in Videssos, he thought, and you'll see murderers under every cushion—but the day you don't, they'll be there.

Caught up in his own rekindled wrath, Thorisin did not notice the tribune's start. He went on, "The dung-faced midwife's mistake hired the knives himself and paid a premium for Ortaias' coin so no fingers would point his way even if something went wrong. But he put everything down on parchment so he could square himself with the Sphrantzai if he did kill me—and put it down on Kybistra's register. Why not? He had the thing with him; after all, he'd collected those taxes, when he ran there after Maragha. After that he could hardly let you see it, but he couldn't send a fake either, now could he?" The Emperor chuckled, imagining his rival's discomfiture.

Scaurus laughed, too. Videssian cadasters were invalid if they bore erasures or crossed-over lines; only fair copies went to the capital. And once there, they were festooned with seals of wax and lead and stamped with arcane bureaucratic stamps —to which, of course, Onomagoulos had no access once he was out in the provinces.

"He must have filched it as soon as he found out I was going to look over the receipts," the tribune decided.

"Very good," Gavras said, making small clapping motions of sardonic applause. Marcus' flush deepened. There were times when the subtle Videssians found his Roman straightforwardness monstrously amusing. Even seemingly bluff, blunt types like Thorisin and Onomagoulos proved as steeped in double-dealing as candied fruit in honey.

He sighed and spelled things out, as much for himself as for the Emperor: "A clerk, even a logothete, wouldn't have made much of some money-changing—probably figured he was lining his own purse and not worried much about it. But he knew I was on that beach, and he must have thought I'd connect things. I recall the fuss he made about its being Ortaias' money, aye, but I'd be lying if I said I was sure a few lines in a dull tax roll would have jogged my memory. He'd have been smarter letting things ride."

This time humorlessly, Thorisin chuckled again. "'The illdoer's conscience abandons the assurance of Phos' path,'" he said, quoting from the Videssian holy books like a Greek from Homer. "He knew his guilt, whether you did or not."

"And if he is guilty, then that means Taron Leimmokheir is innocent!" Marcus said. Certainty blazed in him. He could not keep all the triumph from his voice, but did not think it mattered. There was such perfect logical clarity behind the idea, surely no one could fail to see it.

But Thorisin was frowning. "Why are you obsessed by that gray-whiskered traitor? What boots is that he plotted with Onomagoulos instead of Ortaias?" he said curtly. Recognizing inflexibility when he heard it, Scaurus gave up again. It would take more than logic to change Gavras' mind; he was like a

man with a writing tablet who pushed his stylus through the
wax and permanently scarred the wood beneath.

"Buck up, Roman dear, it's a hero y'are tonight, not the
spook of a dead corp, the which wouldn't be invited to dinner
at all, at all," Viridovix said as they walked toward the Hall of
the Nineteen Couches. He deliberately exaggerated his brogue
to try to cheer up Marcus, but spoke Videssian so Helvis and
his own three companions would understand.

"Crave pardon; I didn't realize it showed so plainly," the
tribune murmured; he had been thinking of Glabrio. Helvis
squeezed his left arm. His right, under its bandages, he
wished he could forget. The smile he managed to produce felt
ghastly from the inside, but seemed to look good enough.

The ceremonies master, a portly man—not a eunuch, for
he wore a thick beard—bowed several times in quick succession, like a marionette on a string, as the Roman party came
up to the Hall's polished bronze doors. "Videssos is in your
debt," he said, seizing Marcus' hand in his own pale, moist
palm and bowing again. Then he turned and cried to those
already present, "Lords and ladies, the most valiant Romans!"
Scaurus blinked and forgave him the limp handclasp.

"The captain and *epoptes* Scaurus and the lady Helvis of
Namdalen!" That one was easy for the fellow; worse challenges lay ahead. "Viridovix son of Drappes and his, ah,
ladies!" The Celt's name was almost unprounceable for Videssians; the protocol chief's brief pause conveyed his opinion
of Viridovix' arrangement. Marcus suddenly groaned—silently, by luck. Komitta Rhangavve would be here tonight.

He had no time to say anything. The ceremonies master
was plowing ahead. "The senior centurion Gaius Philippus!
The junior centurion Junius Blaesus!" Blaesus was a longtime
underofficer and a good soldier, but Scaurus knew he was
hardly a replacement for Quintus Glabrio. "The underofficer
Minucius, and his lady Erene!" Not "the lady," Scaurus noted;
damned snob of a flunky. Minucius, proud of his promotion,
had burnished his chain mail till it gleamed.

Two more names completed the legionary party: "The *nakharar* Gagik Bagratouni, detachment-leader among the
Romans! Zeprin the Red, Haloga guardsman in Roman service!" Despite persuasion, Gorgidas had chosen to be alone
with his grief.

Bagratouni, too, still mourned, but time had dulled the cutting edge of his hurt. The leonine Vaspurakaner noble swept through the slimmer Videssians as he made his way toward the wine. Scaurus saw his eyes moving this way and that; no doubt Bagratouni was very conscious of the figure he cut, and of the ladies among whom he cut it.

The tribune and Helvis drifted over to a table covered with trays of crushed ice, on which reposed delicacies of various sorts, mostly from the ocean. "A dainty you won't see every day," said an elderly civil servant, pointing at a strip of octopus meat. "The curled octopus, you know, with only one row of suckers on each arm. Splendid!" Scaurus didn't know, but took the meat. It was chewy and vaguely sea-flavored, like all the other octopus he'd ever eaten.

He wondered what the gastrophile beside him would have thought of such Roman exotica as dormice in poppy seeds and honey.

A small orchestra played softly in the background: flutes, stringed instruments whose names he still mixed up, and a tinkling clavichord. Helvis clapped her hands in delight. "That's the same rondo they were playing when we first met here," she said. "Do you remember?"

"The night? Naturally. The—what did you call it? You'd know I was lying if I said yes." A lot had happened that evening. Not only had he met Helvis—though Hemond had still been alive then, of course—but also Alypia Gavra. And Avshar, for that matter; as always, he worried whenever he thought of the sorcerer-prince.

They drifted through separate crowds of bureaucrats, soldiers, and ambassadors, exchanging small talk. Scaurus was unusual in having friends among all three groups. The two imperial factions despised each other. The Videssian officers preferred the company of mercenaries they distrusted to the pen-pushers they loathed, which merely confirmed their boorishness in the civil servants' eyes.

Taso Vones, an imposingly tall Videssian lady—*not* Plakidia Teletze—on his arm, bowed to the tribune. "Where are you come from?" he asked with a twinkle in his eye. "How to shoe a heavy cavalry horse, or the best way to compose a memorandum on a subject of no intrinsic worth?"

"The best way to do that is not to," Helvis said at once.

"Blasphemy, my dear; seal-stampers burn people who express such thoughts. But then, I find cavalry horses no more inspiring." With that attitude, thought Scaurus, it was easy to see why Vones held aloof from warriors and bureaucrats alike.

"His Sanctity, Phos' Patriarch Balsamon!" the ceremonies master called, and the feast paused for a respectful moment as the fat old man waddled into the chamber. For all his graceless step, he had a presence that filled it up.

He looked round, then said with a smile and a mock-rueful sigh, "Ah, if only you paid me such heed in the High Temple!" He plucked a crystal wine goblet from its bed of ice and drained it with obvious enjoyment.

"That man takes nothing seriously," Soteric said disapprovingly. Though he did not shave the back of his head in usual island fashion, Helvis' brother still looked very much the unassimilated Namdalener in high tight trousers and short fur jacket.

Marcus said, "It's not like you to waste your time worrying over his failings. After all, he's a heretic to you, is he not?" He grinned as his brother-in-law fumbled for an answer. The truth, he thought, was simple——the Videssian patriarch was too interesting a character for anyone to ignore.

Servants began carrying the tables of hors d'oeuvres back to the kitchens and replacing them with dining tables and gilded chairs. From previous banquets in the Hall of the Nineteen Couches, Marcus knew that was a signal the Emperor would be coming in soon. He realized he needed to speak to Balsamon before Thorisin arrived.

"What now, my storm-crow friend?" the patriarch said as Scaurus approached. "Whenever you come up to me with that look of grim determination in your eye, I know you've found your way into more trouble."

Like Alypia Gavra, Balsamon had the knack of making the tribune feel transparent. He tried to hide his annoyance, and was sure Balsamon saw that, too. More flustered than ever, he launched into his tale.

"Leimmokheir, eh?" Balsamon said when he was done. "Aye, Taron is a good man." As far as Scaurus could remember, that was the first time he'd heard the patriarch judge anyone so. But Balsamon went on, "What makes you think my intercession would be worth a moldy apple?"

"Why," Marcus floundered, "if Gavras won't listen to you——"

"—He won't listen to anyone, which will likely be the case. He's a stubborn youngster," the patriarch said, perfectly at ease speaking thus of his sovereign. His little black eyes, still sharp in their folds of flesh, measured the Roman. "And well you know it, too. Why keep flogging a dead mule?"

"I made a promise," Marcus said slowly, unable to find a better answer.

Before Balsamon could reply, the ceremonies master was crying out, "Her Majesty the Princess Alypia Gavra! The lady Komitta Rhangavve! His Imperial Majesty, the Avtokrator of the Videssians, Thorisin Gavras!"

Men bowed low to show their respect for the Emperor; as the occasion was social rather than ceremonial, no proskynesis was required. Women dropped curtsies. Thorisin bobbed his head amiably, then called, "Where are the guests of honor?" Servitors rounded up the Romans and their ladies and brought them to the Emperor, who presented them to the crowd for fresh applause.

Komitta Rhangavve's eyes narrowed dangerously as they flicked from one of Viridovix' lemans to the next. She looked very beautiful in a clinging skirt of flower-printed linen; Marcus would sooner have taken a poisonous snake to bed. Viridovix did not seem to notice her glare, but the Celt was not happy, either. "Is something wrong?" the tribune asked as they walked toward the dining tables.

"Aye, summat. Arigh tells me the Videssians will be sending an embassy to his clan. They're fain to hire mercenaries, and the lad himself will be going with them to help persuade his folk to take service with the Empire. A half-year's journey and more it is, and him the bonniest wight to drink with I've found in the city. I'll miss the little omadhaun, beshrew me if I won't."

Stewards seated the legionaries in accordance with their prominence of the evening. Marcus found himself at the right hand of the imperial party, next to the Princess Alypia. The Emperor sat between her and Komitta Rhangavve, who was on his left. Had she been his wife rather than mistress, her place and the princess' would have been reversed. As it was, she was next to Viridovix, an arrangement Scaurus thought ill-omened. Unaware of anything amiss, the Gaul's three longtime companions chattered among themselves, excited by their high-ranking company.

The first course was a soup of onions and pork, its broth delightfully delicate in flavor. Marcus spooned it down almost without tasting it, waiting for the explosion on his left. But Komitta seemed to be practicing tact, a virtue he had not associated with her. He relaxed and enjoyed the last few spoonfuls of soup and and was sorry when a servant took the empty bowl away. His goblet of wine, now, never disappeared. Whenever it was empty, a steward would be there to fill it again from a shining silver carafe. Even if it was sticky-sweet Videssian wine, it dulled the ache in his arm.

Little roasted partridge hens appeared, stuffed with sautéed mushrooms. Balsamon, who sat next to Helvis at the tribune's right, demolished his with an appetite that would have done credit to a man half his age. He patted his ample belly, saying to Scaurus, "You can see I've gained it honestly."

Alypia Garva leaned toward the patriarch, saying, "You would not be yourself without it, as you know full well." She spoke affectionately, as to a favorite old uncle or grandfather. Balsamon rolled his eyes and winced, pantomiming being cut to the quick.

"Respect is hard for a plump old fool like me to get, you'll note," he said to Helvis. "I should be mighty in my outrage like the patriarchs of old and be a prelate to terrify the heretic. You *are* terrified, I hope?" he added, winking at her.

"Not in the least," she answered promptly. "No more than you convince anyone when you play the buffoon."

Balsamon's eyes were still amused in a way, but no longer merry. "You have some of your brother's terrible honesty in you," he said, and Scaurus did not think it was altogether a compliment.

Courses came and went: lobster tails in drawn butter and capers; rich pastries baked to resemble peahens' eggs; raisins, figs, and sweet dates; mild and sharp cheeses; peppery ground lamb wrapped in grape leaves; roast goose—sniffing the familiar cheese and cinnamon sauce, Marcus declined—cabbage soup; stewed pigeons with sausage and onions . . . with, of course, appropriate wines for each. Scaurus' arm seemed far away. He felt the tip of his nose grow numb, a sure sign he was getting drunk.

Nor was he the only one. The great count Drax, who wore Videssian-style robes, unlike Soteric and Utprand, was singing one of the fifty-two scurrilous verses of the imperial army's marching song, loudly accompanied by Zeprin the Red and Mertikes Zigabenos. And Viridovix had just broken up the left side of the imperial table with a story about—Marcus dug a finger in his ear, trying not to believe he was hearing the Celt's effrontery—a man with four wives.

Thorisin roared out laughter with the rest, stopping only to wipe his eyes. "I thank your honor," Viridovix said. Komitta Rhangavve was not laughing. Her long, slim fingers, nails painted the color of blood, looked uncommonly like claws.

Dessert was fetched in, a light one after the great feast: crushed ice from the imperial cold cellars, flavored with sweet syrups. A favorite winter treat, it was hard to come by in the warmer seasons.

The Emperor rose, a signal for everyone else to do the same. Servants began clearing away the mountains of dirty dishes and bowls. But even if the food was gone, wine and talk still flowed freely—perhaps, indeed, more so than before dinner.

Balsamon took Thorisin Gavras to one side and began speaking urgently. Marcus could not hear what the patriarch was saying, but Thorisin's growled answer was loud enough to turn heads. "Not you, too? No, I've said a hundred times —now it's a hundred and one!" Rather muzzily, the tribune wished he could disappear. It did not look as though Taron Leimmokheir would see the outside of his dungeon any time soon.

As the guests decided no further trouble was coming on the heels of Gavras' outburst, the level of conversation picked up again. Soteric came over to tell Helvis some news of Namdalen he'd got from one of Drax' aides. "What? Bedard Woodtooth, become count of Nustad on the mainland? I don't believe it," she said. "Excuse me, darling, I have to hear this with my own ears." And she was gone with her brother, exclaiming excitedly in the island dialect.

Left to his own devices, the tribune took another drink. After enough rounds, he decided, Videssian wine tasted fine. The interior of the Hall of the Nineteen Couches, though, wanted to spin whenever he moved his head.

"Piss-pot!" That was Komitta Rhangavve's wildcat screech, aimed at Viridovix. "The son of a pimp in your joke would be no good to any of his wives after he had his ballocks cut off him!" She threw what was left in her goblet in the

Celt's face and smashed the cut crystal on the floor. Then she spun and stamped out of the hall, every step echoing in the startled silence.

"What was that in aid of?" the Emperor asked, staring at her retreating back. He had been talking with Drax and Zigabenos and, like Scaurus, missed the beginning of the scene.

Red wine was dripping from Viridovix's mustaches, but he had lost none of his aplomb. "Och, the lady decided she'd be after taking offense at the little yarn I told at table," he said easily. A servitor brought him a damp towel; he ran it over his face. "I wish she had done it sooner. As is, I'm left wearing no better than the dregs."

Thorisin snorted, reassured by the Celt's glib reply and by what he knew of Komitta's fiery temper—which was plenty. "All right, then, let's hope this is more to your taste." He beckoned a waiter to his side and gave the man his own goblet to take to Viridovix. People murmured at the favor shown the Gaul; the room relaxed once more.

Gaius Philippus caught Marcus' eye from across the hall and hiked his shoulders up and down in an exaggerated sigh of relief. The tribune nodded—for a moment, he'd been frightened nearly sober.

He wondered just how much he had drunk; too much, from the pounding ache that was beginning behind his eyes. Helvis was still deep in conversation with a couple of Namdalener officers. The dining hall suddenly seemed intolerably noisy, crowded, and hot. Marcus weaved toward the doors. Maybe the fresh air outside would clear his head.

The ceremonies master bowed as he made his way into the night. He nodded back, then regretted it—any motion was enough to give his headache new fuel. He sucked in the cool nighttime air gratefully; it felt sweeter than any wine.

He went down the stairs with a drunken man's caution. The music and the buzz of talk receded behind him, nor was he sorry to hear them fade. Even the tree frogs piping in the nearby citrus groves grated on his ears. He sighed, already wincing from tomorrow's hangover.

He peered up at the stars, hoping their calm changelessness might bring him some relief. The night was clear and moonless, but the heavens still were not at their best. Videssos' lights and the smoke rising from countless hearths and fireplaces veiled the dimmer stars away.

He wandered aimlessly for a couple of minutes, his hobnailed *caligae* clicking on the flagstone path and then silent as they bit into grass. An abrupt intake of breath made him realize he was not alone. "Who the—?" he said, groping for his sword hilt. Visions of assassins flashed through his head—a landing party from Bouraphos' ships out there, perhaps, stealing up on the Hall of the Nineteen Couches.

"I'm not a band of hired killers," Alypia Gavra said, and Scaurus heard the sardonic edge that colored so much of her speech.

His hand jerked away from the scabbard as if it had become red-hot. "Your pardon, my lady," he stammered. "You surprised me—I came out for a breath of air."

"As did I, some little while ago, and found I preferred the quiet to the brabble back there. You may share it with me, if you like."

Still feeling foolish, the tribune approached her. He could hear the noise from the dining hall, but at a distance it was bearable. The light that streamed through the Hall's wide windows was pale, too, the princess beside him little more than a silhouette. He took parade rest unconsciously, a relaxed stance from which to savor the night.

After they stood a while in silence, Alypia turned to him, her face musing. "You are a strange man, Marcus Aemilius Scaurus," she said finally, her Videssian accent making the sonorous sounds of his full name somehow musical. "I am never quite sure what you are thinking."

"No?" Scaurus said, surprised again. "It's always seemed to me you could read me like a signboard."

"If it sets your mind at ease, not so. You fall into no neat category; you're no arrogant noble from the provinces, all horsesweat and iron, nor yet one of the so-clever seal-stampers who would sooner die than call something by its right name. And you hardly make an ordinary mercenary captain—there's not enough wrecker in you. So, outlander, what are you?" She studied him, as if trying to pull the secret from his eyes.

The question, he knew, demanded an honest answer; he wished his wits were clearer, to give her one. "A survivor," he said at last.

"Ah," she said very low, more an exhalation than a word. "No wonder we seem to understand each other, then."

"Do we?" he wondered, but his arms folded round her as her face tilted up.

She felt slim, almost boyish, under his hands, the more so because he was used to Helvis' opulent curves. But her mouth and tongue were sweet against his—for a couple of heartbeats, until she gave a smothered gasp and wrenched herself away.

Alarmed, Marcus tried to flog his brain toward an apology, but her sad, weary gesture stopped him before he could begin. "The fault is not yours. Blame—times now gone," she said, casting about for a circumlocution. "No matter what I wish to feel, there are memories I cannot set aside so easily."

The tribune felt his hands bunch into fists. Not the least of Avshar's crimes, he thought once more, was the easy death he gave Vardanes Sphrantzes.

He reached out to touch her cheek. It was wet against his hand. She started to flinch again, but sensed the gesture was as much one of understanding as a caress. Her wounded strength, the mix of vulnerability and composure in her, drew him powerfully; it was all he could do to stand steady. Yet however much he wanted to take her in his arms, he was sure he would frighten her away forever if he did.

She said, "When I was a painted harlot you showed me a way to bear what I had been, but because of what I was then, I can have no gift for you now. Life is a tangled skein, is it not?" Her laugh was small and shaky.

"That you are here and healing is gift enough," Scaurus replied. He did not say he thought he might be too drunk to do a woman justice in any case.

But that was one thought Alypia missed. Her drawn features softened; she leaned forward to kiss him gently. "You'd best go back," she said. "After all, you are the guest of honor."

"I suppose so." The tribune had nearly forgotten the banquet.

Alypia stayed beside him no more than a second before drawing back. "Go on," she said again.

Reluctantly, Marcus started back toward the Hall of the Nineteen Couches. When he turned round for a last look at Alypia, she was already gone. A trace of motion among the trees might—or might not—have been her, slipping toward the imperial residence. The tribune trudged on, his head whirling with wine and thought.

He knew most mercenaries, if offered a chance at an imperial connection, would cut any ties that stood in the way. Drax would, instantly, he thought; the man who was too adaptable by half. What was the nickname that Athenian had earned during the Peloponnesian War? "The stage boot," that was it, because he fit on either foot.

But Scaurus could not find it in himself to imitate the great count. For all the attraction and fondness he felt for Alypia Gavra, he was not ready to cast Helvis aside. They both sometimes strained at the bond between them, but despite quarrels and differences it would not break, nor, most of the time, did he want it to. Then, too, there was Dosti. . . .

"We missed you, my lord," the ceremonies master said with another low bow as Marcus stumbled back into the hall. The Roman hardly heard. For a man who called himself a survivor, he thought, he had an uncommon gift for complicating his life.

XIII

"PHOS BLAST THAT INSOLENT TREACHER BOURAPHOS INTO A thousand pieces and roast every one of them over a dung fire!" Thorisin Gavras burst out. The Emperor stood on Videssos' sea wall, watching one of his galleys sink. Two more fled back to the city, closely pursued by the rebel drungarios' ships. Heads bobbed in the water of the Cattle-Crossing as sailors from the stricken vessel snatched at spars or swam toward Videssos and safety. Not all would reach it; tiny in the distance, black fins angled toward them.

Gavras ran an irritable hand through his hair, ruffled by the sea breeze. "And why have I no admirals with the sense not to piss into the wind?" he grated. "A two-year-old in the bathhouse sails his toy boat with more finesse than those bullheads showed!"

Along with the other officers by the Emperor, Scaurus did his best to keep his face straight. He understood Thorisin's frustration. Onomagoulos, on the western shore of the Cattle-Crossing, led an army far weaker than the one Gavras had mustered against it. What did it matter, though, when the Emperor could not come to grips with his foe?

"Now if you had some ships from t'Duchy—" Utprand Dagober's son began, but Thorisin's glare stopped even the blunt-spoken Namdalener in mid-sentence. Drax looked at his countryman as if at a dullard. Everyone knew the Emperor suspected the islanders, his eye seemed to say and to ask what the point was of antagonizing him without need.

Cross as a baited bear, Gavras swung round on Marcus. "I

291

suppose you'll be after me next, telling me to turn Leimmo-kheir loose."

"Why, no, your Majesty, not at all," the tribune said inno-cently. "If you were going to listen to me, you would have done that long since."

He scratched at his arm. It itched fiercely. Still, it was healing well enough that Gorgidas had pulled the pins from it the day before. The feel of the metal sliding through his flesh, though not painful, had been unpleasant enough to make him shudder at the memory.

"Bah!" Thorisin turned his gaze out to the Cattle-Crossing again. Only scattered timbers showed where his warship had sunk; Bouraphos' vessels were already resuming their patrol. As if continuing an argument, the Emperor said, "What would it gain me to let him go? He'd surely turn against me now, after being shut up all these months."

Unexpectedly, Mertikes Zigabenos spoke up for Leimmo-kheir. The guards officer had come to admire the older sailor, who showed repeatedly while the Sphrantzai held Videssos how a good man could keep his honor under a wicked regime. Zigabenos said, "If he grants you an oath of loyalty, he will keep it. No matter what you say, sir, Taron Leimmokheir would not forswear himself. He fears the ice too much for that."

"And besides," Marcus said, thrusting home with a plea-sure for which he felt no guilt at all, "what's the difference if he does betray you? You'd still be outadmiraled and hardly worse off, whereas—" He fell silent, leaving Thorisin to work the contrary chain of logic for himself.

The Emperor, still in his foul mood, only grunted. But his hand tugged thoughtfully at his beard, and he did not fly into a rage at the very notion of releasing Leimmokheir. His will was granite, thought the tribune, but even granite crumbles in the end.

"So you think he'll let him go?" Helvis said that evening after Scaurus recounted the day's events. "One for you, then."

"I suppose so, unless he does turn his coat once he's free. That would drop the chamber pot into the stew for fair."

"I don't think it will happen. Leimmokheir is honest," Helvis said seriously. Marcus respected her opinion; she had been in Videssos years longer than he and knew a good deal about its leaders. Moreover, what she said confirmed everyone else's view of the jailed admiral—except the Emperor's.

But when he tried to draw her out further, she did not seem interested in matters political, which was unlike her. "Is anything wrong?" he asked at last. He wondered if she had somehow guessed the attraction growing between himself and Alypia Gavra and dreaded the scene that would cause.

Instead, she put down the skirt whose hem she had been mending and smiled at the tribune. He thought he should know that look; there was a mischievous something in her eyes he had seen before. He placed it just as she spoke, "I'm sorry, darling, my wits were somewhere else. I was trying to reckon when the baby will be due. As near as I can make it, it should be a little before the festival of sun-turning."

Marcus was silent so long her sparkle disappeared. "Aren't you pleased?" she asked sharply.

"Of course I am," he answered, and was telling the truth. Too many upper-class Romans were childless by choice, beloved only by inheritance seekers. "You took me by surprise, is all."

He walked over and kissed her, then poked her in the ribs. She yelped. "You like taking me by surprise that way," he accused. "You did when you were expecting Dosti, too."

As if the mention of his name was some kind of charm, the baby woke up and started to cry. Helvis made a wry face. She got up and unswaddled him. "Are you wet or do you just want to be cuddled?" she demanded. It proved to be the latter; in a few minutes Dosti was asleep again.

"That doesn't happen as often as it used to," Marcus said. He sighed. "I suppose I'll have to get used to waking up five times a night again. Why don't you arrange to have a three-year-old and save us the fuss?" That earned him a return poke.

He hugged her, careful both of her pregnancy and his own tender arm. She helped him draw the blouse off over her head. Yet even when they lay together naked on the sleeping-mat, the tribune saw Alypia Gavra's face in his mind, remembered the feel of her lips. Only then did he understand why he had paused before showing gladness at Helvis' news.

He realized something else, too, and chuckled under his breath. "What is it, dear?" she asked, touching his cheek.

"Nothing really. Just a foolish notion." She made an inquisitive noise, but he did not explain further. There was no way, he thought, to tell her that now he understood why she slipped every so often and called him by her former lover's name.

"Let's have a look at that," Gorgidas ordered the next morning. Marcus mimed a salute and extended his arm to the doctor. It was anything but pretty; the edges of the gash were still raised and red, and it was filled with crusty brown scab. But the Greek grunted in satisfaction at what he saw and again when he sniffed the wound. "There's no corruption in there," he told the tribune. "Your flesh knits well."

"That lotion of yours does good work, for all its bite." Gorgidas had dosed the cut with a murky brown fluid he called barbarum: a compound of powdered verdigris, litharge, alum, pitch, and resin mixed in equal parts of vinegar and oil. The Roman had winced every time it was applied, but it kept a wound from going bad.

Gorgidas merely grunted again, unmoved by the praise. Nothing had moved him much, not since Quintus Glabrio fell. Now he changed the subject, asking, "Do you know when the Emperor intends to send his embassy to the Arshaum?"

"No time soon, not with Bouraphos' ships out there to sink anything that sticks its nose out of the city's harbors. Why?"

The Greek studied him bleakly. Marcus saw how haggard he had become, his slimness now gaunt, his hair ragged where he had chopped a lock away in mourning for Glabrio. "Why?" Gorgidas echoed. "Nothing simpler; I intend to go with it." He set his jaw, meeting Scaurus' stare without flinching.

"You can't," was the tribune's first startled response.

"And why not? How do you propose to stop me?" The doctor's voice was dangerously calm.

"I can order you to stay."

"Can you, in law? That would be a pretty point for the barristers back in Rome. I am attached to the legions, aye, but am I of them? I think not, any more than a sutler or a town bootmaker who serves at contract. But that's neither here nor there. Unless you choose to chain me, I will not obey your order."

"But why?" Marcus said helplessly. He had no intention of putting Gorgidas in irons. That the Greek was his friend counted for less than his certainty that Gorgidas was stubborn enough not to serve if made to remain against his will.

"The why is simple enough; I plan to add an excursus on the tribes and customs of the Arshaum to my history and I need more information than Arigh can—or cares to—give me. Ethnography, I think, is something I can hope to do a proper job of."

His bitterness gave Scaurus the key he needed. "You think medicine is not? What of all of us you've healed, some a dozen times? What of this?" He held his wounded arm out to the physician.

"What of it? It's still a bloody mess, if you want to know." In his wretchedness and self-disgust, Gorgidas could not see the successes his skill had won. "A Videssian healer would have put it right in minutes, instead of this week and a half's worth of worry over seeing if it chooses to fester."

"If he could do anything at all," Marcus retorted. "Some hurts they can't cure, and the power drains from them if they use it long. But you always give your best."

"A poor, miserable best it is, too. With my best, Minucius would be dead now, and Publius Flaccus and Cotilius Rufus after Maragha, and how many more? You're a clodhopper to reckon me a doctor, when I can't so much as learn the art that gave them life." The Greek's eyes were haunted. "And I can't. We saw that, didn't we?"

"So you'll hie yourself off to the steppe, then, and forget even trying?"

Gorgidas winced, but he said, "You can't shame me into staying either, Scaurus." The tribune flushed, angry he was so obvious.

The Greek went on, "In Rome I wasn't a bad physician, but here I'm hardly more than a joke. If I have some small talent at history, perhaps I can leave something worthwhile with that. Truly, Marcus," he said, and Scaurus was touched, for the doctor had not used his praenomen before, "all of you would be better off with a healer-priest to mend you. You've suffered my fumblings long enough."

Clearly, nothing ordinary would change Gorgidas' mind. Casting about for any straw, Marcus exclaimed, "But if you leave us, who will Viridovix have to argue with?"

"Now that one strikes close to the clout," Gorgidas admitted, surprised into smiling. "For all his bluster, I'll miss the red-maned bandit. It's still no hit, though; as long as he has Gaius Philippus, he'll never go short a quarrel."

Defeated, Scaurus threw his hands in the air. "Be it so, then. But for the first time, I'm glad Bouraphos joined the rebels. Not only does that force you to stay with us longer, it also gives you more time to come to your senses."

"I don't think I've left them. I might well have gone even if—things were otherwise." The Greek paused, tossed his head. "Uselessness is not a pleasant feeling." He rose. "Now if you'll excuse me, Gawtruz has promised to tell me of his people's legends of how they overran Thatagush. A comparison with the accounts by Videssian historians should prove fascinating, don't you think?"

Whatever Marcus' answer was, he did not wait to hear it.

The tribune stood at stiff attention, below and to the right of the great imperial throne. For this ceremony he did not enjoy the place of honor; Balsamon the patriarch was a pace closer to the seated Emperor. Somehow Videssos' chief prelate contrived to look rumpled in vestments of blue silk and cloth-of-gold. His pepper-and-salt beard poured down in a disorderly stream over the seed pearls adorning the breast of his chasuble.

At the Emperor's left side stood Alypia Gavra, her costume as somber as protocol would permit. Scaurus had not seen her save at a distance since the feast two weeks before; twice he had requested an audience, and twice got no reply. He was almost afraid to meet her eye, but her nod as they assembled in the throne room had been reassuring.

With no official status, Komitta Rhangavve was relegated to the courtiers who filed in to flank the long central colonnade. In that sea of plump bland faces her lean, hard beauty was like a falcon's feral grace among so many pigeons. At the sight of the Roman, her eyes darted about to see if Viridovix was present; Marcus was glad he was not.

An expectant hush filled the chamber. The Grand Gates, closed after the functionaries' entrance, swung slowly open once more, to reveal a single man silhouetted against the brightness outside. His long, rolling strides seemed alien to that place of gliding eunuchs and soft-footed officials.

Taron Leimmokheir wore fresh robes, but they hung loosely about his prison-thinned frame. Nor had his release robbed him of the pallor given by long months hidden from sun and sky. His hair and beard, while clean, were still untrimmed. Scaurus heard he had refused a barber; his words were, "Let Gavras see me as he had me." The tribune wondered what else Leimmokheir might refuse. So far as he knew, no bargains had been struck.

The ex-admiral came up to the imperial throne, then paused, looking Thorisin full in the face. In Videssian court etiquette it was the height of rudeness; Marcus heard torches crackle in the silence enveloping the courtroom. Then, with deliberation and utmost dignity, Leimmokheir slowly prostrated himself before his sovereign.

"Get up, get up," Thorisin said impatiently; not the words of formula, but the court ministers had already despaired of changing that.

Leimmokheir rose. Looking as if every word tasted bad to him, the Emperor continued, "Know you are pardoned of the charge of conspiracy against our person, and that all properties and rights previously deemed forfeit are restored to you." There was a sigh of outdrawn breath from the courtiers. Leimmokheir began a second proskynesis; Thorisin stopped him with a gesture.

"Now we come down to it," he said, sounding more like a merchant in a hard bargain than Avtokrator of the Videssians. Leimmokheir leaned forward, too. "Does it please you to serve me as my drungarios of the fleet against Bouraphos and Onomagoulos?" Marcus noted that the first person plural of the pardon had disappeared.

"Why you and not them?" Prison had not cost Leimmokheir his forthrightness, Scaurus saw. Courtiers blanched, appalled at the plain speech.

The Emperor, though, looked pleased. His answer was equally direct. "Because I am not a man who hires murderers."

"No, instead you throw people into jail." The fat ceremonies master, who stood among the high dignitaries, seemed ready to faint. Thorisin sat stony-faced, his arms folded, waiting for a real reply. At last Leimmokheir dipped his head; his unkempt gray locks flopped over his face.

"Excellent!" Thorisin breathed, now with the air of a gambler after throwing the suns. He nodded to Balsamon. "The patriarch will keep your oath of allegiance." He fairly purred; to a man of Taron Leimmokheir's religious scruples, that oath would be binding as iron shackles.

Balsamon stepped forward, producing a small copy of the Videssian scriptures from a fold of his robe. But the drungarios waved him away; his seaman's voice, used to overcoming storm winds, filled the throne room: "No, Gavras, I swear no oaths to you."

For a moment, everyone froze; the Emperor's eyes went hard and cold. "What then, Leimmokheir?" he asked, and danger rode his words. "Should your say-so be enough for me?"

He intended sarcasm, but the admiral took him at face value. "Yes, by Phos, or what's your pardon worth? I'll be your man, but not your hound. If you don't trust me without a spiked collar of words round my neck, send me back to the jug, and be damned to you." And he waited in turn, his pride proof against whatever the Emperor chose.

A slow flush climbed Thorisin's cheeks. His bodyguards' hands tightened on their spears. There had been Avtokrators —and not a few of them—who would have answered such defiance with blood. In his years Balsamon had seen more than one of that stripe. He said urgently, "Your Majesty, may I—"

"No." Thorisin cut him off with a single harsh word. Marcus realized again the overwhelming power behind the Videssian imperial office in its formal setting. In chambers, Balsamon would have rolled his eyes and kept on arguing; now, bowing, he fell silent. Only Leimmokheir remained uncowed, drawing strength from what he had already endured.

The Emperor still bore him no liking, but grudging respect slowly replaced the anger on his face. "All right, then." He wasted no time with threats or warnings; it was clear they meant nothing to the reinstated admiral.

Leimmokheir, as abrupt as Gavras, bowed and turned to go. "Where are you away so fast?" Thorisin demanded, suspicious afresh.

"The docks, of course. Where else would you have your drungarios go?" Leimmokheir neither looked back nor broke stride. If he could have slammed the Grand Gates behind him, Scaurus thought, he would have done that, too. Between them, the stubborn admiral and equally strong-willed Emperor had managed to turn Videssian ceremonial on its ear. The assembled courtiers shook their heads as they trooped from the throne room, remembering better-run spectacles.

"Don't you just wander off," Thorisin said to the tribune as he started to follow them out. "I have a job in mind for you."

"Sire?"

"And spare me that innocent blue-eyed gaze," the Emperor growled. "For all the wenches it charms, it goes for nothing with me." Marcus saw the corner of Alypia Gavra's mouth twitch, but she did not look at him. Her uncle went on, "You were the one who wanted that gray-bearded puritan loose, so you can keep an eye on him. If he so much as breathes hard, I expect to hear about it. D'you understand me?"

"Aye." The Roman had half expected that order.

"Just 'aye'?" Gavras glared at him, balked of the chance to vent his anger further. "Go on, take yourself off, then."

As Marcus walked back to the legionaries' barracks, Alypia Gavra caught him up. "I have to ask your pardon," she said. "It was wrong of me to pretend I never got your requests to see me."

"The situation was unusual," the tribune replied. He could not speak as freely as he would have liked. The path was busy; more than one head turned at the sight of a mercenary captain, even one of the prominence Scaurus had won, walking side by side with the Avtokrator of the Videssians' niece.

"To say the least." Alypia raised one eyebrow. She, too, used phrases with many meanings. Marcus wondered if she had deliberately chosen to meet him in public to keep things between them as impersonal as possible.

"I hope," he said carefully, "you don't feel I was, ah, taking undue advantage of the situation."

She gave him a steady look. "There are many benefits an officer with an eye for the main chance might gain; something, I might add, I am as capable of seeing as any officer of that stripe."

"That is the main reason I hesitated so long."

"I never believed here—" Alypia laid her hand on her left breast "—you were such a man. It is, though, something one considers." She cocked her head, still studying him. "'The main reason'? What of your young son? What of the family you've made since you came to Videssos? At the banquet you seemed well content with your lady."

Scaurus bit his lip. It was chastening to hear his own thoughts come back at him from the princess' mouth. "And you claimed to have trouble reading me!" he said, embarrassed out of indirection.

For the first time Alypia smiled. She made as if to put her hand on his arm, but stopped, remembering better than he where they were. She said quietly, "Were those thoughts not there to read, the, ah, situation—" Her mockery of the tribune's earlier pause was gentle. "—Would never have arisen."

The path divided. "We go different ways now, I think," she said, and turned toward the flowering cherries that concealed the imperial residence.

"Aye, for a while," Marcus answered, but only to himself.

"Look what Gavras gives me to work with!" Taron Leimmokheir shouted. "Why didn't he tell me to go hang myself from a yardarm while I was about it?" He answered his own question, "He thought my weight'd break it, and he was right!" He looked disgustedly about the Neorhesian harbor.

The capital's great northern anchorage was not a part of the city Scaurus knew well. The Romans had patrolled near the harbor of Kontoskalion, on Videssos' south-facing coast, and had also embarked on campaign against the Yezda from there. But Kontoskalion was a toy port next to the Neorhesian harbor, named for the long-dead city prefect who had supervised its building.

There were ships aplenty at the docks jutting out into the Videssian Sea, a veritable forest of masts. But all too many of them belonged to fat, sluggish trading ships and tiny fishing craft like the one Marcus had sailed on when Thorisin's forces sneaked over the Cattle-Crossing. These, by now, rode high in the water. Their cargoes long since unloaded, they were trapped in Videssos by Elissaios Bouraphos outside. As had been only proper—then—Bouraphos had taken the heart of the Empire's war fleet when he sailed for Pityos and kept it when he joined Onomagoulos in rebellion.

Leimmokheir had precious little left: ten or so triremes, and perhaps a dozen smaller two-banked ships like the ones the tribune knew as Liburnians. He was outnumbered almost three to one, and Bouraphos also had the better captains and crews.

"What's to do?" Marcus asked, worried the drungarios thought the task beyond him. After his outburst, Leimmokheir was staring out to sea, not at the choppy little waves dancing inside the breakwater, but beyond, to the vast sweep of empty horizon.

The admiral did not seem to hear him for a moment; he slowly came back to himself. "Hmm? Phos' light, I truly don't know, left here with the lees to drink. Wait and watch for a bit, I expect, until I understand how things have gone since I was taken off the board. I've come back facing a new direction, and everything looks strange."

In the Videssian board game, captured pieces could be used against their original owners and change sides several times in the course of a game. It was, Scaurus thought, a game very much in its makers' image.

Seeing the Roman troubled by his answer, Leimmokheir slapped him on the shoulder. "Never lose hope," he said seriously. "The Namdaleni are heretics who imperil their souls with their belief, but they have the right of that. No matter how bad the storm looks, it has to end sometime. Skotos lays despair before men as a snare."

He was the living proof of his own philosophy, Scaurus thought; his imprisonment had dropped from him as if it had never been. But the tribune noted he had still not answered the question.

The last clear notes of the pandoura faded inside the Roman barracks. Applause, a storm of it, followed swiftly. Senpat Sviodo laid aside his stringed instrument, a smile of pleasure on his handsome, swarthy face. He lifted a mug of wine in salute to his audience.

"That was marvelous," Helvis said. "You made me see the mountains of Vaspurakan plain as if they stood before me. Phos gave you a great gift. Were you not a soldier, your music would soon make you rich."

"Curious you should say that,", he answered sheepishly. "Back in my teens I thought about running off with a troupe of strummers who were playing at my father's holding."

"Why didn't you?"

"He found out and stropped his belt on my backside. He had the right of it, Phos rest him. I was needed there; even then, the Yezda were thick as tax collectors round a man who's dug up treasure. And had I gone, look what I would have missed." He slid his arm round Nevrat beside him. The bright ribbons streaming from his three-peaked Vaspurakaner cap tickled her neck; she brushed them away as she snuggled closer to her husband.

Marcus sipped from his own wine cup. He had nearly forgotten what good company the two young westerners made, not just for Senpat's music but for the gusto and good cheer with which he—indeed, both of them—faced life. And they were so obviously pleased with each other as to make every couple around them happier simply by their presence.

"Where is your friend with the mustaches like melted bronze?" Nevrat asked the tribune. "He has a fine voice. I was hoping to hear him sing with Senpat tonight, even if Videssian songs are the only ones they both understand."

"'Little bird with a yellow bill—'" Gaius Philippus began, his baritone raucous. Nevrat winced and threw a walnut at him. Ever alert, he caught it out of the air, then cracked it with the pommel of his dagger.

The distraction did not make her forget her question. She quirked an eyebrow at Scaurus. He said lamely. "There was some business or other he said he had to attend to; I don't know just what." But I can make a fair guess, he thought.

Nevrat's other eyebrow went up when she saw him hesitate. Unlike most Videssian women, she did not pluck them to make them finer, but they did nothing to mar her strong-featured beauty.

In this case, Marcus was immune to such blandishments. He wished he had no part of Viridovix' secret and would not spread it further.

Nevrat turned to Helvis. "You're a big girl, dear. You should do more than pick at your food."

Said in a different tone, the words could have rankled, but Nevrat was obviously concerned. Helvis' answering smile was a trifle wan. "There'd just be more for me to give back tomorrow morning."

Nevrat looked blank for a moment, then hugged her. "Congratulations," Senpat said, pumping Marcus' hand. "What is it, the thought of going west that makes you randy? This'll be twice now."

"Oh, more than that," Helvis said with a sidelong glance at the tribune.

When the laughter subsided, Senpat grew serious. "You Romans will be going west, not so?"

"I've heard nothing either way," Scaurus said. "For now,

no one goes anywhere much, not with Bouraphos at the Cattle-Crossing. Why should it matter to you? You've been detached from us for months now."

Instead of answering directly, Senpat exchanged a few sentences in guttural Vaspurakaner with Gagik Bagratouni. The *nakharar's* reply was almost a growl. Several of his countrymen nodded vehemently; one pounded his fist on his knee.

"I would rejoin, if you'll have me," the younger noble said, giving his attention back to Scaurus. "When you go west, you'll do more than fight rebels inside the Empire. The Yezda are there, too, and I owe them a debt." His merry eyes grew grim.

"And I," Nevrat added. Having seen her riding alone through them after Maragha and in the press when the legionaries fought Drax' men, Marcus knew she meant exactly what she said.

"You both know the answer is yes, whether or not we move," the tribune said. "How could I say otherwise to seasoned warriors and bold scouts who are also my friends?" Senpat Sviodo thanked him with unwonted seriousness.

Still caught up in his own thoughts, Bagratouni said hungrily, "And also Zemarkhos there is." His men nodded again; they had more cause to hate the fanatic priest than even the nomads. Likely their chance for revenge would come, too, if the legionaries went west. On the way to Maragha, Thorisin had mocked Zemarkhos, and so the zealot acknowledged Onomagoulos as his Avtokrator. His followers helped swell the provincial noble's forces.

The hall grew silent for a moment. The Romans were loyal to the state for which they fought, but it was a mercenary's loyalty, ultimately shallow. They did not share or fully understand the decades of war and pogrom which tempered the Vaspurakaners as repeated quenchings did steel. The men who styled themselves princes rarely showed that hardness; when they did, it was enough to chill their less-committed comrades.

"Out on the darkness!" Senpat Sviodo cried, feeling the mood of the evening start to slide. "It's Skotos' tool, nothing else!"

He turned to Gaius Philippus. "So you Romans know the little bird, do you?" His fingers danced over the pandoura's strings. The legionaries roared out the marching song, glad to be distracted from their own thoughts.

"Are you well, Taron?" Marcus asked. "You look as if you hadn't slept in a week."

"Near enough," Leimmokheir allowed, punctuating his words with an enormous yawn. His eyes were red-tracked, his gravelly voice hoarser than usual. The flesh he had begun gaining back after his release looked slack and unhealthy. "It's a wearing task, trying to do the impossible." Even his once-booming laugh seemed hollow.

"Not enough ships, not enough crews, not enough money, not enough time." He ticked them off on his fingers one by one. "Outlander, you have Gavras' ear. Make him understand I'm no mage, to conjure up victory with a wave of my hand. And do a good job, too, or we'll be in cells side by side."

Scaurus took that as mere downheartedness on the admiral's part, but Leimmokheir grew so insistent the tribune decided to try to meet with the Emperor. Exhaustion had made the drungarios of the fleet irritable and unable to see any viewpoint but his own.

As luck would have it, the tribune was admitted to the imperial presence after only a short wait. When he spoke of Leimmokheir's complaints, Thorisin snapped, "What does he want, anchovies to go with his wine? Any fool can handle the easy jobs; it's the hard ones that show what a man's made of."

A messenger came up to the throne, paused uncertainly. "Well?" Gavras said.

Recognized, the man went down in full proskynesis. When he rose, he handed the Avtokrator a folded leaf of parchment. "Your pardon, your Majesty. The runner who delivered this said it was of the utmost urgency that you read it at once."

"All right, all right, you've given it me." The Emperor opened the sheet, softly read aloud to himself: " 'Come to the sea wall and learn what your trust has gained you. L., drungarios commanding.' "

His color deepened at every word. He tore the sheet in half, then turned on Scaurus, shouting, "Phos curse the day I heeded your poisoned tongue! Hear the braggart boasting as he turns his coat!

"Zigabenos!" Gavras bellowed, and when the guards officer appeared the Emperor profanely ordered him to send troops hotfoot to the docks to stop Leimmokheir if they could. He grated, "It'll be too bloody late, but we have to try."

The fury he radiated was so great Marcus stepped back when he rose from the throne, afraid Thorisin was about to attack him. Instead Gavras issued a curt command: "Come along, sirrah. If I must watch the fruit of your folly, you can be there, too."

The Emperor swept down the aisleway, an aghast Scaurus in his wake. Everything the Roman had believed of Leimmokheir looked to be a tissue of lies. It was worse than betrayal; it spoke of a blindness on his part humiliating to contemplate.

Courtiers scurried out of Gavras' path, none daring to remind him of business still unfinished. Swearing under his breath, he stalked through the grounds of the palace compound; he mounted the steps of the sea wall like an unjustly condemned man on his way to the executioner. He did not so much as look at Scaurus.

What he saw when he peered over the gray stone battlements ripped a fresh cry of outrage from him. "The pimp's spawn has stolen the whole fleet!" Sails furled, the triremes and lighter, two-banked warships were rowing west from the Neorhesian harbor. Sea foam clotted whitely round their oars at every stroke. Marcus' heart sank further. He had not known it could.

"And look!" the Emperor said, pointing to the suburban harbor on the far shore of the Cattle-Crossing. "Here comes that cow-futtering Bouraphos, out to escort him home!" The rebel admiral's ships grew swiftly larger as they approached. Thorisin shook his fist at them.

Boots rang on the stairway. A swearing trooper trotted up to the Emperor. He panted, "We were too late, your Majesty. Leimmokheir sailed."

"Really?" Gavras snarled. The soldier's eyes went wide as they followed his outflung arm.

Leimmokheir's ships shook themselves out into a line facing the rebels, his heavier galleys in the center with the Liburnians on either wing. Even in an element not his own, Marcus knew a tactical maneuver when he saw one. "That's a battle formation!" he exclaimed.

"By Phos, it is!" Thorisin said, acknowledging his presence for the first time. "What boots it, though? Treacher or zany, your precious friend will wreck me either way. Boura-phos'll toy with him like a cat with a grasshopper. Look at the ships he has with him."

Whether or not Gavras thought Leimmokheir a turncoat, plainly Elissaios Bouraphos did not. His entire fleet was there to form a line of battle, its horns sweeping forward to flank the smaller force it faced. The curses Thorisin had called down on Leimmokheir's head he now switched to Bouraphos. Zigabenos' messenger listened admiringly.

Marcus scarcely heard the Emperor. Watching a fight in which he could take no part was worse than combat itself, he discovered. In the hand-to-hand there was no time to reflect; now he could do nothing else. His nails bit into his palms as he watched the rowers on both sides step up the stroke. Their ships leaped at one another. The tribune wondered if Leim-mokheir had in fact gone mad, if the egotism that seemed to lurk in every Videssian's soul deluded him into thinking his powers godlike.

The fleets were less than a furlong apart when one of Bouraphos' two-banked craft swerved inward to ram the tri-reme next to it square amidships. The heavier galley, taken utterly by surprise, was ruined. Oars snapped; faint over the water, Marcus heard screams as rowers' arms were wrenched from their sockets. Water gushed into the great hole torn in the trireme's side. Almost with dignity, the stricken ship began to settle. The Liburnian backed oars and sought another victim.

As if the first treacherous attack had been a signal, a score and more of the rebel admiral's ships turned on their comrades, throwing Bouraphos' line into confusion. No longer sure who was friend and who foe, ships still loyal lost momentum as their captains looked nervously to either side. And into the chaos drove Taron Leimmokheir.

On the sea wall Thorisin Gavras did three steps of a jig. "See how it feels, you bastard!" he screamed to Bouraphos. "See how it feels!" Scaurus abruptly understood Leimmo-kheir's sleepless nights; the drungarios had been sowing this field for many days and come to harvest it now that it was ripe.

But for all the sowing, the sea fight was far from won. Even with his suddenly revealed recruits, Leimmokheir was still outnumbered, and Elissaios Bouraphos a resourceful com-

mander. It was his ships, though, that were pressed back into
a circle, with Leimmokheir's prowling round them. And when
he tried to strike outward, a galley of his that had bided its
time drew in its starboard oars and sheared away its neighbor's
portside bank with its projecting bulkheads. The crippled ship
wallowed helplessly; its conqueror joined the enemy; Bouraphos' attacking squadron, daunted, pulled back.

To add to the disorder, both sides flew the imperial pennant
with its central sun. Tiny in the distance, Marcus saw another
banner at a trireme's bow, this one scarlet barred with gold—
the emblem of the drungarios of the fleet. Bouraphos must
have decided the only way out of his predicament was to kill
his rival admiral, for four of his own galleys surged toward
Leimmokheir's, sinking a Liburnian as they came.

No ships were close by to help. The drungarios' trireme
spun in the water, backing oars to port while pulling ahead on
the starboard side. It turned almost in its own length and sped
away from the attackers. Some of Leimmokheir's fleet might
not be perfectly trained, but he tolerated no slackness on his
flagship.

The wake foamed up under the galley's bow; it was driving
almost straight back toward Scaurus, past the slowly settling
hulk of the first trireme sunk when Bouraphos' ships began
changing sides. One after the others, the rebels gave chase.

"Skotos and his demons take them, they're gaining," Thorisin said, his hands clutching the battlements until knuckles
whitened. Where minutes before he had been ready to dip
Leimmokheir an inch at a time into boiling oil, now he was in
an agony of suspense lest the drungarios come to harm.

But Leimmokheir knew what he was about. Even at a
range of more than a quarter of a mile, his mane of gray-white
hair made him recognizable. His arm came down to emphasize an order. Twisting like a snake, the trireme darted round
the sinking galley and rammed its leading pursuer before the
startled rebels could maneuver. Bouraphos' other three ships
stopped dead in the water, as if Leimmokheir had shown himself to be a dangerous wizard as well as a seaman.

His daring put new heart into his fleet and seemed to be the
blow that broke his foes. In a desperate charge across the
water, about twenty of them broke through his line, but all
fight was out of them. They fled toward the suburbs of the
opposite shore. Another group, seeing the way the wind was

blowing, went over to the winners and fell on their erstwhile comrades.

Thorisin began to dance in earnest. Heedless of the imperial dignity, he pounded Marcus and the messenger on the back and grinned as he was pummeled in return.

One squadron of about fifteen ships kept up the fight; Scaurus was unsurprised to spot a second drungarios' pennant among them. Game to the end, Elissaios Bouraphos and his surviving loyal followers gave their fellows the chance to escape. They tried to be everywhere at once, whirling and dashing forward to the attack like so many dogs at bay.

Facing so many, the battle could have had only one result, but the end came quicker than the tribune had expected. All at once the coordinated defense dissolved into a series of single-ship actions. White shields came up on poles as the last of Bouraphos' captains began to yield.

"Sink 'em all!" Gavras shouted, and then a moment later, reluctantly, "No, we'll need them against Namdalen one day." He sighed and said to Marcus, "I'll turn forethoughtful yet, damn me if I won't. This wretched job will see to that." He sighed again, remembering the freedom of irresponsibility.

By the time the Emperor reached the Neorhesian harbor he was jovial again. The space by the docks was filled with a milling crowd of civilians and soldiers. To the people of the city, Leimmokheir's triumphal return was a spectacle to make the day pass more quickly. The soldiers knew how much more it meant. Now at last they could face Baanes Onomagoulos; the shield that had separated them was hacked to bits.

Thorisin nodded to every captain coming ashore. He carefully made no distinction between the men who had sailed out with the drungarios and former rebels. The latter, knowing his reputation for a swift temper, approached him warily, but found their role in the victory outweighing earlier allegiance. They left the imperial presence quite relieved.

Taron Leimmokheir's galley was among the last to put in. It had taken damage, Marcus saw. Some oars trailed limply in the water for lack of men to pull them, and a ten-foot stretch of the port rail was smashed to stove-wood.

Gavras' soldiers cheered the admiral, who ignored them until the trireme was tied up at the dock. Then a single short wave sufficed him. With the agility of a much younger man, he scrambled up onto the pier. He elbowed through the press until he stood before the Emperor.

He bowed low, saying, "I trust my message sufficed to lay your concern to rest." Holding the bow, he tipped a wink to Scaurus with his left eye, which Thorisin could not see.

The Emperor, coloring, inhaled ominously. But before he could blast Leimmokheir, he spied Marcus trying to swallow a grin. "Then you're too fornicating trusting by half," he growled, but without sincerity. "I've said so for years, you'll recall."

"So now my task is done, it's back to the cell, eh?" The drungarios returned Thorisin's banter, but Scaurus heard nothing light in his tone.

"After the scare you threw into me, you deserve a yes to that." Gavras' eyes swung to the flagship. "What have we here?"

Two corseleted marines brought their prisoner before the Emperor. They had to half support him; the left side of his handsome face and head was bloody from a slingstone's glancing blow. "You would have done better to stay at Pityos, Elissaios," Thorisin said.

Bouraphos glared at him, shaking his head to try to clear it. "We were nearly holding our own till that cursed rock flattened me, even with the bolters. I'd bolt 'em proper, I would." The wordplay was feeble, but Marcus had to respect the rebel's spirit for essaying it at all.

"You're not likely to have the chance," Thorisin said.

"I know." Bouraphos spat at Taron Leimmokheir's feet. "When will you fight for yourself, Gavras? You used me to counter this bag of turds, and then him against me. What sort of warrior does that make you?"

"The master of you both," the Emperor replied. He turned to the marines, who came to attention, expecting the order. "Take him to the Kynegion."

As they began to lead Bouraphos away, Gavras stopped them for a moment. "In memory of the service you once gave me, Elissaios, your lands will not stand forfeit to the fisc. You have a son, I think."

"Yes. That's good of you, Thorisin."

"He's never harmed me. We can keep your head off the Milestone, too."

Bouraphos shrugged. "Do as you like there. I'll have no

further use for it." He eyed the marines. "Well, let's go. I trust I don't have to show you the road?" He walked off between them, his back straighter and stride firmer at every step.

Unable to hold the thought to himself, Marcus said, "He dies very well."

"Aye, so he does," the Emperor nodded. "He should have lived the same way." To that the tribune had no good reply.

The small crowd studied the ship moored at the pier. "What's that written on its stern?" Gaius Philippus asked.

The letters were faded, salt-stained. "*Conqueror*," Marcus read.

The senior centurion pursed his lips. "It'll never live up to that."

The *Conqueror* bobbed in the light chop. Beamier than the lean Videssian warships, it carried a wide, square-rigged sail, now furled, and a dozen oarports so the crew could maneuver in and out of harbors at need.

Gorgidas, who knew more of ships than the Romans, seemed satisfied. "It wasn't built yesterday or the day before, either, but it'll get us across to Prista, and that's what counts." He stirred a large leather rucksack with his foot. Having helped him pack it, Marcus knew that rolls of parchment, pens, and packets of powdered ink make up a good part of its bulk.

The tribune remarked, "The Emperor wastes no time. Less than a week since he gained the sea, and already you're off to the Arshaum."

"High time, too," Arigh Arghun's son said. "I miss the feel of a horse's barrel between my legs."

Pikridios Goudeles gave a delicate shudder. "You will, I fear, have all too much chance to grow thoroughly used to the sensation, as, worse luck, will I." To Scaurus he said, "The upcoming campaigns, both against the usurper and against the Yezda, shall be difficult ones. Good Arigh's men will be too late for the first of them, it seems, but surely not for the second."

"Of course," Marcus said. That Thorisin had enough faith in Goudeles to send him as ambassador surprised the Roman —or was the Emperor clearing the stage of a potential danger to himself?

Whatever Gavras' reasons, his trust for the smooth-tongued bureaucrat plainly was not absolute. Goudeles' fellow envoy was a dark, saturnine military man named Lankinos Skylitzes. Scaurus did not know him well and was unsure whether he was brother or cousin to the Skylitzes who had died in the night ambush the year before. In one way, at least, he was a good choice for the embassy—the Roman had heard him talking with Arigh in the nomad's tongue.

Perhaps knowledge of the steppe was his speciality, for he said, "There's another reason for haste. A new set of dispatches came from Prista last night. Avshar's on the plains. Belike he's after soldiers, too; we'd best forestall him."

Marcus exclaimed in dismay, and was echoed by everyone who heard Skylitzes' news. In his heart he had known the wizard-prince escaped Videssos when the Sphrantzai fell, but it was always possible to hope. "You're sure?" he asked Skylitzes.

The soldier nodded once. No garrulous imperial here, Scaurus thought with a smile.

"May the spirits let us meet him," Arigh said, pantomiming cut-and-thrust. Marcus admired his bravado, but not his sense. Too many had made that wish already and got no joy when it came true.

Gaius Philippus undid the shortsword at his belt and handed it to Gorgidas. "Take it," he said. "With that serpent's spawn running free, you'll need it one day."

The Greek was touched by the present, but tried to refuse it, saying, "I have no skill with such tools, nor any desire to learn."

"Take it anyway," Gaius Philippus said, implacable. "You can stow it in the bottom of your duffel for all of me, but take it."

He sounded as if he were taking a legionary to task, not giving a gift, but Gorgidas heard the concern behind his insistence. He accepted the *gladius* with a word of thanks and proceeded to do just what the senior centurion had advised, packing it away in his kit.

"Very moving," Goudeles said dryly. "Here's something with a sweeter edge to it." He produced an alabaster flask of wine, drank, and passed it to Scaurus. It went down smooth as cream—nothing but the best for Pikridios, the tribune thought.

A gangplank thudded into place. The *Conqueror*'s captain,

a burly man of middle years, shouted, "You toffs can come aboard now." He wagged his head in invitation.

Arigh left Videssos without a backward glance, his right hand on the hilt of his saber, his left steadying the sueded leather bag slung over his shoulder. Skylitzes followed, equally nonchalant. Pikridios Goudeles gave a theatric groan as he picked up his duffel, but seemed perfectly able to carry it.

"Take care of yourself," Gaius Philippus ordered, thumping Gorgidas on the back. "You're too softhearted for your own good."

The physician snorted in exasperation. "And you're so full of feces it's no wonder your eyes are brown." He embraced the two Romans, then shouldered his own rucksack and followed the rest of the embassy.

"Remember," Marcus called after him, "I expect to read what you say about your travels, so it had best be good."

"Never fear, Scaurus, you'll read it if I have to tie you down and hold it in front of your face. It's fitting punishment for reminding me you're my audience."

"That's the lot of you?" the captain asked when the Greek came aboard. Getting no contradiction, he called to his crew, "Make ready to cast off!" Two half-naked sailors pulled in the gangplank; another pair jumped onto the dock to undo the fat brown mooring lines that held the *Conqueror* fore and aft.

"Hold on, avast, belay, whatever the plague-taken seaman's word is!" The pier shook as Viridovix came thudding up, his helmet on his head and a knapsack under his arm. He was crimson-faced and puffing; sweat streamed down his cheeks. He looked to have come from the Roman barracks on the dead run.

"What's happened?" Marcus and Gaius Philippus asked together, exchanging apprehensive glances. Except in battle and wenching, such exertion was alien to the Gaul's nature.

He got no chance to answer them, for Arigh shouted his name and leaped out of the *Conqueror* to greet him. "Come to see me off after all, are you?"

"Not a bit of it," Viridovix replied, dropping his bag to the boards of the pier with a sigh of relief. "By your leave, I'm coming with you."

The nomad's grin flashed white in his swarthy face. "What

could be better? You'll learn to love the taste of kavass, I promise you."

"Are you daft, man?" Gaius Philippus asked. Pointing to the *Conqueror*, he went on, "If you've forgotten, that is a ship. Your stomach will remember, whether you do or not."

"Och, dinna remind me," the Celt said, wiping his face on a tunic sleeve. "Still and all, it's that or meet the headsman, I'm thinking. On the water I'll wish I'm dead, but to stay would get me the wish granted, the which I don't fancy either."

"The headsman?" Scaurus said. Thinking quickly, he shifted to Latin. "The woman turned on you?" As long as no names were named, Arigh—and the listening sailors—could not follow.

"Didn't she just, the fickle slut," Viridovix answered bitterly in the same tongue. His happy-go-lucky air had deserted him; he was angry and self-reproachful. Catching the gleam in Marcus' eye, he said, "I've no need for your told-you-so's, either. You did that, and rightly. Would I were as cautious a wight as you, the once."

That admission was the true measure of his dismay, for he never tired of chiding the Romans for their stodginess. "What went awry?" the tribune asked.

"Can you no guess? That one's green as the sea with jealousy—like a canker it eats in her. And so she was havering after me to set aside my Gavrila and Lissena and Beline, and I said her nay as I've done before. They'll miss me, puir girls, and you must be after promising not to let herself's wrath fall on 'em."

"Of course," Scaurus said impatiently. "On with it, man."

"Och, the blackhearted bitch started shrieking fit to wake a dead corp, she did, and swore she'd tell the Gavras I'd had her by force." A fragment of the Celt's grin appeared for a moment. "Belike she'd make himself believe it, too. She's after seeing enough of me to give sic charge the weight of detail, you might say."

"She'd do it," Gaius Philippus said without hesitation.

"The very thought I had, Roman dear. I couldna be cutting her throat, with it so white and all. I had not the heart for it, to say naught of the hurly-burly it'd touch off."

"What did you do, then?" Marcus demanded. "Let her go

free? By the gods, Viridovix, the imperial guards'll be on your heels!"

"Nay, nay, you see me revealed a fool, but not a damnfool. She's swaddled and gagged and tied on a bed in the sleazy little inn where we went. She'll be a while working loose, but I'm thinking the exercise'll not improve her temper, and so it's away with me."

"First Gorgidas, and now you, and both for reasons an idiot would be ashamed to own," the tribune said, feeling the wrench as his tightly knit company began to unravel. Again he gave thanks that the Romans had not had to split themselves between Namdalen and Videssos; it would have torn the hearts from them all.

Impatient with the talk in a language he did not understand, Arigh broke in, "If you're coming, come."

"I will that, never fear." Viridovix clasped Scaurus' hand. "Take care o' the blade you bear, Roman. It's a bonny un."

"And you yours." Viridovix' long sword hung at his right hip; he would have seemed naked without it.

The Celt's jaw dropped as he noticed Gaius Philippus weaponless. "Wore it out, did you?"

"Don't be more foolish than you can help. I passed it on to Gorgidas."

"Did you now? That was a canny thing to do, or would be if the silly lown had the wit to realize what grand sport war is. As is, like as not he'll lose it, or else slice himself." Viridovix' lip curled. A second later he brightened. "Och, that's right, I'll have the Greek to quarrel with. Nothing like a good quarrel to keep a day from going stale."

Marcus remembered his own words to Gorgidas when the doctor told him he was leaving. At the time they had been a desperate joke, but here they were coming back at him in all seriousness from the Gaul's mouth. Viridovix lived to wrangle, whether with swords or with words.

The captain of the *Conqueror* made a trumpet of his hands. "You there! We're sailing, with you or without you!" The threat was empty—while Viridovix meant nothing to him, he could hardly set off without the Arshaum, who meant everything to the embassy.

The aggrieved shout underlined Arigh's unrest. "Let's do it," he said, taking the Celt's arm. Viridovix' rawhide boots clumped on the planking of the dock; the nomad, shod in soft calfskin, walked silent as a wildcat.

Looking like a live man going to his own funeral, the Gaul tossed his duffel to a sailor. Still he hesitated before following it down. He sketched a salute to Scaurus, waved his fist at Gaius Philippus. "Watch yourself, runt!" he called, and jumped.

"And you, you great bald-arsed lunk!"

To the captain's shouted directions, his crew backed water. For a few seconds it seemed the *Conqueror* was too bulky to respond to the oars, but then it moved, inching away from the pier. When well clear, it turned north, ponderous as a fat old man. Marcus heard ropes squeal in pullies as the broad sail unfurled. It flapped loosely, then filled with wind.

The tribune watched until the horizon swallowed it.

With regained mastery of the sea, Thorisin Gavras threw Drax and his Namdalener mercenaries at Baanes Onomagoulos. Leimmokheir's galleys protected the transports from rebel warships; the men of the Duchy landed in the westlands at Kypas, several days' march south of the suburbs opposite Videssos.

A great smoke rose in the west as Onomagoulos fired his camp to keep Thorisin from taking possession of it. Baanes retreated toward his stronghold round Garsavra. He moved in haste, lest the Namdaleni cut him off from his center of power. Thorisin, acting like a man who feels victory in his grasp, retook the western suburbs.

Marcus waited for a summons from the Emperor, expecting him to order the legionaries into action against Onomagoulos. He drilled his men furiously, wanting to be ready. He still had doubts about the great count, despite the successes Drax was winning for Gavras.

No orders came. Thorisin held military councils in plenty, but to plan the coming summer campaign against the Yezda. He seemed certain anyone fighting Onomagoulos had to be his friend.

Scaurus tried to put his suspicions into words after one officers' meeting, saying to the Emperor, "The nomads attack Baanes, too, you know, but not in your interest. Drax wars for no one but Drax; he travels under your banner now, but only because it suits him."

Thorisin frowned; the Roman's advice was clearly unwelcome. "You've given me good service, outlander, and that sometimes in my despite," he said. "There have been stories told of you, just as you tell them now against the Namdalener. A prudent man believes not all of what he sees and only a little of what he hears. But this I tell you: no rumor-seller has ever come to me with news that Drax purposed abandoning me at the hour of my peril."

Scaurus' belly went heavy as lead—how had that report reached the Emperor? Unsure how much Gavras knew, he did not dare deny it. Picking his words with care, he said, "If you believe such tales, why hold me and mine to your service?"

"Because I trust my eyes further than my ears." It was dismissal and warning both—without proof, Gavras would not hear charges against the great count. Glad the Emperor was taking the other question no further, Marcus left hastily.

He had expected a great hue and cry after Viridovix, but that, too, failed to materialize. Gaius Philippus' misogyny led him to a guess the tribune thought close to the mark. "I'd bet this isn't the first time Komitta's played bump-belly where she shouldn't," the veteran said. "Would you care to advertise it, were you Gavras?"

"Hmm." If that was so, much might be explained, from Thorisin's curious indifference to his mistress' tale of rape to her remaining mistress instead of queen. "You're getting a feel for the politics hereabouts," Marcus told the senior centurion.

"Oh, horseturds. When they're thick on the ground as olives at harvest time, you don't need to feel 'em. The smell gives them away."

In the westlands Drax kept making gains. When his dispatches arrived, Thorisin would read them out to his assembled officers. The great count wrote like an educated Videssian, a feat that roused only contempt in his fellow islander Utprand.

"Would you listen to that, now?" the mercenary captain said after one session. " 'Goals achieved, objectives being met.' Vere's Onomagoulos' army and w'y hasn't Drax smashed it up? T'at's what needs telling."

"Aye, you're right," Soteric echoed vehemently. "Drax greases his tongue when he talks and his pen when he sets ink to parchment."

Marcus put some of their complaint down to jealousy at Drax' holding a greater command than theirs. From cold experience, he also knew how much such complaints accomplished. He said, "Of course the two of you are but plain, blunt soldiers of fortune. That you were ready to set Videssos on its ear last summer has nothing to do with intrigue."

Utprand had the grace to look shamefaced, but Soteric retorted, "If the effete imperials can't hold us back, whose fault is that? Ours? By the Wager, they don't merit this Empire of theirs."

There were times when Scaurus found the islanders' insistence on their own virtues and the decadence of Videssos more than he could stomach. He said sharply, "If you're speaking of effeteness, then betrayal should stand with it, not so?"

"Certainly," Soteric answered; Utprand, more wary than his lieutenant, asked, "W'at do you mean, betrayal?"

"Just this," Marcus replied. "Gavras knows we met at the end of the siege, and what befell. By your Phos, gentlemen, no Roman told him. Leaving Helvis out of the bargain, only four ever learned what was planned, and it never went beyond them. Some one of your men should have his tongue trimmed, lest he trip on it as it flaps beneath his feet."

"Impossible!" Soteric exclaimed with the confidence of youth. "We are an honorable folk. Why would we stoop to such double-dealing?" He glared at his brother-in-law, ready to take it farther than words.

Utprand spoke to him in the island dialect. Marcus caught the drift: secrets yielded accidentally could hurt as much as those given away on purpose. Soteric's mouth was still thin with anger, but he gave a grudging nod.

The tribune was grateful to the older Namdalener. Unlike Soteric, Utprand had seen enough to know how few things were certain. Backing what the officer had pointed out, Marcus said, "I didn't mean to suggest deliberate treachery, only that you islanders fall as short of perfection as any other men."

"You have a rude way with a suggestion." Soteric had a point, Scaurus realized, but he could not make himself regret pricking his brother-in-law's self-importance.

* * *

"A priest to see me?" the tribune asked the Roman sentry. "Is it Nepos from the Academy?"

"No, sir, just some blue-robe."

Curious, Marcus followed the legionary to the barracks-hall door. The priest, a nondescript man save for his shaved pate, bowed and handed him a small roll of parchment sealed with the patriarch's sky-blue wax. He said, "A special liturgy of rejoicing will be celebrated in the High Temple at the eighth hour this afternoon. You are bidden to attend. The parchment here is your token of entrance. I also have one for your chief lieutenant."

"Me?" Gaius Philippus' head jerked up. "I have better things to do with my time, thank you."

"You would decline the patriarchal summons?" the priest said, shocked.

"Your precious patriarch doesn't know my name," Gaius Philippus retorted. His eyes narrowed. "So why would he invite me? Hmm—did the Emperor put him up to it?"

The priest spread his hands helplessly. Marcus said, "Gavras thinks well of you."

"Soldiers know soldiers," Gaius Philippus shrugged. He tucked the parchment roll into his belt-pouch. "Maybe I'd better go."

Putting his own invitation away, Scaurus asked the priest, "A liturgy of rejoicing? In aid of what?"

"Of Phos' mercy on us all," the man replied, taking him literally. "Now forgive me, I pray; I have others yet to find." He was gone before Marcus could reframe his question.

The tribune muttered a mild curse, then glanced around to gauge the shadows. It could not be later than noon, he decided; at least two hours until the service began. That gave him time to bathe and then put on his dress cape and helmet, sweltering though they were. He ran a hand over his cheek, then sighed. A shave would not be amiss, either. Sighing as well, Gaius Philippus joined him at his ablutions.

Rubbing freshly scraped faces, the Romans handed their tokens of admission to a priest at the top of the High Temple's stairs and made their way into the building. The High Temple dominated Videssos' skyline, but its heavy form and plain stuccoed exterior, as always, failed to impress Scaurus, whose tastes were formed in a different school. As he did not worship Phos, he seldom entered the Temple and sometimes forgot how glorious it was inside. Whenever he did go in, he felt transported to another, purer, world.

Like all of Phos' shrines, the High Temple was built round a circular worship area surmounted by a dome, with rows of benches north, south, east, and west. But here, genius and limitless resources had refined the simple, basic plan. All the separate richnesses—benches of highly polished hardwoods, moss-agate columns, endless gold and silver foil to reflect light into every corner, walls that imitated Phos' sky in facings of semiprecious stones—somehow failed to compete with one another, but were blended by the artisans' skill into a unified and magnificent whole.

And all that magnificence served to lead the eye upward to contemplate the Temple's great central dome, which itself seemed more a product of wizardry than architecture. Liberated by pendentives from the support of columns, it looked to be upheld only by the shafts of sunlight piercing its many-windowed base. Even to Marcus the stubborn non-believer, it seemed a bit of Phos' heaven suspended above the earth.

"Now here is a home fit for a god," Gaius Philippus muttered under his breath. He had never been in the High Temple before; hardened as he was, he could not keep awe from his voice.

Phos himself looked down on his worshipers from the interior of the dome; gold-backed glass tesserae sparkled now here, now there in an ever-shifting play of light. Stern in judgment, the Videssian god's eyes seemed to see into the furthest recesses of the Temple—and into the soul of every man within. From that gaze, from the verdict inscribed in the book the god held, there could be no appeal. Nowhere had Scaurus seen such an uncomprising image of harsh, righteous purpose.

No Videssian, no matter how cynical, sat easy under that Phos' eyes. To an outlander seeing them for the first time, they could be overwhelming. Utprand Dagober's son stiffened to attention and began a salute, as to any great leader, before he stopped in confusion. "Don't blame him a bit," Gaius Philippus said. Marcus nodded. No one tittered at the Namdalener; here the proud imperials, too, were humble.

Fair face crimsoning, Utprand found a seat. His foxskin jacket and snug trousers set him apart from the Videssians around him. Their flowing robes of multicolored silks, their high-knotted brocaded fabrics, their velvets and snowy linens served to complement the High Temple's splendor. Jewels and gold and silver threadwork gleamed as they moved.

"Exaltation!" A choir of boys in robes of blue samite came down the aisles and grouped themselves round the central altar. "Exaltation!" Their pure, unbroken voices filled the space under the great dome with joyous music. "Exaltation! Exaltation!" Even Phos' awesome image seemed to take on a more benign aspect as his young votaries sang his praises. "Exaltation!"

Censer-swinging priests followed the chorus toward the worship area; the sweet fragrances of balsam, frankincense, cedar oil, myrrh, and storax filled the air. Behind the priests came Balsamon. The congregation rose to honor the patriarch. And behind Balsamon was Thorisin Gavras in full imperial regalia. Along with everyone else, Marcus and Gaius Philippus bowed to the Avtokrator. The tribune tried to keep the surprise from his face; on his previous visits to the High Temple, the Emperor had taken no part in its services, but watched from a small private room set high in the building's eastern wall.

Balsamon steadied himself, resting a hand on the back of the patriarchal throne. Its ivory panels, cut in delicate reliefs, must have delighted the connoisseur in him. After resting for a moment, he lifted his hands to the Phos in the dome, offering his god the Videssians' creed: "We bless thee, Phos, Lord with the right and good mind, by thy grace our protector, watchful beforehand that the great test of life may be decided in our favor."

The congregation followed him in the prayer, then chorused its "Amens." Marcus heard Utprand, Soteric, and a few other Namdalener officers append the extra clause they added to the creed: "On this we stake our very souls."

As always, some Videssians frowned at the addition, but Balsamon gave them no chance to ponder it. "We are met today in gladness and celebration!" he shouted. "Sing, and let the good god hear your rejoicing!" His quavery tenor launched into a hymn; the choir followed him an instant later. They swept the worshippers along with them. Taron Leimmokheir's tuneless bass rose loud above the rest; the devout admiral, his eyes closed, rocked from side to side in his seat as he sang.

The liturgy of rejoicing was not commonly held. The Videssian notables, civil and military alike, threw themselves into the ceremony with such gusto that the interior of the High Temple took on a festival air. Their enthusiasm was contagious; Scaurus stood and clapped with his neighbors and followed their songs as best he could. Most, though, were in the archaic dialect preserved only in ritual, which he still did not understand well.

He caught a quick stir of motion through the filigreed screening that shielded the imperial niche from mundane eyes and wondered whether it was Komitta Rhangavve or Alypia Gavra. Both of them, he thought, would be there. He hoped it was Alypia.

Her uncle the Emperor stood to the right of the patriarchal throne. Though he did no more than pray with the rest of the worshipers, his presence among them was enough to rivet their attention on him.

Balsamon used his hands to mute the congregation's singing. The voices of the choir rang out in all their perfect clarity, then they, too, died away, leaving a silence as speaking as words. The patriarch let it draw itself out to just the right length before he transformed its nature by taking the few steps from his ivory throne to the altar at the very center of the worship area. His audience leaned forward expectantly to listen to what he would say.

His eyes twinkled; he plainly enjoyed making them wait. He drummed his stubby fingers on the sheet silver of the altartop, looking this way and that. At last he said, "You really don't need to hear me at all today." He beckoned Gavras to his side. "This is the man who asked me to celebrate the liturgy of rejoicing; let him explain his reasons."

Thorisin ignored the irreverence toward his person; from Balsamon it was not disrespectful. The Emperor began almost before his introduction was through. "Word arrived this morning of battle just east of Gavras. Forces loyal to us—" Even Gavras's bluntness balked at calling mercenaries by their right name. "—decisively defeated their opponents. The chief rebel and traitor, Baanes Onomagoulos, was killed in the fighting."

The three short sentences, bald as any military communique, touched off pandemonium in the High Temple. Bureaucrats' cheers mingled with those of Thorisin's officers; if the present Avtokrator was not the pen-pushers' choice, he was a paragon next to Onomagoulos. For once, Gavras had all his government's unruly factions behind him.

Master of his own house at last, he basked in the applause like a sunbather on a warm beach. "Now we will deal with the Yezda as they deserve!" he cried. The cheering got louder.

Marcus nodded in sober satisfaction; Gaius Philippus' fist rose and slowly came down on his knee. They looked at each other with complete understanding. "Our turn to go west next," the senior centurion predicted. "Still some work to do to get ready."

Marcus nodded again. "It's as Thorisin said, though—at least we'll be fighting the right foe this time."

ABOUT THE AUTHOR

HARRY TURTLEDOVE is that rarity, a lifelong southern Californian. He is married and has two young daughters. After flunking out of Caltech, he earned a degree in Byzantine history and has taught at UCLA and Cal State Fullerton. Academic jobs being few and precarious, however, his primary work since leaving school has been as a technical writer. He has had fantasy and science fiction published in *Isaac Asimov's*, *Amazing*, *Analog*, *Playboy*, and *Fantasy Book*. His hobbies include baseball, chess, and beer.